Saint Mary Blue

Saint Mary Blue

Barry B. Longyear

AN AUTHORS GUILD BACKINPRINT.COM EDITION

Saint Mary Blue

All Rights Reserved © 1988, 2000 by Barry B. Longyear

AN AUTHORS GUILD BACKINPRINT.COM EDITION

Published by iUniverse.com, Inc.

For information address:
iUniverse.com, Inc.
5220 S 16th, Ste. 200
Lincoln, NE 68512
www.iuniverse.com

Originally published by SteelDragon Press

The characters and events described in this book are entirely
fictitious. Any resemblance to actual persons or events is coincidental.

Works quoted in this book:
Alcoholics Anonymous (the "Big Book").
New York: Alcoholics Anonymous World Services, Inc., 1976.
A Day at a Time. Minneapolis: CompCare Publications, 1976.
Twenty-Four Hours a Day. Center City, MN: Hazelden Foundation, 1975.
Why Am I Afraid to Tell You Who I Am?
John Powell, S.J. Niles, IL: Argus Com-munications, 1969.

ISBN: 0-595-13885-3

Printed in the United States of America

To
June Qualy, Marion Mann,
and
The Animals

DECEMBER 30TH

1

Jacob Randecker was trying to remember a joke. It was very funny, he recalled.

—Very funny, unless you happen to be the joke. But it's all relative. Hell, relativity's relative. Reality is the problem, you see. And if you aren't part of the problem, you're part of the solution.

—God, I feel sick. No. It's more like I'm covered with a thick layer of bread mold.

—What was that joke?

—Oh, yes. This drunk comes into a bar, see. And he orders a Martini from the bartender. While the bartender is getting the drink, the drunk looks down the bar and notices this little monkey sitting on top of an upright piano.

—Yeah, that's the way it went. And I better keep my eyes shut. I feel like I'm moving, and I can't remember any good reason why I should be moving. But if I push the feeling down, I won't have to deal with it. Never do today what you can put off until tomorrow....

He felt for the reassuring lump of the pillbox in the pocket of his sweater vest.

—It's all illusion, anyway. A dream, this day, this life, this nightmare. What was the rest of that dumb joke, anyway?

—Shit.

Something lurched against his shoulder. He nodded to himself as he
concluded that he really was moving. He studied the problem of trying
to open his eyes.

—First there is the deeper issue to consider: should I open my eyes?
You can't ever tell what's going to be there.

—The joke. Concentrate on the joke.

—As soon as the bartender puts down the drink, the little monkey
scoots off the piano, runs down the bar, and plants his ass right in the
guy's Martini. The drunk bends down, looks through the side of the
glass, and sees the monkey's two fuzzy little balls right next to the
olive....

Another lurch against his shoulder and a horn honking. He opened
his eyes. The world was a blur of grays. He opened his eyes further and
saw that he was looking at a pair of gloves. He wiggled the fingers of his
left hand and decided that his hands were in the gloves. His head tilted
back, and above a red plastic oblong, there was a dark brown melon
perched on a dark blue rug....

The world looked very silly. Jacob closed his eyes.

—"Bartender!" says the drunk, "this monkey has his balls in my
Martini."

—The bartender checks it out and shrugs. "I'm sorry, mister. The
monkey belongs to the piano player, and the boss likes the piano player,
so we have to put up with the monkey. I'll get you a fresh drink."

Jacob opened his eyes again.

The melon resolved into the back of a head, the rug was a coat,
the red plastic oblong was the back of a couch. He looked up and saw
a face glowering at him. It was a picture in a plastic holder, the kind

they have in taxicabs.

—Taxicabs?

He turned his head to the right and saw men and women moving rapidly past. But they weren't walking. "What in the hell am I doing in a taxi?"

—Questions.

—Where am I? Where am I going? Where was I? Why....

—A taxi? This might be a problem.

As the motion of the cab pushed him against the right-hand door, he wiped his gloved hand over his bearded face, tried to work up enough spit to counter the dryness in his throat, and then let his eyelids fall shut from their own weight.

—I could ask the driver where I am, but I'd sound like a real jerk. What the hell. Look on the sunny side. At least it's not a police cruiser, or an ambulance, or a hearse. Concentrate on the joke.

—As soon as the bartender puts down the second drink, the little monkey scoots off the piano, runs down the bar, and plants his ass right in the fresh Martini. The drunk looks down and sees those two fuzzy little balls....

Jacob saw a face from outside looking back at him. A woman dressed like a blue snowball. Was she laughing? Laughing at him? The face disappeared as sick fear spread through him.

—What is the point? Life. What is the damned bleeding point of it all? I could see going through this pain if I was doing some kind of good somewhere. But what? Where?

—I can't figure out the rules. I just can't. Whatever it is that you have to know to live on this planet, I just can't figure it out.

He fought down the tears as he reached for his little green plastic pillbox. As he placed one of the little white oblongs on his tongue, he teased himself with the memory of the time he had once died. Back-to-back heart attacks. In the hospital's intensive care unit, all feeling, all sensation, all thought leaving him. Absolutely nothing whatever was important or unimportant. No pain, no hurt, no loneliness, no hate, no nothin'. The pleasant neutrality of death. Infinite universes of warm, black cotton.

Jacob Randecker never could understand why people feared death.

"What's so funny?" asked the cabbie.

Jacob looked up and nodded. "Death."

"Death?" The cabbie looked over his right shoulder, his face dark with concern. No, Jacob discovered. He's black. But concerned. "Are you all right, man?"

Jacob waved his hand back and forth, then let it fall to his lap. "Not death. That people are afraid of death."

"That's funny?"

"That's funny."

Jacob managed to focus on a street sign. Hiawatha? He giggled.—Now I know where I am. By the shores of Gitchee-Goomy….

He looked into the open palm of his right glove. The green plastic pillbox sat there. He enclosed the box with his fist and gently shook it, listening with his sense of touch. There were still a few left.

—Death. Soft, black, nothingness. The ultimate downer. It is such a plus next to the abject negative of my existence, death. It's there: my ticket out, if I want out badly enough….

He rolled his head to the right and looked out the window at the snow, the ice, the huddled masses yearning to be any place except except…

—Where in the hell am I? Where are the shores of Gitchee-Goomy?

He closed his eyes. That's right. Who cares? Like that guy in one of his stories. Sitting at a bar putting away his third keg. The bartender points at his glass and says, "You know, buddy, there aren't any answers in there."

The guy looks up at the bartender, then looks back at his glass. "I'm not looking for answers; just less questions."

—Less questions. Let's hear it for less questions. Amen.

—"Mister, the monkey belongs to the piano player, and the boss likes the piano player, so we have to put up with the monkey. I'll get you another drink."

—So the bartender pulls the monkey's ass out of the Martini....

"That's the new stadium. The dome is held up by air pressure."

"What?" Jacob Randecker opened his eyes and leaned forward. "What did you say?"

The taxi driver, his gaze never leaving the icy street, cocked his head toward his left. "That's Minneapolis's new stadium. It's paid for by a nickel-a-drink tax. Isn't that a sonofabitch? I'm getting laid off from work tomorrow, I can't afford the price of a drink, but I got me a brand new stadium, if I can come up with the bread for a ticket...."

Minneapolis.

The driver kept talking as Jacob rubbed his eyes and tried to squeeze some kind of sense out of existence.—Minneapolis is in Minnesota. Minnesota is...somewhere west or south of Michigan. They have iron mines in Minnesota. And Saint Mary's Rehabilitation Center....

Panic edged into his intestines as memory crept through the fog.

Just before Christmas they came to eat dinner. That was the cover story. Ulterior motives were dripping from the rafters. But Jacob hadn't noticed. He had spent the day examining the inside of nothing; exactly as he had spent the previous six days.

After the meal, there was some television. They watched a video tape of *Apocalypse Now.* Talk about your heavy symbolism.

Della, Jacob's part-time secretary, said that they wanted to talk.

"Okay," said he, "let's talk."

The words came through distorted as if they had been reflected from the audio equivalent of funhouse mirrors. He could tell that they were worried.

—But, why? What about? Lay it on good ol', I can fix anything, Jacob. Put down your burden—

"We're worried about you, Jacob."

"Why? What about? I stopped drinking on the seventeenth."

He glanced at Ann, demanding her support, but her eyes were closed, her arms folded, a frown crouching upon her brow. The three friends sat before him like a jury, their accusations couched in phrases of concern. Jacob played with the words, deflecting the concern, trying to keep the subject on anything but Jacob Randecker. But they were persistent.

"Now, listen," said Kate.

Della's hands were occupied with wringing the life out of a scarf. "We have a friend who went through Saint Mary's." The scarf was unwrung and rewrung in the opposite direction. "We've been talking with him, and he says that Saint Mary's is just what you need."

"What for? I said I stopped drinking."

Larry rubbed his eyes and shook his head. "Six days ago?"

"Seven."

Larry smiled. "Seven, then. Why did you stop?"

"Not that it's any of your business, but I made a fool of myself. I went to get my Ativan prescription refilled. I had been up the night before drinking..." Jacob shrugged and smiled sheepishly. "I smelled bad. The doctor wouldn't write the new prescription."

Della began throttling the opposite end of her scarf. "Jacob, how do you feel?"

"Feel?"

"Yes. Happy, sad, mad—"

"—Depressed. Very, very depressed."

"Saint Mary's can show you the way out of that. It's not just stopping drinking. They can show you how to live."

"What kind of program is it, anyway? I don't want to get near any bible-thumping bunch like A.A."

"What do you know about A.A., Jacob?"

"Not a damned thing, and that's the way I want to keep it."

"Saint Mary's isn't a religious program."

"Oh? That's why it's called Saint Mary's? Hmmm?"

"The Catholic Church runs the place, but it isn't a religious program."

"Just think about it," said Larry.

Jacob sat, staring at his friends. They were overreacting. He couldn't just hack a month out of his life on a whim and go to wherever. Minneapolis. Minneapolis is a joke. Mary Tyler Moore, WJM, and Ted Baxter....

"Think about it," Larry repeated. His friends got up to leave.

"I will." He closed the door after them and stood muttering, "Yeah, I'll think about it. I'll think about it a whole bunch. So why don't you go home? Why don't you go the fuck home and mind your own fucking business."

He looked at the couch. Ann was fast asleep. Jacob roused his wife, and they went to bed. "You don't look so good," he said.

Her words were clipped, all emotion ironed out. "Are you going to go to Saint Mary's? What did you tell them?"

"I didn't say yes or no."

"Will you at least see Dr. Hamund, tomorrow?

"Sure. I'll see Don the shrink."

Ann went to bed and Jacob stood in front of the bathroom mirror eating a quadruple dose of Ativan topped off with a Librium. In bed with the lights out, he put his head on his pillow and dropped to sleep through a cloud of quiet tears and silent curses.

It wasn't anyone's business. And they read it all wrong.

—If they could look through my eyes for a second, they'd understand. Talk to the shrink, my ass....

—That's how the joke goes.

—"Like I said, mister, the monkey belongs to the piano player, and the boss likes the piano player, so we have to put up with the monkey."

—The drunk looks at the monkey, then back at the bartender. "There must be something I can do."

"Maybe you can talk to the piano player."

The cab lurched and Jacob ate another Ativan as he thought about Christmas Eve in Don the wigpicker's office.

Sitting in front of the shrink being very confused, talking to himself.

—I don't know what's going on. Why is everybody on my ass?

At some point he thought about what his wife and friends had risked in giving him their little talk, however misguided it might have been. It would have been so much easier in the short run to avoid scenes and confrontations, risking friendships, marriage…keep ignoring the problem, whatever they thought it was.

They had risked a lot. Jacob couldn't think of a situation that would move him to take a similar risk.

"It also shows a lot of care," said Don the shrink.

Jacob frowned. Don's statement was both true and contradicted one of the laws of the Randecker Reality, one of the supporting structures of the universe. That anyone could care a damn for him was not possible. That's why he cared not a damn for anyone. Driving everyone away, letting no one get close, was his rock.

—If you don't let them get close to you, they can't hurt you. But these people care. They're not stupid or gullible. Is there something about Jacob Randecker worth caring for?

—Questions. Always questions. And no one gives a damn that all of this is embarrassing me.

"Why can't you treat me?"

"Jacob, all I know about alcoholism is that I can't do anything for you.

"Given that I'm an alcoholic."

A smile. "Of course."

"What if I'm not alcoholic?"

"Then, don't you want to find out? There are some other options."
Don talked about Antabuse, the puke pill. Makes it impossible to
metabolize alcohol. If you take a drink, it won't kill you. Only makes
you wish you were dead.

"No. It scares me."

"There's Alcoholics Anonymous. it

"Forget it. It can't work for me."

"Separation from Ann."

Suddenly he was wide awake. "Why? What's that have to do with
anything?"

"She needs a rest from you, Jacob."

"That—That's a hell of a thing to say!"

"You need a rest, too, Jacob."

"No, I can't agree to that. That won't work."

"It doesn't look as though you've anything left that will work, Jacob."

"Don't play shrinker games with me. Say what you mean."

"For every suggestion, you have an objection." Don's Ticonderoga
doodled avant-garde nudes on a prescription form.

What was that dumb joke, thought Jacob. I just found out that my
analyst wears elevator shoes. How many shrinks does it take to change a
light bulb? Only one. But the light bulb really has to want to change—

"And there's St. Mary's in Minneapolis."

"Jesus! Can't you people think of anything else? What is this thing
with Minneapolis?"

"Do you really want to change, Jacob?"

Panic. "Why me? I mean, why am I the one who has to change?"

"I'm not going to argue with you, Jacob. You can talk circles around
me. You need help and I told you where you can get it."

"This is a hell of a thing you people want me to do. What if being
without me takes? What if Ann discovers she prefers it?"

"Cross that bridge when you come to it."

Jacob stared, paralyzed, as what he really wanted to say scrolled behind his eyes:

—Gee, I wish I'd said that.

—Did you screw the government out of $150,000 in student loans to learn that?

"Wotthehell."—Jacob Randecker is always good for a grand gesture. "I'll go to St. Mary's. I could use a vacation. It's second on my list to suicide, and I can always exercise that option.

"They say that suicide is a permanent solution to a temporary problem."

"Pick that up in the playground at psychiatrist school, did you?"

—And Jacob Randecker doesn't have temporary problems.

Some Christmas Eve. And it's going to be some great New Year, as well, he thought as he stared out of the window at the Minneapolis snowstorm, feeling awfully alone and like he had been talked into something.

He began fishing another Ativan out of his pillbox when the cab driver hit the brakes for a red light. The cab slid on the ice right through the intersection. A red panel truck coming from the right did an end-forend, just missing the cab's rear bumper. Jacob noted the near disaster as an inconsequential, not too terribly interesting event in the environment, and concentrated on what was important: finding the tablet he had dropped on the floor. He found it in the mud next to a cigarette butt.

He brushed the dirt off, erased where it had been from his memory, tossed it into his mouth, and settled back to watch miles of ugly grain elevators through the grimy window.

"Damn, man!" said the driver. "Sorry about that. The road's like a skating rink."

Jacob nodded and continued looking at the dull, stained, frozen buildings as he spoke. "Do you people really believe that Mary Tyler Moore lived here?"

The cabbie didn't answer. Jacob didn't notice. All he noticed was the color gray. Gray buildings, gray sky, gray snow, gray people dressed in gray....

Inside there was a feeling. Something that said to Jacob Randecker: you should be crying right now, or cursing, or screaming—not making Jokes.

—Numb jokes, dumb Jokes.

—Oh, yeah. That's how the joke went.

—So the drunk gets off his stool and walks over to the piano. He taps the piano player on the shoulder and says "Do you know your monkey has his balls in my Martini?"

—The piano player shakes his head. "No, man. But hum me a few bars and I'll fake it."

A voice woke him out of his semi-doze. The cab driver was looking back at him. Jacob's lips were numb. An electric tingle skittered across his scalp. "What?"

The cabbie pointed with his finger. "Where to?" Jacob leaned forward, looked out of the windshield, squinted, and saw a chocolate-brown collective sign stacked with the names of several institutions. It identified the mass of snow-covered, red brick buildings beyond it as St. Mary's Hospital. In the center of the aggregate was a specific. Jacob picked it and slumped back in the seat. "The rehab center."

The cabbie raised an eyebrow, then went back to the job. The taxi moved off, turned right, and stopped in front of a five-story building. The fare on the meter was over ten dollars. Jacob handed the driver a twenty and said, "Keep it," as he reached for the door.

"Thanks." The cab driver pointed at the building with his thumb. "What's it like in there?"

Jacob shook his head, got out of the cab, and pulled his bag out after him. "I don't know anything about it." He closed the door and the driver spoke through his open window. "Think it'll do you any good?"

Jacob turned around and looked up at the building. "These people have an impossible task: trying to convince me that there is a good reason for being in this world alive and sober at the same time."

The driver didn't laugh. "I hear you, man. Good luck."

Jacob heard the cab crunch off through the fresh snow, and he lowered his gaze to the building's double glass doors. Icy wetness trickled down the back of his neck. The image blurred.

"Damn. Damn, but I'm scared."

A guy in shirtsleeves was shaking his am. "Hey! Hey, what's your name?"

Jacob frowned. He was still standing in front of the glass doors. The guy, wide eyes and close-trimmed brown beard, seemed to have appeared out of nowhere. "Where did you come from?"

The bearded youth pointed toward the doors. "Are you supposed to be in there?"

"Why?"

"You've been standing out here in the snow for the last twenty minutes." He rubbed his arms, and paused as his face softened. "Look, man, you've come to the right place. But let's get inside. I'm freezing."

The man's image blurred as tears obscured Jacob's vision. "I don't know. I don't know."

The man took Jacob's arm and removed the bag from his stiff fingers. "Let's go." He began pulling Jacob toward the glass doors. "You can make it. You can make it if you can be honest. You know what I mean by honest?"

Jacob smiled, then laughed. "No. man. But hum me a few bars and I'll fake it."

2

Farmer Jones
Who's bald on top
Wishes he could
Rotate the crop.
Burma-Shave

Eden Valley, Minnesota.

From the darkness of the barn, Earl Nelson recited the ancient shaving cream rhyme as he watched the steady fall of the snow. The curtain of white almost obscured the dark, lifeless house. The Dodge was still broken down. "Which means paying the Novak kid again to plow us out in the morning."

—And Alice bitching at me for having to pay the Novak kid. God, that woman has a mouth on her. And she wants to know why I drink so much.

"If you loved me, Earl, you'd stop drinking," he whined in a mocking falsetto. He spat on the floor. "I guess that gives you your answer, bitch."

Again he looked at the falling snow. It was so dark that it might as well be night. He realized that he hated everything that he could see. He hated the snow, the house, the barn, the planet Earth.

"Why don't they have Burma-Shave signs anymore?" As a kid, Earl delighted in the red-and-white roadside rhymes. Earl and his two sisters would be in the back seat of the DeSoto, and when a string of the signs would appear, Dad would cry out, "Avast, there: Rhyme on the horizon."

And all of them would shout out the pieces of the rhyme as the signs flashed past, and then collapse in laughter. Good times. They were good times.

But one day, the roads glazed with old ice, Dad wrapped the old DeSoto around that big boulder at the forks. Earl thought he could still see the mark on the boulder left by the splash of blood thirty years before. You could smell the gin a hundred feet from the wreck.

Mom wasted away for two years, never leaving the house except to attend her own funeral. Earl hated her anyway. If she had been different, maybe Dad wouldn't have been drinking that day, January Sixth, Earl's eleventh birthday. And the girls?

—Jilly married that drunk from St. Paul, divorced, married that other drunk from Tampa, divorced, then disappeared. Shana went to college in California. Her body was sent back eight months later. An overdose of something. And there's me. Stuck in the middle of a snow-storm with a wife and kid who hate me and a Dodge that doesn't work. And no more Burma-Shave signs.

—Such a beautiful name, Eden Valley. Eden Valley, Minnesota. "Eden Valley my ass."

Earl yanked the barn door shut and turned on the lights. Beneath the cobweb-hung glare were the skeleton and scattered remains of the tractor Earl had been working on for the past month. He shook his head as once more he laid eyes upon his nemesis.

The thing crouched there, waiting.

—Here, Earl, try this. No? Well, try that. No? Well, try that other thing. Cut yourself, eh, Earl? Gotcha again, asshole.

Did the simple piece of inert machinery possess a spirit? A demon? Some form of intelligence? Not so much as to walk and talk, but enough to frustrate the heroic efforts Earl had employed to repair it?

He couldn't understand why he took the tractor's inertia so personally. It was like the piece of machinery had singled him out for destruction. Like the Burma-Shave signs. Years ago in some corporate boardroom, the motion was put forward: *Resolved: Screw Earl Nelson— take down the signs.*

"Aw, shit!"—The damned tractor will never work again. I know it, the family knows it, even the damned bank knows it. I know the equipment dealer knows it. Shiny color brochures every damned month. I'm sure that the damned tractor knows it! But a new tractor, with interest rates like they are….

There was a table littered with tools and odd parts. Next to the table was an empty nail keg. He sat upon the nail keg and glared at the lifeless machine.

"Bastard. You bastard. You greasy, dead-assed lump of shit." He clasped his hands, elbows resting on his knees, and let his head hang down.

"If I do get you to run, so what? Where am I going to get the money for gas and oil? Fertilizer? Seed? The damned mortgage? All of the damned mortgages?"

Pushing himself upright, he leaned against an empty stall. "If I could get a crop in, what'll it do next year? Dry up? Burn out? Flood? Bugs?" He pointed at the tractor. "And I get a bumper crop, and you'll fall the hell apart before I could—"

He shook his head and rubbed his eyes. "And if you don't fall apart, some new government regulation, prices won't pay me to burn the damn place down. Anyway, if everything works out just fine, I'll still be here in the middle of a farm and a family I can't stand. Nothing works. Nothing the hell works."

The tractor seemed to grow until it filled his vision. Earl closed his eyes, but it was still there. He pulled off his right glove, reached to his pocket, and pulled forth a pint bottle.

Whiskey. He never could stand the taste of gin. Gin always tasted like hair tonic. Seagrams tasted like shit, too, but not as bad as gin.

—Gin was Dad's poison.

"No. Mom was Dad's poison."

Holding the cap in his left hand, he tilted the bottle to his lips. Only enough drops to raise a smell fell on his tongue. He lowered the bottle, looked at it then threw it at the tractor. The bottle bounced off one cleated tire and fell unbroken to the plank floor. Earl stood, picked up a ten-pound sledge hammer from the table and advanced on the bottle.

His first swing smashed the bottle and continued through the rotten floor, wrenching Earl's shoulder. With one hand on the hammer, the other gripping his shoulder, he glowered at the hammer.

"You son of a bitch! You rotten sonofabitch!"

He yanked the hammer from the floor, held it in both hands, then saw the tractor. He swung the hammer down upon the engine block, again and again. Before he could understand what he was doing, he reduced the remains of the tractor to yard scrap. He dropped the hammer and staggered backwards until his back stopped against the tool table. Sweat dribbled from his eyebrows onto the lenses of his glasses, but he paid no attention to the funhouse images dancing before his eyes.

—Now the tractor is impossible to fix.

A strange terror ate at the edges of his fog. There was an old feed box in the next stall. He always kept a couple of quarts in there.

—Jason says it's hiding. What a pain in the ass he is. Won't even talk with me if I'm having one little drink. I'd stay the hell away from him if he wasn't the only person I know who'll listen to me without giving me a bunch of shit. He said that hiding booze isn't normal; it's sick.

Earl tried to remember. It was weeks—months—ago.

"Hell, Jason, if I didn't put something aside for a rainy day…Anyway, Alice keeps taking the stuff and tossing it down the drain. I'm just trying to keep from letting her bankrupt us, prices and all…."

"Alice is still doing that? Isn't she in Al-Anon?"

"Al-Anon! That bunch of nosy old bitches! Christ, what she must say about me there!" Earl shrugged and shook his head. "No. She doesn't take the stuff anymore. But it's just easier for me to…it's just easier, that's all. And don't give me any more shit about A.A. I went to five meetings, didn't I?"

"What about St. Mary's, Earl? You know, the place I went for treatment?"

Earl laughed a laugh that felt more like a cry. "Working eighteen hours a day, I can't make ends meet. Where am I going to come up with a month free and clear? And for what? *To sit around in some damned hospital?*"

He shouted at the closed doors of the barn. "Tell me, Jason! For what?"

He pushed himself away from the table and walked until he stood before the old feed box. He lifted the lid and looked inside. The bottles weren't in their usual place. He pushed the lid up and back until it thudded against the wall. The bottles were gone. In their place was his shotgun. There was a note on it. Earl bent over, picked up the note, and opened it. It was his son's handwriting. He read:

Dad—

Be a good father, for a change. If you are going to do it, do it right. The bottle takes too long.

There are more shells in the kitchen in case you miss with these.

—Joey

Joey was twelve years old. The note fell from Earl's fingers as waves of shame washed over him. His hands gripped the edge of the feed box. Slowly he went to his knees until his forehead rested on the backs of his hands.

"Jesus, Joey. I haven't been that bad to you. Not that bad:" The shame was forced sideways, distorting itself, becoming white-hot rage. Earl pushed himself up and ran to the door, kicking it open to the snowstorm. "Joey!" He listened but could hear no reply. He wouldn't be at school, would he? No, they're still out on Christmas break.

"Joey! I am a good father! Do you hear me? Do you hear me, Joey? Do you hear me, you little snot-nosed piece of shit? *I am a good man!*"

The scream was muffled by the snow. Earl lowered his hands from his eyes to see that he was kneeling in the icy white powder.

—Funny. I used to like snow as a kid. Before Dad died....

Earl pushed himself to his feet, turned, and walked mechanically to the feed box. Just before he reached it, he remembered that the bottles were gone. He slumped against the box, leaned over, and stared at the dull blue light reflected from the shotgun's barrel. Leaning over, he picked the weapon up by the small of its stock and stood up as his left hand gently gripped the barrel.

The hand was bare. He frowned at the bare hand, not remembering taking off his left glove. He shook his head and looked at the gun's safety. The safety was on.

"Good. Joey at least learned that much from me."

He pulled back the hand grip and looked into the breach. A brass-capped red cylinder looked back. All loaded and ready to go. He thumbed off the safety and chambered the shell.

"You little bastard. I'll give you something to think about." Earl aimed at the plank floor, placed his index finger on the trigger, and pulled.

A roar instantly numbed his ears as a piece of the floor vanished in a cloud of splinters and ancient dust. His shoulder ached, the acrid stench of burnt powder stung his nasal membranes. He turned to the open barn door and waited.

A minute passed. Ten minutes passed. He lowered the shotgun to his side. Fifteen.

No one was coming.

—Is this what it amounts to, then? Is this what it all means? Your husband, your father, blows the shit out of himself, and no one cares enough to look?

Twenty minutes passed. Earl walked out in the snow, still carrying the shotgun, heading for the house.

Flashes of scenes went through his mind, shards of reality mixed with splinters of fantasy:

Grooming the mare with Larry for 4-H, helping Larry's friend Bessy with her pigs. Alice screaming at him, tearing at his face with fingernails like knives. Alice on their sixth anniversary dressed in that dreamy black wisp, Earl too drunk to do anything but call her names and laugh. The note.

—the note from Joey.

"Why? Why are they doing this to me?"

The storm door to the kitchen slammed shut behind him. As he flicked on the overhead light, he saw the box of shells on the kitchen table. Earl pumped the weapon, chambering a fresh round. Holding the gun at the ready, he took a step toward the living room. "I'll show you, you little bastard."

At the foot of the stairs he paused and looked down at the shotgun, his tears splashing on the softly glowing hand-rubbed stock. "Dear God. Dear God, what am I doing?"

Without volition he watched as his left hand moved the muzzle of the weapon beneath his chin while his right thumb reached for the trigger.

—Just let it stop. Just let it stop the buzzing in my head. I just don't want to hurt anymore.

—God, what if I miss? What if I only fuck up my face? Blow off my jaw. The mess in the kitchen. Alice'll be furious.

"God. God. God, what in the hell did I ever do to you?"

He lowered the shotgun, walked back to the kitchen, and placed the weapon gently on the kitchen table.

Just before leaving the last time, Jason had said something. *"When you finally run out of answers, Earl, call me. Before you do anything, Earl, call."*

Earl stood alone in the center of the floor. "I guess I am all out of answers." He looked at his watch. The crystal was smashed, the hands missing. "Aw, look at that."

Reaching to his wallet, he pulled out a slip of paper, then went to the wall phone and dialed. A woman's voice, a voice that sounded much too happy, answered. "Yes? Hello?"

"Hello. This is Earl. Earl Nelson? Can I talk to Jason?"

A long silence, then a man's voice came on the wire. "Earl?"

"Yeah."

"What is it? What's the matter?"

"Jason, that place you talked about. St. Mary's?"

"What about it?"

"I'm ready. For about another fifteen minutes, I'm ready. Past that I don't know."

"I'll be there in five minutes."

"I was going to kill my son. Get me out of here, Jason. You got to get me out of here."

"Hang in there, Earl, okay? Five minutes."

Earl nodded as he heard Jason hang up.

"Hang in there."

He replaced the receiver, turned and saw the shotgun on the table.

He picked it up, ejected the shell, and leaned the gun against the wall. Turning up his collar, Earl went outside to wait in the snow on the front steps for the last friend he had in the world.

3

Jacob Randecker opened his eyes. He was sitting in a chair in front of a desk. He frowned and looked around, trying to remember where he was and why he was there. How had he gotten to this particular office? It was always possible that he would have to find his way out again. That edge of terror again tugged at his intestines, and he took out his pillbox and put an Ativan into his mouth. He noticed that he still had one of the blue-and-white Libriums left. He put that into his mouth as well, washing down both with the cup of coffee he took from the edge of the desk.

As he waited for the edges to soften, he studied the office. There was a stupid little Nativity scene hanging on the wall. A polystyrene Madonna grinning evilly at an Aryan Jesus. That's right; Christmas was back there someplace.

A woman entered the office and sat down across from Jacob. She was one of those youthful, clean-scrubbed, naturally beautiful, wholesome bitches that Jacob Randecker hated. She probably jogged, too. He looked in his hand and found the check that he was supposed to do something with. It was made out to St. Mary's Rehabilitation

Cent—oh, yeah. Minneapolis.

The check was his deposit. "What about my insurance?"

She handed him back his Blue Cross card. "We still require the deposit." She took the check and turned her attention to a form. "Occupation?"

"I'm a writer."

Her eyebrows went up. "Really?"

"Yes, really." Jacob felt very threatened.

"What have you written?"

"I don't know. What have you read?"

She smiled and returned to the form. "Wife's name?"

As the questions were asked and answered, Jacob wanted to take back his wisecrack and prove to her that he was a writer. He was somebody.

—I am a writer. There are the books, the stories, the awards; all of those things that seem to impress everyone in the world but me.

—Everybody but me.

The Ativan and Librium began, at last, to work on the edges.

"Jacob? Jacob?"

He frowned as he felt the weight pulling on his arms.

He wasn't sitting; he was standing.

He looked down and saw the armload of books he was carrying. Up went his head. A brightly lit hallway—doors, railings, and light fixtures running down the walls. Posters and pitiful holiday decorations everywhere. The office was gone.

—Why is reality all in bits and pieces? Who tore this day into a thousand scraps and threw them into the wind?

"You'll need those materials for your work here." There was a woman standing in front of him. She was a pleasant-faced smiler with dark blond hair, sweater and slacks.

"Work?" He looked at the books in his arms. "I thought this was supposed to be a hospital."

She kept smiling. "It is." She pointed toward a door. He carried in the books and dropped them on a small desk. His bags and coat were already on the bed.

—So, I must have been in here before. Yes?

Harsh fluorescent light from fixtures above the beds filled the room. He stood at the foot of one of the two beds as the woman began searching through his belongings.

"Lady, are you just nosy, or what?"

"We have to search for medications. Any medications you need will be prescribed for you."

Jacob took a deep breath and shook his head. "I don't do any drugs. My problem is drinking and I haven't had anything to drink since the seventeenth of December."

She began stuffing things into her pockets. His Alka-Seltzer Cold Plus, his aspirin, his vitamin C.

"What—Hey, what are you *doing?* Swipe that stuff and my sinuses will curl up and die."

"Anything you need will be prescribed for you." She held up a small brown plastic container. "What's this?"

"Ativan. It's a prescription for anxiety." She opened the bottle and poured the pills into the palm of her hand. Among the little white Ativan oblongs were several blue-and-whites.

"Those blue and white capsules are Librium. My doctor prescribed them when I stopped drinking."

Into her pocket they went, along with Jacob Randecker's heart, followed by his Alka-Seltzer regular.

"What if I get heartburn?"

"Any medications you need—"

"I know, I know." Jacob sighed as she topped off her bulging pockets with his Preparation H.

"Not that, too."

"Yes, that too."

Jacob rubbed his eyes, thinking.—"Hey, man, what're you in for?"

—"I was doin' H."

—"You wuz shootin' smack?"

—"No. Ah duz Preparation H, straight up the old kazoo—with a dirty finger!"

"Did you say something?"

Jacob smirked and shook his head.

"Remain in your room. Someone will be by in a little while to brief you and give you your schedule. And until you detox, you'll be getting your vitals taken four times a day, every day. Morning vitals are taken in the lounge at the end of the wing. Go to the nurse's station for the other three. The times are on your schedule." Out the door she went, looking for more poor Alka-Seltzer junkies to rip off.

—"Hey, man. I'm sick."

—Plop, plop. Fizz, fizz.

—No relief in sight.

"I don't need to detox," he said to the empty doorway. "Hell, I haven't had anything to drink since the seventeenth."

Jacob sat on the edge of his bed, his fists thrust into his coat pockets, and stared out the window at his first night in Minneapolis. Dark, cold, and everything covered with ice and snow. The streets and walks were deserted, a frozen confetti of flakes curling around in the cones of lonely brightness cast by the widely spaced street lights. "How did I ever wind up here? God, what a hole."

Jacob turned around. There was another bed in the room. His stomach knotted as his imagination took over and assigned him a succession of socially undesirable roommates. It's a rehab center. Drunks and junkies.

"I'll probably be bunkies with the guy who taught Charlie Manson the ropes." He thought of the television junkies shaking it out on the block, slitting throats for enough bread to score another fix.

"I'm sure glad I was too smart to get into drugs." He felt a headache beginning, and he began reaching for his pills, stopping himself when he remembered the shakedown. He reached into his sweater-vest pocket for his pillbox. Even before he opened it, he knew that it was empty. He tossed it into the wastebasket, not relishing the prospect of trying to get a few aspirin from the goons at the nurse's station.

He lit his pipe and comforted himself with the thought that he had a round-trip ticket and plenty of money in his wallet. Anytime he wanted to, he could split. That time was getting close. Ann would be disappointed. So would the friends who had pushed him in this direction. Don the shrink, too. But they didn't know; they didn't understand. A terrible mistake had been made.

"I don't belong here."

He said it, and it sounded friendly. Reasonable. Rational. Sane.

He glanced at the pile of books. *I'll Quit Tomorrow.* He remembered reading that one before, but couldn't remember anything about it. Ann had given it to him. Some coincidence. *The Recovery of Reality.* Hmm. A big blue book: *Alcoholics Anonymous*—

He bolted upright, his eyes widening. "They told me that Saint Mary's has nothing to do with A.A.!"

There was a skinny light blue book titled *Twelve Steps and Twelve Traditions: A Co-founder of Alcoholics Anonymous Tells How*—

"Damn!" *Living Sober: Some Methods A.A. Members Have Used*—

And every rock Jacob turned over exposed another snake. *A Day at a Time*, a tiny tome filled with daily doses of religious claptrap; and *Twenty-Four Hours a Day*, more daily doses of more religious claptrap. Even a handy wallet-sized item containing the selfsame twelve steps and twelve traditions on the inside, and a little prayer on the outside: *God grant me the serenity to accept the things I cannot change*—

"Well, goddammit, I can certainly change this!" Jacob shredded the little white card.

"There's no smoking in patient rooms."

Jacob tossed the pieces of the card on the floor, pulled the pipe from his mouth, turned and saw another female clad in slacks, but this time the woman was wearing black curly hair instead of blond. "What do you mean, no smoking?"

"Smoking is allowed only in the lounges designated as smoking areas." She smiled. "It's the Minnesota Clean Indoor Air Act."

Jacob shook his head as anger reduced his despair and confusion to righteous certainty. "That tears it."

"What do you mean?"

He pointed at the mountain of treatment texts. "What is this shit?"

"What?"

"This." He slammed his hand down on top of the texts. "I was told Saint Mary's didn't have anything to do with the A.A. program!"

"The program here is based on the A.A. pro—"

"I sort of figured that out for myself!" Jacob turned abruptly, his eyes narrowed, the tip of his beard an inch from the woman's nose.

"Honeybuns, do I have a news flash for you. I'm no spook-sucking religionist. This halfwit bible society doesn't have a godfuckingdamned thing to teach me."

He stormed around her and marched down the corridor past the nurse's station. He needed a cup of coffee, a smoke, and to go home. "I am in the wrong place," he muttered. A blond woman in a lavender jogging suit came out of a room. Jacob said to her, "Why is everybody around here so stupid?"

Her expression didn't change. "Don't worry about it. If you stick around long enough, they'll smarten up."

4

The Georgia evening was cold and wet as the Reverend Roger Sanders stood on the doorstep of Bishop White's plantation-style manor. He shivered as he stood there, thinking that he hadn't had enough to drink after all. He ate two more Clorets to prepare for the meeting on the other side of the door.

—The only reason I am here is because I am black. I can name a dozen men and women in the church who drink more than I do, including the haystack bishop who called me here. I bet some of them use cocaine, pot, and other drugs. I was singled out for just one reason: color.

"Might as well be done with it." He stabbed the doorbell button with his finger, twisting his knuckle in the process. As he was flexing his finger, the door opened to reveal the duchess of the manor, Sandra White. Whitey White's whitey wife. She looked too pleasant, was dressed too well, and acted too, too polite.

"Good evening, Roger. Please come in. Gale is expecting you."

She pronounced Gale, gay-yul, and Roger, Rah-juh. She talked with one of those mouthful-of-mush southern accents that Roger swore was a put-on. He nodded curtly and stepped into the vestibule, his hat defiantly upon his head. He glowered down at her. "I told him I can't stay for too long. I'm very busy."

"I'm sure he understands." She held out her hands and smiled. "Roger, you can keep wearing your hat and coat if you wish, but they are soaking wet. Wouldn't you like to let me have them?"

Roger paused in mid-glower, thinking that she was making him feel like a fool. Swallowing hard, he closed his eyes, removed his coat and hat and gave them to her.

"These are wet, aren't they? Go right on in, Roger."

She stood there nodding toward the bishop's door until he began walking toward it. He opened the door and saw Whitey busily scribbling at his football-field sized desk. The bishop looked up at Roger and grinned. "Come in, Roger. Come in. I was just finishing up a few things. Thank you for dropping by. Sit down and I'll be with you in a second."

Unable to mouth meaningless pleasantries, Roger simply nodded, closed the door, and sat down in the chair facing the bishop. The chair was a heavy wooden piece of furniture with all of the domestic charm of an electric chair. Whitey went back to his scribbling.

—Me sitting in this chair like some criminal, or a bad little boy called into the principal's office.

Roger studied the robust white-haired man on the other side of the desk.

—Whitey White. And is he ever white. Sitting in his brown leather throne, leaning over his antique, mahogany desk, his manicured nails and pink hands, that rum and coke on the desk next to his elbow....

"There." Whitey pushed his papers aside, clasped his hands together and looked straight at Roger. "Do you remember that little meeting you and your family had here in my office two months ago?"

—Little meeting, my ordained ass. Inquisition. The things they said.… "Of course."

—You can't say a thing to me, Whitey. Not with that rum and coke next to your elbow, you can't.

Whitey White nodded his head, took a sip from his drink, and smiled. "Good. Do you remember the agreement you made with me and your family?"

"Agreement?"

"You were going to try to stop drinking on your own."

Roger shook his head. "I was…I am doing just fine. Just fine. And things would be much better if everyone would mind his own business!"

Whitey leaned forward, his elbows on the desk, his hands clasped together. The smile left his face. "I'm your bishop. Your work is my business. Denise is your wife. Her husband is her business. Carmel is your daughter. Her father is her business. Now, how have you been doing with your drinking?"

"I said, just fine."

"That's not what Denise and Carmel tell me. They told me that last week you ran your car into a ditch and passed out in the middle of your front lawn. They said they had to drag you in, undress you, clean you—"

"They make it sound worse than it was." Roger interrupted. "Sure, I lost control of the car, but the roads were wet. I tripped going into the house, and—"

"Roger, do you really want me to bring them in here for a little questioning? Denise and Carmel have had seven weeks of Al-Anon. If I bring them in here, they're going to tell you what you need to hear, not what you want them to say. Shall I bring them in?"

"I didn't know they were here," he whispered. Roger moistened his lips as a terrible pressure mounted inside his skull. "If I had known—"

"Shall I bring them in?"

Roger glanced at the door to Whitey's office, closed his eyes, and slowly shook his head, remembering the last time he had seen them.

Sitting in the living room, covered with dried mud, the sofa cover spread with more dried mud. Permanent red Georgia mud. Denise, kneeling on the floor in front of him. "Why, Roger? Why?"

His sixteen year old daughter, Carmel, standing over him. "I'm tellin' you, Papa, this's the last damn time I haul your sorry ass in so the neighbors won't see another shitfaced nigger out cold on his front lawn. *How do you get up before those people every Sunday and preach that sanctimonious shit? I'd choke—*"

"No," he whispered. "Don't bring them in here." He racked out a harsh sigh and nodded. "Okay. I'm drinking. But—"

"No buts," interrupted Whitey. "I'm not interested in your excuses, Roger. And I don't want to hear any more promises. Do you remember what you agreed to if you couldn't make it on your own?"

"To go to that place for the cure."

"There's no cure, Roger. But you'll learn all about that."

Roger pushed against the chair's armrests. "Bishop, I didn't say I was going!"

Whitey sat back in his chair. "We have an agreement, Roger. I insist that you live up to your end."

Roger sat back in his chair, hid his face behind a mask of indifference, and motioned with his hands. "I'm sorry if there was some misunderstanding, bishop But I have no intention of going. Isn't this the place way out west? Minnesota? There are simply too many things for me to do here."

"What do you have to do that's worth dying for?"

Roger chuckled. "Come now. Isn't that overstating the case just a bit? I know I ought to do something, and I'm taking serious steps—"

"Don't feed me any of your bullshit, Roger." It was said with an even, friendly voice. Roger couldn't have been more shocked if Whitey had reached across his desk and slapped Roger's face. Bishops don't say bullshit.

"If you don't go, Roger, you will no longer be the pastor at Saint John's, nor will you be anywhere else within this church. That was the agreement."

Roger laughed. "You mean I'll be fired?"

"Not only can you bet the farm on that, Roger, you can bet your narrow little ass."

Roger stood up, his arms quivering at his sides. "Who do you think you're talking to? Don't...don't ever talk to me like that! I don't care who you are, you honkey...muth...You...you...."

Whitey smiled. "Are you finished? Our plane leaves in two hours. Our bags are packed and in my car. It's up to you. Do we go to Saint Mary's, do you rent a store front and start up your own church, or do you go and look for another line of work?"

Roger lowered himself into his chair. "We?"

"I'm going to escort you to St. Mary's."

"No. I remember now, Whitey. You said you went to Saint Mary's."

"That's right. Class of June, Seventy-Eight." The bishop said it like he was proud of it.

"You drink!" Roger stood and pointed at the bishop's glass. "That: I've seen you drink a hundred times! You're drinking right now!"

"Want one?" Without waiting for an answer, the bishop swung around in his chair, opened a small refrigerator, and returned, placing an unopened can of Diet Pepsi on the desk. Roger reached past the can, picked up Whitey's drink and sniffed it. Then he tasted it. Nothing but cola. Whitey grinned. "Roger, Saint Mary's will give you a whole new meaning for the term Pepsi Generation."

5

At the sound of his own scream, Jacob opened his eyes, the rapidly fading horror of his nightmare still making him breath hard.

The room was strange. The hospital. St. Mary's.

He saw that he was sitting up in his bed, the lights above his back were on. The other bed was still empty. Reaching to his nightstand, he picked up his watch. It was one-thirty in the morning. The last time he had checked his watch it had been a couple of minutes after one.

With his hands he wiped the sweat from his face as he tried to ease the tightness in the back of his neck. "Christ, the heat in here."

He swung his feet to the floor, walked to the window, and slid it partly open. As crisp, clean air entered the room, Jacob examined the scene outside. The ugliness of the Minneapolis night had only deepened. Snow and more snow. "I thought Maine had it bad."

He returned to his bed, sat down, and listened to the crackle of the plastic mattress cover. "No wonder I'm hot." He pushed at the two pillows with his left hand and listened to their plastic covers crackle. Together the two pillows were no thicker than the fuzz on Jacob's tongue.

He felt at the pillowcase for his wallet. Money, airline ticket, credit cards.

—Can't have some light-fingered junky swiping and flashing my Masterfraud card. Paranoid is simply the definition of being realistic.

He satisfied himself that the wallet was there.

—Will that be enough, or should I check inside? The cards might have walked away on their own. Or a really skilled junky could have placed the wallet back in the pillowcase while I was asleep.

—Checking inside the wallet would be silly.

He checked. "Hell, no. I'm not paranoid."

Ann's comments on the phone a few hours before about protecting the cards from his new classmates had been pointed.

No. Threatening.

Everything was in order. He replaced his wallet in the pillowcase. He reached for his pipe, but as he picked it up, he remembered the Minnesota Clean Indoor Air Act. He lowered the pipe to his lap and looked toward the door leading to the bathroom his room shared with the adjoining room. "Thirty-nine years old, and sneaking smokes in the shithouse. My how the mighty have fallen."

He turned on the light and slid shut the accordion door. He lit his pipe and sat on the toilet. To accommodate the handicapped, the toilet was so high Jacob's toes hardly touched the floor. The toilet paper seemed to be that super-stiff, institutional test of a man's ability to withstand pain: Brillo Cloud. There was a hissing air vent in the ceiling that should suck out the smell of the tobacco smoke.

He stared at the vent.

—What if there's a smoke detector in there? Or a TV camera?

He knew he was being silly, but the anxiety wouldn't leave. The tension in his neck and shoulders was nothing compared to the headache. He finished his pipe and got up to leave. The door to the bathroom would not unlock.

"What the hell?" He shook the door and shook it again. "Open up, dammit." He looked around the bathroom for something to pry open the lock. He saw the emergency pull-cord next to the toilet.

He could call the nurse's station to get the door open, but there he would be, smoking pipe in hand. Even without the pipe, they'd know why he had gone in there. "I don't believe this. How did I wind up in this situation?" His bag of toilet articles was on the counter. He looked through it, thinking that it seemed awfully empty without his various medications. He found his nail file.

Several minutes and a broken nail file later, he escaped to the relative freedom of the bedroom. Again he looked at his watch. 1:58 a.m..

He checked his wallet again, turned off the lights, put his head on his pillow, and tried again to sleep. Time passed. More time passed. He realized that his hand was inside the pillowcase, and that he had a death grip on his wallet. If the cards fell into evil hands, Ann would see to it that he never heard the end of it.

"Rip Van Winkle couldn't sleep like this." He got up and took his wallet into the bathroom. He pulled the small set of scissors out of his kit and cut his cards into tiny pieces. After flushing the pieces down the toilet, he tried to sleep again. After a few moments more, he sat up and turned on the lights.

"I can't sleep." He looked at his pillows. They told him that sleep for the night was a lost cause. His gaze wandered to the pile of texts on his desk. Hot anger immediately flushed his face.

There was a steno pad that was part of the book issue. Jacob picked it up, turned to the first clear page, picked up a tome, and continued preparing his brief tentatively titled, "Why Jacob Randecker Doesn't Belong Here."

At the top of the page he scribbled *December 30th*.

Another browse through the Big Book, *Alcoholics Anonymous,* and he began writing:

The A.A. program is founded on substituting the religion/philoso-phy of moral altruism & helplessness for a chemical dependency—sub-stituting religion for alcohol (and not such a great religion, at that).

Jacob was an atheist and believed that he always had been. The book said that's okay. It's not a religious program.

"Like the Inquisition wasn't a religious program," Jacob snorted.

He turned to "The Chapter to the Agnostic."

I get the impression that the only atheists A.A. has ever seen are dis-illusioned religionists—and that the program will lead to a restoration of faith. Preach it, bro'.

I also get the very loud impression that A.A. holds that my only two options right now are continued destruction through alcohol or "spiri-tual" salvation.

Which brings us, in turn, to A.A.'s questionable "success record." "One million recovered," if I understand the program, is the same as saying "One million drunks turned into Jesus freaks."

Although more socially acceptable, I find religionism as bad or worse than alcoholism.

More reading and still more. A few words made him stumble. He read them again, then wrote.

If A.A. is right—and they've been in the business a long time—I am dead. However, reason would seem to indicate the possibility that one can remain true to what little truth one has nailed down and still be sober—we must all keep open minds.

"Okay, then. Let's just answer a few of these questions."

Why am I here? I am here because…because I guess I'm an alco-holic, and that St. Mary's was represented to me as a non-religious, non-A.A. treatment program. They've made a religion out of not drinking.

More reading, and the walls seemed to get closer and closer. The writing continued.

This crap is just a bunch of gross generalities.

Bored should be on this list of emotions. One of my big ones for drinking—and I don't make myself bored.

More reading, more writing.

Nitrous oxide is a drug? Now that I think about it, I didn't drink as much before that spate of dental work. After that one three-hour session under gas, I just didn't want to come down. Went straight to the liquor store after leaving and didn't come down until—

He thought very hard.

I didn't come down until my heart attack. That was on my thirty-sixth birthday.

He shook his head. "Well, according to *their* definition, I'm chemically dependent."

At harmful dependency level—hurting self and others. Still, they want to move the psychological dependency from alcohol to religion.

I have the chemical dependency

The program is still in question.

A few more pages, and he was wide awake.

Chemical dependency—psychological dependency includes Ativan whether drinking or not! Holy shit!

There was the lecture last evening after that inedible dinner. Jacob hadn't been paying very close attention. He had been sitting on the new fish row, the back. Something the lecturer had said stuck.

"The most prominent symptom is that it's the disease that tells you that you haven't got it."

Someone from the front. "You mean alcoholism?"

"Yes."

"What about drug addiction?"

"Are you one of those curious persons who believes that ethanol isn't a drug?"

"I know it's a drug, but aren't the diseases different? Isn't alcoholism different than drug addiction?"

"The difference between drugs and alcohol: it's like changing seats on the *Titanic.*"

Jacob had laughed. It was a good line.

He shook his head. "Ativan isn't a drug. Technically, I suppose it is. But it's not a real drug, like them neat things the street shooters use." He read some more on the progression of the disease. One-by-one the addict gets rid of his straight friends and replaces them with other addicts. Now here was something that just didn't apply.

I never lost any friends. I never had any friends to lose.

I never had any blackouts.

Alibi system—These people are blaming everything, all problems, on alcohol. There can be problems without alcohol.

Jacob nodded and said "Don't I know it." He looked at the pad one last time and wrote.

I don't know. I just don't know.

He put down the pen and looked at his watch. 3:21 a.m. Jacob tossed the steno pad on the desk, rubbed his eyes and noticed that a backache and sinus inflammation had joined the stiff neck and headache.

"It's only tension. I've got to relax."

He closed his eyes, leaned back upon his plastic pillows, and tried to make sense out of the past twenty-four hours. Sense would not come.

After his first encounter with Honeybuns, the floor counselor with the aversion to smoking, and storming out of his room, he had gone to the tiny kitchen on the fourth floor placed there for the convenience and salvation of the patients. Picking up a tiny foam plastic coffee cup from a stack on a shelf, Jacob had drawn coffee from the automatic dispenser and pushed his way through a swinging door into the adjoining recreation room. Ping pong table, pool table, a piano, record player, and lots of chairs.

Everything had been in use. There were lots of patients. Jacob had paused to reflect on the company he would be keeping for the New Year holiday. Sorry fathers, mothers, husbands, wives, children, rejected by their families, condemned to spend this moment of renewed family resolution whining it out along with a hundred other rejected souls.

"Christ, is New Year's going to be f-u-n, fun." He made his way to a couch facing the center of the room, sat down, and sipped at his coffee.

The anger at the woman proselytizing the canons of the Minnesota Clean Indoor Air Act faded to fear. The room was full of patients: teens, twenties, thirties on up to one old guy who sat telling jokes with a Swedish accent. Strangers. The room was full of strangers.

Jacob Randecker was terrified of strangers. The voices around him talked in cheery voices about smack, coke, ope, dust, reds, 'ludes, pot, and the ever popular John Barleycorn. Strange words: chemical dependent, co-dependent, concerned person, family week, enabling, higher power, group, getting staffed.

He listened in amazement about the variety and quantity of substances that can be shot into a vein, ingested, rubbed into an eye, inhaled, snorted. One fellow, doing nostalgia, was an opium smoker.

Jacob put his fear aside long enough to satisfy his curiosity. "No kidding? You smoke opium?"

The man nodded. He was young, narrow faced, with large, deep-set brown eyes. The smile came easily to his lips. "I once read something about Edgar Allen Poe."

"Isn't smoking ope a little old fashioned?"

There was a bitter glitter to his eyes as he looked away. "I guess I'm just an old fashioned sort of a guy."

And he heard it isn't what you use, or when you use, or how you use, or even how much you use. It's what it does to you.

After running out of coffee for the fifth time, Jacob remembered the brown plastic cup he had been issued. The one with the little prayer upon it. Almost everyone in the room was carrying a similar one, and the reason was obvious: the brown cup held about three times as much as one of those white foam cups. Those folks certainly could put away the coffee. If everyone used those little foam cups, the asphalt floor tile wouldn't last a week.

Jacob had returned to his room, found that the counselor had gone, and picked up the brown cup. On one side there was a curious coat of arms crowned by the enigmatic interrogative: "How does that make you feel?" On the other side that clever little prayer: "God grant me the serenity to accept the things I cannot change, courage to change the things I can, and wisdom to know the difference." Jacob was grinding his teeth so hard, they ached.

He took the pressure sensitive name strip they had given him to identify his cup, removed the backing, and attached the strip diagonally across the prayer.

Before returning to the kitchen, he scanned the room to see if the counselor had left a copy of the schedule. Jacob found it and read that they were on a special holiday schedule. The next two days would be taken up with New Year's Eve and New Year's Day, followed by the weekend. Except for an odd-lecture or movie, there wouldn't be anything to do except smoke, drink coffee, and grind teeth. His plans for returning to Maine were already in the works.

He had two hundred dollars and the remaining half of his round trip plane ticket in his pocket. But it was late, he was tired, and it was cold outside. Tomorrow would be soon enough to plow his way to the airport.

A little white card fluttered to the floor. Jacob frowned and picked it up. The Twelve Steps and Twelve Traditions of A.A. "Where in the hell did this come from?"

Back in the recreation room, Jacob telephoned Ann. Ann's voice had sounded weary and very, very frightened.

"Hey, I'm sorry I was so silent driving to the airport. I was pretty tired. And I guess I was waiting for you to ask me not to go."

Her voice, very small. "You'll never know how much I wanted to."

"Yeah, well, I just wanted to let you know that I showed up in one piece. By the way, the program here is based on the A.A. program. I might not stay."

"Jacob, I didn't know anything about the place—"

"Yeah, well, good night. I'll let you know when my plane will get in."

Silence from the other end of the line, and Jacob had hung up.

That night he had read all of the books at light speed, looking for things to fight about, finding plenty, and making notes, preparing his brief for when he stepped off the plane in Portland a month early.

Afterward, he had gone to bed and tried to get some sleep. Both the pillows and the mattress crackled with every movement. They were all encased in heavy plastic. And he began to sweat. For a moment he slept, then came the nightmare.

That one guy in the lounge had called them St. Mary's Revenge. About St. Mary's ball-busting dreams, another one had asked, "You ever hear of paying the piper?"

Jacob nodded.

"That's the collection agency." Another fellow in the lounge had called the dreams Saint Mary blue.

Jacob opened his eyes and looked again at his watch. 3:59 a.m. "How long can a night be?"

He looked again at his collection of patient schedules. The facility festivities would begin at 7:15 a.m. Vitals in the wing lounge. He figured that he may as well spend the rest of the night some place where he could smoke and drink coffee. He got out of bed, grabbed his brown plastic coffee cup and headed for the door.

6

Between lights out and morning call, the fourth floor lounge and recreation room was a lonely dark cavern illuminated by a single dim corner light. Earl Nelson sat in pajamas and bathrobe, looking through the recreation room's double doorway at the brightly lit nurse's station. Crushing his twenty-second cigarette since abandoning his efforts at sleep, he sipped at his coffee and leaned back in the couch. He couldn't tell for certain, the room was too dark, but he thought there were three or four other patients scattered throughout the lounge.

—Why can't they sleep? It's such a lonely place. Maybe I shouldn't have come here.

He looked down at the bathrobe. If Jason hadn't packed a quick bag of his own clothes, Earl would have arrived with nothing but the clothes on his back. Earl had quit trying to figure out Jason's angle. Maybe Jason just cared.

Earl sighed, finished off his coffee, and pushed himself to his feet to get another cup. As he moved toward the kitchen door, the shadow of another patient stood in front of him. Earl's breath stopped, then resumed as the shadow moved toward the hall. A third patient, blond with a gray-shot beard, gold-rimmed glasses and a tan bathrobe, was approaching the recreation room.

As they passed, the shadow asked the beard: "How are you doing?"

"How am I doing what?" came the sarcastic response.

The shadow shook his head. "It'll get better, man. The first few are Mary blue, but it evens out. Welcome to the Nighthawks."

The beard turned and watched as the shadow continued down the darkened hallway. Earl turned and made his way around the ping pong table, seeking the safety of the kitchen's bright lights.

—There are too many weird people at St. Mary's. Who knows where they've been, or what they've done? The angry one with the beard looks like some kind of flipped-out psycho-killer.

Once inside the kitchen, Earl placed his cup in the automatic dispenser and held the button until the cup was full. As he withdrew the cup, the door to the recreation room swung open and in came the bearded, flipped-out psycho-killer. The beard gave a curt nod. "I guess you're a Nighthawk, too."

Earl nodded. "I guess. My name's Earl. Earl Nelson."

"Jacob Randecker."

"Jake?"

"Sure. Why not?"

"If you don't want to be called Jake, tell me."

Jake waved his hand and stuck his cup in the dispenser. "It doesn't make any difference." He nodded at his cup as he pulled it from the dispenser. "Fresh from the kidneys of a diseased moose" He glanced at Earl as he opened the small refrigerator for some milk. "How long've you been here?"

"Just since tonight. You?"

Jake frowned for a moment as he lightened his coffee and replaced the cardboard container. "Yesterday, I think. Yesterday afternoon, or evening." He cocked his head toward the recreation room. "Want to sit down?"

"Sure."

They worked their way through the dark until they found two easy chairs. Jake sat in one and crossed his legs as Earl sat in the other. They remained silently sipping at their coffee until Earl spoke. "How did you wind up here?"

Jake burst out with a sharp, hard laugh. "I'd give worlds to know. I'm not too damned sure how I got here. Maybe I got talked into something." Jake sipped at his coffee and lowered it to an end table. "What about you?"

Earl sat immobilized. "Me?" He leaned forward, his elbows on his knees, his face resting on his palms. There were terrible things clawing at the inside of his chest. "I heard about this place from a friend of mine. His name is Jason. I met him through A.A." Earl pulled his hands away from his face. As they drew away, they became fists.

—This is not what I want to say.

He lowered his hands and looked at the shadow sitting across from him. "Jake, a few hours ago I was on my way up to my son's room with a shotgun to kill him. A split second later I had the muzzle of that gun aimed at my own head."

Jake leaned forward and placed a hesitant hand upon Earl's shoulder. Earl shook his head. "I don't know what it was. My boy wanted me to kill myself. He wrote me a note and put it where I keep a bottle. He put a shotgun there and—God. The note told me to go kill myself." Again Earl shook his head, amazed at the amount of pain, amazed that he couldn't seem to stop talking, and amazed that the guy sitting across from him was still there, listening.

"Alice, my wife, hasn't talked to me in years. Not really talked. She nags like a bitch." He took several deep breaths. "It seems like everything I do—the farm. All shit. It's all shit. I had to get out. Just had to get out."

Earl waited for Jake to excuse himself and begin edging out of the room. But Jake simply sat there, his hand upon Earl's shoulder, his eyes fixed upon some unseeable point. Earl reached up and placed his hand upon Jake's arm. "Jake?"

"Huh?" Jake looked surprised, then he squeezed Earl's shoulder and let go as he slumped back in his chair. "I don't know how you can just blurt it out like that."

"Sorry—"

"No. No, Earl, don't be sorry."

Jake picked up his coffee and held the cup with both hands. "God, if I could—" Jake glanced up at Earl, then back down at his coffee. "I just spent a week trying to argue myself into staying alive." He shook his head. "I wasn't coming up with any answers. See, I stopped drinking on the seventeenth. But ever since then I've been going down and down. I don't know."

Jake finished his coffee, lowered his cup, and lit his pipe. "Yeah, I was going to kill myself. Seems funny to say it. I never put it into words before. I hadn't figured out how, hadn't figured out when. But I knew the why. Christ, Earl, this planet can be a bastard…."

Earl listened as Jake shared the intimate details of the nightmare of his life. As Jake listened, Earl spoke to him about his own horror. They listened and talked the night away. It didn't matter what was said; there seemed to be no taboos. Wishing death on close ones, failing at work, at marriage, at parenthood, at sex, at love, at life, at being a human.

They talked, each one finding in the other a person who had walked in the same footsteps. Each one doubling the number of humans who could understand them from one to two.

"…And like I said, Earl, the planet sucks."

"Tell me about it. I'm a farmer."

"No kidding? I always thought you had to have a screw loose to farm, or a death wish."

Earl chuckled. "I don't know about loose screws. Anyway. I got the death wish. What do you do?"

"I write. Mostly science fiction."

"No kidding? What name do you write under?"

"My own."

"What do you write? Books, magazine stories?"

"Both," answered Jake. "Seemed like a big deal, once."

"It is. Is anything you've written available around here?"

Jake shook his head. "I don't know. With the load of shit they handed me on the way in here, it doesn't look like anybody on the unit will have time to do any outside reading."

Earl thought for a moment. "I think there's a newsstand on the first floor. I saw it when I was admitted."

"I don't remember any newsstand. But then I don't seem to remember much about being admitted. I guess I was pretty angry." Jake was silent, deep in thought, then he looked at Earl and smiled. "But if there's a newsstand, I'll have a story there."

"How can you know that? It looked pretty small."

"*Omni* is everywhere. Newsstand operators who don't handle *Omni* get their knees broken."

"You have a piece in *Omni?*"

Jake nodded. "January issue. It ought to be on the stands now."

"Well, I'll check it out."

"If you don't like the story, Earl, keep it to yourself, okay?"

Earl laughed. Then he sat upright. Jake leaned forward. "What is it? Earl?"

"That's the first time I've laughed in I don't know. Years."

"Don't be surprised. I'm a riot."

Earl laughed again, then took a gulp of his coffee. Lowering the cup, he looked thoughtfully at Jake. "Have you talked much with the people around here?"

"No. Not much."

"I've gabbed with a few. Peculiar, but if I was a writer, I'd write a book about this place."

"I'm not going to be here that long." Jake waved a hand in the negative. "This A.A. stuff, it's not for me. Do you know anything about A.A.?"

"I went to five meetings, read some literature. But drinking isn't my problem. I just agreed to go here because I had to get away from home. Once I can think straight, I'll have to figure out what I'm going to do next."

Jake puffed on his pipe, then slowly nodded. "I guess I'm going to have to do the same. I don't know what, though. I could sure think a lot better if this damned headache would let up."

The lights in the hall went on, and Jake glanced at the recreation room windows. Cold gray light attempted to force its way through the heavy frost. He faced Earl. "It's New Year's Eve."

Earl stood, looked around at the windows, then looked down at Jake. "I want to say that I feel a lot better—you letting me cry on your shoulder."

Jake looked up and closed his eyes. "It's okay. I feel better, too. I ought to feel like shit, and I guess I do. But I feel better." Jake grinned. "We must do this again, sometime."

Earl chuckled, waved a hand at Jake, and headed for his room. As he passed the nurse's station, Earl talked to himself. "This place has nothing to offer me, but, baby, if anybody belongs here, it's one Jake Randecker."

Jake stood up, stretched, then winced at the pain in his lower back. As he walked back to his room to change for breakfast ("Patients are required to attend all meals"), he pondered the case of Earl Nelson, Minnesota farmer. Whatever else Jake knew or didn't know, he knew that at least one shotgun-wielding sodbuster was in the right place.

DECEMBER 31ST

7

Back in his room, Jake had just pulled on his trousers when a young blond girl in a lab technician's uniform knocked and entered carrying a rack full of stoppered test tubes. Half of them were filled with a suspiciously red fluid.

"Randecker?"

"Yeah?"

She put her rack on the chair. "Blood."

"Not before breakfast?"

"Blood." She wiggled a yellow rubber hose in the air making it look like an angry snake.

"I may not stay here. I was thinking of going home today if I felt well enough, and—"

"Blood!"

Jake presented his right arm. The bloodsucker immediately trapped his wrist beneath her left arm and began tying the snake above his elbow. The needle went in, a spring catch was released, and what seemed to be a quart of blood blooshed into the container. She removed the container, but left the needle. "Hey, what about the needle?"

She inserted another container into the exposed end of the needle. "More."

"I bet you can't speak in sentences of more than one word."

"You lose."

The second container was removed and replaced by a third. "More." She grinned. "For my brother, the count." Then she flapped away, trying to make it back to her coffin before the sunlight caught her.

As Vampira left, a red-haired woman in civilian clothes entered. She was carrying a little white cup. "Here. Fill it up to the line and turn it in at the nurse's station."

Jake's stomach writhed as he took the cup. "I take it breakfast isn't the big meal at this hotel."

"You should've made reservations at the Holiday Inn." She left.

After filling the cup to the specified mark and performing minimal freshening up motions, Jake put on his shirt. As he picked up his urine specimen, a sharp pain stabbed into his right eye and the room began to whirl. He put the specimen on his nightstand and sat on the bed until the dizziness passed. The headache remained.

"God, the bloodsucker really drained me."

When he was certain the room would remain stationary, he picked up his specimen and made his way out into the hallway with great care. He got in line at the nurse's station to turn in his mello-yellow. The patient behind him whispered that he was going to play a joke.

"Heh, heh. See, heh, heh, after I peed in the cup, I dipped it in warm water. Makes the cup wet on the outside, see? Makes the nurse think she's gotten pee all over her fingers, hey?"

After Jake turned in his cup, he watched as the nurse took the next patient's cup, looked shocked, jerked her hand, and slopped piss down the front of the joker's pajamas.

Jake nodded at the comedian. "Some joke." Jake suspected that the joke had been played before.

Back in his room, Jake juggled the regular patient schedule, week-end schedule, new patient schedule, and special holiday schedule—all of which appeared to refer to each other several times. It was like reading selections from the tax code. They made no sense at all. He couldn't understand why the schedule was so bewildering. Finally he tried to write down what he hoped he was supposed to attend.

Breakfast (remembering to make bed, clean up bod, and straighten up room, first), morning lecture, except for holidays, New Year's Eve being one of those, during which there would be no morning lecture, unless there was a movie, except following the weekend schedule, when you could stay in bed, if the part of the weekend schedule you were looking at happened to be Sunday, in which case you didn't have to attend breakfast, the new patient schedule, however—

A head poked into the room. "Morning vitals. Down at the end of the wing in the lounge."

"Thanks."

The head vanished and Jake balled up his schedules, tossed them into the wastebasket, and decided to follow the crowd. "I've got to get some aspirin. This headache is murder." It was like someone was trying to pry his right eye out of its socket with an electric ice pick. He wiped the palm of his hand across his forehead. Even with the window open, it was very hot.

The red-haired one did the morning vitals: temperature, pulse, blood pressure. Jake sat down in the chair at the left of the card table in west wing's tiny lounge. As instructed, he put a new cover on the probe of an electronic thermometer and stuck it under his tongue as the woman attacked his right arm.

As soon as the arm was shucked of its sleeve, the band of the BP began crushing Jake's upper arm as the electric thermometer beeped at him. The illuminated display read 96.2. The nurse wore a light green sweater over tie-dyed something. Jake closed his eyes.

—Doesn't anybody wear uniforms around here? I thought this was a Catholic hospital. Where are all the little old nuns? Where is Ingrid Bergman?

"Temperature?" demanded the nurse.

"It said ninety-six point two."

"How did you sleep last night?"

He opened his eyes. "I didn't."

"How do you feel?"

"For some curious reason, like I haven't had any sleep."

As she wrote something on a clipboard, others, some in bathrobes, some dressed, began wandering into the lounge, sleepily joking with each other. Both men and women, they seemed to range in age from eighteen to eighty. They lined up behind Jake, passing the thermometer along the line.

"Hold out your hands." Jake held out his hands, and the red hair and green sweater looked at them. "You're shaking."

"I'm nervous."

"I bet you are." She held his hands, then looked at the perspiration dribbling down his face. "You're sweating."

"You don't miss a thing. You people keep this place like a furnace."

"Sure we do. Later on today you have an appointment with your doctor for an interview. It'll be in your room. Someone will let you know when. Next."

When he returned to his room, he stopped dead in the open doorway. There were clothes spread out on the other bed. Jake's intestines moved into his throat. Somewhere there had been a hope that he would get out of having a roommate.

Loud noises came from the bathroom. Familiar loud noises. The accordion door had snagged another one. Jake opened the room door, turned right, and addressed the folds of the closed accordion. "I'll get you out in a minute. Are you my new roommate?"

A mellow voice, tinged with edges of hostile humor, answered. "I guess so. My name's Robby. I'm Jewish; I'm not supposed to be here."

Jake chuckled as he knelt and stuck the blade of his pocket knife into the jaws of the lock. "I'm Jake. Atheist. I'm not supposed to be here either."

Robby turned out to be an executive with a microchip manufacturing concern. He possessed a drug and liquor history that would probably make the textbooks and an angry streak a mile wide. His anger took the same form as Jake's: humor. They instantly became brothers. This was Robby's fourth day and he had just been assigned to a group. A group of what, Jake didn't know, and wasn't about to ask.

After making his bed, Jake stretched out and closed his eyes. The headache seemed to ease for a moment, and finally he felt tired enough to sleep. He was halfway there when hell assaulted his eardrums. Horrible clanging all around him. Sitting bolt upright and covering his ears, he looked and saw that there were intercom speakers built into the night stands. The boiler-works sounds ceased, and Jake removed his hands from his ears. "Holy shit, what was that?"

"Cowbells. They ring 'em into the intercom for chow call."

As Jake passed by the nurse's station on his way to a breakfast that he would just as soon have skipped, he saw the cow bell on the counter. It was not just an ordinary cow bell. This one was eight inches high. The hangover buster. He looked at the black-bearded man behind the counter. "Why cow bells?"

The man looked at the bell, frowned as though he were seeing it for the first time, then shrugged. "I don't know. They've always been here."

For breakfast Jake drank a glass of orange juice and six cups of coffee. He added an acid stomach to his stiff neck, lower back pain, sinus inflammation, headache, toothache and other complaints.

—It's only tension. I'm in a strange place. It's only normal to be a little tense in a strange place. I've got to try and relax.

After more coffee and smoking his pipe in the wing lounge, the bells of St. Mary's rang out the call for the morning lecture in the third floor lecture hall.

No beverages, no smoking, no talking, no sleeping.

New fish sat in the back row. Jake felt singled out. The outsider. Robby sat with his group.

—Here I am, the new kid in school once again.

The rest of the room's hundred and fifty chairs were arranged to leave a wide aisle down the center. Every other row had a name above it on the wall. The name was printed in large block letters on white poster board. Harry, Jane, Vivian, Bill, Mark, Angela. Robby sat beneath the Mark sign.

A skinny blond guy climbed up on the stage, beat the hell out of the microphone while attaching it to his coat, and commenced to scribble with a black marker on the glossy white board mounted on a stand. From Jake's vantage point, the glare off the board from the two spotlights wiped out the drawing. His headache seemed to be compressing the sounds around him, making everything unintelligible anyway. The noise that got through seemed perversely amplified.

—I wonder where reality's treble control is.

"My name is Mark, and I'm an addict."

"Hi, Mark!' the patients shouted. Jake held his head. "The thing scribbled on the board," Mark informed everyone, "is a feeling chart."

"Sounds positively repulsive," muttered Jake.

Mark's act rolled into high gear. Chemical dependency is a disease, not a matter of willpower, intelligence, or morals. It can be described in medical, physiological terms; it has a definable onset and a predictable outcome. The American Medical Association elected chemical dependency a disease in the 'Fifties, and then promptly forgot all about it. It's the nation's number three killer, yet the majority of medical students only learn about the disease by getting it. By occupation, doctors appear to be among those who are most frequently found heavy with the bug. Thus the old physician's definition of alcoholism: anyone who drinks more than his doctor.

Jake laughed, despite the effect this had on his aching head.

"Unless arrested," continued Mark, "the outcome of chemical dependency, what you call your prognosis there, is one hundred percent dead. It's a fatal disease, friends. Sorry about that."

"Very funny," muttered Jake. He was puzzled as he listened to the other patients laughing.

—They're going to die, and they think it's funny. I don't get the joke.

Mark plowed on. "The disease of chemical dependency affects you physically, emotionally, and spiritually as well as socially and economically. It touches everything. It is a primary disease, which means that before any progress can be made in improving any of these other areas, the addiction must be treated first. Can it be cured?" Mark rubbed his chin and leaned on the lectern with his elbows.

"Remember all of those TV shows and novels where a character addicted to ethanol, heroin, or something else, locks himself up or has a buddy sit on him while he 'kicks' the habit? Well, it's all very amusing, but you don't 'kick' addiction. Once you lose control over your use of chemicals, you can never get it back. Once you are addicted, the bug is yours for the rest of your life.

"This doesn't mean that a recovering addict or alcoholic cannot lead a fairly normal life. It simply means that the bug is always there waiting for you. The Big Book of Alcoholics Anonymous says that the disease is cunning, baffling, and powerful. It is also very patient.

"You remember those movies and books where a guy has what you call a 'drinking problem,' but he searches his past, finds out why he drinks, and then—miracle of miracles—he's cured? Great fiction, gang, but it's not going to do a thing for you. Wallow in your past until you pass out from the stink, and it won't do a thing for you except keep you in the jug or on your needle. Perhaps, long ago, you began easing yourself through reality with chemistry because of some problem you had. But once you became addicted, the chemical became its own reason. Old Oriental saying: First the man takes a drink, then the drink takes a drink, then the drink takes the man.

"The habit is no habit; it is an incurable disease. It is permanent, and why you drink or drug is because you are an addict. That never changes. The addict in you will always be there. In addition, the chemical or chemicals you are addicted to will always be there. The two-joint coffee break is every bit as common as the three-Martini lunch. Those entrepreneurs are still on the street corners, in the playgrounds, in the schools, the saloons, and the drugstores. The billboards are still up and the ads still on television. This is a using culture. You can't change the culture, but you can change you.

"The disease can't be cured, but it can be arrested, and that's what we do here at Saint Mary's. We have been at it since nineteen sixty-eight, and thousands of recovering addicts are still alive today because of the work they did here. We consider ourselves the West Point of rehab centers."

Laughter. Jake smiled.—Doesn't that create a mental image or two,
—"What are you on, Mr. Dumbjohn?"
—"Shit, sir!"
—"What's a pound of coke worth?"
—"Every cent, sir!" or
—"Mr. Dumbjohn, what's the definition of leather?"
—"I dunno, man. I forgot. You have any garlic dip for these donuts?"

"It's a feeling illness," said Mark. "Mood altering chemicals alter moods. And the addiction is to the process of mood change, not to a particular formula. It's a family illness. Family members get sucked in and experience many of the same symptoms experienced by the addict. Family members need treatment and recovery too."

Jake sat back and folded his arms.—Ann is going to be tickled to hear that.

"It's a progressive illness. If you stop using now and go back ten years from now, you don't pick up where you left off. Instead, you will rapidly degenerate to where you would have been if you had never stopped. It's incurable. That means you can never safely go back to using. Treatment means total abstinence from all mood-altering drugs. Every single last one of them. It's a fatal disease. That means dead. Physical failure, such as heart or liver; suicide; traffic accident. One way or the other, you buy a one-way trip on the meatwagon.

"Do you have the bug? How do you know if you are an addict? Drunk or junk? We call it harmful dependence. If the use of the chemical is causing continuing disruption in your personal, social, spiritual, or economic life, and if you do not stop using, that constitutes harmful dependence. In short, if you use, and using is screwing up your life, and you continue to use, you've got the bug."

The bug, thought Jake.—But beer wasn't screwing up my life. Christ, that was the only thing I had left that was making it bearable. That and the Ativan.

Mark was saying more on the bug as a disease of delusion. Why the chemically dependent person is unable to look at his own behavior with objectivity. Then a look at the results of treatment.

"The numbers don't lie. On average, a third will make it the first time around, a third will have to go out and suffer some more, making it after a second or third treatment, and a third will die. Out of the hundred and twenty patients in this lecture hall, forty of you are already dead."

"Shit," Jake heard someone sitting in the new fish row whisper, "That's what I call a real up message."

"Addiction is a fatal disease, and there is no cure. We can help you to arrest it, but we can't cure it. We also can't predict who will make it and who won't. St. Mary's has one of the most complete follow-up programs in the nation, but we still haven't been able to predict in treatment who will succeed, who will have to retread, and who will die."

Mark stood to the right of the lectern and leaned on it with his elbow. "While you are here, assume you are going to make it. Try your best. Leave tomorrow up to your Higher Power. Are there any questions?" A hand went up in the front. "Yes?"

"You said that addiction is a killer, right?"

"Right."

"What about alcoholism?"

Mark stood staring at the patient who had asked the question. "What week are you in?"

"Second."

"You've managed to make it to your second week and you haven't figured out that alcoholism is the addiction to the drug ethanol? An addict is an addict is an addict. Next."

Another hand, left rear. "Yes?"

"The third you mentioned that has to go through treatment again. Do you mean that some of us can go out and drink or use again if later we come back for another treatment?"

Mark looked down, thrust his hands into his pockets, shook his head, and looked up. His face was angry, but his voice deadly quiet. "Wake up, kid. There is a high-speed freight train barreling down on your ass this very second, and you still want to play on the tracks. We haven't been talking about a case of emotional jock itch. We are talking about addiction. Addiction is a killer. A killer, son. And you've got it."

Jake began to doze.—It's all very interesting, but what does any of this have to do with drinking beer? Anyway, no sleep last night.

He was startled awake to the sound of loud applause. Everyone was filing out of the lecture hall. He rubbed his eyes, whispering, "Where to now?" As much as it hurt his pride to do so, he would have to retrieve his schedules from the wastebasket. He got to his feet, noticing that his toothache had been joined by another toothache.

8

In Cleveland a woman named Nancy Coffee knelt over the lifeless body of her lover trying to fathom how—from where they started out—how she and Mike had arrived here. Was it only months ago they had met in treatment at St. Mary's?

"Everything was going so good." She shook her head slowly, back and forth, observing the things on the dirty floor. She was kneeling in spilled beer, puke, piss, and blood. She was holding an open can of beer. Miller's Lite. Diet beer.

—Think of all the calories I save.

She sat back on her ankles and looked at the ceiling's cracked plaster. "Mike, you sonofabitch, you said you'd fix the ceiling." Her gaze wobbled down and came to rest on the still body. Next to the body was a revolver. "You never fixed the ceiling."

She reached out her free hand and slapped the body's shoulder. "Broke my antique table. Sonofabitch." She slapped the shoulder again. "Mike? Get up, Mike." She grabbed the shoulder and shook it. "Come on, honey. Please? Please get up."

She sat back on her ankles and frowned at him. Mike had gone for ten months after getting out of treatment. Ten months straight. Back on the force, back on patrol. Mike the cop. The force had a terrific alcoholism program. But there was a little slip. Nancy was hurting, and she sought relief from an ancient source. The pain eased, but then he started bitching at her about her drinking. Tried to get her to go back to meetings. Back to St. Mary's. One day he said to hell with the Antabuse. A few days later he came home with a case of beer. Then there were some pills and powders, spoons and needles. A week later he was in the middle of the kitchen floor, lying in a puddle of piss, dead.

"Get up, honey. Oh, honey, get up. I need you, Mike. Mike?"

She shook her beer can, dropped it on the floor, and pushed herself to her feet. She stood above the body, weaving, looking through the open door of the refrigerator. Its contents were a black banana, a plastic container of something spoiled, and the six-holed plastic holders from several expired six-packs.

Her gaze moved around the room—rags, cracks, trash, filth, until she saw the six-pack of Lite perched on the back of the ripped-up easy chair. She looked down and kicked the body's right leg.

"Sonofabitch. Never put it in the icebox. It's warm. I don't know how you can be so stupid." She stumbled toward the chair, placed her hands on the cans, and pulled one free. Leaning against the back of the chair, she opened the can, drank deeply from it, then let her gaze settle upon a dark shape curled in the corner.

She waved a hand. "Lucky? Lucky, come. Come. Lucky!" The dark shape didn't move.

It was back there somewhere; back there in the dark of her mind.

Mike throwing the empty beer case out the window...the neighbor yelling at Mike. Mike yelling back—

"You got something to say to me, muthafuckah!! Muthafuckah!." Mike getting his police revolver, waving it out the window.

"Muthafuckah, I got somethin' for ya! Heyyyy muthafuckah."

The neighbor closing his window. Lucky tried to get out the door, Mike kicked him, and Lucky bit Mike's leg.

"You son of a bitch—"

—and Nancy had laughed at Mike, because Lucky was. A son of a bitch, that is.

Mike had screamed, jumped at the dog, landed his full weight on the animal. Mike had rolled off, went to the bedroom, and started a little needle work on the collapsed veins of his right arm.

Lucky had crawled off to the corner, curled up, and—

"Oh." Nancy nodded. "Lucky's dead. Lucky's dead; Mike's dead."

She picked up the remainder of the Lite, went back to Mike's still form, and sank down next to him. "Didn't have to kill Lucky." She jabbed at the body. "Didn't have to kill my dog."

She finished off the can in her hand, threw it across the room, and opened another. After a long swallow, she sat back in the urine and picked up Mike's revolver. She frowned at it. It wasn't where it belonged. After waving it out the window, Mike brought it back to the bedroom. Left it there—

She swallowed again, the can falling from her fingers, the remaining fluid in the can mixing with the urine and a growing pool of red. Her eyes closed.

"Why is your gun here? What were you going to do with the gun? What, huh? Gonna kill me? Gonna shoot me?"

She aimed the revolver at the body's head. "Bang! Bang!" She laughed. "Bang, bang, bang: Who's goin' to be at the Silver Bullet tonight, Mike?"

She dropped the revolver on the floor, bent over, and picked up Mike's head. But there was no back to his head. Her hands came away covered with blood and a smear of brains.

Mike staggering in from the bedroom.

"Bitch! Lookit this, bitch!" Opening his mouth, sticking in the revolver....

"Mike?" She tried to wipe away the tears with the back of her hand. "I can't live without you." She shook her head again and again. "How'd I ever get here?"

It was there somewhere; that dim memory of how good it had been for those ten months. How the world and her future had seemed to open up before her. She could always go back for a retread. They must have told her that at St. Mary's a hundred times.

She lifted the revolver, aimed it between her breasts, placed both thumbs on the trigger, and pulled. As the last of her life dribbled out onto the floor, a memory—something someone had said at St. Mary's—came back to her.

—A third makes it the first time around, a third has to retread, and a third is already dead. It just takes them a while to lie down.

9

Third floor, east wing lounge, evaluation group. Roger Sanders felt uncomfortable—naked—without his collar. Just before he had left, Whitey had suggested leaving the clerical badge in the bottom of a drawer. Roger had taken the suggestion, but now he wished he hadn't. Without the collar he looked just like everybody else. He was beginning to feel self-conscious about the number of times being a minister popped up in his conversation.

He surveyed the house. The walls of the lounge were ringed with faces. Old, young, male, female, hip, straight. Blue jeans, golf slacks, skirts, and pin-stripes. Bare chests, love beads, lace, and neckties. Red and yellow, black and white. No one in the evaluation group looked like an alcoholic: dirty gray overcoat, six day stubble, vacant eyes, brown paper sack, the stink. Such an apparition would have stood out like a rock band in a cemetery.

"Let's begin by introducing ourselves and saying a little about why we're here. I'm Michelle, chemically dependent, and I am your evaluation counselor."

Roger studied the speaker, Michelle, the evaluation counselor.

—What kind of woman does this kind of work? She said she was chemically dependent. Seems like an almost respectable way of saying junky.

Michelle was sort of chunky with tightly curled dirty-blond hair, wearing a brown suit, with a holiday decoration in her left lapel. She looked enthusiastic. Roger never could stand anyone who bubbled before noon.

The person immediately to Michelle's left, a young, shaggy-headed boy with a short brown beard, let his hands hang over his knees. His long fingers rubbed nervously at the ugly purple scars on the backs of his hands. He wore a green football Jersey, faded jeans, ragged jogging shoes. He smiled sheepishly.

"My name's Ken. I don't know what the fuck I am." A weak chuckle worked its way around the group. Ken held out his hands. "I mean I'm, I'm fucked up on *everything*. Fucked up on life." Ken was silent for a moment—a moment in which his face seemed to age twenty years. His eyes closed. "I don't know where to begin."

Michelle leaned toward him. "How did you get here, Ken?"

"My dad. He said he'd pay for it if I came and went all the way through treatment." Ken opened his eyes and looked down at his hands. "Either that, or get the fuck out of his house."

"How old are you Ken?"

"Nineteen." He inhaled sharply, letting his breath out as though all of his resistance was released with it. "If I had a kid like me, I'd kill the little fucker. Dad, he talked to me after the accident. It was the third fuckin' car I racked up. But this one—I was doin' speed. That and pot, a few drinks. My sister was in the car. Look at me!"

He pointed his open hands toward his chest. "Look at me. Not a fuckin' scratch. My sister is in the hospital right now and they still don't know if she'll walk again."

Michelle reached out and squeezed Ken's arm. "That's not something you have any control over. When did you start using?"

"Sixth grade. I was eleven and a few friends and me got hold of some pot...."

Roger listened. The stories seemed to be an infinite number of variations on a common theme. The banker, the college student, the professional athlete, the auto mechanic, the street punk, the drug dealer, the housewife, the prostitute, the businesswoman, the manufacturer, the sports announcer, the farmer, the artist, the clergyman, the rock musician, the union steward, the writer—

The young, the old, the hip, the straight; after a few minutes they seemed to unconsciously accept that they were all tight in their own subculture, their own brother and sisterhood. The addicted. Acid, dope, mo, coke, liquor, beer: chemicals.

Better living through chemistry: our motto.

And this new fellowship talked about and listened as others talked about all of their lives. Experimentation, use, abuse, preoccupation—productive lives boiled down to a single purpose: use. Destined to a single end: death. Listening to the tales, it wouldn't have been so bad if death was the only result. But getting there was at least half the horror.

First there is the trip through that narrow, tiny, dark universe where nothing works, hope does not exist, and nothing can be done for love except trying to remember if it ever existed. It is a place where self-loathing is raised to the level of a religion; where despair becomes an art form; where accumulating and dispensing pain is a science. It is a world of perpetual torture where death—any kind of death—eventually becomes the greener grass.

And then, part of the package deal, all of those others, close to you, who get crippled or destroyed as you're painfully lurching your way toward oblivion, who are forced into the same tiny universe. While you have to have that drink or drug, they have to try to control your addiction. In the process they get sucked down too.

The stories all led to Saint Mary's. It was a place that to someone—addict, friend, employer, wife, child, lover—seemed like a glimmer of hope in a hopeless universe. Roger listened, and for the first time regretted that he had said nothing to Whitey before he had left. He had said nothing to Denise or Carmel, either.

—All of them must have cared for me a great deal. Otherwise I wouldn't be here,

Glen the athlete said, "I figured if I wanted to kill myself, that was my business. I wasn't hurting anyone else. At least I didn't think so until my daughter tried to kill herself. I can't believe how much that powder meant to me—"

The banker: "My wife and I must have spent a million dollars on psychiatrists, counselors, hospitals…I thought she was crazy. After a while, I had her convinced. Eventually, she went crazy for real. About all I could do was use it for another excuse to drink—"

A farmer named Earl: "A friend of mine from A.A. told me about St. Mary's. Yesterday…"

Roger saw the farmer look across the room at a chubby white guy with glasses and a gray-blond beard. The beard nodded and smiled back at the farmer. Earl closed his eyes, his body bent over, his hands clasped together, holding on to each other for lack of anything else to hold on to.

"Here goes. I was drinking. I ran out, and I knew there was a bottle in the feedbox in the barn. But there wasn't. My boy Joey had taken it and left my shotgun in its place. The gun was loaded and there was a note. My son wanted me to kill myself." The farmer rubbed his eyes, his voice dropping to a whisper. "I took that gun and I was going to kill him. I was going to kill my own son." He looked at Michelle. "That's when I called this friend from A.A. to bring me here."

Michelle sat back in her chair and studied the farmer. "That note must have hurt you very deeply."

"It did."

"Earl, do you think you're an alcoholic?"

Roger watched with amazement as the farmer transformed from a weeping wreck to a wired-down mountain of barely-controlled fury. "Maybe I drink more than I should. I don't know about being an alcoholic."

Michelle marked down something on her clipboard, then nodded at the big time drug dealer, Austin.

"...I couldn't come up with the bread anymore, man, y'know? This monkey I had to feed was a go-rilla. The only way I could stay alive was to deal the shit. The shit, y'know? Before I got busted I was up to eight hundred dollars a day. A day, man. Man, do you know what you got to do to get eight hundred dollars a day? More'n deal...."

The businesswoman: "...I can't figure out why. One second I'm at my daughter's wedding reception, the next I'm screaming at her, ripping off her wedding dress. I ruined it. It was over a hundred years old. My husband and son-in-law dragged me out of there. All I could come up with for an answer was the same answer I had used for years: Valium. This time I washed it down with scotch. When I woke up I was over there in the main hospital. One of the doctors there told me about this place. He said he was a drug addict, too."

A young geology professor with a full-length cast on his right leg: "...When I woke up and tried to get out of bed, I found my leg was broken. I found out later that it was broken in two places. I didn't even have time to think about it before two cops pounded on the door. I had to tell them to get the landlady to let them in with her key. I was scared to death. Once in my room they told me that what was left of my pickup was spread all over I-94 at the route fifty-two interchange. They thought it was real funny and didn't even give me a ticket, although I had to pay to clean up the crash site. I never did figure out how I got to my bed.

But there was that moment when I thought I might have killed some-one. I called here a few minutes after the cops left…."

Next spoke the chubby guy with the beard that the farmer had looked to for support. His name was Jacob Randecker, a writer, and he talked about needing a prescription refilled and walking into his doctor's office drunk. "So when I went into the doctor's office, the smell knocked him on his ass. He told me 'You stink!'" There was laughter, and Roger could see that the one called Jake played to laughs. He looked red-faced and angry, but he was laughing. "Then my wife and a few friends got together, handed me a plane ticket, and told me to get out of town before sundown."

Although the other patients laughed, Michelle's face remained impassive throughout the monologue. Then she asked, "Did anything your doctor say lead you to suspect that you might be an alcoholic?"

"Yeah. He said I stink."

Roars of laughter from the audience. Michelle scribbled down a note and the black marble moved on.

There was a nurse who couldn't believe she could have been so stu-pid as to get addicted.

Michelle looked up from her clipboard and said, "It's not a disease of stupid people. It's just a disease."

There was another nurse, a retired grandfather from Florida, a nine-teen-year-old student from New York, a pharmacist from Wyoming, a Baptist minister from Oregon.

Roger clasped his hands together and looked at the floor as the per-son to his right finished introducing himself. Roger wasn't even listen-ing. Instead he was teetering on the brink of prayer. But God had been so remote for so many years. The room was silent. His turn had arrived.

Roger didn't look up. "My name is Roger Sanders. I'm from Georgia and I'm here as the result of an intervention."

"Roger," Michelle began, "who was there at the intervention?"

"Just my bishop." Roger looked quickly around the room. "I'm a clergyman."

"Wasn't your family involved at all in the intervention?"

Roger felt the heat coming to his face. "Sort of. A few weeks ago my wife and daughter, along with the bishop and an intervention counselor, saw me—"

"Do you mean there was more than one intervention?"

Roger glared at the counselor. "I guess you could say that."

Michelle's eyebrow's went up. "What do you say?"

"Yes. There were two interventions."

Michelle made a notation on her form and without looking up asked, "Are you an alcoholic, Roger?"

Roger folded his arms and sat back. "Isn't that what you're supposed to tell me?"

"No. You're the only one who can answer that question. No one here is ever going to call you an alcoholic."

"Then I guess I don't know whether I am or not."

Michelle nodded made another mark, and the woman sitting to Roger's left spoke. "My name's Larissa, and there ain't no doubt about it. I'm an alcoholic and drug addict...."

10

After evaluation group, Jake collapsed in the large recreation room on the fourth floor, took a large swallow of coffee, lit his pipe, inhaled deeply, and began the long process of letting his muscles unkink—the process being complicated by the absence of Jake's usual muscle unkinkers.

"Jacob Randecker?"

Jake opened his eyes, looked up, and saw a man wearing jeans and a mustache holding a slip of paper. "Yeah?"

"Go on down to your room. Your doctor will be there soon to conduct your initial interview."

"What about my coffee?"

"Bring it with you."

"What about my pipe?"

The man slowly shook his head. "The Minnesota Clean Indoor Air Act strikes again."

Jake knocked the smoldering ashes from his pipe into an ashtray, stood, picked up his brown plastic cup, and headed for his room, muttering. Once inside his room, he looked at the books on his desk and picked up his steno pad. He knew there were a lot of very good reasons in it for why he shouldn't be at St. Mary's. If he could just shake this headache—

The doctor entered the room and Jake knew that he was not going to like that doctor. His face carried a beatific expression of such sheer joy and serenity that Jake wanted to stick his foot in it.

"My name is Tony." He sat down on one of the desk chairs and placed a clipboard upon his knee. "Let's see, now. Age?"

"Thirty-nine.

"Occupation?

"Writer."

"Really?"

"Yes. Really."

There was the usual run of housekeeping questions, then: "On your entrance form, it says you had a heart attack?"

"That's right. On my thirty-sixth birthday."

"Do you worry about having another heart attack?"

Jake laughed, "Hell, no." He told Tony about his frequent expressions of anger by trashing the house, knocking holes in walls, ripping doors from their hinges, reducing furniture to splinters. "Very athletic stuff."

"Do you get angry a lot, Jake?"

Jake thought upon the question for a long time. "It's the only emotion I've been able to feel for years."

"What about medications? Are you on anything?"

"Ativan. Some time after the heart attack it was prescribed for anxiety."

"Did you abuse the drug?"

"No, I just followed the prescription."

"Ever have any blackouts?"

"No."

"Did you ever pass out?"

"No."

Tony nodded, rubbed the spot between his glasses and the bridge of his nose, then began writing on his clipboard. "I'm going to prescribe Dylantin and a decreasing dosage of Librium. Withdrawal won't be easy, but the medications should make it tolerable."

"I don't need anything. I haven't had anything to drink since the seventeenth."

Tony's black eyebrows rose above the frames of his glasses. "You're refusing medication?"

"Yes. I don't need it."

Tony nodded and made a note.

"Look, doctor, I'm not sure I belong here. In fact, I 'm almost certain I don't belong here."

"Why's that?"

"I'm not a religionist."

"You don't have to be. It's not a religious program."

"Bull." Jake pulled out his notes and read off a few of the highlights. By the time he was finished, Tony was having a difficult time not falling out of his chair he was laughing so hard. The more he laughed, the angrier Jake got.

"Look, I don't see what point there is in swapping one psychological dependency for another, religion for alcohol!"

"Psychological dependency?" the doctor managed to gasp.

"Yes! I obviously don't have a physical dependency. I haven't had anything to drink since the seventeenth. If I had a physical dependency, I would have experienced some withdrawal symptoms by now, wouldn't I?"

"Why are your hands shaking?"

"Dammit! I'm angry, that's why!"

Jake glanced at the pile of books, looking for the little white A.A. card, remembering that he had wasted his second one and found a brand new one on top of the pile. He told himself that he would deal with where it came from later. He picked up the card and read off the first step: 'We admitted we were powerless over alcohol—that our lives had become unmanageable.' This just doesn't fit my case. I quit on my own, and I haven't gotten any withdrawal symptoms. And this one here. Step three, 'Made a decision to turn our will and our lives over to the care of God, as we understood him.' I'm an atheist. I'm not going to jump out of some damned window because some spooky vapor says to."

Tony got to his feet. "Maybe you will some day, if you're lucky."

"But, doctor, this isn't—"

"Jake, you're just bound and determined to make this as hard on yourself as possible, aren't you?"

"What about my questions?"

"You'll answer them for yourself in time." He paused, assumed an expression somewhere between a smile and a grimace, and looked at Jake over the tops of his glasses. "Jake, if all you get out of this program is to wind up not drinking, will that be enough?"

"Sure. Sure. That's why I'm here."

Tony smiled. "You know, Jake, one of these days—real soon, now—you are going to be shocked to hell to find out that we know what we're doing here."

As the door closed behind Tony, Jake realized that he had unwittingly agreed to stick it out at St. Mary's.

—Well, maybe I need to know a little more before heading back to Maine. I am scared of drinking again. Besides, the lack of sleep and tension is working my body to death. There aren't any locks on the doors. I can go home anytime.

He felt with his tongue and counted. "Shit. Now I have four toothaches. I simply have got to relax."

For lunch he had half a piece of buttered whole wheat and four cups of coffee. His earlobes felt like they had fallen asleep. There was nothing scheduled for the afternoon, and he stretched out on his bed and tried to sleep. After a fruitless hour wandering through every humiliating memory he could dredge up, he moved to the big lounge, lit his pipe, and consumed additional mass quantities of coffee.

After dinner, which consisted of more coffee, there was a movie in the lecture hall. It was an impressionistic documentary about a bunch of recovering drunks coming from all over the nation to gather in a stadium and listen to recovering alky Dick tell jokes in the rain.

Jake squinted against his headache and tried to read the faces. Were the laughter and happiness the real articles, or were they the masks that people wore to hide from themselves and from reality? Allow the slightest crack to appear, stand back, and listen to the screams.

He shook his head and muttered, "Might as well join the goddamned Moonies." He closed his eyes and let the images play.

—Randecker at the airport, holding out a flower. The irate passenger shakes his head. "No, thank you."

—"Jesus loves you."

—"I said no."

—"Then, fuck you buddy!" He jams the flower into the guy's mouth.

—Jake drummed out of the cult for conduct unbecoming a religious fanatic.

—Reverend Moon breaks Jake's flowers over his knee—

Applause. The movie was over and the New Year's Eve festivities about to begin. Jake pushed himself to his feet and shuffled out of the lecture hall.

11

Stayin' alive,
Stayin' alive,
Stayin' alive,
Stayin' alive,
Ah—hah—hah—hah,
Stayin' aliiiiiiiiiiiiiiiii—

—Hell, thy name is disco.

Roger Sanders closed his eyes against the scene in the recreation room, sipped coffee from his brown plastic mug, and wished that his lobes were long enough to fit inside his ears. The pain of Hell is one thing, he reflected; ancient disco is cruel and unusual punishment. Where did they ever get those old recordings?

—And Whitey loves this place.

He rubbed his eyes as he remembered the bishop on the plane trip from Atlanta to Minneapolis. Roger had felt that he was just a handy excuse for Whitey to go back to visit his old rehab.

—I don't get it. I really don't.

Roger opened his eyes and looked at the people, sitting around tables, munching food from carts brought up from the kitchen, playing cards, other games, just sitting and talking. Many of the patients, local yokels from the twin cities of Minneapolis and St. Paul, had visitors. Wives, parents, children, looking around wide-eyed at the zoo.

Someone laughed loudly and Roger wondered what Denise and Carmel were doing. It was New Year's Eve. He should call, but still couldn't bring himself to do it. He could never find anyone who could understand his fear of telephones. Everybody in the place was paranoid to one degree or another. But telephones? C'mon, man. Grow up.

A mob surrounded the pool table, cheering on, or trying to mess up, a particularly difficult shot. Again the ping-pong ball ricocheted around the room, came to rest, and was tossed back in the general direction of the players. The cigarette smoke in the air was barroom grade.

There were only five other black faces in the room. All kids. One boy was all do-rag, comb, and "man!" The second boy sat alone in a cor-ner, his eyes staring in terror at the whiteness of his new academy. The third—it seemed to Roger that the third boy hated him for, among other reasons, pronouncing the 'g' at the ends of words ending in 'g.'

Vietnam had done the third boy. The only war that took the veteran and threw him away "like a used condom," to hear the boy tell it. He didn't want to hear about Korea.

Roger would have liked to have talked to him about Korea. For thirty years Roger had been silent on the subject. Something had hap-pened there, something that festered within Roger's soul. There would be no relief from the disease until the past subjected itself to change. There was not much hope of that happening. Not for Roger, not for the Vietnam vet.

For that Vietnam vet, Korea may as well have never happened. Still, thought Roger, I would like to *try* to talk about it. Perhaps, thought

Roger, I am taking his anger too personally. He looks as if he is angry at the world and everything and everyone in it.

The one girl was locked into a permanent Butterfly McQueen impression. Entertaining her new circle of acquaintances, confirming every hairbrained stereotype ever devised. The second girl seemed to be from another planet—laughing her way through a thousand horror-packed drug stories from open heart surgery to attempted murder.

The put on, the terror, the hostility, the giddy brainlessness, the hardened laughter at horror—all walls. Armor plate covering…what?

He shook his head. "I have troubles of my own."

"What?"

Roger looked to his right. A white guy, late thirties or early forties, glasses, beard, and coffee cup, was looking back. Not just white. The man's skin was the color of chalk. He recognized the face from evaluation group. He was the one whose doctor told him that he stank. "Excuse me?" Roger had to raise his voice to overcome the boom-boom-boom of the disco.

The man pointed in the direction of the stereo. "Disco. Can't stand it. Couldn't hear what you said." He leaned to his left and held out a hand. "Jake Randecker."

Roger shook hands with him. The hand he grasped was damp and cold. "Roger Sanders. I was saying that I have troubles of my own."

Jake nodded, his eyebrows raised. "Been here long?"

"First week."

"Me too." Jake rubbed his eyes, rubbed his temples with both hands, then let his head loll back to ease the strain on his neck muscles.

Roger moved his chair closer to Jake's. "Are you all right, Jake? You don't look at all well."

Upon closer inspection, Jake's blond hair was soaking wet. The head shook, very gently. "I just didn't get much sleep last night. I guess it's getting to me." He looked for a moment at the crowd in the recreation room and closed his eyes. "I don't think I'll stay up for the New Year." His eyes opened and he smiled. "I need the sleep. But right now I sort of like having people around."

Roger nodded. "I feel the same way. What do you do for a living, Jake?"

An unreadable series of emotions put on a split-second demonstration across Jake's face. "I'm a writer. Mostly science fiction.'

"I never read much sci-fi."

Jake seemed to wince. "In the business, we call it either science fiction or SF. Only the rubes call it sci-fi." Jake slowly shook his head. "Among all of the other terribly important issues of our time. What do you do?"

"Clergy."

"There certainly is a bunch of you guys here." Jake's hand swept in a circle. "All Episcopal priests."

"I'm Methodist."

"So much for my theory."

"What theory?"

"Forget it. How come there aren't any Catholic priests here? This is a Catholic hospital."

"The Catholic Church has its own separate facility just for priests."

"A rehab with nothing in it but priests?"

"So I've been told."

"Now, *that's* depressing."

"Jake, did you ever consider writing a book about this place?"

"What a novel idea."

"You sound a little sarcastic."

"Sorry." The boom-boom-boom of the disco appeared to have Jake wincing in time with the music. He stood up. "I can't take it any more, Rog. I'm heading for some more coffee and then the sack." He extended his hand and Roger shook it. Still damp and cold. "See you tomorrow, should I live so long."

Roger slumped back in his chair as Jake moved through the people into the hallway. Jake did not look well. Which is probably why he's in a hospital, thought Roger. He devoted one thinly-split second to recalling the last time he was just as cold and almost as pale as the recently departed Jake.

Carmel, leaning against the doorjamb. "I'm tellin' you, Papa, that's the last damn time I haul your sorry ass in so the neighbors won't see another shitfaced nigger out cold on his front lawn in the mornin'. How do you get up before those people every Sunday and preach that sanctimonious shit? *I'd choke—*"

He held out his hands and watched as they slowly closed into fists, his mind letting nothing through but the thud-thud-thud of the disco, the miasma of tobacco smoke, the endless, incomprehensible chatter, the almost hysterical din raised by a hundred junkies and drunks celebrating New Year's without chemicals.

Roger closed his eyes. There was something he ought to do. Something he ought to do soon. He pushed himself to his feet, navigated through the crowd, and headed for the stairwell. In his third floor room, the lights off, Roger got down on his knees and did something that he had faked pretty well for the benefit of his several congregations over the past eleven years. He prayed, trying to feel again that presence that led him so long ago to believe that he wasn't alone.

12

Jake pushed open the door to his room and saw Robby writing at the desk. "What're you up to?"

"The Micky Mouse Penis Itcher." Robby threw his pencil on the booklet and clasped his hands behind his head. "It's a test. The M.M.P.I., otherwise known as the *Minnesota Multi-phasic Personality Inventory.*"

"Penis Itcher." Jake entered and began changing into his pajamas. "Does everybody have to take it?"

"They'll get around to you." Robby turned and looked at his roommate. "Are you okay? You look like hell in a microwave."

"Sleep. I need some sleep." He nodded at the desk. "The test. What's it about?"

Robby looked back at the booklet. "A five hundred and some odd question exercise that now wants to know if I am afraid of doorknobs."

"Not unless you sneak up behind me." As he buttoned his pajama tops, Jake walked over and looked over Robby's shoulder. "You weren't kidding...'I have smelly, black-looking bowel movements.'"

"Something I must have asked myself a thousand times. True or false. On most of these questions I want to do essay answers. But true or false is the only choice you get."

Jake shook his head, sat down on his mattress, and swung his legs up from the floor. "Rob, I think the theory is that if the patient goes through and answers all of those questions, he's crazy."

"You mean that the only way to pass this test is to throw it back in their faces?"

"Now you've got it."

"You might have a point, there. But keep your head away from pencil sharpeners and it may eventually wear down."

"Yuk, yuk."

Robby flipped through a few pages and stopped. "Here's one you'll like: 'I believe I am a special agent of God.'"

"What? That's a joke."

"Oh, that it were. Doorknobs. I wonder what ward they put you in if you say you're afraid of doorknobs. They give you twenty-four hours to turn in the answers."

"What if you don't?"

"I don't know."

Jake reached to his nightstand, punched the buttons controlling his set of lights, and settled down on his right side. "You can leave your lights on. I'm just crapping out early."

Robby turned off the floor lamp next to the desk and stood up. "I think I've itched my penis enough for one night. I'm going to go and see what's doing with the rest of the inmates. Don't wait up."

The door closed and Jake tried to make his mattress absorb his left shoulder. He adjusted the pillows. Kicked off the blanket. Pulled up the sheet.—Dammit, I'm so tired I can hardly see straight. Sleep! Sleep! Sleep! I don't ever want to go through another day like today. I need some sleep!

He rolled forward, picked up his watch. and looked at the dial. 10:37 PM. Plenty of time. Holiday schedule tomorrow. Easy duty.

He closed his eyes, relaxed his arm muscles, leg muscles, wriggled until his back muscles felt loose, rocked his head to ease his neck muscles, eased the constant tension his jaw muscles kept on his teeth, waiting for sleep...opened his fists and wiggled his fingers, letting his hands hang limp. Toes, feet...waiting....

Faces swam into his mind. A friend, a foe, a wife who was somewhere in between, an agent who had joined the other side.—Treason in exchange for his goddamn ten percent. That damned old bitch who told me that my mother was dead...easy does it.

Again, relax the arms, legs, back, neck, jaw—his tongue counted eight toothaches.

"Fuck it."

He sat up, swung his feet to the floor, and leaned forward, his weight upon his arms. "What in the hell do I have to do to relax? I can't keep this up. I must get some sleep."

He inventoried his muscles. All of them ached as though he had gone through some strenuous athletic event the day before. The stiff neck was beginning to throb, as was the headache, sinus pain, and that sensation in his teeth. It wasn't just eight toothaches. All of his teeth hurt. Not a sharp pain. Dull, maybe this will go away in the morning kind of pain. Joints. All of his joints ached.

And the sweat. He wiped his hands across his face up through and past his hair.—Christ, I'm soaking.

He reached to the nightstand, put on his glasses, and walked to the bathroom. He turned on the light and looked at himself in the wall mirror. For once he looked like he felt.

He removed his glasses, doused his face with cold water, and dried off with a towel. He picked up his glasses to put them on, noticed some dirt on the frames, and tried to rub it off beneath the running water. It wouldn't come off. He looked closely at the frames. It wasn't dirt. Wherever his frames had been in contact with his skin, the gold plating had been eaten off. The frames were brand new.

He lowered his glasses and looked in astonishment at his reflection in the mirror. "My sweat dissolves gold!"

—Don't think about it. I have to get some sleep. No upsets right now. Try and look on the positive side. There must be a simple, logical explanation. Pearle Vision Center, shopping mall frames, probably coated with some cheap metallic-looking plastic.

"My sweat dissolves plastic?"

—Not much better.

He turned off the light and returned to bed, wondering if he would find himself on the floor in the morning, having burned his way through the bed, springs, mattress, plastic mattress cover, and all.

—Sleep. I must get some sleep.

He picked up his watch and looked at it. 10:58 PM. Still plenty of time.

Laughing voices from the hall came through the door. Light from outside the window glittered on the frosted windowpanes. A blast furnace of dry, hot air issued from the heater. A twinge came from his shoulder.

—I can't sleep with all of these little aches and pains nagging at me.

He sat up, put on his slippers and bathrobe, and walked to the nurse's station. Behind the counter was a woman dressed in a strange costume: all white, with white stockings and white shoes, with a strange little white cap nailed to her head. Gray hair, wire-rimmed glasses—she's in a nursey uniform!

She looked at him. "Can I help you?"

"Uncle."

"What?"

"Uncle. I'm crying uncle. I can't get to sleep. It's been I don't know how long. Can I have a sleeping pill?"

"Name?"

"Jake. Jacob Randecker."

She began pawing at some papers. Robby had said that the last time he had asked for an aspirin the nurse had called out two fellows named Guido and Carmine who had adjusted his kneecaps.

"We usually don't give out sleeping pills."

Jake nodded. "I figured it wouldn't hurt to ask."

"Here." She opened a blister pack and handed him a single capsule. She pointed at the water jug and a stack of tiny paper cups on the counter. "Take it here and then go to bed."

"I will. I will. Thank you." He popped the pill, chased it with a thimble of water, and headed back to the rack.

As he climbed into bed, he saw again the little wooden and gold crucifix hanging on the wall between the two patient desks. He jumped out of bed, took the icon from its nail and tossed it into his desk drawer, closing it with a slam.

He went to bed, stretched out, and turned off the lights. An hour of waiting later, he heard cheering, along with the recreation room's piano grinding out a butchered version of "Auld Lang Syne."

There was an old man,
Name of Lang,
He had a yellow sign,
And every time he hung it out,
They said: There's Old Lang's sign....

Jake checked his watch and was not terribly surprised to find out that it was two minutes past midnight. "Happy New Year."

Earlier in the lounge he had called Ann. But she had been out with friends. Don the shrink and his wife Betty.

—Friends, hell. Co-conspirators. I've never been away from Ann on New Year's. Not since we were married.

"Let it go," he whispered, "Got to rest." Again he looked at his watch. Closed the eyes, relaxed the muscles. "Mister Sandman, I'm so alone...."

—Sleep, dammit! Sleep: The lousy pill was probably powdered sugar!

He rolled to his other side and folded his arms.—Give it a chance. It's only been an hour. Placebos take longer.

He sat up and looked again at his watch. "Sleeping pill, my ass."— Recite the mantra. Recite the mantra when you're lying down, and off you go to sleep. Meditation never worked without a few drinks, but what the hell. Give it a shot.

He turned the pillow to a dry side and placed his head upon it.— Now, what was that mantra? Sounded like it rhymed with key ring. That's it: Heer-r-r-ing, and don't forget to trill those r's. Heer-r-r-ing, heer-r-ring, heer-r-ring, heer-r-ring, hee—Ann wanted to try the meditation course. Supposed to be for stress. Goddamn Maharishi. Little bugger cracked me up—hee-r-ring, heer-r-ring, heer-r-ring, heer-r-r— hee, hee, hee, god what an accent! Guy was cute as a bug's ear, but I couldn't listen to those lecture tapes without rolling on the floor. Hee, hee—heer-r-ring, heer-r-ring, heer-r-rinq—gonna kill my agent when I get out of—heer-r-ring, heering, hearing, steering, fearing, queering—

"To hell with it."

He stood up in the center of his bed, held his hands up to the ceiling, palms open, and shouted. "I do! I *do* believe I'm a special agent of God! And that means I get ten percent of *everything!*"

He let his arms come down slowly, then climbed down from the bed, put on his robe, and re-enlisted for another six in the Nighthawks.

JANUARY IST

13

Morning vitals.

"Happy New Year, Jake."

"Not yet."

"How did you sleep last night?"

"In a bed."

"How do you feel?"

"With my hands."

"Hold out your hands."

"My hands are fine; your eyes are shaking."

"Still nervous, eh? You're sweating. Are we still keeping it too warm for you?"

"Yes."

"It'll get warmer. Next."

Breakfast. Patients have to stay in the dining room for at least ten minutes. The seconds on Jake's watch crept away. Three cups of coffee. The nausea level climbed. Sinus, neck, and dental pain increased. The headache convinced him that his brain pan could probably melt steel ingots. The pain in his knees became particularly noteworthy not by its intensity half as much as by its sudden appearance.

—Tension. Only tension. Got to relax.

He flexed his fingers. There was a sharp ache in every single joint. He gently shook his head.—Got to relax.

…four, three, two, one, zero.

He turned in his tray and almost passed out from the pain as the elevator to the fourth floor accelerated beneath him, placing pressure on his knees and back.

More coffee in the recreation room. Jake met a patient who spent the past five years stumbling her way along this nation's economic coil as a surgical nurse. She had been heavily into perks, ludes, and Valium. The nurse's name was Candy.

Candy laughed, "It sort of makes you wonder about getting your hemorrhoids operated on, doesn't it?"

—Jesus.

Jake laughed nervously and turned to see the man with the jeans and mustache come in with three slips of paper.

"Jacob Randecker?"

"Uh huh?"

"Here." He handed the first slip to Jake. "This is your group assignment. You've been assigned to Angela Gwynn's group, lucky you. Which means," he handed Jake another slip, "you are being moved to third floor, north wing."

"What?"

"You're being moved to third floor north."

"Why?"

"You have to be on the wing where your group lives. Angela's Animals hang out on third north."

"Where?"

"What, why, where—are you auditioning for *Welcome Back, Kotter* reruns? Everything you need to know is on the slip. Move today."

"I like the roommate I have."

"Recite the Serenity Prayer three times and call me in the morning." He handed Jake the third slip of paper. "After the morning movie, report to Michelle for an interview."

"About this new room assignment—" But the mustache and jeans was gone. Jake looked down at the paper and said to himself, "Besides, I don't want to meet anybody new."

Candy placed a hand on Jake's shoulder. "You'll find out that what you want doesn't have a damned thing to do with recovery."

Jake listened to Candy and found out that it's great he's in Angela's group. So was she. Angela's Animals considered themselves the unit's aristocrats. "Don't worry about a new roommate, Jake. All of the rooms on third north are private, except for Room 356."

Jake looked at the room assignment slip. Room 356.

Candy waved at another face. A pleasant-looking fellow came over. He reminded Jake of a Walt Disney puppet-maker. He reached down and shook Jake's hand. "I'm John Pennoyer."

Candy informed Jake that the group calls John D.T. and that D.T. got his name because of this problem he has when he isn't drinking or evening things out with Valium. These rats keep crawling up his legs. D.T. turned out to be a surgeon.

Others came over and there were more introductions. Some were in the Animals, some not. A banker—explains a lot about today's economy—a union steward—the rest of the explanation—an airline pilot— oh, shit—an alcoholism counselor named Brandy—

Brandy was the blond in the lavender jogging suit who had spoken to him on his first night on the unit. He couldn't remember what she had said. Jake shook his head and looked at her. "Goddammit, Brandy, isn't anyone exempt?"

She laughed and said to Jake, "You're cute."

The union man, short red hair, a body built like an abbreviated locomotive, a beergut the size of a medicine ball, was named Dave. Dave liked his beer with grass. He wandered off to talk to his best friend on the unit, another Animal, about to be discharged, named Harold. Harold was a steel executive. Harold was into fruit salad.

"What's fruit salad?"

Candy raised her eyebrows. "You're not kidding? Pills. That's a bowl full of just everything. You reach in, pop away twenty or thirty, and see what happens."

—Ah, adventure.

Candy and Brandy—Christ, will this comedy never end?—were in Angela's group, as was D.T., Harold, and the union man. The airline pilot was in Bill's group—Thank whoever, because I don't want to have to deal with that. When I get out of here, I have to *fly* back to Maine.

"Let me put your mind at ease," Lyle the airline pilot offered. "Pilots in rehab don't bother me half as much as all those air traffic controllers who are still out there doing lines on their radar screens."

"Thanks, Lyle."

"Anytime, Jake."

A young kid, Ron, was introduced as a member of Angela's Animals, in addition to being third floor north's wing leader. Ron spent a month on the psychiatric floor of the main hospital before being allowed on the unit.

Young, crazy, loose. Jake guessed that Ron must be the group's duster; PCP. It turned out that Ron was orthodox alcoholic. Strictly ethanol. One of the few in the group.

"You know," said Jake to Brandy, "this place is doing severe damage to my poor head's favorite collection of pigeonholes."

"It'll do that. What do you do, Jake?"

"Beer, mostly."

She laughed. "I mean, for a living."

"I'm a writer."

"Really?"

"Really." Little creatures with splitting mauls were having a gang rumble behind Jake's eyes.

"You know," said Brandy, "if I was a writer, I'd write a book about this place."

"Jake!" a voice shouted. Jake saw Earl Nelson waving a copy of *Omni* in the air as he walked. "I'm glad I ran into you. Would you mind autographing your story for me?" As Jake tried to focus on the page and steady his hand, Earl said that he liked the story.

"Thanks, Earl."

"No, I really mean it."

"So did I."

Earl frowned. "Are you okay, Jake?"

—Nothing that a half-hour in a bar wouldn't cure. "I just need some sleep."

Earl picked up Jake's cup. "More coffee?"

"Thanks."

While Earl was on his coffee run, Jake finished signing the magazine, leaned back in his chair and rubbed the back of his neck. Lowering his hand, he noticed that everyone except Candy had wandered off. Candy was nervously burning her way through her fifth cigarette since she met Jake.

"Candy, why do they call this group Angela's Animals?"

She picked some tobacco off the tip of her tongue. "Angela gets the toughest nuts to track. If Angela won't take you, no one will."

"You mean I've been sorted into some kind of hard-luck bunch?"

"That's not a bad description."

"What's this Angela like?"

Candy looked off in the distance, then shook her head. "I don't know. Angela is somewhere between Saint Mary and the Marquis de Sade in drag."

"That narrows it down."

Candy nodded and lit another cigarette.

The morning movie: Carol Burnette in *"Women and Alcoholism."*

Jake moved off of the back row of the third floor lecture hall and sat with his group for the first time. Roger the clergy sat next to him. Roger was an Animal. Earl Nelson sat down in front of Jake. Earl was an Animal, too.

Carol wasn't very funny. As with most other things, women appear to get a raw deal with alcoholism. Among society's collection of grotesque scales of value, the female alcoholic is less acceptable than the male. And there are numbers. Ten percent of the women married to alcoholics leave their husbands; ninety percent of the men married to alcoholics leave their mates. Married female alcoholics hide their alcoholism with great skill, and for good reason.

Jake glanced at the women in his group, Candy, Brandy and someone he hadn't met yet, suddenly aware that he wasn't the only patient in the joint with problems. After the movie he gulped down three cups of coffee and smoked four pipes before heading down to the second floor for his interview with Michelle.

Jake sat down in a chair facing Michelle's desk. "Are you one of those militant non-smokers, Michelle?"

She pulled out a weed, lit it, Jake stoked up his pipe, the cloud grew and the interview began. Name, age, occupation—

"Writer."

"Really?"

"Really."

"What a wonderful gift to have." Michelle paused. "You know, if I was a writer, I think I'd write a book about this place."

"No kidding?"

Something in Jake's voice caused Michelle's face to grow a wry smile. "Marital status?

"I haven't been home for a while."

"What was your marital status before you left?"

"Tentative."

"Children?"

"Not guilty."

The questioning seemed to go on forever. Jake's headache made it impossible to do anything but give mechanical answers. As he lifted his pipe to take another drag, he frowned.—I get headaches from smoking too much. Maybe that's it.

He removed the pipe from his mouth as Michelle moved into a new category. "Were you closer to your mother or your father?"

"I don't know. Dad was hardly ever around. Maybe I was closer to him because of that."

"Is there anyone who knows how you really feel inside?"

Jake thought, searching his mind for someone. The question had been equivalent to asking "Do you have any friends?"

—The shrink! Don the shrink.

Jake shook his head. He had lied his ass off to Don the shrink. The only thing he had really wanted out of that relationship was another prescription.

"I can't think of anyone," he said very quietly. "Maybe a guy upstairs, one of the patients here named Earl. I talked to him some that first night I was here."

"Do you take any medications?"

"Ativan. For anxiety."

"Did you ever abuse the drug?"

"No. I just followed the prescription."

"Have you ever passed out?"

"Not from drinking. I passed out in a parade once."

"Did you ever overdose on drugs?"

"No."

"Have you ever had any blackouts?"

"No. Anyway, how would you know?"

"Partying in St. Paul and waking up a week later in Teheran on trial for flashing the Ayatollah might give you a hint."

"No. Nothing like that."

So many questions. Many of them overlapped with the questions he had been asked by Tony in his first interview. Whatever. He faded in and faded out with the pain in his head. Then Michelle asked a question that made Jake's mind frighteningly clear:

"Jake, what's your earliest memory?"

It was as though a giant hand had grabbed his guts and was twisting them from him through his chest. "Nineteen forty-five. It was late afternoon and chilly. I was three and a half years old and my father...."

Daddy worked for Washington, Mama was sick, and the Ford pulled over to a stopping place on the bridge. Daddy walked around and opened the passenger door. Jacob climbed down from the passenger seat and went to a place to look at the city.

Chicago was all over the place. He forced himself to take an interest in the buildings, the people. He was to be left alone someplace, and the longer he could drag out the ride, the longer Daddy would still be there. He wanted to vomit. But he couldn't. There wasn't time for things like that.

A hand shook his shoulder. Jacob looked around and Daddy was capping a bottle and putting it into his overcoat pocket. "C'mon, fella, we have to go."

The huge hallway was dark and quiet. "How old is he?"

"Three and a half."

The lady spoke in hushed tones to Daddy, then Daddy hugged him and he went away through those huge wood and brass doors. The lady pointed Jacob toward a huge staircase that seemed to circle upwards forever. The lady had apple cheeks, rimless glasses, a cheery smile. She looked like Mrs. Santa Claus. Jacob held her hand with both of his.

It was dark and they were in a large room walled with double bunk beds filled with sleeping children. Mrs. Santa Claus folded his clothing and placed it into a dresser. Jacob had questions, but kept quiet.

He had tried to ask about Mama before, and Mrs. Claus had told him to "Shoosh." It was a strange place, and he was frightened. He began crying. The silent tears grew into sobs, then Mrs. Claus shooshed him again.

"I want to go home."

Mrs. Claus shook her head. "You can't go home."

"Why can't I go home?"

"Shoosh!"

"Why can't I go home?" Louder.

Mrs. Claus bent over, her great floppy breasts straining against the dark flowered print dress that covered them. She grabbed his chin with a soft, powdered hand, forcing him to look at her eyes. They were dark, narrowed, unwavering.

"Now you shoosh! You can't go home. Your mother is dead."

—Dead.

A great emptiness opened beneath him and he tumbled into it.

Dead.

His head was light. Mrs. Claus undressed him as though he were a lifeless rag doll.

Dead.

The question built up inside of him until he had to give it voice or explode. It forced its way out, half choked down for fear of the answer.

"Daddy? What about my daddy?"

The lady turned her back and began pulling down the covers on a bottom bunk. When the covers were arranged to her satisfaction, she looked at him and pointed at the bed. Jacob climbed onto the cold sheet, put his head on the cold pillow, then felt the chill of the sheet and blanket being pulled up to his neck.

"What about my Daddy?"

The lady stood, pressed her hands against the small of her back, then yawned. After that she looked at him, shook her head, and patted Jacob on his left cheek.

"Your Daddy doesn't want you anymore. That's why he left you here. So behave."

She turned her back, extinguished the small light on the dresser, then closed the door to the room.

He didn't move.

The impossible—the unthinkable—had happened. He was alone. Not by himself. Alone. All alone in that room, in that city, on that planet, in that galaxy, in that universe.

Alone.

Jake felt the tears burning his eyes, he turned his head away from Michelle, and lit his pipe. "My mother wasn't dead, and my father hadn't taken off, of course. That was just Mrs. Santa Claus's way of getting her babies to do what she wanted. It was very effective, too."

Jacob turned back and saw that Michelle was wiping her eyes. She shook her head and spoke. "That was a hell of a thing to do to a child."

Jacob looked away and stared at one of the blank walls. "Yes. Wasn't it?"

—I can always jerk a tear with that story. It never fails. I ought to write it up and sell it. Too bad that it was just as bad as I thought it was. Too bad it's true.

Michelle blew her nose, then it was back to the job. "Complete this sentence: God is...."

"A word."

"Did you understand the question?"

"Yes."

Lunch. Jake theorized that part of the reason why he didn't feel well was because he hadn't ingested anything but coffee for two days. Lasagna was being served. Jake took two helpings and forced himself to eat all of it. He felt better for a moment, then ran from the dining room and hit the first floor shithouse, just managing to reach the toilet in time.

When the retching, at last, ended, Jake leaned with his elbows on the edge of the toilet bowl. "What in the hell was wrong with that lasagna?"

Noon vitals at the nurse's station.

"How do you feel, Jake?"

"I've felt worse."

"Your blood pressure is down."

"Isn't that good?"

"If it goes down much lower, someone will throw dirt on your face. How have you been eating?"

"With my mouth."

Jake and Robby swore to keep in touch with each other for life. Jake picked up his books and bag, walked past the nurse's station, and headed down north wing. Coming out of the fire stairs onto third floor north's lounge, he looked to his right. Room 355. It was open and housekeeping was polishing the floor. There was a desk, posters on the wall, a green chalkboard, stacks of chairs. A metal card holder to the left of the doorjamb said "Angela Gwynn." A black plastic sign in the center of the door said "Counselor."

Across the hallway was Room 356. There was a pair of feet on the bed farthest from the door. Jake took a deep breath and entered the room. "Hi. I'm Jake Ran—"

His new roommate stood up. He was black, at least six-foot six, and at least three hundred pounds, give or take a hundred.

Jake felt faint.

The man held out a hand and smiled. "I'm Frank Kimbal."

Jake's hand vanished inside Frank's. What was he? Professional football player? Cop? Prison guard? Bouncer? Horror film extra? The gang rumble behind Jake's eyes escalated to the Normandy Invasion.

"What do you do for a living, Frank?"

"I'm a teacher. Elementary school."

"Really?" Frank grimaced. Jake suspected that Frank had gotten that "Really?" about a million times. "That's great."

Frank released Jake's hand and sat on his bed. "What do you do?"

"I'm a writer."

"No kidding? What do you write?"

"Novels. Short stories. Science fiction, mostly."

"No kidding?" Jake nodded. Frank sat on his bed, put his legs up, and stretched out with his hands behind his head. "If I was a writer, I think I'd write a book about this place."

Jake nodded again as he began putting away his clothes.

—You'll get no argument from me, Godzilla. The proposal is in the mail. "What week are you in, Frank?"

"Second. You're lucky to have Angela for your counselor."

"Is she pretty good?"

"She scares the shit out of me."

Jake turned around and frowned at his roommate. "She scares *you?*"

"That's a fact, Jack."

He wasn't kidding. Jake turned back to his unpacking, while images of the Masked Mangler in drag performed body slams in his head.

Limping his way to dinner, Jake's preoccupation with his pain was interrupted by a look from one of the civilian-clad nurses behind the counter of the third floor nurse's station.

Jake stopped and looked at her. —Why are all these people so perky looking? Perky little face, perky little smile, perky little hairdo, perky little boobs. "I'm Jake."

"Hi. I'm Tess."

"Was there something you wanted?"

She shook her head and looked down. "No. Nothing."

"My mistake." Jake turned away and dragged himself to the stairwell.

"Happy New Year," she called from the station.

Jake frowned back at her then looked up at Frank. "Is she trying to be funny?"

Frank laughed as he led the way down the stairwell.

14

Jake sat in the fourth floor recreation room, his head in his hands, trying to maintain sanity between the thump-thump-thump of the disco alternating with the whine-whine-whine of the country & western. The clatter of billiard balls, the incessant pok-dok pok-dok of the ping pong game, talk, laughter, singing, smoke. The slosh of eternal coffee.

His head felt like a rotten pumpkin filled with broken bottles. His stomach felt like he had eaten his head.

—It's only tension. Maybe a sinus problem. Maybe an abscessed tooth. Well, maybe thirty abscessed teeth. Everything aches because I'm making a hundred pains out of one by favoring my stiff neck and backache. Got to relax.

"Excuse me."

He looked up, forced his eyes to focus, and saw a woman, late twenties, large round glasses, handsome in a wrung-out sort of way, brown strands of hair of uneven lengths averaging shoulder-duster.

"What?"

"I'm Diane."

He closed his eyes, nodded, and held out his hand. "Jake."

She shook the hand and sat down across from him. "What do you do for a living, Jake?"

Jake performed a slow count to ten. "I am a writer. I have absolutely no intention of writing a book about this place."

She laughed. "Tom told me you were a writer. I see you've run into it, too."

Tom. The issue of just who in the hell is Tom was tabled. "Too?"

"I write. Every time I tell someone that, I hear 'you know, if I was a writer—'"

"'—I'd write a book about this place,'" Jake completed. He grinned and held out his hand again. "What was your name again?"

"Diane Cook."

"Jacob Randecker. Science fiction."

"Is that the name you write under?"

He nodded.

"I can't say I'm familiar with your work."

"Do you read SF?"

"No."

"That's probably why. I haven't met any of my readers here yet. Either they're all straight or beyond hope. What do you write?"

"Trade mag freelance. Interviews and eyeball openers mostly."

"The you'll never guess why or how often Senator Ted Kennedy changes his underwear sort of thing?"

"Jeez, Jake, you get mean when you're not drinking."

He chuckled and lit his pipe. "I apologize. At the moment I feel like reprocessed shit."

"You look like it." She leaned forward. "Is there anything I can do?"

"The only thing that would cheer me up right now is to find out that my agent was admitted today." Jake looked around the room, letting his gaze stop on Diane. "Why do they want a book about this place?

They've got to hate it as much as I do."

"I think I know. If you could step outside of it and look in for a moment, there's quite a story."

Jake grimaced. "*Human Misery for Fun and Profit.*"

Diane smiled and looked at the faces in the lounge. "It isn't so difficult to understand. Imagine an entire community going through a 180° change in life and personality all at the same time. These people are going through the most profound experience of their lives. They can talk about it, and they will. But it'll be like, 'Yeah, man, it was something else.'"

She leaned forward, her elbows on her knees. "But they don't have the skills necessary to communicate the power and meaning of what they're experiencing. That's why God invented writers."

"Diane, why don't *you* write a book about Saint Mary's? You could call it *Shitfaced Again.*"

She laughed and held out her hands. "Oh, no! It's way too close. Besides, I'm on an eighty-proof sabattical."

"Come again?"

"No one knows I'm here. Little Diane has gone away for a little vacation. And someday soon she'll come back all refreshed and happy. I'm not about to announce it in print that I've been put away."

"Hmmm. That's exactly what I already did: announce it. I sent notices to all of the SF trades and fanzines. Jake is in the joint."

"Jesus!" She shook her head. "Whatever made you do that?"

"Seemed like a good idea at the time...said the naked man in the cactus patch upon being asked why he jumped in." His shoulders gave a tiny heave. "I suppose it's better than leaving it up to the rumor mill."

"As long as you've done that, why don't you write a book about it? As for a title, I'd call it *The Miracle Factory;* that's what they do here: manufacture miracles."

"There's a million drug stories on the shelves."

"I never read any about treatment."

Jake shook his head. "I was handed two on my way in here."

"*I'll Quit* and *Recovery*? Those are nonfiction. I mean fiction."

"Remember me? Science fiction."

"You are some piece of bullshit, Jake. What would you say to a tyro who wouldn't write for the excuses you're dishing up?"

Jake leaned forward, a little of the color coming back to his face. "Okay, how about this? A treatment center located in a galaxy far, far away. This alien is admitted; a large feline-looking creature. His drug of choice? Remember Three-Mile Island?"

Diane frowned. "Yes."

"Well, some of the radio-active leakage makes some bizarre DNA changes in the catnip along the river. See, this alien is hooked on Susquehanna Gold. Kitty's killer nip—"

Diane stood up. "Bye, Jake." She turned and walked off into the crowd.

Jake wrapped his arms around his quaking stomach. "I could call it *The Superfluous Earthman*, or *I was an Extra Terrestrial*." It began feeling like long, sharp, steel needles had been thrust into his eyes and were sticking out the back of his head. He stood up and began making his way through the crowd. "Probably make a million dollars."

Down the stairwell to the third floor, past the nurse's station. There was another broad in civvies giving him the fisheye. "Yeah?"

In another time, another place, she would have been beautiful. To Jake she was just another affliction. She looked down and shook her head. "Nothing."

Jake turned down north wing, grabbed the railing on the right and began pulling himself down the nine miles to his room.

—Got to relax. Can't let this tension get to me. Relax. Sleep. Good. Sleep. Try and get some sleep. First, get back to the room, then sleep.

He opened his eyes, saw that he was half on the floor, hanging from the railing by one arm. He pushed himself up, looked toward the nurse's station in time to see nursey with the white-blond hair look away. She looked back and Jake grinned and called out, "Must've twisted my ankle."

She smiled and went back to work. Brandy, walking toward the recreation room, paused to speak. "How are you doing, Jake?"

Jake nodded, grinned, took a renewed grip on the rail. "Fine. Just fine."

"That's certainly the way it looks to me." Brandy continued on her way, not looking back.

—Nobody likes a smartass, lady.

Jake adopted an attitude of grim determination and continued the task of returning to Room 356. For reasons he hadn't the energy to explore, returning to his room seemed to make child's play out of completing his first novel, or getting out of the Army without doing stockade time, or—

—It's only tension. Got to relax. Got to get some sleep.

He closed his eyes, took several deep breaths, and wiped the perspiration from his face. A feeling almost of well-being descended upon him. He pushed himself away from the railing, stood upright, and walked the remainder of the way to his room.

—There. I said it was only tension.

15

On the floor above, in the recreation room, Frank Kimbal stood up from making a complete botch of an easy corner shot, handed his cue to Ron, and shook his head. "This table must have warts."

"Unh, huh." Ron bent over, lined up, and began cleaning up the table. Frank leaned against the window sill, crossed his arms, and watched Ron at work. Not a wasted motion, just enough of a tap to sink the ball he was aiming at, and just enough English to leave the cue ball lined up for the next shot. It looked effortless.

Frank looked around and saw a hand waving at him. Sharp looking lady in dark sweater and slacks. Marnie. Nurse from the third floor. He pushed off from the window sill and made his way through the crowd of patients, stopping next to the nurse. "Did you want me?"

The nurse took him by his left arm. "Out into the hall for a minute, okay?"

"Sure." Frank followed Marnie out into the relative quiet of the hall and stopped when she stopped. She looked up at him. "Frank, do you understand what's happening with your roommate?"

"Is there anyone on the unit who doesn't know—besides Jake?" He nodded. "How can I help?"

"He has to go through this by himself, but he's carried it on a bit longer than Doctor Caccia thought he would. Tony's been on an open line to the nurse's station for the past hour."

"Afraid Jake'll kick off into the D.T.'s?"

Marnie nodded. "Or worse. I don't want you to hold his hand— unless he asks for help. But look in now and then and keep me posted. Will you?"

"Sure."

"And don't be too obvious about it."

Frank grinned and shook his head. "Aren't we cool, calm, and unconcerned? You look terrified."

"I've seen too many needless deaths, Frank. I can accept it out on the street; I can't accept it on my floor." She glanced up. "Thanks." He watched her back as she walked to the stairwell.

Why was she like a sister to him? Two days before another patient had made a lewd remark about Marnie, and Frank had threatened to kill him. Why shouldn't the turkey make whatever comments he felt like making? Marnie's the kind of voluptuous beauty that naughty little boys have been making lewd comments about since the invention of naughty little boys. Frank must have heard it in at least ten lectures: emotional development stopped when your chemical dependency began. The unit was filled to the rafters with little boys and little girls, sixty going on six, thirty going on thirteen.

But Marnie was a sister. She cared. For all the drunks and junks, she cared. She treated everyone like a human. She also insisted on everyone treating themselves like humans, too.

Frank scratched his head, went into the recreation room to rescue his cup, and headed for the kitchen. As he pushed his way through the door, he saw the kitchen cart in the middle of the floor and a woman from the main kitchen restocking the small refrigerator next to the sink. The coffee dispensers were located on the other side of the cart.

Leaning against the dispensers was the new fish who had been shaking it out all day in the kitchen, talking a mile a second, smoking an endless chain of Salems. Just then he was burning off the kitchen helper's ears.

Frank held out his cup. "Mind getting me one?"

Brandy entered the kitchen from the opposite door and stopped to wait for the cart to clear the room.

The kid, white in between the new stitches on five different cuts that ran into his hairline, held up Frank's cup. "Sure, bro'. How you want it?"

"Black."

The kid nodded, filled the cup with scalding hot coffee, then turned and handed the cup across the cart to Frank. "Just like you likes your women, huh? Hot and black."

Frank's face resembled carved stone. Without blinking his eyes, he took the cup, tossed down the coffee with one gulp, and handed the cup back to the kid.

"More!" His deep voice reverberated in the tiny room.

The kid's eyes bugged as he took the cup and quickly stuck it in the dispenser. "Shi...sure. Sure, man, sure." He pulled out the full cup and handed it to Frank. The extended hand shook. "Here."

Frank took the cup and let his eyes narrow. "Thenk you veddy much." He turned and went through the door to the recreation room. Brandy followed him out and pulled on his sweater to stop him.

"You stupid shit. How badly did you burn yourself?"

Frank waved his hand in front of his mouth and sucked air in. "Why do you ask?"

"Was it worth it?"

"In the long run, when I become more mature and responsible, I suppose I will look back upon this moment as the exercise of childish resentment. But right now? Shit, yes!"

"How's Jake?"

"I'm going now to check."

She turned back to the kitchen. "Just so it was worth it."

Still waving his hand in front of his mouth, Frank headed for the stairwell. Shaky Jake was back in the room trying to prove that he didn't have a problem, and Marnie needed a watchdog to make certain that Jake didn't blow into a rat-and-cockroach festival, or simply end it all to stop the pain.

Watching Jake was no burden. Frank knew what Jake was playing with and was going through. Frank's visitors had been snakes. Millions of yard-long, slimy black coils. Screams wouldn't send them away. Not all of the screams in the world.

As he walked down the stairs, Frank remembered some saying. The words were foggy, but the sentiment was somewhere along the lines of there being no love greater than that of one drunk for another. Whoever had come up with that one obviously had never witnessed the love one recovering drunk has for another recovering drunk.

16

Jake sat on the edge of his bed in his pajamas and bathrobe, his slippers on his feet, his hands out to his sides on the mattress. His arms were elastic supports helping him to keep his purchase on the bed as it rocked and twisted. Jake whispered an old joke, "You're not drunk if you can lie down on the floor without hanging on."

The door opened, but the pain in Jake's neck made turning to look to see who it was an exercise in self-abuse. "Frank?"

"It's me. How are you doing?"

"This headache. I don't believe this headache. I tried to get some sleep, but every time I lie down and close my eyes, my toes go over my head and my stomach—" Jake stood up. "To hell with it. Same thing happens sitting down."

Frank pulled out his chair, sat down at his desk, and opened his steno pad. "I'll be here working on my first step if you need anything."

Jake waved a hand back and forth. "I'm okay. I'll walk around a little, take the kinks out. What's a first step?"

"Angela will give you an outline Monday. It's the history of your chemical usage and how it affected you."

Jake laughed. "That ought to take all of five minutes. The war stories I've heard around here make my tale pretty pale. I'll be around." He turned and walked through the door, the brightness of the hall lights hurting his eyes.

Using the wall to hold himself up, he entered the north wing lounge. It was deserted. He looked to his right. One Honeywell thermostat. Set at 72°F. "They *do* keep this place like a furnace!"

He turned, centered himself in the hallway, and began walking briskly toward the nurse's station. He rounded the corner, made it to the west wing lounge, and checked the thermostat. 73°!

"I was right!" He ran his fingers through his hair and they came away wet and sticky. "God damn them! I was right! It *is* too damned hot!"

As he passed the nurse's station on his way to east wing, he asked one of the nurses, "Doesn't anyone check the thermostats around here? I haven't found one set lower than seventy-two."

No one answered and Jake continued down the east wing hall until he reached the lounge. The east wing thermostat read 74°.

Seventy-four! Jake sat down on the arm of the couch and rubbed his eyes. Tears were very near the surface. He was vindicated.

"At home it's always set to 68". No wonder I'm perspiring."

As a wave of nausea rolled over him, Jake got to his feet and began walking.

—74°. Goddamn.

As he passed the nurse's station, he said to a face, "Seventy-four degrees. I told you. Someone should check it out."

And he continued down west wing. At the west wing lounge, he turned around and headed east.

—I can walk it out. If I walk far enough, I'll get tired enough to sleep. I have to get some sleep.

East, west, north, south to the nurse's station, then west, east, north, south....

Another patient came from the opposite direction. "How's it going?"

"Fine. Just fine."

Time after time, up one hall, down another, the throbbing in his head keeping double-time with his footsteps. The pains in his legs moved up and down from his knees, the muscles in his shoulders protested at the weight of his arms.

West, east past the nurse's station down to the east wing lounge, about face, west until the nurse's station, turn north, walk, walk, walk until north wing lounge, about face—

Another patient. "How's it going?"

"Not real great."

South, turn right at the nurse's station....

Endless circuits of endless corridors. Thousands of pale gray asphalt tiles polished to a high gloss. He began counting them one at a time.

—Damned things are staggered. The halls are eight tiles across. Nine counting the indentations for the doorways. East, one, two, three, four....

Another patient. "How's it going?"

"Fuck you."

—West, hundred and two to the big black crack. Must be an expansion joint. Step on a crack, break your mother's back. Hundred and nineteen, turn at the nurse's station. North, hundred and something, eight times one hundred and nineteen...screw it. North wing lounge, tired, legs cramping. Got to sit down.

He sat on the couch; the wormy pattern in the ceiling's acoustic tile began crawling. An army of worms swimming through an ocean of fly specks. His stomach flipped, he sprang to his feet; south to the nurse's station, he turned, stumbled, fell flat on his ass, made a joke, got up

again, no problem, just slipped, go west until you reach the west wing
lounge, turn around....

—Eight times one nineteen. Nine eights, seventy-two. Carry the
seven. Nine'n' seven...something.

"How's it going?"

He shook his head.

—How long?

He stumbled toward...west, east wing? He was confused. He lifted
his arm, looked at his watch, couldn't make out the time. Ten thirty?
Eleven thirty? He couldn't hold the arm up forever, so he dropped it.

—Some lounge. Turn around and head the other way. Figure out
where you are once you get to the nurse s station. Can't walk. Use rails.
Pull, step, pull, step, pull, step, pull...God damn these thoughtless bastards who don't close their doors.

—Reach, step, pull, step, pull, step, pull....

"Gimp, gimp, gimp, the crips are marching...."

—Fucking tension. Got to relax. Need sleep. Feels like I'm on the
Bataan Death March. Pull, step, pull....

—Door. Open.

The distance between the end of the handrail he was gripping and
the beginning of the next one on the opposite side of the door seemed
impossible to traverse. Slowly he lowered himself until, still hanging
onto the railing, he was squatting. The floor and walls of the hallway
seemed lined with a thin film of moving bubbles, like dirty, slightly
soapy water on a windshield. The bubbles were black and had legs. The
walls were covered with billions of tiny black spiders.

"No. Now that can't be."

To avoid the spiders, he looked up at the ceiling. Up there was a
white ocean of pulsating earthworms. They flowed, wriggled, and
writhed. They began crawling down the walls—

Up he leaped, reaching across the door. There was no muscle that didn't scream for attention, no joint that didn't feel filled with grit, no nerve that didn't vibrate with bad news for his neural centers.

—The pain. God, what's wrong?

He opened his eyes and found himself facing the nurse's station, weaving like a top running out of spin. One of the beauties behind the counter was looking back. "Y'know," he said to Marnie. "I feel terrible." He looked around, got his bearings, found a railing, and headed north. Marnie walked up to him.

"Would you like to talk about it, Jake?"

"Talk?" Jake managed a shrug, then a nod. "Yeah. Gotta be in the lounge, though. Smoke. Minnes…Cleanair Act. Smoke."

He pulled himself down the hallway, Marnie holding onto his left arm. Then he was frightened. There was something very important, something he had forgotten.

"My name?"

"Jake. You're Jacob Randecker. You write."

"Yes. Remember now." Jake nodded and continued to pull himself down the hall. "Your name?"

"I'm Marnie."

"Marnie, how do you know?"

"How do I know what?"

"Marnie, how do you know I write?"

"Your story in *Omni*. I read it." She smiled. "I'm a fan."

"No shit?"

They reached the lounge and Jake lowered himself into a loveseat. Marnie sat to his right and held his hands. He was trembling, his body switching from hot to cold then back again.

"What's going on, Marnie? Why's this happening?"

"What was your drinking like, Jake?"

"Not like this, you can bet. Beer. Up to my heart attack I was killing a fifth of Seagrams a day. After that I only drank beer. I guess it was a lot.

Maybe I fit some whisky in there, but not a lot—"

The room went totally black, all was silence, then light and noise again, ultra bright and loud. "Shit. I haven't had anything to drink since…the seventeenth." Black, then light again, and the lights turned about him, their brilliance a smear of colored streaks. A voice came through.

"What was your drinking like, Jake?"

The room whirled, and Jake would have gladly vomited could he have located his stomach. "Three…six-packs at a crack at the end. Sixteen-ounce cans. Just beer, though. A little whisky now and then. Some rum. Spent half my life with my dork in the john pissing away my time. Fill it up, piss it out."

"Were you on any medications, Jake?"

"After the heart attack. They put me on Valium for a short time. Then Ativan. Sort of like Valium. I had this backache, see? Anxiety. Ativan's just a little muscle relaxant. Minor tranquilizer."

"Did you ever abuse the drug?"

"No! No, I just followed the prescription—"

The universe became deadly silent for Jacob Randecker. His mind could see it as clearly as if it were yesterday.

Ran out of Ativan early that one time. Squirmed in bed for three days until….

Until he had Ann call the hospital's emergency room. There was a doctor on duty that didn't know him. *He had the doctor phone in a new prescription, to another drugstore—*

"Just followed the prescription! *Both* of them! *Both* of them!"

He made her release his hands so he could hold his head. "I'll be a— I'm a son of a bitch! *Both* of them! Double!" He looked at her, still holding his head. "And when I was drinking hard, I wouldn't take *any*. So when I wasn't drinking, I could triple, quadruple—Marnie?"

"Yes, Jake?"

He reached out a finger and touched her cheek, bringing away a tear. He examined the tear, enclosed it in his fist, then closed his eyes and shook his head.

"We've been very concerned about you, Jake."

He couldn't deal with the tear right then. "I came here with a lousy little beer habit. Now, I'm…" He sighed and covered his eyes with his palms. "Marnie, I'm a drug addict." It seemed too much to hear, even from his own mouth. He tried to get up from the loveseat. His legs collapsed beneath him.

Frank was called, and he and Marnie helped Jake to bed. Jake sat up while Marnie went to get the Librium and the anti-convulsant, beginning the medication that had originally been prescribed for withdrawal.

Frank, sitting on his own bed across from Jake, reached out a hand and clasped Jake's shoulder. "It's going to be okay, man. They say the rest of the way is downhill."

"Frank, I have never before felt so defeated."

"You're up against one powerful opponent, Jake. No one's ever beaten it."

"What are you saying?

Frank reached out, picked up the little white card atop Jake's books, and opened it. "Can you read the first step?"

"Oh, hell, Frank. Not literature. Not now."

"Read it. Especially now."

Jake forced his eyes to focus. His neck muscles jerked as he read. "We admitted we were powerless over alcohol—that our lives had become unmanageable."

Frank returned the card to Jake's desk. "What you've just done is what we call taking the first step on your knees."

Jake laughed weakly. "You mean, on my ass."

"On your ass."

Marnie returned, Jake took the medication, and she left. He stretched out in bed, wept for a few moments, and drifted off to sleep.

17

In bed in the dark, Frank lit a cigarette, blew the smoke toward the ceiling, then looked at the warmth in his cigarette's glowing coal. While on Shaky Jake watch, he had actually started on his first step, the history of his use of chemicals illustrating his powerlessness over them and just how unmanageable things had gotten. He ran that old tape, that last day in group before the New Year holidays.

Angela had rolled her chair across the floor until she was directly in front of him. The seated circle of the other patients in the group issued looks of everything from sympathy to "Better you than me." Angela was bent over, leaning her elbows on her lap, that sharp glitter in her eyes. He felt like a bug under a microscope.

"Frank, you've been pretty quiet."

He grinned, shrugged, nodded.

"Frank, are you ready to give your first step yet?"

He shook his head. "No, not yet."

"Why?"

"I can't seem to get into it." He tried to look and feel unconcerned.

Inside his springs were compressed to the limit.

Angela sat back, placed her elbows on her chair's armrests, placed her fingertips together, played spider-doing-pushups-on-a-mirror, and put on The Grin. The Grin was a slight pulling back of the right corner of her mouth. The Grin was the needle pinning the bug to the observation deck. The Grin seemed to go on forever.

"Well, Frank?"

He sat back, folded his arms, his eyes half closed, his jaw muscles twitching. "Well, what? I don't know what to answer—"

Angela pushed her chair back to her desk. "You know the answer, Frank. I don't want to play games with you."

His arms unfolded and he grabbed his knees. "I don't—I don't know what you're talking about!"

Both sides of Angela's mouth went back, exposing her teeth in Grin Rampant, and she looked up at the ceiling. "Oh, Frank, Frank, Frank."

Frank moistened his lips. "I've admitted I'm an alco—"

Angela came forward, her chair scooted across the floor, and screeched to a halt in front of Frank. "I don't want to listen to your games, Frank. I don't have the time to waste. We have important work to do in here."

Angela's face went in and out of focus in time with the mad pounding in Frank's head. "I've done what the A.A. first step says. I don't see why I have to go into all of this other stuff! I've admitted I'm an alcoholic, that my life was unmanageable, and I don't want to drink or use pot any more."

Angela closed her eyes, nodded, her face displaying her Grin Covert. "How about it, group?" Slowly her chair moved back to her place in the circle.

Frank looked around the room at the faces. Somewhere inside he knew that he had at least half of the group intimidated. But there were exceptions. Dave, the union thug, clasped his hands beneath his belly, raised his eyebrows, and looked in Frank's direction. "Frank, you're an asshole."

Angela reached out a hand and placed it on Dave's arm. "Now, don't be judgmental, Dave. What do you see; what do you hear?"

Dave nodded at Angela. "Okay." He looked at Frank. "We been told a hundred times that doing the first step—Angela's version—is supposed to show us just how powerless we are, and just how unmanageable things got."

Dave scratched his chin, looked at the floor, then back at Frank. "I don't think you want to know that. Every time you talk since you joined the group I hear you saying the same thing. You say all I gotta do is quit drinking and all my problems will be solved."

Frank jabbed his finger in the air in Dave's direction. "That's right! If I can stop drinking, all *my* problems will be solved!"

"Bullshit!" answered five members of the group.

Frank sat back, shocked. Before he knew it, Angela's face was again in front of him. "Your Higher Power is talking to you, Frank. Listen to it. On Monday I want you to be ready to give your first step. Do you understand?"

"Yes."

The Grin. "How do you feel right now, Frank?"

"Feel?"

Angela closed her eyes, nodded, then opened them again. That blue, sharp, glitter that seemed to penetrate to Frank's backbone. "Yes, how do you feel right now? Mad, sad, glad."

"I guess I'm mad."

"I guess you are." She reached out and touched his arm. "How mad are you, Frank?"

He could hardly keep his eyes in focus, keep his breakfast down. He kept his fists clenched, or else…or else—

"Do you want to hit me, Frank?"

He saw the care in her face, the same face that he wanted to smash. He didn't reply. Couldn't reply—

"Shit!" he hissed, sitting up in his bed. He had frozen in group. He had been numb ever since. Up until he watched the power of the disease to deny itself in his new roommate. Jake was like a guy standing in the middle of a burning house, explaining away the smoke, the heat, the crackle of the flames, throwing desperate words at reality, only admitting to the fire when the burning beams began falling on his head.

Opening his nightstand drawer, Frank put out his cigarette in the ashtray concealed there. He waited for twenty minutes, his eyes closed, and then put on his slippers and bathrobe, grabbed his cigarettes, coffee cup, and steno pad and looked at Jake, struggling in his dreams the same way he had been struggling awake.

The disease affects everything: body, mind, and spirit, they say. Write down the big first and you'll understand that better, they say. And for the first time since entering treatment, Frank wanted desperately to understand the nature of the monster and what it had done to him.

"Thanks, Jake," he whispered. He walked around Jake's bed, opened the door, and closed it silently behind him. In the small wing lounge, he sat next to a bright light, opened his pad, and got to work.

JANUARY 2ND

18

The penny belt.

On a kid's TV show. Jacob watched. Take one strip of Scotch Brand cellophane tape and lay it sticky side up on a flat surface. Then, take penny after penny and lay them on the tape until they are in a bright, straight row. Then take another strip of Scotch Brand cellophane tape and place it sticky side down on top of the row of pennies. Eureka, a penny belt.

Jacob watched the little girl on the TV screen showing her mother the belt and how delighted her mother was at the dexterity and cleverness of her daughter.

He knew where the Scotch Brand tape was, and his penny jar was full. He selected the pennies with care. Each one a different date. Then he took the Comet Brand cleanser and scoured the pennies until they were all the same copper-pink color. He dried the pennies, and as per instruction, he made the penny belt, dates in ascending order.

Jacob ran from his room and showed the penny belt to Mama and awaited her approval—

—hours later—

—left Mama's room, her endless tirade against the waste of Scotch Brand cellophane tape still smashing against the insides of his head.

Jacob knelt in front of the upstairs toilet and vomited.

He was out the pennies. too—

A dark shape holding a light. Jake started from his sleep, sat partway up. "Who's that?"

Before the dark shape answered, Jake remembered. Saint Mary's. Room check. "Just doing the room check. Sorry."

The floor nurse prowled the halls like some denim-clad Diogenes burning up his Ray-o-vacs in search of a man who can be honest with himself.

"Brother, did you get the wrong number."

The door closed and the room went to dark split by ghosts of blue-white from the lights outside the building. Jake rolled onto his back and looked at the ceiling, trying to sort the images buzzing through his head.

—I haven't thought about the penny belt for years. Decades. The dream was so vivid.

Jake whispered to the dark, "I couldn't have been more than ten or eleven years old." There were tears inside, and he didn't know why. He didn't want to know why. He reached out his right hand, felt around for his watch, then felt a stab of fear.

—Stolen. My watch...stolen!

He felt with his hand and found the watch on his left wrist. Last night he hadn't taken it off. Jake frowned in the dark. "I always take my watch off at night. I can't stand sleeping with it on." He moved the band and felt the ridges the expandable band had embossed into his skin. "Why didn't I take off my watch?"

He blushed in the dark as he remembered. "Oh. yeah. I sort of had other things on my mind." A feeling of despair washed over him as he became aware of his newly understood circumstances. His new status:

addict. No longer a fellow with a little beer habit, a "former" drinking problem. *Drug* addict. No one had called him one. Self-admitted addict.

—Junky, junky, junky; he got himself a monkey.

He thought about what he had read. The alcohol and Ativan were interchangeable. That's why no hangovers. Pop a pill first thing in the morning. He didn't feel high, but he didn't hurt too much. There was his morning ritual of Arm & Hammer Baking Soda for the acid stomach, the Bufferin for his headache, the Alka-Seltzer to back up the Arm & Hammer and the Bufferin, the Alka-Seltzer Plus to blast open his sinuses, along with the Afrin nasal spray to urge on the Alka-Seltzer...Visine to lube the eyeballs...another Ativan....

"Jesus." He shook his head. "Hell, no, Randecker. You never had any hangovers."

...Pabisol to kill the gut pain and stop the trots. Sort of like Pepto-Bismol mixed with opium—contained paregoric—another Ativan....

And when things began crumbling around noon, or eleven, or ten in the morning, it was time for Miller's Lite. Or rum, or whisky, or vodka, or gin—

"No, stupid, you saved up all of your hangovers to have at the same time. Last night."

—Everybody on the unit must've known. Everybody watching me do a number on myself.

"Shit!" Jake remembered the urine specimen he had turned in and the blood that Vampira had sucked out of him.

—That doctor—Tony—when I refused medication. He knew! He knew then! He knew what I was going to go through! With that smug little grin on his face. He could have at least told me—

"No. stupid." Jake rested his face in his hands and shook his head. "No. He couldn't have told you a god damned thing. You didn't need it, remember? All you had was a psychological depen...."

The memory of Tony trying to gasp out "Psychological dependency" flashed before Jake's eyes. His blush grew deeper as more came back. There were his answers to all of those questions:

Did you ever pass out?

"Well…see, I used to plow into bed every now and then and take these fourteen-hour naps. But I never passed out." He shook his head. "I used to nap at parties every now and then, too."

Did you ever have any blackouts?

—What about all of those times Ann seemed to think something horrible happened the night before, I couldn't remember anything about it and told her she was crazy. What about coming to in that taxi? Standing in front of the rehab doors for twenty minutes and not remembering? Coming to on the fourth floor shouting at that nurse?

He felt the heat of shame on his face as tears welled in his eyes. "Dammit. Can I repent by wearing a sign that says 'Asshole'?" Jake nodded. He already had been wearing the asshole sign. Everyone had been able to read it except him.

The door opened and the size of the shadow standing in the doorway could only be Frank. "Jake?"

"Yeah."

"I heard talking. Are you okay?"

"I'm okay. I'm sore as hell, but the headache is gone."

Frank came in, closed the door, and sat on his bed. He left the lights off. "What was the talking all about?"

Jake snorted out a laugh. "I was giving a jerk a good talking to." Frank lit a cigarette. Jake turned to face Frank. "Everybody knew and I didn't have a clue?"

"Yes. You'll get used to that. It happens a lot around here. They say it's the disease that tells you that you haven't got it." He tapped his steno pad against his knee. "You're not unique."

Jake looked at his watch. 4:43 a.m.. "Hell, Frank, haven't you gone to bed yet?"

"No. Did you have some talking you want to do?"

"It can wait. Get some sleep." Jake pulled on his bathrobe, grabbed his coffee cup, climbed out of bed, and opened the door. The hallway was dark, the only lights white from the nurse's station and red from the emergency exit signs in the lounge. He patted his pocket to verify the location of his pipe and tobacco, closed the door to his room, and headed for the kitchen.

After filling his cup, Jake headed back north, past his room, to the north wing lounge. The heavy frost on the lounge windows obscured and diffused the lights from the city. A woman in a metallic gold gown and robe sat in the love seat next to the only illuminated light in the room. Her legs were pulled up beneath her, and for a moment she didn't notice Jake enter the room.

She was smoking super-long tipped cigarettes, and the ashtray on the end table to her left was flowing over with butts. She turned her head and smiled at Jake. "You must be the morning shift."

"Say again?"

"Frank just left."

"Oh." Jake took a seat on the couch facing the love seat and placed his cup on the coffee table. "Frank's my roommate. My name's Jake Randecker."

"Lydia Marx. What week are you in, Jake?"

"First. I haven't really gotten started yet. I came here on the thirtieth."

She slowly nodded. "Yes. Then you haven't met Angela yet."

"No. I start group Monday. From all of the stories I've heard, she sounds like she wears black leather and brass knuckles."

Lydia studied a spot on the floor, then glanced toward room 355. "They say the third time's the charm."

"Excuse me?"

Lydia turned her head toward Jake. "I said, they say the third time's the charm. I've been through here twice before."

"What happened?"

Lydia crushed the life from the butt she was smoking and reached to the pack onher lap for another. The pack was empty. "Do you have a cigarette?"

"No. I smoke a pipe."

She crumpled the empty pack and dropped it on the end table. "I don't know what happened. Everything is going great one minute, the next minute I'm waking up in an airline terminal on the other side of the world, lost, hung over, and scared." She looked at him,, her large brown eyes misting with pain. "Why? As certain as I know anything, I know what will happen if I drink. Then I go and do it anyway. Why? Why do I do things like that?"

Jake closed his eyes and shook his head. "I wish I could help, but I'm fresh out of answers. I'm just getting around to figuring out that I have a problem myself."

"This is your first time?"

"Yes."

"Good luck."

"You too."

Jake turned his head as he heard footsteps. Brandy entered the lounge wearing her lavender jogging suit. She nodded at Lydia, and collapsed into the room's lone easy chair. "How are you feeling, Jake?"

He snorted out a laugh. "Sore, contrite, silly as hell."

She smiled. "Now you know why they say watch out for that first step; it's a big one."

Not as big as the second step, he thought. Drugs are reality. That second step is something else. "Came to believe that a Power greater than ourselves could restore us to sanity." He picked up his cup, realizing that he was terrified. That power that was greater than Jacob Randecker wasn't something he was resisting; he simply couldn't imagine such an entity.

Brandy yawned. "I'm bored. These nights can get pretty long."

Jake pointed at Lydia. "Have you met?"

Brandy nodded, took a cigarette from the pack she was carrying and lit it. Lydia smiled. "Could you spare one for a sister in need?"

"Sure." Brandy threw the pack across the lounge. Lydia caught it, took a cigarette and tossed back the pack. Brandy caught it with her left hand and dropped it to her lap. Jake sat back and sipped at his coffee. He had never been very good at catching anything but colds. That, alcoholism and drug addiction. He shook his head.

"What are you thinking on so hard, Jake?" asked Lydia.

He didn't look at Brandy or Lydia, but kept staring at his cup. "I'm scared. I'm so scared I don't know whether to pee, panic, or pass out." He glanced up, then back at his coffee cup. Lydia and Brandy were both listening. It made the confession easier, and harder.

"I don't know what I'm going to do. Okay, I've got the bug. I admit that. But the program wants me to crawl in bed with this Higher Power fiction called God, and I can't do it. I'd have to lie to do that, and I'm just discovering that everything has been lies. The Great Juju just doesn't talk to me."

Lydia sat forward. "Jake, I don't swallow this God shit either. But believe me, it's a lot easier getting through this place if you say the words. Just go along with it, and you'll avoid a lot of flak."

Brandy chuckled and pointed at Lydia. "Is that what you did?"

"Yes."

"Both times before?"

Lydia nodded. "Right."

"Is that what you're planning on doing this time, too?"

"It worked before."

Jake sat back and crossed his legs. "It doesn't seem to be working very well if you have to keep coming back here."

Brandy nodded. "That's the way it looks to me—"

"If I need professional help, Brandy, I'd just as soon that it didn't come from a counselor who is in treatment herself."

Lydia abruptly stood and walked from the lounge. Jake glanced at Brandy. She was staring down the hallway at Lydia marching through the shadows. There was the rather distinct slam of a door closing.

It wasn't much of a scene, but it was enough to make Jake's stomach crawl. Ever since he could remember, "scenes" were things to be avoided—at any price. But there was something else. "Brandy?"

The woman lit another cigarette, her first still burning in the ashtray. She took a long drag, blew the smoke at the ceiling, then closed her eyes as she rested her head against the backrest of the easy chair. "Yes?"

"How come we can see it,, and she can't?"

"Insanity." She noticed Jake chuckling. "I'm serious. Addiction is a form of insanity."

"I don't think I'm insane."

"Crazy people rarely do. Check out your second step sometime. 'Came to believe that a power greater than ourselves could restore us to sanity.' You don't need to be restored to sanity if you're already sane."

"I don't define insanity like that."

Her eyebrows went up. "How do you define it?"

"I don't know exactly. Maybe there is no exact definition."

"Jake, if you are an addict, and if you adopt as your operating premise that you cannot be an addict, and therefore search for other reasons to explain what is happening to you and by you, you tend to bend your perception of reality to fit your convictions. You see things that aren't there, and don't see things that are. You hear things that aren't there, and don't hear things that are. Your picture of yourself and the universe around you is exactly the opposite of the truth. And you swear by the fiction and ignore, even malign, the real. And when it comes time to act, you are guided by the fiction in hopes of attaining goals that can exist only in fantasy. Every thought, every action, becomes dedicated to attaining a better life through self-destruction."

Brandy laughed and shook her head. "I don't know about you, Jake, but that strikes me as a pretty fair definition of insanity."

Jake rubbed the back of his neck. "That's right. You're in the business, aren't you?"

She nodded and got to her feet. "And you were about to ask what's a nice alcoholism counselor like me doing in a dump like this."

"As a matter of fact, I was. You know so much about it, how…" Jake couldn't find another way of saying, Didn't you know better?

She answered the unasked question. "Everything I know about addiction is in the real world, Jake. But addicts and alkys don't live in the real world. That's why they're insane." She waved and quietly left the lounge.

Jake sat back, put his feet up on the coffee table, stoked up his pipe, and exhaled a satisfyingly blue cloud of smoke toward the ceiling. He lowered the pipe, closed his eyes, and said to the empty room: "Randecker, m'boy, you are in big trouble."

10:00 a.m.. Sunday morning vitals at the nurse's station.

"How do you feel, Jake?"

"Okay. Stiff, but okay."

"Your hands are shaking. Still nervous?"

"Yeah, I'm nervous. But I think we've all figured out why the hands shake."

"You're still perspiring."

"You said it was going to get warmer. Look, I have trouble sleeping at night. Do I just wait it out or is there something I can do?"

"Do you drink coffee?"

"Yes."

"How much?"

"I don't know. Maybe twenty or thirty cups a day."

"And you're having trouble sleeping? I can't understand that."

19

In back of the nurse's station is the hideout. It's a small room containing supplies, a counter, a few chairs, and the staff mailboxes. During the week, group counselors sometimes gather there to eat lunch or talk. Sometimes they stay alone in the hideout to catch up on the endless patient charting and other paperwork. Sometimes it's used just to get away from the patients. It's called screaming distance. Sometimes it's handy for a quiet cry. During the weekends and evenings, however, the hideout is taken over by the floor nurses for much the same purposes.

Coral Nation was camping out in the fourth floor hideout, letting bitter tears flow. The memo on her lap was in the wrong place. It was for Angela Gwynn, and it had been months since Angela's office had been moved from the fourth to the third floor. But some people never seem to get the word.

The memo was a note to Angela informing her of the death of Nancy Coffee. Coral shook her head. These little bits of reality flowing into the counselor mail never seemed to stop.

"Christ," she whispered, "counselors aren't immortal. Why do they keep rubbing death in their faces?" But every time they are asked, the counselors say the same thing: we want to know. If you love someone, you want to know when they die.

Coral pulled a tissue from an open box, wiped her eyes, and crumpled the tissue in her hand. Monday Angela will read the memo and forget everything she knows about grief and what to do with it. Right before morning group there is no time for grief. There is a fresh circle of fish to fry, and the job demands it all. The better the job is performed, the fewer of those memos show up in the mailbox.

Coral remembered Nancy. She had been so proud the day she left, showing her Saint Mary's medallion to everyone on the floor, giving misty hugs to all of the people she loved, which was everyone. The world was hers.

Angela had been at the nurse's station when Mike Remick came to drive Nancy home. He had gotten his medallion the week before and was still on medical leave from his job. He looked good. Angela's smile seemed to have a tremble in it.

"How has aftercare been, Mike?"

"I haven't arranged for it yet. Too many things to do. I'm getting in four meetings a week, though."

"Aftercare is very important—"

"I know, I know. Hey, there's Nancy."

Mike gave Angela a quick hug, reached across the counter and patted Coral's cheek. "Be seeing you, buddies."

Yeah, Coral had thought at the time, be seeing you Mike. So what if the program says stay away from forming any new love relationships until a year after treatment. So what if alcoholics and addicts aren't equipped to handle love. So what if they simply substitute each other for their chemical, sucking each other dry. There are exceptions. There's growth group, A.A., and N.A. It can work. Besides, Nancy and Mike have traveled hell from pole to pole. They deserve happiness. They are too good to fail. That's what Coral had thought.

Mike and Nancy, loaded down with books, boxes, and bags, had waved as they passed the nurse's station and hurried to the open elevator. The door closed and there was another patient who had a question, needed to be found for vitals or meds, a new book issue to hand out, charts to update, an endless series of things to do.

Coral had glanced at Angela's face before the counselor had turned north and headed toward her office. Afternoon group coming up. Things to do. But the look on her face. It had been haunted.

"And now Nancy is dead." Coral picked up another tissue and blew her nose.

—Did Angela see the black mark on Nancy? The sign that said this one is already dead? They say they can't predict it. But still there was the look on Angela's face. But maybe Angela had other things on her mind. Counselors do have lives away from the unit. Homes, families, joys, nightmares.

Mike was in Janet's group on the third floor. When she brought the memo down, Coral would ask the third floor station crew about Mike. Coral wanted to know. It's true. If you love someone, you want to know when they die. Even if it's only in your heart, you want to say good-bye.

Coral pushed herself to her feet. "God only knows why I'm in this damned business."

She reminded herself. A father, husband, and two brothers dead from the disease and a teenage son with an inquiring mind were some of the original motives.

—But, Christ, sometimes this shit gets hard. And old. And tired. Goodbye Nancy Coffee.

Coral tossed away her tissue and headed out to the nurse's station on her way to deliver the memo to the third floor. A familiar face was waiting on the other side of the counter. Beard, glasses...Jake Randecker, moved to the third.

"Can I help you?"

He nodded, his face slightly red. He glanced at her nametag, then back at her face. "Coral, I wanted to apologize for how I acted when I was admitted." He stood up, tapped his fingers on the counter, and shrugged. "I seem to be apologizing to a lot of people lately."

"I'm glad to see you're getting better, Jake." The lump in her throat was very large, painfully so.

"Well, that's all I wanted to say. I'll be seeing you around."

—Goodbye Nancy Coffee; Hello Jake Randecker. God, what am I doing in this funny farm?

As Jake moved toward the stairwell, the elevator door opened. A frightened face surrounded by silver fox fur poked out. It was soon followed by the rest of the lovely coat and several matching pieces of gray cowhide luggage. The woman put down her bags and looked nervously around at the strange people that populated her new universe. She spoke to Jake, and Jake turned and pointed back toward Coral.

New fish.

Coral sat down in a chair behind the station's counter, picked up a plastic holder, and began making up a new name tag.

"Excuse me?"

Coral glanced up. "Name?"

"James. Susan James."

As Coral printed the name on a white card, slipped it into the plastic holder, and stapled the assembly together, Snake Dooley, the floor cowbell-ringer, reached over the counter, flicked on the floor's intercom system, and gave an enthusiastic shake of fourth's killer cowbell. Snake Dooley looked and smelled like a shaved bear. Susan James stared in disbelief as the bell ringer headed for the stairwell. On the back of his sleeveless denim jacket appeared the inscription: "Born To Kill."

"That's the lunch bell," said Coral. "As soon as we get you settled in, you can go down and eat." Coral held out the nametag. "Wear this at all times."

Susan James stared at the nametag in Coral's outstretched hand as she unconsciously wrapped her beautiful coat more tightly about herself. Her eyes grew even wider. "I'm sorry, but I—I don't know if I'm in the right place."

"You and me both, sister." Coral grinned warmly and shook the nametag at the new fish. "Welcome to the club."

20

Jake waited in line with his group in the hallway to the cafeteria, his back against the rail, his stomach rumbling. He wasn't just hungry. Hungry is such a feeble word. Famished, ravenous. There was a reproduction of a painting hanging on the wall across from him. It was a black and tan affair, mostly black. An abstract guillotine in a bad mood. On the wall against which he was leaning were four small framed prints of hot air balloons. The frames had been swung around on their permanent mounts, stacking the frames on top of each other.

D.T. pointed at the quad display. "The Anonymous Avenger strikes again."

The word passed down the line from the front. Mystery burgers, enigmagel, and white knuckles. Plenty of chef's surprise.

"What's chef's surprise?" Jake asked.

Frank grinned. "Apricot juice. They serve it in containers that look suspiciously like urine specimen cups."

Jake nodded. "You stick out your cup, another guy sneaks up behind the chef and gooses him—"

"Surprise, chef!"

D.T. shook his head. "I can't stand mystery burger. I'd rather have the Fido patties."

"Or turd-on-a-stick," added Candy.

Jake raised an eyebrow, then gave an almost imperceptible nod. "Just think," Jake reminisced, "only a few days ago I was on my way to Kentucky Fried Snot. Goin' on down to the Colonel's to get me a bucket o' boogers—"

Candy backed away and looked in horror at Jake. "Jesus Christ, Jake! You're sick!"

"No shit. Why do you think I'm in a hospital?"

The one called Harold joined the line; Candy stepped behind him and maneuvered him until he was between her and Jake. He looked at Jake. "What did you do, win the gross out?"

Jake grinned and held out his hand. "Jake Randecker."

"Harold Rose." They shook hands.

"You get out tomorrow, don't you?"

Harold nodded. "Seems like only yesterday that I showed up. I think I'll miss it."

"Yeah, this place, hemorrhoids, and the income tax."

The line spaced and they moved up. Frank came to a rest against the rail and pointed with his thumb at Harold. "He's responsible for the name of our favorite restaurant: the Constipated Eagle."

Harold nodded. "Look when you pick up your tray. Above the door to the kitchen is a huge gold eagle that looks like it's sitting on a pot, grunting away, and not having a lot of success."

"Are you responsible for the other names, too?"

Harold shook his head. "Mystery burgers and Fido patties were here when I was admitted. I named enigmagel, though. That's a salad that looks like huge orange and yellow grubs stuck in Palmolive soap. The Sweeny Todd stew was here, and white knuckles." He looked at Frank.

"What did Jake come up with? Candy looks positively green."

"Kentucky Fried Snot. A bucket o' boogers."

Harold nodded at Jake. "I sense a military school education."

"Staunton Military Academy, Class of '60."

"Valley Forge, '64:"

They shook hands again. "Tell me, Jake. What do you do for a living?"

Jake paused, then looked at Harold. "I'm an undertaker."

Harold leaned his back against the railing and nodded. "You know, if I was an undertaker, I think I'd write a book about this place."

Jake frowned at Harold, Frank laughed, Harold joined in. "I read your *Omni* story, Jake. Very good."

Jake was relieved of the task of accepting the compliment by being next at the trays. He picked up a tray, napkin, silverware, and waited for Frank to move on. True, the gold eagle above the door to the kitchen looked like it had an immovable load on. Mystery burgers were hamburgers; easily guessed. The enigmagel seemed to be lime gelatin mixed with mayonnaise and citrus fruit of various kinds. The white knuckles?

Jake looked up at the chalkboard menu mounted on a pillar behind the servers.

Cold turkey.

—Very funny. Ha, ha.

At the table, the group sat together generating a cloud of talk.

"I figure if I got to do this higher power thing I'll get into devil worship. The program says to stick with the winners, and—"

"So this new kid comes into group smelling like scotch, his hands jammed into his pockets, wearing a U.S. Olympic Drinking Team sweatshirt. He drops into a chair, slouches down, glares at me, and says 'Fuck you.' I suspected he might have a bad attitude—"

"I picked the Cosmic Comedian for my higher power. Let's face it, if God exists, he's got to be the original practical joker—"

"I think I've solved the mystery of the mystery burger."

"Shut up. I don't want to hear about it. I'm trying to eat."

"Okay, but don't blame me if you get hoof 'n' mouth—"

"—or maybe I'll take up Islam. Wouldn't that yank Angela's chain? See, she puts me in the hot seat and I don't respond. I just whip out my prayer rug, aim at Mecca, and do my thing. What would she do—"

"—and this minister says to Angela, 'If I ever need a heart transplant, Angela, I hope I get yours, because it's never been used.' Isn't that a hell of a trip from a minister—"

"Maybe I'll take up voodoo. Stick pins in my Angela doll and get in touch with my higher power."

"——with family week starting tomorrow, I'm scared shitless—"

"Use whatever you want for a higher power. You don't have to have an Old Testament Jehovah. Plenty of fish here just use the group."

"Worship the group?"

"No, no. Worship doesn't have anything to do with it. HP is what you put in your tank to outrun the bug—"

"You can't lie about a thing like that, Lydia. If you're lying, then you don't have a higher power at all. You can't do it by yourself."

"I guess you're right, Frank."

"That's right, Lydia. Always be sincere, whether you mean it or not."

"Kiss my ass, Brandy.

"Check out Chapter Five in the Big Book, Jake. Just because a bunch of drunks want to call their higher power God, what's that to you? You can call it anything you want. A higher power can be anything that works better than you do, and you don't work at all—"

"As a minister, I suppose I feel professionally obligated to pick God as my higher power. Jake, I can't see how you can be an atheist."

"I feel the same way about goddies and Jesus freaks, Rog."

"If you don't believe in God, how do you explain the miracles, Christ talking to Satan in the desert?"

"If you wandered around under the hot sun for forty days eating nothing but them funny little cactus buttons, you'd see devils, too."

"God works!"

"Yeah, but how much does he charge? Anyway, we're both here. So what's God done for you lately?"

"What I am is *my* failing, not God's!"

"It's a disease, Roger. It isn't a moral failing. It's a bug. You've got it, that's all."

"Nonsense, Ron. Why me?"

"Why not you?"

Back in his room, Jake sat at the desk and made another try at writing the letter.

January 2nd

Dear Ann,

He sat back and stared at the top sheet of letter paper.

"Dear Ann." he said out loud, "Dear Ann, I'm dead." That one he crumpled up. "Shit, Randecker, can't you do anything but whine?"

Dear Ann,

I don't know what to do. I don't know where to go. I don't know who to ask.

"The violins'll be playing in a second." The second joined the first.

Dear Ann,

I've got the bug. I'm convinced I can't do anything about it by myself. And I don't have a god to pull out of the hat. I almost envy those who do...

Jake shook his head. "No I don't."

The third followed the second. "This is one hell of a situation to be in for a guy who is used to cranking out five thousand words a day. Can't write a simple letter."

—A simple letter. Putting into words things you've not allowed yourself to feel for decades. To someone you've refused to love. and refused to allow to love you.

"Screw it."

He stretched out on his bed and closed his eyes. Only to rest them. After one's third dose of Saint Mary's Revenge, one does not nap on a whim. He thought about his most recent interview with Michelle:

"Do you think your wife will participate in your family week?"

"What's family week?"

"The concerned persons show up, attend lectures, learn about the disease, how it's affected both you and them. They attend and participate in their own family group, and in patient group."

"I don't see what good that'll do. I'm the addict."

"You don't have to see, right now. You'll learn later about the family aspects of the disease, and how family week can help the patient's co-dependent relations. Right now all you have to worry about is answering my question. Will your wife participate in family week?"

"I don't know. January is her big month. She's in the tax business. Besides, it costs to fly out here from Maine. I don't know if she'd want to. Some things have been coming back, and if I were in her shoes, Jake Randecker wouldn't exactly be tops on my list of favorite people. Besides, we didn't know anything about family week when I came here."

"She knows now."

"How?"

"We sent her a package. Things to do. We'll be talking with her, too."

There were those old questions again, but this time some different answers:

"Were you on any other medications?"

"Ativan."

"Did you abuse it?"

"Yes. I doubled up on prescriptions, quadrupled dosages, used them with alcohol, lied to obtain more prescriptions."

"Did you ever have any blackouts?"

"Yes."

"Did you ever pass out?"

"Yes. You know, Michelle, I'm not trying to keep my story straight from one interview to the next."

"That's good."

"But there are some differences in the versions."

"That's even better."

"Jake?"

Jake opened his eyes and looked at the door to his room. Brandy was looking in. "What?"

"Telephone."

"Thanks." He sat up, rubbed his eyes, and felt sick. Fear. The outlines of the fear were in sharp focus. The things Ann could say to him; the things she had every right to say to him.

He pushed himself up from the bed. "C'mon, Jake, keeping those tongs hot forever wastes energy. What with the price of whips, bamboo splinters, and rack straps these days. The Office of Inquisition was terrific basic research for opening up a rehab." He left the room and headed for the phones located in the corridor between the third floor kitchen and east wing.

Two of the phones were occupied. The center one had the receiver off the hook. He picked it up and held his hand over his left ear to block out the voices of the other callers. "Hello?"

"Jake, honey?" It was Ann. She had been crying. "Jake, I want you to come home."

He lowered his receiver, found a chair, and sat down with a thud. He felt lightheaded, his gut in knots.

"Jake?"

"Yeah, Ann. I'm here."

"Did you hear me? I want you to come home. I'm so frightened, and I miss you so."

Jake nodded silently. Take his ticket, his money, pack his bag, he could be home before Monday.

"Jake?"

"Yes. I heard you. Ann. I can't. I can't come home."

"Why? You said you were coming home two days ago."

"I know." He shook his head and wiped his cheek with the back of his hand. "I'm where I belong, Ann. I can't come home. Not yet."

There was a long silence on the other end of the line. Then Ann's voice, tiny, puzzled. "Goodbye, Jake." A click. A dead line.

Jake reached up and replaced the receiver. He stared at the telephone, stunned that he had flatly turned down his free ride out of recovery. "That was a stupid thing to do," he muttered. He debated calling her back and saying that he had changed his mind, but the spiders and worms were still fresh in his mind.

—What would I be going back to?

The patient on the phone to his right began shouting, "Look, you told me this place didn't have anything to do with A.A.! Shit! The program here is based on A.A.!" He looked like a cross between a hippie and a U.S. Marine. "I'll let you know when I'm coming home, y'hear?" The patient hung up his receiver with a bang and looked at Jake. "Can you fucking believe that?"

Jake stared as the angry man stormed into the east wing hallway.

21

That night there was a terrible snowstorm. Nothing on the streets of Minneapolis moved. Earl Nelson looked past Jake at the lecture hall windows. He felt guilty, wondering how Alice and Joey were keeping themselves plowed out.

—Have to pay the Novak kid again. I really ought to be at home.

There were some men and women milling around down front toward the stage. Earl jabbed Jake with his elbow. "What's the holdup?"

"The scheduled A.A.s couldn't make it because of the storm. I guess the second string's trying to decide whether or not to put on the meeting."

Earl looked toward the stage. Every Sunday night after dinner, there was a mandatory A.A. step meeting in the third floor lecture hall. A.A. members from a local squad—they call them squads in Minneapolis—show up and tell their stories, making an effort to relate them to A.A.'s Twelve Steps. The stories were of three types classified by length: drunkalogs, drunkaramas, and drunkathons.

There was some talk about scrubbing the performance among the few members who did show. They were nervous, several of them never having spoken before. Then one of the members, a woman, said, "Oh, let's do it." Earl, thinking about the snowstorm, found it difficult to pay attention. Therefore, he didn't. His ass bones felt as though they were grinding against the seat of his chair. A man climbed up on the stage, introduced himself, stated his affliction, and the audience responded with a "Hi, Albert."

Earl put his elbows on his knees and rested his head in his hands as the man led the meeting in reciting the Serenity Prayer, gave the reading of the A.A. preamble, and began on his qualification.

The life and times of Albert the Alcoholic. Earl suspected that he might not live long enough to hear the end of it, and he was tuned out completely by the time Albert entered the ninth verse of the third chapter of "How Albert Found God."

"I didn't know he was lost," muttered Earl to no one in particular.

Then Albert the Alcoholic concluded his yarn and introduced the next speaker. A young woman dressed in jeans and a brief multi-colored fur coat climbed up on the stage. She looked to be about twenty years old. She smiled at the frys.

"My name's Wanda, and I'm an alcoholic."

"Hi, Wanda!!!" shouted her buddies and half the patients in the room, causing Earl's buttocks to levitate six inches off his chair.

She rubbed her hands together, grinned, and did a fair impression of Shirly Temple needing to go pee-pee. "I'm kind of nervous."

Earl nodded. —No shit.

"I started drinking when I was fifteen. I liked it a lot. At first I only drank at parties or with my friends on weekends. But by the time I was sixteen, I was getting drunk every night and having a couple in the morning to steady myself to go to school. Then I was introduced to pot, and one boy friend I cultivated had the local coke franchise. I'm not talking about the pause that refreshes. I'm talking about the real thing."

Earl's mind moved off of his troubles as he listened to Wanda. How she went from being an honor student to quitting school. How she turned pro at sixteen to make enough money on her back to support her three hundred dollar a day monkey. A brief tour through her tricks, rapes, beatings, incarcerations. How, at the age of eighteen, she freaked on angel dust and took a razor to her little sister's face. The treadmill of her tiny, dark, universe. Using, getting money however it could be gotten, using, getting more money. The monkey was demanding, it was expensive, it was a jealous god and would allow no other.

Earl jabbed Jake's arm with his elbow. He turned and Earl whispered into his ear. "I thought *I* had problems." Earl nodded and turned back toward the speaker.

He felt Jake's elbow jabbing him back. "What?"

Jake bent over and whispered into Earl's ear. "You *do* have problems."

Earl felt stunned. "Nothing like that."

Jake shrugged. "I suppose going after your son with a shotgun is more technologically advanced than a razor."

Earl raised a hand, opened his mouth, then closed his mouth and lowered his hand. His head slowly turned toward the stage, a lost feeling in his gut. He watched as Wanda told about finishing off her last pint in the street, then walking through the doors of Saint Mary's. She had just celebrated her eighth continuous year of sobriety. A little calculation told Earl that Wanda was not twenty. She was crowding thirty.

Applause. There were two more speakers, then a break. Earl was immobilized as he faced it. It was written out for him a dozen times in the A.A. book. He had heard it again in Wanda's story, everybody's story.

—I'm an alcoholic.

He looked at Jake, hating him for the comment he had made. If he had just kept his mouth shut.

Someone got up in front and announced that after the break, there would be an optional Father Martin movie. Earl stood and joined the few patients who were leaving the lecture hall. As he came to the stairwell he couldn't make up his mind about where to go. He frowned as he said it out loud for the very first time. "I'm an alcoholic."

"Don't brag about it, buddy, or everybody'll want to be one." Whoever said it slapped him on his back and scooted down the stairwell.

22

Back in the lecture hall, Jake noticed that very few of the patients had left. The favorable comments about Father Martin movies by the local fans intrigued Jake into sticking around for the feature.

The film began past the credits, throwing upon the screen a gray-headed, bespectacled dynamo wearing Jake's least favorite suit: death black and collar. Father Martin, as the name might have suggested, was a priest. The camera panned the audience, and the priest was addressing a crowd of several hundreds. Jake noticed a large sprinkling of service uniforms on both men and women. Father was talking about intervention and treatment.

Jake laughed, cried, and listened. This was no ordinary cleric belched forth from some Roman assembly line. God, could he speak. Great delivery on his punchlines, and great punchlines.

Jake heard Roger ask "Is he an alcoholic?"

Frank answered "Yes."

Dave, the union man, disagreed. Frank leaned over the back of his chair and practically shouted at Dave, "If he isn't an alky, he certainly knows one very well."

Later, lying in bed smoking, Jake thought about the movie. He tried to figure out and understand the good feelings soothing his aching body. Where did his new tolerance for the goddies come from? He couldn't figure it out. Only a few days ago he would have walked out of such a movie the second he laid eyes on the bad suit. But this time he didn't. And when the priest talked about his god, that was okay. Okay for the priest, and no obligation to Jake.

He sat up in bed. When Father Martin talked about higher powers, he also said that his God wasn't necessarily Jake's or anybody else's answer. A phrase from the movie stuck in Jake's head.

"Whatever works."

There was something in the Big Book. Jake twisted around, opened his copy of *Alcoholics Anonymous* and leafed through "Bill's Story." Bill W., one of the co-founders of A.A. Old Bill had been the route until he met a sobered friend who had "found religion." Goddies were a sticking point with Bill, also. Not to Jake's degree, but a sticking point all the same. Bill would have no part of it. But then his friend had suggested, "Why don't you choose your own conception of God?"

The idea rang Bill W.'s chimes. It wasn't doing a thing for Jake R. But Bill wrote: "It was only a matter of being willing to believe in a Power greater than myself. Nothing more was required of me to make my beginning."

Was there a power on earth greater than Jacob Randecker?

"That is the question, isn't it?" He puffed on his pipe, thinking about his decades of self-training in rugged Ayn Randian individualism. Could John Galt or Howard Roark take the second of A.A.'s Twelve Steps? "Came to believe that a power greater than ourselves could restore us to sanity."

No, they couldn't. But what if they were addicts? No one has an exemption. No race, no religion, no society, no economic class, no social set, no follower of any particular philosophy. They'd be dead, that's what.

"There's no smoking allowed in patient rooms."

Jake glanced up and saw one of the male floor nurses. "This isn't a patient room."

"What?"

"This is an impatient room."

The nurse cocked his head to one side and pointed at Jake's pipe.

"The Minnesota Clean Indoor Air Act says—"

Jake stood up and walked around the nurse. "It's all right. I'm not from Minnesota."

23

On the second floor, south of the nurse's station, is the unit chapel. It has dark stained wooden doors set with tall, narrow windows. Jake peered through one of the windows.

The altar was of marble or plastic and had a third-grade drawing of a fish on it. Above the altar was a large light source that bathed it in heavenly hundred-watt florescence. The altar faced the hundred or so ochre-colored chairs, and behind the altar was dark-stained bat'n'board that provided a contrasting backdrop to the uneven tan brickwork that curved in towards it from both sides. The carpet was light green and it rose up to provide a stage for the celebrations and blood sacrifices. It had all of the sacred charm of a Holiday Inn lobby.

Jake pulled open the door, looked at all of the seats. satisfied himself that he was the only occupant, and entered. He wondered which would be the greater violation of his values: being in church, or being caught in church. Roger had recommended the place as being the only quiet spot on the unit.

—What the hell. It is quiet.

He took a seat in the back row, noted the many spotlights set into the ceiling, then lowered his gaze to the light of the lone candle that flickered in its black wrought iron holder on the brick wall to the right of the altar. If memory serves, thought Jake, the candle light is supposed to signify the presence of God.

He held out his hands. "Okay. Here I am." His hands fell into his lap and he shook his head.

—Yeah, burn that bush, part them waters, let me see some locusts! Bring on the show!

Jacob stared at the flame, his eyes glistening as he spoke. "And the bishop waited until after the service to meet with and talk to the inebriated priest. 'Father,' said the bishop, 'I congratulate you on the force and enthusiasm of your message this day. However, I would like to correct a small error that you made in your text. I believe that Samson slew the Philistines with the jawbone of an ass; he did not kick the shit out of them.'"

Jake chuckled and sadly shook his head. "What am I doing here?" He slouched down in his chair, thrust his hands into his pockets, and crossed his legs. The stiffness in his neck still made the back of his head throb. But it was tolerable, like Tony the Doc said. He had answered his own question about whether or not he had a physical dependency on chemicals, like Tony the Doc said. He had been shocked as hell to find out that the people at Saint Mary's knew what they were doing, like Tony the Doc said.

—From there it is only a small step to Jake Randecker is a dead man. "I just can't take that damned second step."

Jake leaned forward and spoke to the candle through clenched teeth. "C'mon Jupiter, Pluto, Goofy, L. Ron Hubbard! Give me a reason. Some little scrap of something." He slumped back in his chair. "Piss off."

—What did Mark Twain call faith? Believing what you know ain't so.

Jake rubbed his eyes. The delusion, the self-deception of addiction. How many fictions had he lived by; how many truths had he ignored?

Jake stood and walked to the eight narrow stained glass windows set into the wall to his right. He saw the tiny organ in the corner of the chapel, he glanced over the little brass dedication plaques beneath the stained-glass windows, walked along the wall beneath the candle, and came to the railing separating the seats from the altar. He walked around the railing, stepped up on the stage, and stopped behind the altar. He looked out over the empty seats and stood in silence.

—So what's the big deal with God anyway? Just about everyone in the joint believes in a god, and look what it's done for them.

—And look at what believing only in Jacob Randecker has done for you.

"Touché."

He walked around the altar, stepped down, walked around the railing, and sat down in a front row chair. When he opened his eyes, he was looking at the light from the candle. His tears diffused the light, filling his vision with flickering yellow.

—I don't want to go back. I don't.

"This is as much as it will ever be for me unless I can take that second step. Otherwise, I might as well go home right now. And how long would it take, Jake?"

—At home, feeling lost. alone, destroyed. How long before saying "I quit!" and heading for the liquor store. A week? A month? A day?

"You say you'd probably pick up something on your way back from the airport, Jake? Yeah." He nodded. "Yeah."

So many of those conventions put on by science fiction fans. He'd show up, hadn't been drinking for a week or two, and then a free drink would be at hand, or a wet bar, or a bathtub full of beer. Another editor or publisher would invite him to the hotel bar to talk business. Jake would say, "Why not?"

—Why the hell not.

There was that one convention in Halifax where, as a joke, he offered to autograph one of his books in exchange for a drink. In a matter of minutes, there was a line of fans, each carrying a favorite book or story and a drink. An astounding variety of drinks. Everything from rye and ginger through straight scotch to crème de menthe. Jake drank them all to celebrate his fifth day without a drink. The signs had said "Drink Canada Dry," and he had damn near done it.

"They do say that the problem isn't stopping drinking; the problem is staying stopped." He wiped his eyes as he looked around. He and the candle were the lone occupants. God was playing hard to get, the close-mouthed sonofabitch. It was quiet. Jake could hear his heart beating in his ears. Something came to him.

"It was only a matter of being willing to believe in a Power greater than myself..."

There were only about a million things Jake could think of that were and could be greater than he. The President, the nation, AT&T...

"But the something ought to have something to do with life, being a human. I can believe in Bell Telephone, but I don't want to be a telephone." Jacob reached up a hand and slapped himself in the face. "Idiot!"

—It was there all the time. Father Martin's "Whatever works." A science fiction writer, and it took me all this time to discover method? The scientific method?

In the lounge he had heard it a hundred times: using the group, the program, for a higher power. You don't have to believe in a god. It's not a religious program. Tony the Doc said that, too, the sneaky little weasel. Whatever works. If the program works, that will become part of it. If group works, that will become part of it.

A glimmer of hope seeped into Jake's chest. He pulled out his pipe, lit it, and looked at the candle flame.

—And if you ever deign to show yourself, maybe—

A heavy hand landed on his shoulder.

"Yowwww!!"

Jake leaped into the railing, jackknifed over it to the floor, landing on his back. He pulled himself up to his knees, shaking. Standing behind the chair in which he had been sitting was a rather stout woman sporting the latest in polyester nunwear.

"I didn't mean to startle you," she said.

As he got up from the floor, Jake held his hand on his chest to keep his heart from giving birth to a baby alien. "Lady, I almost had my spiritual awakening in the seat of my pants!"

"I apologize." She pointed at the floor. Upon it was Jake's pipe, glowing coals merrily burning their way into the carpeting. Jake quickly picked up the pipe and extinguished the conflagration.

"I wouldn't have dropped it if you hadn't snuck up on me like that."

"Smoking is not permitted in the chapel."

Jake glanced around, then looked back at the nun. "I don't see any no smoking signs."

"You don't smoke in church! Ever!"

"Okay, okay."

"What are you? *Protestant?*" She pronounced the word like its syllables had been dipped in alum.

"No. I'm a Secularist."

She squinted at him with her left eye. "Secularist? Is that some new cult?"

"That's an atheist who doesn't want to argue about it."

"Well. Well, Secularist, you don't smoke in *my* church! The Minnesota Clean Indoor Air Act, in addition, states that you can only smoke in areas designated as smoking areas. This," she pointed at her left foot, "is *not* such an area!"

Jake mumbled an apology and stuck his pipe into his trouser pocket. Sister Mary Torquemada, as Jake instantly named her, turned abruptly on her heel, genuflected at the door, and stormed out into the hallway.

Rubbing the back of his neck, Jake turned and faced the altar. "Sort of breaks the mood."

He pulled out his pipe, noted that most of the tobacco was gone out of the bowl, and walked to the doorway. He paused, knocked the remainder of the ashes into one of the receptacles mounted there, and pushed open the door. Still holding the door open, he noticed in the hallway the wall-mounted ashtray located between two of the elevator doors. It was much larger than the ones inside the chapel.

—If you don't ever smoke in church, what—

Jake backed into the chapel and looked. They were holy water fonts. The yellow sponge at the bottom of the east holy water font was covered with ashes. "Oh, shit." Inside the stainless steel bowl was a clear plastic liner. Making certain that the hall was deserted, Jake pulled the liner out of the bowl and held it at his side as he walked to the nurse's station, turned left, and entered the floor's public rest room.

Locking the door, Jake rinsed the liner and washed the sponge until all hint of its defilement had been removed. He replaced the sponge in the liner, gave it a shot of Minneapolis Municipal, and went back to the chapel. No one at the nurse's station seemed to have noticed his coming or his going.

Jake put the liner back into its bowl, then remembered that a ritual was necessary to make the municipal sludge holy. Come morning, the faithful will trudge in at some silly hour, dip in their fingers, and those dipping right will be cleansed while the lefties….

—Maybe if I squeezed a little from the right sponge into the left bowl?

—Diluted salvation.

"Nuts." Jake passed his hand over the font in the sign of the cross and muttered "Dommi dommi, gobbi gobbi." He glanced at the candle. "Hey, all I can do is my best."

JANUARY 3RD

24

Looking out of the mirror, the sounds of claws from the darkness behind—

Jake opened his eyes. The dream left an odd feeling; he couldn't remember much about it. He took a deep breath, rolled over and looked at his watch. 6:27 a.m. Monday.

Monday, the first day of treatment. Jake put down his watch and picked up his pipe. There had already been so many changes. Admission of the problem, a real desire to do something about it, this new tolerance of goddies. It seemed strange to think of this as the first day of treatment. As he lit his pipe, he heard Frank roll over in his bed and make a grab for his cigarettes.

"Did I wake you up?"

Frank lit up and rolled back on his bed. His voice came out of the shadows. "No. Did you get any sleep?"

"A new record. Almost two hours."

Frank grunted, then his voice came. Low, almost timorous. "Could you stand a little talk?"

"Sure."

Frank sat up, hung his legs over the edge of his bed, and faced Jake. "I'm supposed to give my first step this morning. That's where I take all my dirty laundry and hang it out for the group to sniff at." The coal of Frank's cigarette brightened as he took a drag, illuminating his face. Whether his eyes were puffy because of just waking up or crying, Jake couldn't tell.

"I can do my first step. It'll hurt, because I still feel like most of this is nobody's business but mine. But I can do it." Another drag. "There's this other thing, though. I swear if that bitch starts yanking my chain this morning about being black, I'll kill her."

"Angela?"

"Yeah. She's convinced being black is the be-all and end-all of my excuses for drinking." His breath came hard, the words excreted from a pain that Jake didn't understand. "It has *nothing* to do with it! *Nothing!*"

Jake swallowed and took the plunge. "Are you sure?"

"What'd I just say?"

"Why does she think it does?"

The orange coal danced in the air as Frank punctuated his words with movements of his hand. "What does that little old white bitch know about me? Or about being black? Understand?"

"I suppose—"

Frank put out his cigarette and stretched out on his bed. "Shit!"

"If it's not part of your problem, Frank, why worry about it?"

"Why? I'll tell you why. "He sat back up again. "She makes me mad. I know they say here that no one makes you mad but yourself, but that little old white bitch makes *me* mad. I start talking, she interrupts me with some off-the-wall question, and the next thing I know I can't see straight I want to wring her neck so bad."

Tears entered Frank's voice. "She...she asked me last group if I wanted to hit her. Hit her! I wanted to so bad. I don't like feeling like that. I hate it. But, I could have torn her to little teeny pieces, danced in the blood, and gone back to my room happy. Why? Why does she have to make me feel like that?"

Jake didn't have any answers. He cleaned his pipe, refilled it, and lit up again. Then Frank asked a simple question. "Jake, did you ever call a black kid nigger?"

Jake sat up, the lie on his lips. An instant headache came near to the bursting point as he killed the lie. "Yes."

"Why?"

Jake took a deep breath. "There aren't any good reasons. It's a cheap shot, and I guess all kids are into cheap shots. At one time I was, anyway. It's a word that pops right into mind when you want to hurt someone. You know you can stab right through the cool with it. Most black people I know can't roll with that word. They take it square between the eyes every time. I guess it's because they don't have a word of equal power they can throw back. It's like a gunfight between a pea shooter and a howitzer. Honkey, gray, haystack, whitey. Those words can't hurt anybody. Not as much...."

—Randecker, you are running off at the mouth.

Frank lit another cigarette. "Thanks."

"For what?"

"For being honest."

Jake chewed on his pipe. His headache was back for keeps. —I feel so guilty.

Frank stood up, walked to the window, and pulled open the drapes. He looked down at the snow for a long time, silently smoking his cigarette. "Nigger. I never let that word hurt me. Get at me. Never felt it. Pop told me not to feel it. See, we lived in a good neighborhood. Mixed. None of this ghetto shit. Nobody in that neighborhood wanted trouble of any kind. Nobody but kids being what kids are.

"Back in Baltimore, when I was twelve, this white kid called me nigger. I'd been called that a thousand times before. I just didn't allow myself to get angry. I'd just get cold. But this time—" He took another drag from his cigarette. "This kid, Kenny Vitali. He was just a little kid. A full head shorter than me. I grabbed him and I beat his little white ass. He had it coming, dammit. But once I started, I just couldn't stop." Frank's breaths came in sobs.

"I beat him. With these." Frank turned from the window and held out his fists. "I permanently blinded that little ten-year-old boy. For calling me a name."

Jake's headache was splitting atoms. He sat up and stuck his feet into his slippers. "So you don't allow yourself to get angry any more."

"Oh, I'm angry. I'm angry all the time. I just don't let it loose. I never show it—can't show it."

Jake scratched his beard, rubbed the back of his neck, and looked at his roommate. "Frank, I'm going to be real honest with you. And with myself for a change."

"Okay."

"You scare the shit out of me."

"What?"

"You heard me. Besides being bigger than most barns, you walk around here like a time bomb. I don't suppose I'm any more paranoid than anyone else is around here. I'm not very brave, but I do have this twisted sense of integrity. The rule here is honesty, and I'm trying to live by that."

"So what's your point?"

"So I think that little old white bitch hit the nail right on the head."

Frank turned back to the window, shook his head, and took a deep breath, letting the air escape in a hiss. Then he laughed. "Yeah. She usually does. Damn her."

Jake held up his cup. "Coffee?"

"No. Thanks. I think I'll take a shower."

As Frank went for his towel, Jake put on his bathrobe and walked out into the darkened hall. Once outside of the room, he leaned against the railing and took a deep breath. Something fearsome had come, touched him, and passed.

—Dammit, why am I so afraid of people? Paranoia is just a word. I want to know why. And from where did I ever get the guts to be honest with Godzilla in there?

He shook his head and pushed off from the railing. At the nurse's station, he noticed that the hall lights for east and west wings were on, their door knockers busily turning out the inmates.

A young fellow with a barely viable blond beard sat behind the counter. He looked up as Jake nodded, glanced at north wing, then turned back to Jake. "The north wing knocker hasn't gotten up your wing yet. Would you mind waking them up?"

"What?" Panic-streaked terror filled Jake's chest.

"Could you get up the patients on north wing?"

Jake closed his eyes, shook his head, and waved his hand back and forth.

—Are you out of your fucking gourd?!

"No, man. I'm sorry, but I can't handle something like that just now."

"What?"

Jake pointed at his own mouth. "Read my lips. No way."

"You're kidding."

"Observe." Jake turned and fled for the safety of the kitchen. As he filled his cup at the dispenser, his hands shook with a beat that had absolutely nothing to do with withdrawal. Instead, it had a lot to do with the thing Ron had been talking about in the lounge. People pleasing. People pleasers are terrified of doing anything that will risk causing people *not* to be pleased with them. Like being a cop, an honest politician…a Saint Mary's wing door knocker. You can't please anybody, so you wind up being terrified of everybody.

The electric icepick again stabbed into the right side of Jake's head. He placed his right palm over his eye. "Shit. I get the feeling that all my troubles haven't quite ended."

25

D.T., alias John Pennoyer, put on his bathrobe, grabbed his towel, and held his left hand out. It still shook. He made a fist. "That's just the kind of thing to inspire confidence in your surgeon."

He stepped into the hallway and headed for the showers, his mind crowded with yesterdays and tomorrows. His family week would begin that afternoon. After Harold's family week, Harold had said that it was sort of like having a vise crush your testicles with care and understanding.

Jake was coming from the kitchen carrying a cup of coffee and the weight of the world. D.T. noticed that the male nurse was knocking on the doors, blasting out the north wing inmates. Wondering why the wing's elected doorknocker, Stan from Bill's group, wasn't doing the wakeup, D.T. opened the door to the showers.

Frank was leaning against the left wall, waiting for the individual shower room on that side to open up. D.T. saw that the door had just closed at the far end of the hall. That one would be tied up for some time. Even the room with the bathtub was occupied. He leaned against the wall opposite Frank and waited for the handicapped shower, which only had a curtain opening onto the tiny hallway, to open up.

"I can't believe how early all these drunks get up."

Frank nodded. "Are you ready for family week?"

"How in the hell can you get ready for something like that?" D.T. laughed nervously and shook his head. "For two cents I'd grab my hat and head for far places."

"Like Angela says, D.T., it won't kill you—"

"Hey!" A voice came from behind the shower curtain. "Hey, I heard a good one yesterday—anybody out there?"

"Yes," Frank and D.T. replied.

"Listen to this. What did God say after he made the second nigger?"

D.T. felt the blood drain from his head as he watched Frank's face turn to stone. Frank pursed his lips, folded his arms, and closed his eyes. "Oh, I don't know. What did God say after he made the second nigger?"

"Ooops! Burned another one!" Shrill laughter came from behind the curtain.

Frank stared at D.T., then back at the shower curtain. He paused, pushed himself away from the wall, removed his bathrobe, and handed the robe, his soap, and his towel to D.T. Monstrously big, black, and naked, Frank entered the shower and pulled the curtain closed behind him. D.T. winced as a blood-curdling scream came from the shower. Then there was silence. Frank emerged, took his towel from D.T. and began drying his hair.

"What did you do?" inquired D.T. who, as a surgeon, suspected his skills might be needed. If for nothing else, the autopsy.

Frank grinned, put on his bathrobe, and went into the hallway.

D.T. pulled the curtain aside. The needle fiend who usually hung out in the kitchen was scrubbing, rinsing, soaping, and rescrubbing his head. "What happened?"

The kid, his eyes wide with terror, pointed toward the hallway.

"Did you see that? Did you?"

D.T. shook his head. "No."

"He kissed me! That big mother came in here, gave me a big hug, and *kissed* me!"

26

7:15 a.m. Morning vitals in the wing lounge: "How do you feel this morning, Jake?"

"Compared to what?"

"Perry said he asked you to turn out north wing this morning and you refused."

"Loose lips sink ships."

"You're still sweating."

"Sometimes my shirt gets so wet that it takes until ten o'clock at night for it to dry out enough to go to bed."

"Jake, you are a seriously disturbed person."

"Everybody has to have a hobby."

After breakfast, 8:00 a.m. med's at the nurse's station. The drug-mobile, a wheeled cart filled with plastic drawers brought over from the main hospital, was at the head of a line of chattering patients.

"Drugs. Gotta have muh drugs—"

"I don't know why I have to keep taking these things. It's not like I was sick with a real disease."

"Hey, man. I'm sick. Can I have a couple o' them purple ones?"

"Anything on sale?"

"Drugs. Gotta have muh drugs—"

"Spent mah money on a bag o'reds, doo-dah, doo-dah—"

"—and he stuck in his thumb and pulled out a plum and said, 'Holy shit am I high.'"

"Spent the next two weeks in bed, oh doo-dah-day—"

"Put mah piss in a cup, hide mah shit in mah shoes, Lordy, Lordy, got dem rehab blues."

"Drugs. Gotta have muh drugs—"

"Jake, you see that guy who came in here with a hotshot?"

"What's a hotshot?"

"Ever see that white stuff on a car's battery terminal? The man gets pissed at you and mixes that in with your smack."

"That's sulfuric acid!"

"Ain't it the sufferin' truth? An armful of that stuff can ruin your whole day. He was bleedin' out of his ears—"

"Get out of the line, Snake. You were through with meds last week. Besides, aren't you on the fourth floor?"

"Drugs, man. Gotta have muh drugs—"

"Get out of here, Snake. You give me the vapors."

Jake picked up his Librium and Dylantin.

"Pop'em on down—"

"—hey, man, what are the fuckin' vapors?"

"Terminal flatulence."

"Say, what?"

"It's glue-sniffing, Snake."

"Man, why don't they say what they mean around here? No fuckin' wonder I can't get this program. You fuckin' people're talkin' fuckin' Sanskrit!"

8:30 a.m. lecture. Roger looked at his schedule. Group Therapy: the animal, its parts, and purposes. He looked up as a short, dark, hairy character climbed up on the stage and impaired hearing for a six-block radius by dropping the microphone. Retrieving the mike, he commenced the show. "I'm an addict and my name is Fred."

"HI, FRED!"

"Hi, yourself. Did everybody have a fun New Year holiday?" There was some laughter in response mixed in with about fifty muttered fuck-you's. The loudest of the fuck-you's seemed to come from Roger's left. He looked and saw Jake glowering at the stage. "That's great," continued Fred as he finished attaching the mike around his neck.

"Today the subject is group therapy, but before we get to that, I want to talk about why we need it. We all have a lot more in common than better living through chemistry. Before we came into treatment or reached for other outside help, we all tried our own do-it-yourself programs to control our using. Another thing we have in common: all of our do-it-yourself programs failed. Sooner or later we went back to the potions, pills, and powders. You can't do it by yourself."

Fred was rubbing Roger's feathers in the wrong direction. "If I put my mind to it, I can do anything I want—"

—But there was the time I switched from whisky to beer to control my drinking. What did that do? About eight inches on the belt line, and ass-deep in beer cans. No other changes, except that I was miserable. Then, because of my weight, I decided to cut down on beer by switching to whiskey. I figured I wouldn't need as much to get the same effect and, therefore, wouldn't drink so much. And what did that do? More on the belt line, ass deep in whisky bottles. I couldn't believe the quantity I was drinking. No matter what I did, it didn't make any difference.

—So maybe you can't do it by yourself. Listen to the guy.

"Now the reason why we failed is because we can't change what we can't see. What you can't see is killing you, and that's what group is for.

Your group can see parts of you that you can't see."

Roger heard Fred say that they were there to discover themselves. Before that was possible, it would be necessary to discover and reduce to rubble the defenses that prevent this discovery. Change is the goal, seeing what needs to be changed is the method, the group is the mechanism, and pain is the side-effect.

"Group is the necessary mechanism of discovery. If you are going to have even a chance at recovering from this disease, you need other people."

Roger felt himself becoming angry. He looked at the anger and saw that it was made up out of fear. He felt very threatened. "Needing others," he muttered. "That's going to be a problem."

Fred was still talking. "In group we aren't interested in what you know or what you think. Remember, your best thinking got you here. In group we want to know you. That means we want to know how you feel. In group we talk on a feelings level."

Roger shook his head as thoughts of leaving treatment crossed his mind.

—I don't want anyone to know how I feel. It's not anyone's business.

"Feelings are facts," continued Fred. "They are neither good nor bad. They just are. Group purpose is to discover and identify feelings. Acceptance of a feeling is necessary before it can be changed...."

Roger tried to blot out what was being said. The whole process was preposterous. He looked to his left and saw Jake staring at the floor, his arms folded. Fred moved on to the mechanics of the "group experience."

"Confrontation. Now we tossed honesty down the drain the first time we started sucking after the approval of others. You know the bit. The guy steps on your toe. He says he's sorry, and what do you say? 'No problem.' Your date calls you up on the phone and says he can't go out with you, he forgot he had already asked Mary Lou. And what do you say? 'I understand.' Your cat dies, the bank forecloses on the old homestead, your father is in jail. and your doctor just told you that you have three months to live. A friend comes down the street and says 'How are you doing?' And what do you answer?" He held out his hands. "Let's hear it."

"Fine, thank you!" shouted back the audience.

Fred clasped his hands behind his back and rocked back and forth between his heels and toes until the laughter died down. The rocking stopped. "Try that in group and you'll be eaten alive."

He leaned on the lectern. "Confrontation is defined as 'presenting a person with himself by describing how I see him.'" He pointed at someone in the front row. "You want to die? This program means nothing to you! It must be. You're not paying attention. You're talking to your neighbor, flouting unit discipline by bringing a coffee cup in here, slouching in your chair, your feet on the edge of the stage, and you look half asleep!"

He looked back at the frys. "You will notice as I held up a mirror to this fellow, I tried to be specific in what I saw—"

"You muthafuckah," was distinctly heard coming from the front of the hall.

Chuckles.

The lecturer smiled. "Although he sounded somewhat judgmental, the fellow down there is doing what we call leveling. That is to respond openly when confronted. The foundation of group, how it works, is made up of confrontation and leveling. Over the years we have carefully constructed the walls that keep others at a distance. Smashing holes in those walls will be frightening, uncomfortable, confusing, and painful. But there is no gain without pain.'

Fred stood to the side of the lectern and leaned his elbow on it.

"Remember this: all we can do here is provide the tools; you have to do the work. A number of you folks do make it through here without a scratch in your defenses. Your walls remain in place, invulnerable. Every

single one of you will go back to using. A month from now, a year, ten
years. Good old alcoholic rigidity can keep you dry—for a while. But
unless you change you, you are going back to using."

Roger's systems seemed to close down. Fear seemed to reach a hand
up from his stomach and through his throat.

—I have spent my entire life avoiding confrontations. I don't confront anyone, and I don't want anyone to confront me. You don't call me
a lying bastard, and I won't call you a lying bastard. Oil on the waters all
around. It's the American way. Don't these people know anything about
politics, business or religion? These people are insane.

"Here would be a good place to mention tough love. If you don't
care anything about a groupmate, keep your mouth shut when he does a
number on himself. Just let him die of kindness. However, if you care,
then tell him what you see; tell him what you hear. If you want to live
yourself, respond to being confronted honestly, openly."

Fred looked at his watch, then smiled back at the frys. "That's it.
Have an awful time at group."

Applause.

On Mondays before group there is a brief wing meeting to elect new
Servants of the Peepul and conduct other housekeeping chores. It is an
effort at democracy that Jake compared to Soviet Russia's: the people get
to vote on the important things like who sweeps up the horseshit while
the unseen powers that be decide the incidentals, such as who will live,
who will die, and who will end eternity thawing pipes in Siberia.

He listened as points were discussed regarding entertainment for the
weekend. The assistant wing leader, Brandy, was the social director. Ron
was wing leader. There were gripes about the use and abuse of floor telephones, accusations against the fourth floor inmates stealing food from
the third floor kitchen, denials against the fourth floor accusations about

the third floor inmates stealing from them, and let's get something done about getting this easy chair reupholstered. There are tacks and staples sticking out all over it.

Volunteers were solicited for the jobs. Table wipers for the dining room, the wing's contribution to the force that's supposed to clean up the lecture hall, someone to neat up the wing's coffee dispenser room, the wing's K.P. for the third floor kitchen. Employment went to Frank, Lydia, Roger, and Earl, respectively.

"And," Ron concluded, "we need a new door knocker. Stan bugged out of treatment last night." The group became deadly silent. Ron faced a stranger who sat just out of Jake's view. "His family week was supposed to begin today."

The person out of sight spoke. "I'm sorry to learn he left treatment."

Candy waved a hand. "How long will they keep Stan's bed open?"

"Forty-eight hours," answered the voice. "Was Stan in Bill's group?"

Ron nodded. "Yeah. He seemed like he really had it together, too." Ron looked back at the group. "Anyhow, we are short one door knocker. Any volunteers?"

There were no volunteers.

"Are there any nominations?"

Jake, under maximum protest, was nominated and elected on the first ballot. The meeting was concluded. A trim, iron-gray haired woman, smartly dressed in a salmon-colored suit, got to her feet and came into Jake's view. "Good meeting. Let's take a ten-minute break and my group reconvene in my office."

Jake studied the woman's face. Could this be Awesome Angela, the terror of St. Mary's?

—Hell, she looks like my maiden aunt.

She turned and walked toward the nurse's station. Jake jabbed Frank in the arm. "Is that her?"

Frank nodded. "Angela."

"She looks harmless enough." He looked around in surprise at the roar of laughter that came from his groupmates.

"Then, again," he amended, "I've been known to be wrong before."

27

The chairs were unstacked, arranged into a circle, the Animals sat down, and the group was formed. All but three persons held in their hands a small black book. The first person without a book was Angela Gwynn, group counselor. The second person was Marnie, floor nurse sitting in. The third person was Jake Randecker, and they all waited while he was sent to get his copy of *Twenty-Four Hours a Day*.

Jake returned, took his seat, opened his book, and tried to ignore the heat coming from his face.

Angela looked around the room for a moment, then looked up at the air vent in the ceiling. "Who's going to read?"

There was a mad flurry of exchanged looks until Brandy, sitting to Jake's left, began reading, her voice steady. "January Third." Jake hurriedly flipped the pages of his black book to the proper date as Brandy continued. "When I came into A.A., I learned what an alcoholic was and then I applied this knowledge to myself…" After the A.A. Thought for the Day, came the Meditation for the Day. "I will be renewed. I will be remade. In this I need God's help—"

God is whatever works, amended Jake silently. It seemed strange that the sound of the word God still rankled him. Actually, it seemed strange that it seemed strange. It still rankled as Brandy concluded with the Prayer for the Day.

"I pray that I may be taught, just as a child would be taught. I pray that I may never question God's plans, but accept them gladly."

This is stupid, thought Jake.

"I'm Brandy Costello, drug addict, and my contract for today is to talk about a resentment I have."

D.T. was to Brandy's left. "I'm John, I'm an alcoholic, and my contract is to listen and provide useful feedback where I can." He looked to his left to pass the black marble, but that was not to be. Angela tapped her fingernails against the armrests of her chair.

"John, you've been here long enough to know how to do a contract. We expect you to listen and give feedback. What are you going to do for yourself?"

D.T. let his hands rest in his lap, his face looked both frightened and resigned to doom. "I guess talk about some concerns I have about this afternoon's group. My family week."

Angela nodded, closed her eyes, and grinned slightly. "I thought you might want to touch on that." She opened her eyes and nodded at the person sitting to D.T.'s left.

"I'm Ron Steward, alcoholic. My contract is to…"

The contracts crept around the room. Ron had a dream that bothered him. Lydia, alcoholic, wanted to talk about why she was there. Angela introduced herself as counselor for the group, Marnie as chemically dependent, floor nurse—

Jake frowned at Marnie until she looked back at him. He quickly averted his glance to the next in turn. While Harold talked, the blood pounded in Jake's head. Marnie? It had never occurred to him that Marnie could be part of the junkyhood. He didn't know how he felt about it.

Dave looked gloomy and contracted to talk about the reasons why he was gloomy. The marble moved on.

"I'm Roger Sanders, alcoholic, and my contract is to talk about a resentment I have against a member of this group."

"I'm Earl Nelson. I'm new and I'm not sure what this contract business is."

Angela smiled. "A contract is simply an agreement you make with yourself and the group about what you need to work on. You might make as a first contract telling the group a little about yourself and why you are here."

Earl nodded. "Okay."

The next in turn was a tall, rawboned woman capped with a short thatch of orange hair. There was not a square centimeter of her visible skin that was not-crowded with freckles. "I'm Gisel Apple, alcoholic, intern."

Does an alcoholic intern do residency in whisky, asked Jake silently.

"I'm Candy, chemically dependent, and my contract today is to talk about gratitude."

Angela leaned forward on her chair and spoke barely above a whisper. "You've had four whole days to think about the little talk we had, and your family week begins today. Don't you think you might want to make a new contract?"

Candy sat back in her chair, her mouth in a pout, her nose reaching for the ceiling. "Very well, Angela. What do *you* want to talk about?"

Angela laughed, and it was laughter that filled every corner of the room. It was the original horse laugh. Guffaw, guffaw. It made Jake's guts crawl.

Angela shook her head, then her bright blue eyes nailed Candy to the wall. "I have been known to discharge members from this group. Members who aren't willing to take their treatment seriously. What do you need to talk about? What's your contract?"

Candy, her face flushed, looked at the floor and shook her head. "I don't know. I guess family week."

"I guess you're right." Angela nodded at Frank.

Frank tapped his steno pad against his knee. "I'm Frank, alcoholic, and my contract is to do my first step this morning."

Angela clasped her hands together, turned her chair until she was looking at Jake, and elevated her eyebrows.

"I'm, uh, Jake Randecker…"

—It's there, Jake. Just say it—

"I'm a drug addict and alcoholic. I'm new also, and I guess my contract is to tell you why I'm here."

Angela nodded, first at Earl, then at Jake. "I want to welcome you both to the group. On your own I want both of you to go one-on-one with each of the other members of the group. Spend about fifteen minutes with each member, telling them why and how you're here. It's the responsibility of all of the group members to show the new ones the ropes. It's your responsibility to ask them to show you."

She glanced to her right. "Lydia, before we start today, I want to welcome you back for your third try."

Lydia smiled and nodded.

Angela smiled and nodded in return. "But I want you to understand that this time you had best get honest with me, with the group, and most importantly with yourself. I won't take you back a fourth time. There are plenty of rear-ends I can stick in that chair that want to get better. If you're not wearing one, then leave. I don't need any chair-time queens."

Lydia, her face red, her eyes looking murder at the floor, nodded. "I want to work."

"Good. I'm glad to hear that." Angela smiled and looked around at the faces. "It's your group."

Frank opened his steno pad. "I'll start."

Angela held up her hand. "Frank, I'd like you to hold off on your first step until later. Group is short this morning because of the wing meeting, and we have a lot to cover before the afternoon session."

"You said you wanted me to give my first step this morning."

Angela slowly shook her head. "No, I didn't. I said that I wanted you to be ready to give your first step this morning."

Hot air snorted from Frank's nostrils. "Well? I am ready!"

The smile on Angela's face vanished. "Good." Her gaze wandered about the room, resting on everyone's face, except Frank's. He had been dismissed. Sitting as he was to Jake's right, Jake could feel the seismic tremors through his buns. Panic nibbled at Jake's insides.

D.T. leaned forward, his elbows on his knees, his hands clasped together. "I don't know if I can face this afternoon." Beginning with Angela, he looked around the group, then at the floor. "I've seen three families go through it, and I've seen the good it's done, but—"

Angela leaned to her right. "What are you concerned about, John?"

He shook his head. "I'm scared, frightened, terrified. I honestly don't feel like I can live through it."

"What are you scared of, John? Mitzi, your wife?"

"Not really."

"Your sons, Mack and Bobby?"

He shook his head. "Not them so much as what they'll say. I think I was honest when I did my first step, so I'm not worried about what they'll say in front of the group. It's…" He sighed and held out his hands. "It's what they'll say to me. That I hurt them, failed them. I don't think I can bear seeing it in their faces—hearing it from them."

"You can survive it, John. We haven't had anyone die in group yet. There have been plenty who wished they had died, but no fatalities to date. Are you really so afraid of what they'll say?"

He nodded. "God, yes."

Angela swung around on her chair, surveying the group. "Well?"

Ron looked to his right. "D.T., I just went through family week. And I see in you the same thing I saw in me. I did a lot of bad things, I admit I was a bad boy, let's begin over again with a clean slate. Just don't lay any heavy trips on me."

John shook his head. "I don't understand."

"I don't think you want to hear what you've done. Not from the people you've done it to. What you're afraid of is the truth; you're afraid of yourself."

"Junior counselor," snorted D.T.

Brandy spoke up. "D.T., I see someone who is sorry as hell for himself. You've got your butterfly net out, and you're collecting all the sympathy you can. You have that po' ol' hangdog look on your face. And we all know what that look means."

Jake watched fascinated as po' ol' D.T. the puppet-maker transformed into one pissed off surgeon. "I leveled with you people—"

Angela reached out and put her hand on D.T.'s arm. "John, you sound like a naughty little boy who has been caught with his fingers in the jellybean jar when it's time to face the music."

"That's a helluva way to put it! You'd think leaving me a little dignity wouldn't be too much to ask."

Harold leaned forward and pointed at D.T. "How much dignity did you leave yourself when you puked on the table at that medical banquet?"

Brandy nodded. "And when you passed out in the lobby of that hospital, and fired your receptionist when she expressed a concern about your drinking. Not to mention slapping around your wife in that restaurant…"

Jake's head swam.—My god, this is a nightmare! I am on my way home! Nobody but nobody is going to grind me like that!

He watched as D.T. sighed, nodded, sat back in his chair, and nodded again. Jake realized that his strong identification with D.T. was based on the same thing. He didn't want to face the music either. It certainly was beginning to look a lot easier staying drunk.

Angela smiled at D.T. "John, you've heard it in lectures, and from other members of the group who have gone through family week. And you've heard it from at least one concerned person: Ron's mother. It will help you to get better. And just as important, it will start your wife and sons on the road to recovery. You want to get well, don't you?"

"Yes."

"You want Mitzi, Mack, and Bobby to get better?"

He nodded. "Yes."

"You've seen it work before. Don't you think it'll work for you?"

He shook his head. "I...I'm just so damned ashamed!" A box of groupwad, institutional tissues, was passed from Lydia, to Ron, to D.T. D.T. took the box, held it in both hands, and shook his head again. "So ashamed."

Brandy reached out a hand and placed it on D.T.'s arm. "It's a disease. It's not anyone's fault."

He looked up at Brandy. "They don't know that."

"They're learning. Everybody has to learn. They're going through the same lectures, learning the same things. You didn't do the things you did because you're a bad person. You were using, drunk, high. You didn't have any choice about that."

D.T. pulled a piece of groupwad and blew his nose. "Angela, I don't know about that."

"What don't you know?"

"That I didn't have a choice."

"You tried to stop on your own?"

He nodded.

"Were you successful?"

"No, but I don't know whether that's I couldn't or just wouldn't."

"Are you an alcoholic?"

"Yes."

"Being an alcoholic means that you didn't have the choice whether or not to drink. An alcoholic only has one choice: drink. The only thing treatment, aftercare, and A.A. can do is to give you back your choice, and maintain your ability to choose. Family week is a critically important part of that treatment."

Angela shook D.T.'s arm. "John, there's only one payoff for continuing to flog yourself. What is it?"

His shoulders heaved as he filled another sheet of groupwad. "To make myself miserable."

"And when I get miserable—"

I drink"."

"Just remember, getting the disease is not your fault. However, your recovery *is* your responsibility." She shook his arm again. "You'll survive, John. I have a lot of faith in you." She turned away from D.T. and faced the group. "Who's next?"

Jake felt Brandy move against his left shoulder. "I wanted to talk about a resentment, but I think I need a new contract." Jake watched her face. It was a different face than the hard-boiled, tough one she wore in the lounge. This face was soft, vulnerable.

"I was pissed at one of the counselors. Listening to D.T., I figured out what was under that. I don't resent that counselor half as much as I…" She looked around at the group and stopped, her eyes on Jake. He couldn't look away, the pain in her eyes was so intense.

"I hate being here. Being an addict." She looked at Angela. "I'm a counselor. I know these ropes better than my own name, and I can't seem to get around them. It's a status thing with me, ego, false pride. I've been confronted I don't know how many times about forgetting I'm a patient and assuming the role of live-in counselor. But…."

Brandy reached and took the box of groupwad from D.T.'s hand. "I don't know how to get around it. Until I do, I won't get any better. But I just don't know. I'm so discouraged."

Harold leaned back in his chair, lifted his arm, and waved at Brandy. "Hi, Brandy! It's great to finally get to meet you. I hoped I would before I left." He lowered his arm to his lap and leaned forward. "Your professional wall is down, and I like what's behind that wall a lot. I'm going to tell you the same thing you told me some time ago. First, you're a human being. That's what you are. That's what makes you somebody. Second," and Harold bent over and held his left hand near the floor, "Second, you're an alcoholism counselor. That's just something that you do."

Brandy tapped her head with her right forefinger. "I know that, up here. How do I move it here?" She tapped her finger over her heart.

Angela frowned, shook her head, and leaned forward. "I don't get this, Brandy. You know the answer as well or better than anyone in here. How do you move it from an intellectual to a feelings level?"

Brandy sat back in her chair, the toughness settling upon her face like a mask. "First admit the feelings I do have, be aware of how the feelings contradict the situation…what's appropriate. Every time it happens, do it over and over again. Repetition."

"What else?"

"Fake It until you make it."

Angela nodded. "And the counselor gets a gold star. Now what I want to do is hear from Brandy. What does Brandy need from the group?"

Brandy looked as though she had resigned herself to throw caution to the winds. "I want the group to tell me what they see, what they hear. What am I doing wrong?"

Angela looked around at the circle of faces, stopping on Ron's. Ron shrugged. "I'd say she's doing everything okay. Brandy's only been in the group a few days, and she's miles ahead of me—"

Angela turned abruptly toward Brandy. "I must congratulate you, Brandy. You really have this bunch snowed." She leaned back in her chair, put her fingertips together, and played spider-doing-pushups-on-a-mirror. "Come on, group."

Guilty, hopeless looks were exchanged, until Angela stood up and pointed to her chair. "Sit here, Brandy."

Brandy hesitated, then walked across the circle and sat down in Angela's black-wheeled runabout. Angela moved until she stood before Brandy's chair. "From all I hear, you're a good counselor. Very effective. Since all we have in group today is Brandy the counselor, I'm going to ask Brandy the counselor what Brandy is doing wrong. The group can't seem to help, so I'm calling out the big guns."

Angela sat down in Brandy's chair, smiled at the group, and continued looking at them, never once letting her glance fall on Brandy. "Hi, I'm Brandy, and I'd like to tell you a little bit about why I'm here." Jake shivered at how accurate Angela's Brandy impression was.

"See, I'm a super alcoholism counselor, and in the process of performing my job, I discovered to my surprise that I have a chemical problem myself." Angela waved a hand, dismissing all problems. "Well, I knew just what to do. That's my job, after all. I did the first step, second step, and third step almost right away. I performed my moral inventory and did my fifth step with my boss before I entered treatment. Of course steps six and seven go without saying—"

Brandy held up her hand. "Stop." Her face was red and she was grinning. "Slow down, Brandy. Slow down. You're here to get better, not to win a most-perfect-drunk competition."

Angela leaned back in Brandy's chair, crossed her legs, clasped her hands in her lap, and fluttered her eyelashes. "Is there anything else I should do?"

"Two things. Get to work on your first step. and—" Brandy stood up. "—get the hell out of my chair."

There was laughter, and when both of them were settled down, Angela looked at Earl, then at Jake. "Let's hear from the new members."

She kept looking at Jake. He squirmed, leaned forward, rested his weight on his elbows, clasped his hands, and looked at the floor.

"Okay. My name is Jacob Randecker. I'm a writer…drug addict and alcoholic, and a few days ago my wife and friends pulled an intervention on me. All the arrangements were made, so here I am."

Angela swung back and forth in her chair. "What led you to think that you are a drug addict, Jake?"

"I didn't think I was. I was on Ativan—a prescription for anxiety—but all I ever thought I did was follow the prescription. So I refused medication when I came in here. I hadn't had anything to drink since the seventeenth, so I didn't need any medications, right?" He shook his head. "I had aches and pains all over my body, and I figured they were tension. My shaking was nerves, and my perspiration—" He laughed. "You people keep the thermostats set too high."

He looked at the floor. "Then I was so crippled up and hurting so badly, I told the nurse's station. Marnie asked me if I wanted to talk, and we talked. That was when I remembered doubling up my prescription. I remembered not using the stuff when I was drinking, so when I was using the Ativan, I'd regularly do up to four times what it said on the prescription. Sometimes more. When I had to give in and take the medication I had to admit that I'm a drug addict."

He glanced up at Marnie, and she was smiling back. "I'm glad to hear you say that, Jake."

Another welcome to the group from Angela, and then Earl talked about himself, saying that he'd read enough and heard enough. He thinks he's an alcoholic and he's not real happy about it.

Marnie whispered something to Angela, got up, and left the room, closing the door silently behind her. Candy talked about her feelings about family week. She's angry. Her husband and daughter, she thinks, are going to tell a bunch of stories, and there're two sides to everything, aren't there?

Angela pointed out that Candy will have her chance to respond to her family on Wednesday. Jake listened as Angela explained the simple ground rules of the "fishbowl."

Chairs are placed into the center of the circle, the patient in one, the family in the others. The family is seated in a straight line facing the patient. When they begin, they tell the patient what he's done, and how it has hurt them—the unabridged version. The patient has to keep his or her mouth shut. For two days. Monday and Tuesday. And on the third day, if he can, the patient is allowed to rise to his own defense and respond.

—My god, thought Jake, I just thought I was kidding about the Office of Inquisition and rehabs!

The group, seated around and observing the patient and his family, are there for feedback, grilling both patient and family members to a golden brown. Jake doubted that Ann could live through such an experience. She's so shy, terrified of others, so vulnerable.

—Take all of those fragile, delicate things that the most intimate lovers never talk about, fling them out into the middle of the floor for a room full of absolute strangers to paw over. Brutal. But, like the man said, no gain without pain.

Jake shook his head thinking that the price of gain just might be a little too high. He frowned as another thought presented itself.

—Very noble indeed, me sitting here thinking about Ann's welfare. What about my own ass?

Angela frowned at Roger. "How about your contract, Roger? You said you have a resentment against a member of this group."

"Yes." He looked at Jake. "Jake is making me very angry—"

"Hold it." Angela leaned on her left elbow, her eyes aimed square between Roger's. "Jake isn't that powerful. He doesn't make anyone in this room, or on this planet, angry. You make yourself angry." She smiled. "Now, why are you angry, Roger?"

"Jake's an atheist."

Angela rocked back and forth in her chair, her gaze never wavering from Roger's eyes. "The world's lousy with atheists, Roger. Are you going to be angry and keep drinking until the last one has seen the light?"

"No. But all those other atheists aren't in this group."

Angela rubbed her chin and glanced at Jake. His face was red, his hands and arms folded into a tight net across his chest. She glanced back at Roger. He was leaning forward, one hand on each knee. Angela waved a hand.

"What's going on here? Jake?"

Jake shrugged, glanced at the floor, then at Roger. "I get the feeling that Roger doesn't want me in this club unless I go out and get myself saved first."

The counselor studied Jake for a long moment. "Do you believe in God?"

"No."

"Do you have a Higher Power?"

Jake quickly glanced around the room, caught Lydia mouthing the words "I told you so," then he looked back at Angela. "I'm using as my higher power whatever works." Jake winced at the sound. The profundity of the night before sounded somewhat lame in the daylight, in front of the group.

Angela's eyebrows went up. "Whatever works?"

—Christ, Randecker, go down in flames if you have to!

"Yes."

"Have you found anything yet that works?"

"All the results aren't in."

Angela's eyeballs almost snapped as she looked at Roger. "Are you powerful enough to change Jake?"

Roger shook his head. "No. I know I can't—"

"—But that doesn't mean you won't try," completed Harold. Harold leaned forward, and looked across Dave at Roger. "Roger, this is the first time you've been in group, but I've watched you over the holiday. The other people in this group who don't believe in your conception of God usually keep their views to themselves. They don't want to offend you. Jake is a smartass and a smartmouth, and he likes yanking your chain. To tell you the honest truth, I enjoy watching him yank it. It's funny. And you're the one who keeps putting that chain in his hands. He couldn't rattle your cage if you didn't require that everyone who enters your presence kneel down and kiss your sanctimonious ass."

Roger looked at Frank, and Frank closed his eyes and laughed as he shook his head. "Don't look for help here just because neither of us looks good in flesh-colored Band-aids." He leaned forward, his steno pad dangling from his hand. "I agree with Harold. You want us all to see and respect Roger the minister and ignore Roger the human being. I'll tell you what I feel. Roger the minister is a big bag of bullshit. I don't know Roger the human being. You've never let us see him."

Angela leaned forward and rested her chin on her hands. "What's your job, Roger?"

"I am a minister of G—"

"What is your *job?* Your job right now. This second."

"I don't know what you're getting at."

"What is your job right now?" Her fingers tapped impatiently against the armrest of her chair.

Roger folded his arms, leaned back in his chair, his eyes closed, his chin on his chest. "I am a minis—"

"Group!" Angela shouted. "Do you hate this man so much you want to let him die?"

There was a mumble of shocked negatives.

"Then tell him what his job is!"

Jake saw it as clearly as anyone in the room. "Your job is to get well."

Roger sprang forward, his trembling finger pointed at Jake. "I'll take it from Frank or Harold or Brandy, but I'll be damned if I'll take that from you!"

"My, my, my," said Angela. "Aren't we selective today. Am I in this privileged jury of yours, Roger?"

Roger sat back in his chair. "Of course."

"Well, Jake is my guest, as are the others you attempt to exclude. The group doesn't divide well. It is either the group or a bunch of individuals. If you won't participate in the group process, the group may very well exclude you. I've seen it happen before. But you can't exclude parts of the group. Neither I nor the group will tolerate it. Now, what is your job here?"

"To get well." Roger's voice sounded close to breaking.

Angela smiled. "Remember what Harold told Brandy. First you are a human being. That is what you are. That's what makes you special. That's what buys you your place in this world. Being a clergyman is just something that you do."

The counselor pushed her chair back to her desk, and looked at Dave. "You're awfully quiet this morning."

Dave nodded, glanced at Harold, then back at Angela. "You know Harold leaves today. I feel like shit about it. I'm glad he's better and all, but I'll miss him."

"Dave," began Candy, "I'm real happy to see that you can say that. Last week you couldn't have."

Dave nodded, smiled and went red all over. "Yeah. I figured if I said out loud that I liked the guy, everybody would think I was a homo."

The group laughed and no one laughed harder than Harold. He put his hand on Dave's shoulder and shook it.

Jake watched the scene. —I hate coming in the middle of a movie. Is Harold a homosexual, or not? I'll be fried in hell before I ask!

Angela turned to her desk, opened the center drawer, and withdrew a coin that looked to Jake like a large cent. She reached to her right and handed the coin to Lydia.

"Lydia, do you remember how this works?"

Lydia nodded as she held the coin. A tear slipped down her right cheek. "I've just gotten to know you over the holidays, Harold, but I like you a lot, and will miss you." She held up the coin. "I've picked up two of these things. I know what they mean. The first one was hard to get. The second one even harder. Follow the program. Do aftercare. Keep going to meetings. Get a sponsor. Don't—don't let your guard down for a second. Good luck."

She passed the coin to Ron. Ron held it, looked at the floor, and slowly elevated his gaze until he looked at Harold. "When you get on the plane back to Indiana, read what I wrote in your Big Book. And if you ever need a strike breaker back at the old steel mill, you know where to reach me."

Laughter and the coin was passed. D.T. took it, held it in his hands and stared at it for a long time. "I had so many things I wanted to say. But my tongue's all in knots." He looked up at Harold. "Take care of yourself. My address and number are in your big book. Use them any time."

Brandy took the coin from D.T., struggled with some unsaid words, kissed it, and handed it to Jake.

He looked at it. It was a bronze medallion the size of a half-dollar. On one side was the same coat of arms that appeared on all of the brown coffee cups in the unit, with the same question: "How does that make you feel?" On the back was the same prayer: "God, grant me the serenity…"

Jake looked up at Harold. "I feel like I've missed out on something not getting to know you better." He smiled. "Good luck." He passed the medallion to Frank. Frank held it and looked at Harold, and talked about the time when Frank had first come on the unit and was looking for faces to smash. Harold had shaken his hand, showed him around the unit, and sat up that entire first night listening while Frank dumped his guts until seven in the morning.

Listening to Frank, Jake felt like he had never heard a bond between two humans expressed with such force and meaning. Frank passed the coin to Candy, and the snotty little brat act ceased for a moment as she told Harold how much knowing him had meant to her. Gisel, the alcoholic intern, took the coin and made noises about how far Harold had grown since she'd known him, and good luck. With an effort, Roger calmed down and wished Harold the best of everything.

Earl took the coin, nodded at Harold, wished him good luck, and passed the coin to Dave, the union man. Dave held the coin, looked at it for a moment, then closed his eyes as tears began dribbling down his cheeks. He shook his head.

"Shit" He wiped his eyes with the back of his hand and said to Harold as he handed the coin to Angela. "It's in the book, asshole. Read it on the plane."

Angela took the coin, grinned broadly, and said, "Well, Harold." The group laughed, and Harold flushed bright red. "Do you remember that first contract you made in here? Your first day in group?"

He nodded. "Yes. God, yes."

Angela looked around at the circle. "That was before any of you were in this group, although you might have heard about it." Most of the group laughed. She grinned at Harold. "Would you mind repeating the contract word-for-word?"

Harold sat back in his chair, crossed his legs, and clasped his hands around his knee. "I said to Angela, if I ever stuck around long enough to pick up one of those fucking juke-box slugs, I'd kiss her ass, first giving her ten minutes to gather a crowd."

After the laughter died, Angela nodded at Harold. "You've come a long way." There was a twinkle of mischief in her eyes, then she stood and handed the medallion to Harold. "I'll settle for a hug."

Harold stood and hugged Angela. Jake could barely hear him speak to her as he held her tightly. "I'll miss you, Angela. I'll miss you a lot."

They parted, Angela held out her hands and said to the group, "Shall we close?"

They stood, joined hands, and said the prayer. "God, grant me the serenity to accept the things I cannot change, courage to change the things I can, and wisdom to know the difference."

Jake didn't say the words. There was still that word God in it. But he listened, Brandy holding his left hand, Frank his right. There was a feeling in the circle. A strange oneness. "Good vibes" the old flower-frys from Jake's generation used to call it. The circle was broken, the chairs stacked as Harold's friends said good-bye, and group was concluded.

Jake walked into the north wing lounge, flopped into the easy chair, lit his pipe, and closed his eyes. Envy was the feeling. He envied Harold. There was a serious doubt in his mind as to the reason. Was it because Harold was getting out? Because all of those people loved him?

Jake shook his head. No. It was because Harold could allow those people to love him. He could accept it, and love them back. Jake's envy turned bright green as he made a lateral move to self-pity.

28

Lunch at the Constipated Eagle.

As he wolfed down his Fido patty, Jake saw D.T. and Candy searching the chow line from the table. At other tables there were other patients taking surreptitious peeks at the chow line. Looking for their CP's—Concerned Persons. For most of them it'd been at least two weeks since they last saw their wives, husbands, parents, children.

As they found their own, a hand waved, and a hand or two in the line waved back. The family members looked nervous, wrung-out, strained, blank, bored, angry. The patients read the faces and projected horror into the coming afternoon session.

There were other patients who didn't search the chow line. Most of them had either finished with family week, or would do theirs next week or the week after. The remainder were doing family week alone. No one would show up for them. For some the disease had managed to eliminate every last person in the universe who gave a damn about them. During family week, they would watch other families painfully begin the healing process, while they sat in the circle that made up the fishbowl. When it came time, they would come across with the most forceful, insightful, and intense feedback ever seen in group. They knew what the family in the fishbowl still had a chance at, and still might lose if they don't stop bullshitting around and get down to the job of getting well.

At night some of them would cry; some of them would scream into their pillows in a cloud of might-have-beens, others would Nighthawk it, cornering a fellow Nighthawk to talk out the pain. A few simply gathered their belongings and walked out into the night. Buggouts. A subtle—but very real—form of suicide.

D.T. smiled and waved at the line. A plump woman of around fifty, dressed in a tan suit, nodded back. Her lips parted in a social smile; the remainder of her face showed no expression. She was followed by two hulking youths neither of whom would look in D.T.'s direction, both of whom Jake had noted knew damn well where D.T. was. The two youths were joking, laughing, making tough.

Farther down the line, just coming to the tray stack, was a slender girl of twenty, with long reddish-blond sausage-curls and wide green eyes. She nodded at the table where Jake was sitting, and he saw Candy wave back, her face in smiles.

"That's Ilene. Doesn't she look lovely? But that blouse she has on. Orange is not her color—"

Candy's prattle halted as a man moved into view and picked up a tray. Where Ilene got her eyes from was obvious. He was gray-haired, trim, wearing slacks and a yellow pullover sweater. He looked over the patients and family members seated in the dining room and saw Candy. He closed his eyes, turned, and began picking out his silverware.

Candy laughed. "Well, isn't Don gloomy? I wonder what the family counselor has been telling him to say to me?"

Frank, seated across from her, lowered his coffee cup. "Careful, Candy. Your shell is cracking."

For an instant Candy looked horrified. Then she laughed, made a kissing sound at Frank, and returned to her lunch and non-stop chatter.

Mid-day meds.

Jake popped his pill ration and began to head for his room. Snake, the shaved-bear biker, blocked the hallway and pointed at Jake. "I heard about you."

"What about me?" Jake looked about for an escape route.

"You write?"

"Yes."

"I wanna ask you to help me."

"Help?"

Snake pulled his steno pad from beneath his rivet-and-swastika littered jacket and opened it. "I gotta problem. See, I don't write so good. People don't unnerstand what I'm talking about, unnerstand? I started to give my first step today 'n' nobody could keep straight what I was talking about, unnerstand?"

"Sure, yeah, I unner—I understand."

"Can you help me organize this thing 'n' maybe punch it up a bit?"

"Punch it up?"

"I don't wanna bore anybody."

Jake nodded. "Sure. When do you want to get together?"

Snake grinned through several missing teeth. "I don't wanna take up a bunch of time, unnerstand? Just a comment here 'n' there."

"Got anything I could look at now?"

Snake glowered at his steno pad, then handed it to Jake. "It's just rough, unnerstand?"

"Gotcha."

Snake waved a hand. "See you at dinner. And thanks."

In the lounge, Jake settled down with his pipe and coffee and began leafing through Snake's notes. Page one, under kinds, amounts, and frequency of use of chemicals. And page two, and three, and four...Jake flipped ahead. Snake had twenty-one pages filled out on that subject alone. "Snake must be the poster-child for the American Pharmaceutical Association."

Jake went back to page one and began reading.

29

In his room, John Pennoyer sat on his bed and looked at the light coming from his window. His mouth moved silently.

—I've put up with it all. The third-degrees in group, Angela treating me like a child, that damned nickname, D.T., making jokes about me like I was some kind of skid row derelict. I have withstood it all. But Mack and Bobby....

He shook his head, remembering the hate in their eyes. "I'm afraid," he whispered. "I'm afraid of them. Physically afraid of my own sons."

John looked at the fingers of his right hand. Sober, they were his livelihood—his excuse to be on the planet. They were how Mack could hurt him. That time—

Mack grabbed his fingers and bent them back. "Scream you old fart! Let me hear you scream, you stinking puddle of shit! Let's see you play the big surgeon without these, motherfucker!" *Two of the fingers snapped. John screamed.*

Later that night, his right hand in a cast, drinking in the car. Mitzi crying, trying to explain away what Mack had done, waiting outside that girl's house for Mack to come out. He would've come alone, but Mitzi forced herself into the car. He had punched her in the mouth, but she still wouldn't leave.

—Bitch. Lilly-white bitch. Martyr. Saint Bitch.

The names he had called her. He had placed the bottle between his legs, reached between the door and the seat with his left hand, his fingers wrapping around the greasy coldness of the gun.

"Come on out now, football hero. Come on out, mother's little hit man."

Mitzi had begun screaming hysterically, and John had swung his cast and smashed her in the mouth. Finally she was quiet. John had looked across Mitzi through the right car window at the front door of the girl's house. "Come on, Mack. Get your hand out of her goddam panties and get out here. Break my fingers, you little—"

The door on the driver's side had suddenly opened. An angry hand had grabbed his shoulder and yanked him from the car. Down he had gone on the asphalt, fists striking his face again and again, a boot kicking his ribs, his face—

He remembered, just for an instant, regaining consciousness, seeing Bobby looking down at him, the gun in his hands, Mitzi kneeling on the street, her arms wrapped around Bobby's legs. There had been a curtain of stars behind them.

"Let me kill him, Mom! Please, just let me put an end to it!"

John rubbed his eyes and his fingers came away wet. When he did his first step, he had included the finger-breaking gun incident. But Mitzi had never said a word about it. Neither had Mack or Bobby. Everyone had gone to their respective corners, licked their wounds, and pretended nothing had happened. John had then given up drinking, had a visit from the rats, and then had numbed out on Valium.

They would talk about the incident during family week. Between Angela and the damned family counselor, they would speak the horrors that they had lived. There would be no more pretending that what was wasn't. Those words would hurt worse than any fists.

"God," said John to his window, "how am I going to make it through family week?"

In the north wing lounge, Candy was maintaining an endless gay chatter about her beautiful daughter, Ilene. She is great this, super that, so lovely, thinks we're sisters, and we're like sisters, famous friends—

The cowbell clanged the first call for the afternoon lecture. Members of the group finished their cigarettes and coffee and began shambling down the corridor, past the nurse's station, to the lecture hall. Candy stubbed out her cigarette, walked part way down the hall, and waited for D.T. to come out of his room.

—They better be careful what they talk about in there this afternoon. If they don't, Don and Ilene will certainly know who they tangled with when I get home.

"Damn this place:"

D.T.'s door opened and he smiled as he saw Candy waiting for him. Brother and sister under the gun. "You look angry, Candy."

"I am!" She looked up at him, smiled, laughed, then closed her eyes as tears began to glisten in her eyes. "No. I'm scared."

They hugged each other, there in the hallway, mixing their tears. No longer surgeon and nurse, bigtime professionals. Just two bruised and frightened scraps of humanity hanging onto each other for dear life.

30

They gathered again in the lecture hall. This time it was to hear about the family aspects of the disease. D.T. was afraid of what he might hear.

"Chemical dependency is a family disease. Those close to the addict or alcoholic become affected. It is difficult for the user of the chemical to see this. It is usually more difficult for those who don't use but are affected to see this."

The lecturer, Counselor Bill, drug addict and alcoholic, leaned on the lectern and began picking faces out of the audience with his fierce blue eyes. "As addicts and alcoholics we put our employers, wives, husbands, children, parents, and friends through hell. Our chemical usage placed these other persons into sick situations. To remain in a sick situation, to rationalize it, you must become sick too. It's been said before: The woman who sticks around long enough to get a second slap in the mouth from a drunken husband is sick. Perhaps even sicker than the user."

D.T. remembered the movie where that had been said. He looked over at Bill's group to see if he could find Norma. After watching the movie, they had talked in the fourth floor lounge. Her father was an alcoholic. She had cried, saying, "The daughter who sticks around long enough to get raped by a drunken parent the second time is sick!" She had shaken her head. "Great. It's not enough I'm a drug addict and alcoholic. Now I have my stripes in Al-Anon, too."

Counselor Bill moved from behind the lectern and looked at a young face in the first row. "Often the members of the alcoholic's family are more affected by the disease than is the alcoholic. Co-dependency is every bit as destructive as alcoholism, and takes almost the identical behavioral form. Lois W., Bill W.'s wife and the founder of Al-Anon, once said that the only difference between her and Bill was the smell."

He looked up at the frys. "You remember how it was, don't you? Everything in your life eventually revolved around obtaining and using your chemical. Things became so oriented around your chemical that if the chemical was removed, life made no sense; it became unbearable. What did you do then?"

A voice out of the frys replied, "Got another chemical."

"You bet. Either you got another chemical, another compulsion like spending or overeating, or you went back to the old chemical. The family members' problem is not addiction to a chemical; they become addicted to a situation. They are addicted to addicts.

"Your life revolved around a chemical. The family member's life revolved around you. Those of you who are divorced, you can almost count on your ex going out and getting hooked up with another alcoholic. That's right. After she ends her nightmare with you, she goes out and moves in with another drunk! Why? We get addicted to chemicals; family members frequently become addicted to addicts. As you all probably know by now, being addicted to something doesn't mean that you like it; it means that you cannot do without it."

Bill moved behind the lectern, leaned on it, and grinned. "Those of you lucky people who begin family week today, your concerned persons are now hearing a lecture on the family response to the illness. They have already been through orientation to chemical dependency and have been through a family group session to prepare them for this afternoon's fun and games."

He rubbed his chin. "Most of them are hearing for the first time that they have a problem, and that the problem isn't you. They have been affected by your use. They have already gone through social isolation and attempts to control the situation, the same as you. They will go through the same route of denial and blaming that you did. The only thing that anyone in the family knows for certain is that addiction cannot be the problem.

"If they are lucky, they will also surrender to the fact that they, too, have the bug. With a little more luck, they will also surrender to the healing process and begin to get better…

D.T. listened to the lecture, trying to bury his feelings of terror in the words. But the words brought back too many things. Enabling, said Bill, is reacting to the behavior of the addict in such a way as to shield him from experiencing the full impact of his chemical usage.

"You make excuses for using your chemical: the job stinks, my boss is out to get me, my wife doesn't understand me, my kids are no good, I have a sick friend, I'm black, I'm white, it's Monday, everybody does it.

"The family member makes excuses for you: he has the flu, he's been under a lot of strain, he's just having a good time, he's out of town, he works odd hours, kids nowadays, well everybody does it."

D.T. couldn't keep it out of his mind. *He had been hung over so bad his hair hurt.* Mitzi had telephoned in to the office. "He's got the flu again. It does seem to be going around."

Mack taking over the father role in the family. "It's okay, Dad, I have to learn to use a checkbook sometime, and you're pretty sick."

Bobby helping him into the house that one night when he had passed out on the lawn, while Mitzi tried unsuccessfully to back the car out of the ditch. Mitzi the next day lying to the neighbors about some rowdy kids who had stolen the car.

Mitzi trying to keep him from killing Mack. Mitzi trying to keep Bobby from killing him—

"The enabler sees this as a sincere desire to help," continued Bill. "The addict's behavior—your behavior—is ignored, tolerated, not seen. Your responsibilities are picked up and fulfilled by the enabler, and the enabler protects you from yourself and the consequences of your actions. Everyone around you settles for less and less. But to function in this manner, the enabler must distort reality. The enabler must see things that aren't there, and not see things that are."

Mitzi on the phone, John watching her from his chair, the drink in his hand. She was saying, "Mother, if you were a little more understanding and accepting of John, there wouldn't be any problem. *You've always hated him, haven't you…*"

"By being an enabler, the family member buys into every little negative projection you have. You have low self-worth? You turn around and hit your enabler with it. 'You act just like your mother. Why don't you lose some weight? You look just like a pig. Your cooking tastes like hell. You can't keep a straight thought in your head, can you? Can't you do anything with your son—'"

"*Dammit, Mitzi, you keep making mountains out of molehills.* It just wasn't like that. Not at all. I really think you have some serious mental problems. Why don't you see…"

Watching her undress for bed, his terror at making sex numbed by a fifth of Jim Beam. "Mitzi, I know a lot of women your age that still look pretty good. *What is it with you?*"

"And the enabler buys it! Every single lousy thing you feel about yourself, the enabler picks up and owns. Now both of you are focusing on the enabler's behavior, and the disease progresses. You tell her she's crazy and ought to see a psychiatrist, and she goes! Your drinking becomes her fault. Your misery is her fault. Your happiness becomes her responsibility, and she takes it all on. No burden is too large. No amount of responsibility too oppressive. Because no one is that powerful, all she can do is fail. That is how the enabler sees herself: a failure. A wretched, negative cipher.

"Eventually Gretchen, her best and only remaining friend, will ask her, 'Why don't you leave the bum?' If her husband began acting like you, of course she'd drop him in a second. Gretchen isn't affected. She doesn't have the bug. She doesn't understand. It's just like some civilian out there asking you, 'If drinking and drugging is screwing up your life, why don't you stop?'

"What does the enabler answer? She'll probably come up with some lame excuse based on the feeling 'After all I've done to him?' But the reason she doesn't leave is the same one that kept you drinking or using: addiction. Addiction is its own excuse."

Bill pointed at one of the frys. "Why do you drink?"

Silence, then the answer. "Because I'm an alcoholic."

Bill looked back at the audience. "It was tough for you to break through your denial and admit that you have a problem. It's even tougher for the family member. They never picked up the drink. You're the alcoholic! You're the problem! You're the one who has to get better! You're the one who has to change!"

Talking to Mack on the telephone. "I want you to come for family week, son."

"Look, old man, I don't care if I never see you again. I don't give a shit whether you get well or not."

"It's not just for me. It'll help you, too—"

"Maybe you convinced Mom that she's crazy, but don't lay your bullshit on me. *I know who the drunk in this family is.*"

"Now I've pictured the enabler as a person who knows only four things: first, the problem can't be addiction; second, if you would just stop drinking and drugging, all her problems would be solved. Third, all her problems and her family's problems are your fault. Fourth, all her problems, her family's problems, and your problems are all her fault.

"And you say, 'Gotcha Bill.' Two flaming contradictions. How could any rational person run his life like that? You're right. No rational person could. That is why Al-Anon, Alateen, and Adult Children of Alcoholics exist. To help those affected by alcoholics. Nar-Anon is for those affected by drug addicts. Gam-Anon for those affected by compulsive gamblers, and so on.

"Every Twelve Step program's Second Step is the same: 'Came to believe that a Power greater than ourselves could restore us to sanity.' If you're already sane, you don't need to be restored to sanity.

"Most of the money and effort in this business is spent on trying to reform *you* characters. That's because you are a highly visible public menace. On the road, on the job, at home you are expensive in terms of lives, property, money, and public and private morals. The persons affected by alcoholics, however, have a lower profile. They usually confine their activities to destroying themselves and their children through attempts at controlling the present and the future. I suppose I've heard it a hundred times or more from men, women and children who have gone through family week here. You people get twenty-eight days of treatment in here. They complain because they only get five days...."

As Bill wound up his lecture, D.T. rubbed his eyes, and looked to his right. Candy was calmly filing her fingernails.

—Very cool, Candy. Very cool, very hard, very sick.

"Are there any sharing speeches?"

Ron, in the row immediately in front of D.T., stood and called out: "Third floor north welcomes back to sanity and sobriety Harold Rose!"

As the frys applauded, Harold stood and walked to the front of the lecture hall. He stopped before the stage, jumped up on it, and faced the audience. Most fish on their way out just talk from their group chairs or stand on the floor in front of the stage. The Animals do sharing speeches from the stage. D.T. had overheard Angela telling Harold, "You've accomplished something very important. Be tall."

The applause died down and Harold's grin diminished to a smile. "It's going to be harder than I thought leaving here. I'll miss you. I'll miss the staff. I'm a bit afraid of the world on the other side. Return visitors have told us often enough that it's business as usual out there. The only thing that's changed is me. But I think that change has been considerable. The new fish that was on the back row of this hall a month ago didn't like himself, he hated the world and everyone in it. He lived in a very cold, very dark, very lonely place. Well, that fish is up here now. He likes himself and he loves you. Thanks."

Harold waved a hand to the applause from the frys. The patients got to their feet, many to shake Harold's hand, most to head for the lounges for smokes and coffee before afternoon group.

31

After the lecture, Jake slouched in the north wing lounge's easy chair, his feet on the coffee table, sipping his coffee and paging through Snake's notes. He reached the last page with writing on it, scanned it, then closed the steno book.

The document was a drama of epic proportions. A life of war, revolution, high finance, adventure, violence, and crime that covered twenty-five years and involved nine countries. Drug smuggling, white slavery, murder-for-hire, arson, political fixing, degradation on a scale unheard of. The main reason it was unheard of was because the document was pure, unmitigated bullshit. Jake told lies for a living. Snake was a rank amateur.

Jake shook his head, lit his pipe, and stared at the steno pad on his lap. The cover had a drawing on it of a swastika intertwined around a Christian-type cross. "And they say *I* write science fiction."

Earl walked in front of Jake, flopped into the love seat, and lit a cigarette. A cloud of smoke, and Earl coughed. "God, I've never smoked so much in my life. That's all we do around here: sit on our butts, get our minds messed with, drink coffee, and smoke."

"Earl, what do you think about this co-dependency disease?"

"You mean the lecture?"

Jake nodded.

"I don't know. I never heard of it before, but the man just spent the last forty minutes describing my wife and boy." Earl shook his head. "I'm going to have to talk to Angela about family week. Neither of them will come." He looked at Jake. "How about your wife?"

Jake thought back to that phone call, the one when Ann asked him to come home. She had been frightened. Perhaps it was a little something she had gotten in the mail. "I haven't asked her yet. I guess there's plenty of time."

Candy walked around Jake's chair and sat next to Earl. Her eyes looked wild. She lit a cigarette, jammed it between her lips, and puffed. "Bastards!" she hissed.

Jake removed his feet from the coffee table and leaned forward. "Candy, what is it?"

She shook her head and continued to stare at the frost-covered windows. Another puff, she ground out the cigarette, and lit another. "Damned bastards. In that family lecture, where they prepare them for group, they tell them to be sure to talk about everything the patient has warned them against talking about."

Earl frowned. "What?"

Candy turned abruptly to her left. "Listen hard, farmer. I warned Don and Ilene against talking about certain things."

"Like what?"

"Bedroom and bathroom stuff! There are just some things that you don't talk about." Another drag, she looked around the lounge like a trapped animal. "Fucking Don. He said he has to talk about...." She shook her head violently. "I'll get them for this. So help me God."

Jake leaned back in his chair. "Maybe they know what they're doing."

"Maybe they don't." She pointed at Jake. "You've never seen a family week before. You have no idea what goes—"

Candy turned her head, frozen, a rabbit caught in the headlights of an oncoming car. Jake turned to look. The door to room 355 was open, a strange woman was at the door with Angela. Several civilians, concerned persons, were in the hall. Jake was surprised that he knew all of their names. Mitzi, Mack, and Bobby for D.T., Don and Ilene for Candy. With the additional six persons—five CP's and their family counselor, it would be Right Guard time in group.

Jake looked around, noticed that everyone was carrying one of the little brown *A Day at a Time* books. "Are there readings in the afternoon group, too?"

Earl wiggled his book in the air. "That's what I was told."

Jake got up, went to his room, dropped off Snake's memoirs, and picked up his copy of *A Day at a Time*. He snorted. "I don't know how much longer I can take this hallelujah crap."

He opened his door and saw the group begin to file into Angela's office. He glanced above the door, almost expecting an "Abandon All Hope Ye Who Enter Here" sign to be posted. There was a knot in the pit of his stomach, and it puzzled him. His headache hovered around the edges of his awareness,

"It's not my family week." He laughed it off and headed across the hall.

32

The circle was formed and everyone was as settled as they could be. Frank opened his brownie and began the afternoon reading. His voice was steady. "My addiction is three-fold in that it affects me physically, mentally, and spiritually. As a chemically-dependent person, I was totally out of touch not only with myself, but with reality...."

As Frank read, Jake looked at the faces in the circle. Earl sat to his left, and next to Earl sat D.T.'s youngest son, Bobby. He slouched in his chair, feet flat on the floor, arms folded across his chest, his eyes half-closed. Mack had his right arm hung behind his chair and was intensely involved in examining the ceiling.

D.T.'s wife, Mitzi, sat with her knees together, her hands in her lap and her back straight. A little girl in finishing school. A thin, barely visible scar ran from the right corner of her mouth to the tip of her chin. She was looking across the circle at D.T., who kept his eyes on his book.

"Have I begun to break away from my old ideas?" continued Frank. "Just for today, can I adjust myself to what is, rather than try to adjust everything to my own desires?"

Next to Mitzi sat Don, his legs crossed, his forehead resting on his right hand, covering his eyes. Beautiful Ilene looked as though she had been charged with putting her favorite pet to death by slow strangulation.

A woman Jake didn't know was next, then Angela, who was looking back at Jake. Jake's eyes returned to the reading.

"I pray that I may not be caught up again in the downward, destructive spiral which removed me from myself and from the realities of the world around me."

Jake glanced up and Angela was watching Frank. To her left sat Gisel, then Dave. Dave was not paying attention, his mind filled with the absence of his friend. Then came D.T., Brandy, Candy, and Frank.

"I pray that I may adjust to people and situations as they are instead of always trying, unsuccessfully and with endless frustration, to bend them to my own desires."

Between Frank and Jake sat Roger. Frank raised his eyebrows and turned to Roger as he concluded with the reading's closing thought. "I can only change myself."

Frank faced the center of the circle. "I'm Frank, alcoholic, and my contract…"

Everybody's contract was the same: to participate in family week.

The family members simply stated their names, except for Mitzi who identified herself as a concerned person for John. The strange woman was Lillian Sterner, family counselor. Lillian Sterner looked like a Hitler Youth housemother.

Jake felt the back of his neck tighten. The tension was as solid as green on lima beans. This was not going to be a family get-together. Angela leaned forward, elbows on her chair's armrests, hands clasped together. "I want to welcome the family members to the first day of family week…" The rules of the fishbowl were explained. No, the patient isn't giving you the silent treatment; the patient isn't allowed to respond for the first two days.

"You need to tell your patient what he or she has done, because the patient might not know. Tell how you felt. This is not only for the patient; it is for you. The healing process is painful, and I wish you a lot of pain." Angela grinned brightly and looked between D.T., Candy, and the family members. "Who's first?"

Candy stood, picked up her chair and placed it near the center of the circle. She waited beside it until Don and Ilene had pulled their chairs out and sat down facing her. Candy slowly took her seat, placed her hands on her knees, and looked at the space between Don and Ilene. Angela pulled her chair up until she was almost between the contestants; the referee explaining the rules.

"We want you to keep to specifics, and to address the patient directly. Being judgmental—name calling—is only destructive. But be frank and honest. Don't rely on clearing things up when your patient returns home, and don't avoid things just because you and your patient have discussed them before. If it hasn't been said here, it hasn't been said. If your patient told you not to talk about something, make certain that you do talk about it—"

No eye-gouging, no foot-stomping, no kicking below the belt. Aim straight for the heart. Jake rubbed his eyes, wishing he were anywhere else.

Angela faced Don and Ilene. "Now, who would like to begin? Ilene? Don?"

Don and his daughter exchanged glances, then Don looked at Lillian. Lillian smiled, nodded, and looked off into the distance. Don opened the yellow folder in his lap, pulled out a wad of papers, checked a point, and looked into Candy's eyes. His voice seemed timid at first. But it was the kind of quiet strength some people achieve through unending pain.

"Candy and I were married in nineteen fifty-eight. I was in college and she—"

Angela pointed at Candy. "Don, talk directly to Candy."

Don lowered his glance, then slowly elevated it until he was looking at her eyes. Candy was smiling back. "You were a wonderful person to be with. Full of life, interested in everything, a delightful sense of humor, loving." He took a halting breath and shook his head. "When Ilene was born in nineteen sixty, you were the mother every child dreams of having."

Jake listened to Don's glowing tribute to what once was. The person he described, although he called her Candy, was a foreigner. Then, when Ilene was eight, there was a period when Candy was depressed. Periods when she didn't want to talk with anyone, minor arguments, tearful scenes. Professional help was sought, resulting in Candy going back to her old job as a nurse.

"Things seemed to get better for a while, then that one morning you had me call you in sick. You said you had a terrible headache. A few hours later, you were up, going through my things. When I caught you going through my desk drawers, you accused me of having an affair."

Angela looked at Don. "How did that make you feel, Don?"

"Feel? I was…stunned. I laughed at her, the accusation was so ludicrous. Then she started smashing the things in my office—I have a home office. She—"

"Talk directly to Candy, Don."

"You shoved everything from my desk onto the floor, picked up my baseball bat, and began smashing windows, lamps, trophies, everything. I tried to stop you and you swung the bat at me."

He shook his head, glanced at Ilene. and looked back at Candy. "You broke my arm. The telephone was totaled and I had to drive myself to the hospital. I told the doctor that I tripped and fell down some stairs. Another time—"

Jake looked at Candy's face. She was still smiling, a twinkle in her eyes. Ilene was looking at her father. Don was struggling through another episode.

"Things were cool between us, but there weren't any more major scenes until Ilene's thirteenth birthday. We had prepared a magnificent party. All Ilene's friends, then you came in the room screaming filth."

He shook his head.

Angela glanced at Candy. "What did she say?"

"My god."

"What did she say?"

"In front of Ilene's friends…" He sat forward, his face red. "Candy, you accused me of sleeping with my own daughter!"

"And you felt…" prompted Angela.

The groupwad was passed from Lillian to Angela to Ilene to Don. Don didn't notice. "And you felt," Angela repeated.

"Horror, shock, outrage…anger." Don looked at Ilene. "And guilty, I guess. Ilene and I had always been very close." He shook his head. "But what ever did I do to get Candy to think that—"

"It was drugs talking, Don. Not candy."

Don sighed and looked at Angela. "My daughter and I stopped doing anything more affectionate than shaking hands."

"Did you know Candy was on pills then?"

Don looked back at his wife. "She had some prescriptions in the medicine cabinet. We had no hint of a drug problem." His eyes closed for a moment, then opened. "Well, after listening to that lecture, I guess we knew and were rationalizing away all of the evidence. We just refused to see what was happening."

Angela looked at Ilene. "How did that make you feel, Ilene?"

The woman looked at Candy, her eyes narrowed, brimming with tears. "Mother, I felt lost, abandoned, and…guilty. Responsible for it all. I didn't know why or how, but I was responsible. But what hurt the most is my father could no longer be a father. He wasn't even a friend. We…" She laughed and shook her head. "Damn it, Mother, we were even afraid to be in the house alone with each other for fear of what you might accuse us of having done."

Angela leaned back in her chair and glanced at Lillian. Lillian, her hands clasped over her belly, studied Candy's face. Candy was still smiling, still studying the space between Don and Ilene. Lillian looked at Candy's husband. "Don, why don't you tell Candy about that Easter three years ago?"

Don's jaw muscles twitched, he looked at Candy and began. "I was sleeping in bed. By then we knew you had a drug problem. You had been fired from the hospital for stealing drugs, and had twice been arrested for possession—"

"Wait!" Candy held up her hand and turned to Angela. "I was never convicted of any—"

"Just listen, Candy.

"Angela, I don't have—"

"Just *listen*, Candy."

Candy grinned, nodded, and turned back, looking straight at Don. Her eyes were very wide, a grotesque smile on her lips. The room almost vibrated with unspoken threats. Her husband looked back and continued speaking. "I was sleeping on my stomach. My back was bare—I only wear pajama bottoms. I woke up in the middle of a nightmare. Candy, you were kneeling on the bed next to me, pressing a hot iron into my back. It took the skin away when I rolled over and tried to fight you off. You kept forcing the iron at my face, burning my arms and hands. Finally I knocked the iron out of your hand and managed to sit up. You got off the bed, picked the iron up and—" He simply shook his head.

Lillian nodded. "Tell her what she said, Don. She might not know."

"Candy, you picked up the iron and said 'Jesus, Don, you can't take a joke at all, can you?" He turned to Angola. "A *joke?*"

"How did that make you feel, Don?"

"I didn't know what to feel. The horror, laughed off as an innocent prank. I couldn't go to the hospital or my doctor's. God, I mean the shape of the iron was burned into my back. How could I explain that away? I was all out of lies. I was ashamed. Hurt. Angry. Frightened."

Ilene reached out a hand and placed it on her father's arm. Don nodded, bit the skin on the inside of his lips, then shook his head. "The burn on my back became infected. I drove out of state, found a doctor, and he entered me in a local hospital—"

Candy sprang forward, her face dark with rage. "How stupid do you think I am? I know you were in bed with one of your little—"

"Candy." Angela had her hand on Candy's shoulder. "Sit down!" Candy sat down, her lips trembling. "Now, *just listen.* You'll have your opportunity to respond Wednesday."

Candy took a deep breath, then her face relaxed, she smiled, laughed, nodded, and resumed staring at the space between her husband and daughter.

Angela rocked in her chair, glanced at the family counselor, then turned toward Ilene. "Is there something you want to say to your mother?"

Ilene opened her yellow folder, withdrew some papers, and began speaking. First came a description of Candy the mother every kid dreams about. After that was a little girl staring in horror as her mother took a pair of scissors and cut the girl's new dress into tiny pieces. A little girl, screaming in pain, feeling filthy, unclean, as Candy took a dry razor and hacked off the little girl's pubic hair. A little girl having her pitifully small breasts whipped by an enraged madwoman—

Jake looked behind Don and Ilene at D.T.'s family members. Playing tough all forgotten, Mack and Bobby were sitting on the edges of their chairs, totally absorbed in the events taking place before their eyes. Mitzi was crying. Jake looked at D.T. He, too, was absorbed in the process, his own coming ordeal forgotten.

Candy was smiling, her eyes closed, her head occasionally shaking.

"Mother, the night before I was to be married to Keith, you were taking one pill after another, fighting with Father, breaking up things. After I fell asleep, you came into my room and sat in the chair next to my bed. I woke up, saw you sitting there in the dark and asked if something was wrong. You—"

Ilene's crying became very agitated. Angela reached out her arm and put it around the woman's shoulders.

"What happened then?"

Ilene shook her head, took a handful of tissues and held them to her face. "She had her big cutting shears. She began stabbing me with them." She shook her head. "I passed out, certain I was going to die. The last thing I saw was your face, covered with my blood, and you were laughing."

Angela patted Ilene's shoulder. They remained that way, the room silent. Then Angela spoke, her voice barely above a whisper. "How did you feel, Ilene?"

Ilene shook her head. English hadn't yet invented a word that could satisfactorily represent how she felt. Angela looked at Candy, and Candy returned the look, her eyebrows raised in a look that seemed to say, "So you've been taken in too, eh?"

Angela turned toward Don, her arm still around Ilene. "Would you like to hear some feedback from the group?"

Don nodded, looked at Candy, and nodded again. "Yes, I would." Ilene remained shaking beneath Angela's wing.

Frank began. "Candy, your entire first step was a fairy tale. You talked about little embarrassments in restaurants, headaches, grumpy arguments with friends and family. We've never heard anything about this person Don and Ilene are talking about. You never once even hinted at the things they've been talking about."

D.T. continued. "In your first step, you said your experience with drugs went back for five years at the most. From what your family said, you had to have been doing pills for at least ten or twelve years."

The rest of the patient group brought up discrepancy after discrepancy between the Candy they knew, the Candy that had been described in her first step, and the Candy that Don and Ilene had described.

"Your behavior was insane, psychotic."

"You've just been denying the existence of a problem."

"You didn't seem to be listening at all."

Jake remained silent, staring at Candy's face. After Dave concluded his observations, the group was silent. Angela studied Candy's face, then looked between the patient and her family at Jake. "Jake?"

Startled, he looked at Angela. "Yes?"

"What's going on with you?"

"Me?"

Angela nodded. "You."

He moistened his lips as he looked at the floor. "While this was going on I was looking at Candy's face—"

"Talk directly to her."

Jake looked at Candy, closed his eyes, and leaned forward in his chair.

—Holy hell, am I scared.

Slowly he opened his eyes and looked at her. "Candy, what were you laughing at? What are you laughing at now?" Candy turned her head toward Angela.

Angela nodded. "Go ahead."

Candy looked at Jake, held out a hand toward her husband and daughter, and laughed. "You don't expect me to take this seriously, do you? Have you been—"

"That is all." Angela removed her arm from around Ilene.

Candy laughed again, "Angela, I can't take—"

"I said that's all, Candy. Be silent." She pointed to the space between Brandy and Frank. "Put your chair back."

Candy sprang up, briskly returned her chair to its place in the circle,

and sat down. After reassuring nods from both Angela and Lillian, Don
and Ilene moved their chairs to the circle.

The fishbowl was clear.

Jake watched in disbelief as Angela nodded at D.T. and his family.—Don't we get breaks between rounds?

D.T. took his place and his wife and two sons sat facing him. D.T.'s
youngest son, Bobby, looked very confused. Twice he looked back at
Ilene. He sat with his hands dangling between his legs. Mack sat flat-
footed, his arms folded, numb anger twitching his jaw muscles.

Flopping back in his chair, Jake closed his eyes as the stiffness in his
neck grew more intense and joined up with his headache. He touched
his forehead and his fingers came away wet. At that moment he admitted that he was sick to his stomach.—Oh, hell. A flashback.

That Valium child in the lounge had told him, "Man, it takes time to
get that shit out of your system. Hell, every time I was in group for the
next two weeks I did flashbacks."

"What are flashbacks?"

"You don't know?"

"Prescription junkies don't have the same educational advantages as
you street shooters."

"Flashbacks. It's withdrawal all over again. The same things, but
shorter. Stress brings it on. *Group brings on stress.*"

You better believe group brings on stress, thought Jake.

Angela completed her second explanation of the rules and Mitzi
waded into D.T. The story was getting familiar. Calling in for him,
explaining him away, embarrassing the family, denying her sex, verbal
assaults, beatings, him threatening to kill Mack, and on and on. D.T.
sat, his hands in his lap, looking at his wife, every word a saltwater
soaked whip stinging his flesh.

Mitzi turned to a new page and continued. "You were drunk, and
we were in the middle of a terrible argument. You were breaking up

everything, slapping me...and then you said you were leaving. In the car. You couldn't hardly walk, but you were going to take the car and drive. When you're drunk angry like that, you use the car like a weapon—"

His eyes still on Mitzi, Jake's mind turned inward as a scene came back to him. *He had been behind the wheel, the passenger door open.* Ann, barefoot and in her nightgown, was standing in the snow, leaning inside the car, fighting with him for the keys.

"Jake. Don't go. You can't drive like this—"

"Get out! Get out! Get away from me, you fucking bitch! What the shit do you care what happens to me? Get out!"

"Jake." She sobbed, coughed. Her asthma making her breath short. Her skin growing blue from the cold and lack of oxygen. "You can't drive. I won't let you."

They had been struggling at it for hours. A crawling battle and grab for the keys from the living room, to the kitchen, to the garage, to the car—

Jake had held the keys inside his fist. "I can wait. Whenever you get tired standing in the cold, bitch, go back inside."

He lit his pipe, folded his arms, and waited. *Ann stood in the snow, half in, half out of the car, sobbing, begging—*

Jake listened to Mitzi. She was fifteen years older than Ann, didn't look a thing like her, but he kept confusing the images, the stories. Tears were streaming down Jake's face.

—Shit, I don't cry. What's happening to me?

Angela spoke to Mack, then nodded at someone. The groupwad found its way to Jake's lap. He blew his nose and tried to follow what was being said.

Mack shrugged his shoulders. "I don't have anything to tell him. No one's ever been able to tell him anything."

Angela smiled at Mack. "It must have been terrible for you. What was it like? How did you feel?"

Mack looked at D.T. "I don't feel a damned thing." He closed his eyes, his face reddened, and the tears flowed. "Shit!"

"What's going on, Mack?"

He shook his head and lowered his chin to his chest. "I smoke pot. When we went to that first lecture they said we had to keep away from dope—chemicals—all the time during family week." He opened his eyes, stared at his father, then looked at Lillian. "I can't do it! Did the old sonofabitch give me this, too?"

Lillian reached across Mitzi and placed a hand on Mack's shoulder. "We'll put you into evaluation, Mack, and see if we can't come up with some answers."

Then it was Robby's turn.

Later, Jake sat in an almost liquid form in the north wing lounge's easy chair, sucking on his pipe, trying to even out the Mary blues. His brain felt like it had been extracted through his left ear, whipped around the block, and stuffed back into his head through his nostrils. He was drained.

The lounge was deserted. Angela's door opened, two men and a woman walked out and headed down the hall to the nurse's station. Angela appeared in the doorway, noticed Jake, then went back into the office. In a moment she returned carrying several pieces of paper. She walked across the lounge and stopped next to Jake.

He grinned. "Hi."

A wry smile crossed her face. "What was happening in there, Jake? Why were you crying?"

He put down his pipe, shook his head. "Something Mitzi was talking about. When she was trying to keep D.T. from driving when he was drunk. My wife and I had a similar incident. Mitzi brought it all back."

Angela nodded and extended her hand. Jake took the papers.

"These are first step outlines and addiction and recovery charts. Later in the week Gisel will go one-on-one with you, Earl, Lydia, and Roger to answer any questions you might have. Could you see that Earl, Lydia, and Roger get a copy of each?"

"Sure."

"There's a tape somewhere on the first step that a lot of patients find helpful. I think Brandy has it. Ask her about it. Perhaps you all could get together to listen to it."

"I'll ask Brandy. When are we supposed to have these first steps finished?"

"It's up to you. I won't chase you down." She folded her arms, leaned back and smiled down at Jake. "Do you have something you want to ask me?"

"I guess so." He nodded and waved his left hand at Angela's open doorway. "Is it…is it like that every day?"

Angela laughed, walked to her door, turned and headed toward the nurse's station, still laughing.

Jake pushed himself to his feet, walked to the end of the hall and watched Angela's back as she laughed her way down to the nurses station. "What's so funny?"

33

At dinner that evening, Jacob Randecker renamed the Constipated Eagle's attempted Oriental offering, previously known to the patrons of SMRC as barfbag. The new name caught the inmates' fancy, and from then on barfbag was known as Chopped Phooey.

After dinner, his stomach prodding him to consider giving Chopped Phooey back its original name, Jake sat in the north wing lounge browsing over his first step outline. There were fifteen major categories. He could see that when Angela whipped this one up she was not screwing around.

Beginning with a complete history from day one, he was supposed to include kinds, amounts and frequency of use of chemicals, examples of his preoccupation with chemicals, attempts to control, effects on physical health, effects on sex life(!), effects on emotional life, effects on social life, effects on spiritual life(?), effects on work, effects on finances, effects on character (list 30 values and give examples of how you have compromised them as a result of your usage), examples of insane behavior, loss of memory, blackouts, examples of destructive behavior, accidents or other dangerous situations produced by use, capped off by twenty-five examples of things he had done that hurt family members and close ones as a result of better living through chemistry.

Brandy and Lydia were seated on the opposite side of the lounge at the card table, working on their first steps. Jake folded up his outline, stuck it into his shirt pocket, and tossed Snake's steno pad on the end table. He cleaned his pipe, loaded it, and fired up. Lydia shook her head. "For the first time I added up total quantities in gallons. I drank enough to fill a damned swimming pool."

Brandy nodded. "The liver's an amazing organ, isn't it?" She sighed. "I just finished adding up what all this has cost. Drugs, hospitalizations, loss of productivity, accidents and so on."

"How much?"

"Almost one hundred and fifty thousand dollars. If you count the value of the drugs I stole, it's about two hundred thousand."

Jake whistled. "That's a bunch of bucks."

"Somewhere on the unit we have a guy who put a three-million dollar inheritance up his nose in less than a year." Brandy shook her head and returned to her steno pad.

Jake leaned back in the easy chair and closed his eyes. Brandy and the three million dollar vacuum cleaner had been fooling with coke, and that stuff costs. Jake had never done coke. In fact he had never done any street drugs. He blushed as he remembered telling a fan at a science-fiction convention "I'm too smart to get into drugs."

He pulled out his first step outline and looked at it.

—How much could a fifth of whisky a day and a bunch of beer cost? There was that heart attack, but that was only five thousand, and insurance covered that. No car accidents. There were a few things in the house that got busted up, but no reduction in income. In fact, the more I drank, the more money I made.

"Jake?"

He looked up. There stood Snake. Jake pointed to a chair. "Have a seat."

"Sure." The hulk lowered itself onto the groaning piece of furniture, and leaned forward in eager anticipation. "What'd you think?"

Jake relit his pipe, clasped his hands over his belly, and looked at the biker. "Snake, what I think is that you are probably the most inept bullshitter I have ever met."

Snake glowered. "I don't unnerstand."

"You don't lie worth a shit."

"That I unnerstand."

Jake reached to his right, picked Snake's steno pad up from the end table, and opened it. "I checked some of this out with one of the doctors. You couldn't have taken all these drugs. Some because they no longer exist, some because they never did exist, some because you wouldn't be alive now if you had taken them." He pointed at the pad. "Only a few of these are mood-altering drugs. The remainder are for things like chemotherapy, crotch itch, poison ivy...this one's used for killing parasites on sheep—"

"Okay! What about the rest?"

Jake removed his feet from the coffee table, leaned forward and dropped the steno pad on Snake's lap. "The rest just has a few minor problems, like being in Los Angeles and Algeria at the same time. Like being in the French Foreign Legion in Algeria several years after the Legion gave the place back to the Arabs. Like being in the Mafia and the Jewish Defense League with a name like Dooley—"

"Awright!" Snake looked down at his pad, then up at Jake. Jake had resumed his slumped back, feet on the table posture. "Nobody talks to me like that."

"Someone should." Jake pulled his pipe from his mouth and pointed it at the biker. "Snake, what are you trying to prove with that?

It's a lousy piece of storytelling, and an even worse first step. It's too clumsy to be a clever little joke you're playing on your group. The language you use in several places shows you know how to use English, so all this grunt-and-groan biker jive doesn't wash. You're not stupid. But what's your game?"

Snake got to his feet, his steno pad in both hands. He looked at Jake, down at his pad, then he turned and walked out of the lounge. Jake shook his head and was about to close his eyes when Brandy croaked out his name. "Jake?"

He glanced over at her. "Yeah?"

She pointed at the empty hallway. "Do you know who that is?"

"Snake Dooley. Biker and bullshitter. Not much of a bullshitter, at that. I've never seen him ride."

"Jake, right now Snake has three charges of attempted murder pending."

"Really? With that first step they should make it four."

She nodded, her eyes wide. "He just might."

"Too bad he doesn't write about it. That might be interesting."

"Are you really that fearless?"

Jake frowned at her and sat up. "No. I'm not fearless at all. In most situations I'm terrified of people, especially of King Kong types like Snake." He fiddled with his pipe as he talked. "But that clown came in on the one spot in my life that works. I'm a writer, and that's really all I have left. About writing, I don't horseshit around. Not for anyone."

Brandy glanced at the hallway, back at Jake, grinned, shook her head, and returned to her first step. Out rang the cowbells for the evening lecture. Jake rubbed his eyes and wondered if the day would ever end.

There is a slide show on the physical effects of alcohol abuse. To kill yourself with alcohol, it seems, one does not necessarily have to be an alcoholic. There are those who have the choice whether to use or not, and choose to abuse. The speaker, a jocular fellow seventeen years off the sauce, does not like the term abuse. He thinks it's misleading.

"Let's face it. No one on this planet ever abused alcohol. Alcohol doesn't care what you do to it. One way or the other, it all comes out in the end. Alcohol abused you."

The slides are in brilliant color. Pieces of human meat are hacked up and spread out on the screen for the edification of the audience.

"Here's a brain sectioned to show you what a non-user's melon is full of. Next, here is the brain of an alcoholic. These large dark areas are holes in the tissue." A little talk about the wet brain, and then to the liver.

"Interesting organ, the liver. Here's a nice purple healthy one. Now, here's our W.C. Fields model. Yellow, covered with alcohol burn scars, enlarged. Hack it open (hack, hack) and we can see the enlarged fatty deposits." There are vessels in the throat distorted into purple-black sacks of blood. Eat a piece of toast, bleed to death and drown at the same time.

"Well, alcohol is just one of the many wonders of science, and it's an ancient one." More modern substances and their consequences: a heart that ripped itself apart, a rotten nose, sinuses that look like a bad dream, uncontrollable bleeding, veins falling apart, enlarged breasts for men, handlebar mustachios for women, hair falls out and begins growing on the palms of your hands, skin shrivels up, balls fall off—

Someone from Janet's group puked on the floor of the lecture hall and the game was called.

In the lounge.

"It's all a big scare," said a new face. His name was Bob. His lawyer had made a smart deal. The prosecution would drop about fifty of the charges if Bob went into treatment. Bob was around thirty-five, looked fifty, and was working on his first step. Bob was pissed. "I was born at the age of twelve. We were too poor to afford a mother."

Jake, slouched in the easy chair, was puffing on his pipe, swearing off liver forever. Brandy, working on how she compromised her values through the use of chemicals, was very, very quiet. Candy was absent, and D.T. left the lounge in search of her.

Ron was at the card table near the balcony door. He was sitting next to a cute dark-haired junky from Mark's group named Paula. It was the third time, according to Lydia, that the pair had cuddled in the north wing lounge. Perhaps, she wondered out loud, is Ron bringing chicky home to meet the folks?

"So what?" asked Jake.

Lydia frowned at him. "Didn't you get briefed on the patient handbook? No romance, no sex, no exclusive relationships?"

"Oh, yeah. But, hell, it seems like any joy you can get out of this place you ought to grab. Maybe, Lydia, you're making too much out of nothing."

"Jake, they have a saying in A.A.: Alcoholics don't form relationships; they take hostages. It sounds very funny until you think about yourself, or the others around here. Our friendly little bottle or pill is gone, and what to do? A lot of us substitute a human and become just as dependent on the person." Lydia leaned back in the loveseat. "That's how I screwed up my first treatment."

"What can you do about it?"

Lydia looked down and shook her head. "Confront Ron. But I should wait to do it in group." She shrugged. "Maybe I ought to concentrate on my own problems, instead." Lydia laughed, got up, and wandered from the lounge.

Jake looked at Ron and Paula and remembered a thing he had once said as a joke: "I don't have to worry about the high cost of divorce nowadays. A bullet costs under a buck. If Ann leaves me, she knows I'll smear her brains all over the house."

—Some joke. Except that it really hadn't been a joke. Alcoholics don't form relationships; they take hostages. "Hmmm."

Frank and Roger were playing cribbage, Earl was studying his first step outline, and Dave was wandering around, looking for something to do. Dave sat in a chair next to Jake, crossed his legs, and pulled out a cigar. It was a Rum Soaked Crook. "Want one?" Dave dangled the bent weed before Jake.

"Who do I have to kill?"

He took the offering and nodded his thanks. In a moment, between the two of them, the lounge attained a sufficient atmosphere in which to select political nominees and apportion available graft. "What do you think of your first day in group, Jake?"

"I still have a headache."

"It's always a little tense the first day of family week."

"A little tense?"

Dave nodded. "It gets real tense tomorrow." Dave puffed, knocked the ash into an ashtray, and looked at the door of room 355. "Yeah, see the family members, first time in front of the group, don't really know what's going on. Kelly, my wife, hardly said anything that first day."

"Things opened up Tuesday?"

"She cut my balls off the second day."

Jake slowly shook his head. "I don't get it. We feel shitty enough already. What's the point? I know it's supposed to help the family members, but it's got to be hell on the patient."

"It's that." Dave removed a flake of tobacco from his tongue. "But I know how it helped me and Kelly. I can't explain it too good, but it's like our whole marriage was nothing but lies. She had this thing she wanted me to be, I had this thing I wanted her to be, and neither of us had what we wanted. We'd never said what we wanted. We never said a lot of things. Family week helped put the cards on the table."

"Dave, I'm just a beginner, but it looked pretty brutal in there. There were things said that just can't be taken back."

"True. But anything that gets blown away by putting the cards on the table was a lie anyway. It's a no-lose play. You don't lose anything by being honest."

"Except peace of mind and a yard of skin."

Dave grinned, stuck the cigar between his teeth, and talked around it. "Do you have peace of mind, Jake? Did you ever?"

Jake thought, then shook his head. "I don't think I ever have had peace of mind. Serenity, I think they calls it here. What I used to call serenity the people around here call passing out. How are you and Kelly doing now?"

"We were separated when I came in to the joint. But we're at least talking now. Look, in the long run it's better to have it out. The stuff you refuse to look at doesn't mean you're done with it. It'll eat at you until you do deal with it." Dave leaned back and looked to his right, grinning as Snake entered the lounge. "Hey, it's Killer Biker. How you doin', Snake? Steal any gumballs or beat up any little old ladies lately?"

"Fuck you, Gompers."

"Wrong union."

Snake fumed and looked down at Jake. "Can I talk to you for a minute?"

"Sure." Jake pushed himself out of his chair and patted Dave on his shoulder as he followed Snake out into the hall. "What's up?"

Snake thrust his hands into his back pockets, looked angrily to his left, then looked down at Jake. "Those things you said to me."

"What about them?"

"I've been thinking about them. They still piss me off."

"If you didn't want my opinion, you shouldn't have asked for it. What's this about?"

"I talked to a couple of my buddies on the unit about what you said.

They said I should kill you."

"What do you say?"

Snake jabbed at his own chest with the thumb of his right hand. "It hurt. It hurt when you said those things."

Jake's eyebrows went up when he noticed, and finally allowed himself to believe, that Snake's eyes were glistening. Tears. "I don't know what to tell you. I'm sorry if I hurt you, but what I said still goes." There was that question. He looked up at the biker. "Snake, why are you here?"

"Don't give me that shit, man—"

"Why are you here? To impress a judge, or to get well? What are you going to do when you get out of here? Crack a beer with your buddies and say 'Yeah, man, I did my twenty-eight in the joint, but they can't make a wimp out of me.'"

"I'm not going to use again."

Jake put his hands on his hips. "If I understand what they've been telling me around here, you can't do it by yourself. You need the program. That's your lifeline. But that program won't be worth a shit to you if you play games with it. That's all that first step was, Snake. Games."

Lydia came out of her room, nodded at the pair, and headed toward the nurse's station. Snake wiped his nose with the back of his hand, shook his head, and looked toward the lounge. "I don't know what it is with you, man. You're a ugly little old fucker that creeps around here like you got one foot in the grave. You must be crazy talking to me like that. I wouldn't have to use more 'n a couple of fingers to break you in half. But you go right ahead and stick your act in my face like you got Bruce Lee in your hand."

An issue suddenly became very clear in Jake's mind. Tough love and what it's all about. Jake laughed. "I'll be damned."

"What?"

"Snake, you're about as likable as a constipated gorilla. But I like you."

"Say, what?"

Jake nodded. "Damned if I know why. Anyway, because I like you, I want to see you get better. Bullshitting you about that thing you wrote isn't going to help you get better." Jake glanced toward the lounge, then back at the biker. "Come on, I want you to listen to someone."

He took Snake by the arm and led him to the lounge where they stopped within earshot of pissed off Bob. Bob was reading his latest version of a first step out loud.

"The effects on my sex life were astounding. Not only could I now do it seventeen times in a row every night, but my dick grew three inches. But I gave up women altogether and resorted to my meat of choice. I was hooked on pork. I just hung around the barnyard, waiting for the farmer to get away from the pigs. As soon as the coast was clear, I'd grab two handfuls of sow and get to work. 'Oink! Oink! 0-o-o-h-h-h! Oiiiiiiink!!!'"

The listeners, except for Snake, laughed. Bob continued.

"But the disease progressed. I was really getting into dead pig. I moved to the city and began hanging out near the delivery entrances to supermarkets. Getting frostbite in meatlockers. I had to go to many different supermarkets so that the butchers wouldn't get suspicious."

Bob looked around like he was trying to make certain he wasn't being observed. Then he leaned to his left and talked out of the side of his mouth to an imaginary butcher. "Got any *rump* roast—"

Snake stood next to Bob and poked him in the chest. "What's your name?"

The man looked up at Snake, swallowed, and peeped out, "Bob."

"Y'know, Bob, you got a real shitty attitude."

In her darkened room, Candy jumped at the sound of the laughter from the lounge. She sat cross-legged on her bed. Reaching to her right, she picked up a cigarette from the pack on the nightstand, and lit it. Holding the lighter in her hand, she fondled the embossed design on its case. She closed her eyes.

Golden masks of comedy and tragedy. Don had given her the lighter that first Christmas after they were married. He knew she loved the theater. That night he had taken her to see a local stock production of *Pygmalion*. Take one dowdy girl, add one romantic superman, and ever after is filled with wonder and fantasy.

The dash, the romance, the elegant glory—

"With where I came from, how did I wind up with an old drudge schoolteacher?"

For the thousandth time she reran the horror of afternoon group in her mind. "Don and Ilene," she muttered, "they shouldn't have told those lies about me. Why did they lie like that? Why do they hate me so much that they'd lie like that?"

Unwanted memories hovered in the dark and her mental hands pushed them away.

—That story of Don's about the iron. It wasn't like that at all. He is really starved for attention. A school assistant principal with all of the romantic dash and flair—

She had a flash of memory. Don screaming at her: *"What do you expect of me, Candy? The Scarlet Pimpernel?* There aren't any more French aristocrats to rescue from the guillotine! To be perfectly frank about it, if I had lived back then, I'd be in the business of sharpening guillotine blades. Don't you know anything about the history of the French aristocracy—"

"There goes the professor, again. Gee, you must know everything."

"You don't live in the real world, Candy."

"Why should I? I want a man. I certainly can't find one here."

Don shook his head, that look in his eyes: Crushed. Candy didn't feel victorious. Instead she felt utterly defeated. He turned and began to walk away. *Candy reached for the antique crystal vase, clasped her hands around the base—*

"I didn't do that," she whispered. "I just didn't do that." She looked into the shadows above her head. Dark, ominous things hung in the darkness. "I'm stronger than you." She felt a painful stab in her chest as tears came running down her cheeks. "Shit. In another two months…I'll be *fifty!*"

She looked at the crack of light beneath her door. "I can't sit in here." She uncrossed her legs, pulled herself off the bed, and placed her attention in a safe place. "Poor D.T.," she whispered. "After the working over he went through this afternoon, he probably feels like he hasn't a friend in the world. I'll see if I can help."

Instantly her head was filled with other people's troubles, leaving no room for her own. Her heart went out to all who suffered. The noise from outside drowned out the noise from inside. She opened her door and turned on the lights before leaving her room.

JANUARY 4TH

34

Nate Koeber thought he was at a hospital somewhere. He heard a voice, but couldn't attach the voice to a talking face.

"There's nothing more we can do. Clear him out. We need the space."

—Nothing more, nothing more, he says. Needs the space, he says. Where is he? Who is he talking to? I'd know better if I opened my eyes, but they won't work. The hinges on my eyelids are stuck.

Nate lifted his arms and swam through the sweet, dark syrup, grabbing handfuls, reaching for the surface, getting discouraged, giving up.

—Fuck it. I can't see anyway.

"How old is he?"

—How old is who?

"Looks around twenty."

Nate laughed, he howled, he screamed, he could hear nothing from himself. There were wheels rolling. A thump of something.

"Hey, Harry?"

"What?"

"You want to take this fried meat down to the icebox? I have to find Harper. We're short-handed as hell."

"What's going on in there?"

"Bus accident. Things are getting crowded and Bennet wants the floor cleared. Drop this one off and hurry back. I gotta get going."

"Sure. Good luck with Harper."

"Yeah."

—Meat? Hey, man, what are you talking about? Meat?

More wheels rolling, doors thumping, the floor falling away beneath him. Nate made another grab at the syrup.

—It's wrong. Something is wrong.

More rolling, another door thumped. He felt himself stop moving.

"Where do you want it?"

"Over there with the other two stiffs."

"Emergency is up to its ass with that bus accident. I'll probably be back with more meat before too long."

Footsteps. Silence. Papers rattling. A phone conversation just out of hearing. Silence. Walking. More silence.

"Fucking Junky."

A chill, then Nate felt a pain in his right big toe.

—Hey, leave my toe alone!

The pain in his toe didn't stop. There was something on it. More footsteps, more silence. Nate tried to open his eyelids. It was like they were glued shut. His left eye opened but there was nothing but a dim blur of white. He pulled up a hand, but couldn't feel anything with it. The hand flopped against his face and pulled the white from his eye. There was a ceiling. The ceiling was white, a large green enameled operating lamp fixture over to the left. The lighting was dim.

Nate closed the eye as the room began spinning. The room slowed and stopped. He turned his head to the right and opened his left eye. There was a still, sheet-covered figure next to him. The sheet covered the figure from head almost to toe. The toe had a tag wired to it. Beyond that one there was another. Nate lifted his head and looked down. His feet were not covered. His right big toe had a tag wired to it.

His head dropped back from exhaustion. "Oh, shit," he said to his two companions. "Not again."

A man's face, mouth open and eyes wide, moved into Nate's field of vision. Nate forced out the words. "Hi. I think I might have a problem with drugs. Could you call somebody?"

The man's face went away as the walls of the morgue appeared to melt revealing the heart of hell. Before it melted, the clock on the wall had said seven minutes after one in the morning. He refused to look, but Nate was certain that the other two bodies in the room were moving.

—I wonder if I'm overreacting about a drug problem.

2:36 a.m.

Jake put down his watch, rolled over in his bed, punched at his pillows, and put his head down. Frank's bed was still empty. Jake still had the aches and sweats. "Christ, when does this stuff let up?"

Give it time. He remembered some of the old A.A. farts in the lounge. Give it time. Not so old junkies from Narcotics Anonymous in the lounge. Give it time.

—The program's nothing but a bunch of threadbare clichés. Easy does it. Easy does what? Let go and let God. *Is* anybody else up there? First things first. Nuts. Have to do laundry tomorrow. I've already sweated through everything.

He smiled, then chuckled. Gary in Bill's group was madder than hell. His wife wouldn't do his laundry. In the lounge he had been ranting, "Dammit, I paid for the washer, didn't I? But, no-o-o-o-o-o. Unit discipline. All you fish're supposed to do your own laundry, make your own beds. I paid for the washer, didn't I?"

Jake rolled over on his back, rubbed his eyes, and looked at the reflections of the lights on the ceiling. "Why am I here?" he said out loud. As always, the ceiling's answer was inscrutable. Jake sat up, put on his bathrobe and collected his smoking, coffee drinking, and first step recording gear.

First he went to the kitchen to fill up on Bill's Brew, then to the north wing lounge. Frank was sprawled out in the love seat reading the pages of his steno pad. Balls of light green paper covered the top of the coffee table. He looked up as Jake entered. "Nighthawking?"

"Yeah."

Jake sat in the couch and fired up his pipe. He pointed at the trash on the coffee table. "Doing some editing?"

Frank smiled. "Yeah. Seeing Candy and D.T. today made me want to revise a few things. My first version…I guess it wasn't very honest."

"How so?"

"Things I left out. Other things that I minimized." His eyebrows went up. "A few things I plain lied about. Like this section on sexuality and sex life." He shook his head. "From reading my first version you'd think using caused me to impregnate half the women on the planet, that I was having one hell of a good time. The truth is that I was—" Frank sat up, lit a cigarette, and removed it from his mouth. "I was scared— terrified—to make love unless I'd been drinking. Do you know what I'm saying?"

Jake pursed his lips. "Yeah. I had the same thing. Couldn't make love unless I was drunk, and once I was drunk I couldn't do anything about it except grunt, sweat, and pass out." He frowned.

"Jake? What is it?"

"I was just thinking. My wife. Christ, what a pig I must have been to live with. I hardly ever showered, came reeling into the bedroom with a couple of extra beers, smelling like the south end of a horse going north, bitching at her because she didn't turn me on." He puffed on his pipe, then looked at Frank. "I'm sorry. You were saying something."

"You already said it." Frank laughed. "Funny, isn't it? It was easy for me to be honest about all of the insane things I've done. But when it came to a thing like keeping clean, I left it out." He took a drag from his cigarette and leaned back in the love seat. "My ex wife's name is Mary. She called me around ten to tell me that she's going to show for family week."

"Do you detect Angela's dainty finger in this?"

Frank nodded. "As much as I hate to say so, I'm glad she's coming."

"Thinking of getting back together?"

"No. Nothing like that."

"How do you feel about that—to coin a phrase."

"Happy—no—grateful that we can both help each other. But scared. That fishbowl scares me. We ought to call it the meat grinder. Have you seen Candy or D.T. tonight?"

"D.T. was in the lounge for a little while. He doesn't look like he's holding up very well." Jake frowned. "Then again it looks like Candy is holding up just fine, and getting no good out of it at all."

Frank looked at his watch. "Hey, Jake, you better get some sleep. The station blasts out the door knockers at six thirty."

"In a bit."

Frank stood up, gave a mighty stretch, then shook himself before picking up his things. "I think I'll give it a try." He gathered up his waste paper, tossed it into the trash can, and waved as he rounded the corner into the room.

Ignoring his pad and first step outline, Jake sipped at his coffee. He looked around at the walls of the lounge.

—This is an interesting place. Sort of like a combination of A.A., boot camp, Oz, and Hell. If I was a writer, I think I'd write a book about it.

"Funny thing you should mention that," he said to the empty room.

He opened his pad, looked at the first step outline, then snapped it shut as he closed his eyes.

　—I haven't written anything new for almost a year. I can't. I just can't write anymore.

　—Let it go, first things first, easy does it, one day at a time. After all, tomorrow is another day.

　Jake put his feet up on the coffee table and closed his eyes. "The days sure start early around here."

35

Trapped in the mirror, pounding on the glass, no one noticing. Behind him, in the dark, were the sounds of claws scraping against a hard surface. He screamed and—

"Jake?"

Jake opened his eyes wide, looked over at Frank—still asleep—then up at the ceiling. He called for the voice. "Yes?"

"Jake, it's time to get up."

He looked to his right. It was the intercom mounted in his nightstand.

—One more spiritual awakening down the crapper.

"Thanks." He looked at his watch. 6:30 a.m.. He slipped it on his wrist and sat up. His sinuses felt like they were smuggling golf balls.

He fired up his pipe, grabbed his cup, and stumbled to the wing's coffee dispenser. He cut the coffee with some of the milk left there the night before. Still in the coffee closet, he sipped his coffee. Again. He finished it and got another cup.

Back in his room he sat on his bed smoking his pipe, fear stalking the hallways. This was his first morning as wing door knocker. Wake everybody up. It's no problem, unless you happen to be paranoid, terrified of people, a people pleaser, terrified of not having everyone in the world love you.

He went and got another cup of coffee, smoked another pipe, then Jake found himself standing near the nurse's station next to the light switches. Perry, the little creep with the attempted blond beard, was wearing the original shit-eating grin.

Jake leaned on the counter. "Perry, did you suggest to Ron that he nominate and railroad me for the door knocker job?"

"Not me."

"Maybe I'm just seeing conspiracies around every corner." Jake nodded and rubbed his beard as he leaned on the counter. "You know Snake Dooley?"

"Yeah. On the fourth floor."

"Snake's working for me now. Did you know that? I hope your family is well. Do your bones knit quickly?"

"Are you...are you threatening me?"

Jake stood up. "And they call me paranoid."

"You were joking, weren't you?"

"Man, I've been in your wallet. I know where you live."

After a look, Perry returned to the magazine he had been reading. His diversion regrettably exhausted, Jake faced the empty hallway.

—Do it. Just do it. You're supposed to wake them up. That's your job! Do it!

He reached out his left hand and flicked on the lights for the hall. He blinked against the brightness, then walked to the first door. The handwritten tag in the ID plate on the left doorjamb identified the room's occupant as Ron Steward. The garishly drawn pair of wings on the poster taped to the door ID'd the room's occupant as wing leader.

—Do it.

Jake closed his eyes, took a deep breath, swung back, hesitated, then beat the door as hard as he could three times in quick succession with the side of his fist and the front of his forearm, the SWAT Team Special. He screamed, "Police! Police! Police!" He beat the door twice more, then moved on, feeling better, alternating his wake up calls between "Police!" and *"R-r-r-raus! Raus!* R-r-r-roll call in fife minutez! *R-r-r-r-raus!"*

Sergeant Schultz would have been proud.

Morning vitals in the wing lounge.

"How are you feeling this morning, Jake?"

"Fine and dandy."

"Ron said that he had one arm in his bathrobe and one leg out the window before he woke up."

"A guy could get hurt that way.

"Maybe you should wake up the wing with a trifle less zeal."

"A job worth doing is worth doing well."

"Did you really threaten Perry with a hit man?"

"A snitch in crime craves slime."

"What's with all of these terribly original lines?"

"We're all in this shit together."

"Jake, you are still a seriously disturbed person."

"I'm working to get turbed."

36

Morning lecture on denial. Q&A time, compliments of Neil, spooker on the God Squad. Dave folded his arms. He had heard this one back in his first week.

Neil pointed. "The fellow in the front, here, has stated that the denial of the disease being a symptom is a Catch-22. If you admit to the disease, you have it. If you say you don't have it, you have it. But what if you don't have it? What does the non-alcoholic or non-addict say when confronted with the possibility he might be addicted to a chemical? Does anybody know?" Eyebrows up, Neil did a visual of the frys.

"Anybody?"

He laughed. "I guess the lack of an answer is due to the scarcity of non-addicts in the hall." Neil pointed at Dave. "You." Dave pointed at himself. "That's right. You. Let's say I'm a doctor. I've just finished examining you, and I give you my professional opinion. 'Sir, I think you might have a terminal form of cancer.' How would you respond?"

"Do you mean after crying, screaming, running around in circles, waving my arms, and cleaning the crap out of my drawers?"

Laughter.

"Right."

Dave shrugged. "I suppose I'd want to be certain. I'd tell him to do whatever tests that were necessary. Maybe get a second opinion. I'd want to know the truth."

"Why didn't you just say, 'Hey, Doc, I can't have cancer.'"

Dave shook his head. "That wouldn't make any sense. I mean, how would I know? If I had the problem, I'd want to know it so I could do what I could to fight it."

Neil nodded. "Do you remember what you said to the first person who said you might have a drinking problem?"

Dave thought back. Was it the company doctor back at the plant? No, it was that teacher back in high school. Yes, he remembered. "Yes. I said I couldn't be an alcoholic."

Neil looked up. "That's one of the basic evaluation tests, folks. How a person responds to the proposition that he might be an alcoholic or a drug addict. If he answers, 'Hey, let's check this out!' then he probably isn't an alky. If he responds 'Yeah, I'm an alcoholic,' then he probably is an alky. If he says 'I can't be,' then he almost certainly is.

"The really amazing part of this symptom is that it works the same way with the family members. When you get out of here, you will see friends and family who you are pretty certain have one end of the bug or the other. To that woman you know whose mother had a 'legitimate' illness, and therefore had good reason to take all those prescription drugs, and who walks and talks like one heavy with bug, try suggesting that she might want to try Al-Anon.

"If she replies 'Maybe I should,' well, maybe she should. She probably is carrying her end of the bug and has gotten to the point of hurting enough to do something about it.

"If she says, 'Hey, I'll check it out. If I have a problem, I want to know as much as I can about it so I can find out what I can do about it,' she might not have the bug. There are a lot of miseries in the world, and not all of them are related to mood-altering drugs. A willingness of the sufferer to examine his or her problem honestly is not normally characteristic of alcoholics, drug addicts, or affected family members.

"Of course, if she says 'I can't have a problem,' and then runs off at the mouth with the usual excuses for herself and the old lady's pills, you can be fairly certain that she does have the bug. Once you have this hot item of information, what can you do with it? Does anyone know?"

From the back, "Polish it up and stick it on the mantelpiece." The voice sounded bitter. "You can't do anything else with it."

Neil stared toward the back. "Ah, the voice of experience. What's the set up?"

"My parents were bugged. They're dead now. The landscape is littered with co-dependents. My two sisters, my brother, two sets of grandparents. None of them think they have a problem. In fact only me and one of my sisters is even willing to consider that our parents had a problem. But I can't get any of them to go to Al-Anon. Hell, I can't even get my wife to go."

Neil rubbed his chin, then leaned his elbows on the lectern. "In other words, you can't control another person." He smiled and looked down. "But there's something else you can do with your information instead of putting it on your mantelpiece. Let it go. It would be better to just consign them to the care of your higher power and let it go. That glare from the mantelpiece has sent a lot of good men and women back to their chemicals."

There was a long pause. The length of the silence made Dave uncomfortable before Neil resumed talking. His voice sounded different. "Those of you who have had some A.A. or N.A. time know—and most of the rest of you are going to find out—that the saddest stories you will ever hear in the program are the guys and gals who have been sober for three or five years, the spouse or the parents never made it to

Al-Anon, and it's gotten to the point where the recovering alcoholic needs a healthier relationship. What's the drunk or junky going to do? In a marriage, here's a spouse who hung in there through all of those years of drinking and drugging. Now that things are starting to get better, does the recovering partner just walk out? But if he stays in the middle of that sickness, eventually he'll go back to the potions and powders. He tries and tries to get her to go to Al-Anon, to get with the program, but she won't go. There are always a thousand excuses—"

Neil took a deep breath. His face became flushed. When he continued his voice was very quiet. "I'm not leveling with you people. This is a decision I have to make, myself." He looked over the audience. "A decision I have to make about myself and my wife. The only one I can change is myself; the only one I have any control over at all is myself. You see, you can't work on a relationship. When you do that, you're trying to change someone else. The only one I can change is me. It's not an easy decision." Two beats of silence. "But then if being sober was easy, everybody would be doing it. Thanks for listening."

Applause.

At the morning break in the north wing lounge, Neil's talk was the subject. Sympathy and self-pity was the mood. Everyone wandered off leaving Dave alone with his own thoughts.

Dave could think of a few persons with the bug, one end or the other. All of the men and women, all of the kids he knew. Every one of his and Kelly's relatives. The bug was there in force. He cared about the ones he knew. He had some answers. But what could he do with his answers? What could he do about the people he knew? His friends? The ones in his family? They would be just as willing to listen to him as he had been willing to listen when using: not at all. There was nothing he could do about them. "That sucks."

A young woman entered the lounge. Her face was bright red. She sat in the couch facing Dave. She looked like she was about to burst.

"Hi. I'm Dave."

"Hi." She looked around the tiny lounge, almost checking under the chairs for eavesdroppers. "Name's Vicky. I'm here for my dad's family week. Do you know Jeff?"

"In Bill's group?"

"Yes."

"Sure, I know Jeff. How was yesterday? You holding up okay?"

Vicky shook her head. "Yesterday was a zoo, but today is getting so weird. God, I'm so embarrassed."

"Why?"

"Do you know who I saw here as a patient? I recognized him out there in the hallway. Jacob Randecker."

"Uh huh."

"Jacob *Randecker,*" she repeated.

"What's your point?"

"You probably don't read science fiction, but I've read all his books. He's a writer."

"I figured."

"I'm so embarrassed. Don't you see?"

Dave grinned. "Why?"

"I mean, to see him here. I mean, I saw him going here as a *patient.* I could just die."

Dave felt a burn beginning beneath his collar. "He's here to get better. If it's good enough for me and your old man, why not for Jake?"

"Do you know him?"

"Yeah. He's in my group."

"Aren't you embarrassed? I mean, to know that he's an *addict?*"

"It's not like you caught him raping a baby seal—"

The cowbells pealed, calling the faithful once more to morning group. Vicky shook her head. "I guess you just don't see."

Dave nodded, his eyes wild. He stood and moved in the direction of Angela's office, his lips silently muttering, "God *damn*, grant me the serenity to accept the things I cannot change!"

37

Jake dropped into his chair for morning group. Dave sat next to him. "I met one of your fans out in the lounge."

"A reader? No kidding?"

"Yeah. It was a real learning experience. What kind of crap do you write?"

Jake noticed Angela's look of rapidly-diminishing patience, and he shut up. Ron did the reading, and Frank contracted for his first step.

There was a youngish stranger in the circle. He wore slacks and a shaggy sweater, and introduced himself as Martin Timberlake, alcoholic, class of October, back for his first return visit. Frank opened his steno book. Angela leaned toward him. "Before you begin with your first step, Frank, I'd like Martin to tell us how the past three months have been."

Frank nodded.

Martin looked very nervous. He grinned quickly and pushed the hair out of his eyes. "Okay. Well, it was a mix. Physically I feel good. Most of the days have been pretty good. I've been doing a lot of meetings, A.A. and N.A. both. But some of those days are bastards. When I went through here, I couldn't imagine ever taking another drink. But I'm getting better and better at letting myself feel things. One of the things I'm letting myself feel is…there isn't any other way to put it. I want to drink. I swear, sometimes I'll be driving past a liquor store, and a chorus of bottles starts calling my name. Once I was in a grocery store shopping with my wife. I felt a little tug on my trouser leg. I looked down, expecting to find a kid who had lost his mother. Instead there was a stack of six-packs."

Laughter.

Angela raised her eyebrows. "Martin, are you an alcoholic?"

He nodded. "Right now I am. But over the past three months I must have talked myself out of it five or six times. I haven't had any slips, but closer you wouldn't want to get. It really gets me in restaurants. Go into a nice place for a quiet, relaxing meal, and the very first question the waiter asks is, 'Would you like to commit suicide before dinner?' The damned part of it is sometimes I want to say yes!"

Dave snorted. "You're playing games with your head."

"True." Martin nodded. "Just be prepared for the same game when you get out. All of the players are still there."

Brandy leaned forward. "Martin, do you have a sponsor?"

"Yes." Martin gave a sheepish smile. "Well, I have this guy who agreed to be my sponsor, but I don't call him much."

Angela arched an eyebrow. "A sponsor you don't use is what?"

The return visitor folded his arms. "A sponsor you don't use is no sponsor at all."

Jake held out a hand. "Excuse me, what's a sponsor?"

Angela looked around the circle. "Anybody." Her group scan halted on Martin.

The visitor shrugged. "Okay. It's someone in the program who has a good deal of sobriety who can show you the ropes, help you on the Steps, and lend you an ear between meetings. I guess if I had used mine

I wouldn't be as uptight as I am right now."

Jake frowned and scratched his beard. "Do you have to have a sponsor to be in the program?"

"No." Martin grinned. "There are no musts in the program, just suggestions. Like the word 'Pull' on a parachute's D-ring. You don't have to do it, it's only a suggestion, but if you don't pull it you better come up with another answer fast."

There was some more discussion on white-knuckle serenity, Martin made a contract to get a sponsor that he would use, and then Angela's attention drifted to Frank.

Frank again put in his bid for a first step. The bid was accepted, and the subcontractors were briefed. Jake listened as Angela looked around the group. "While you're listening to Frank give his first step, listen for the progression—the stages—of the disease. Watch for words that minimize either the chemical usage or its effects, such as I *only* had five drinks, or the car accident *only* crippled three people; it wasn't *that* bad. Listen for the powerlessness over chemicals and the unmanageability of his life. The main question is this: is Frank honestly in touch with his past and what it was like?"

She nodded at Frank and Jake remembered what he had been told about an Animal's Step One. The Animals have a ritual that opens the performance of a first step. It is the flawless recital of the first of A.A.'s Twelve Steps from memory. On the surface this doesn't appear to be much of a task. It's short: "We admitted we were powerless over alcohol—that our lives had become unmanageable." But a first step is usually given in one's second week of treatment. By that time the patient has seen Angela rip up two or three other Animals who flubbed their line.

When Angela means flawless, she means not an emphasis out of place, no transpositions, no added or deleted words, no mispronunciations, and loud enough for the entire first floor staff to hear. And she wants to "hear" that long dash. There is a story handed down over the

years from Animal to Animal that it took one fellow who had a heavy
New England accent four years to get to his first step in Angela's group.
The ghost of former-Animal Sam the Stutterer is rumored to be stalking
the halls of Saint Mary's still issuing his mournful cry: "Wuh-wuh-wuh."

Animals preparing to do a first step can be seen silently mouthing
the words in lectures, in the chow line, in the bathroom, in the showers,
in their sleep. Of course, as soon as the patient's turn comes in group, his
mind goes totally blank.

It is considered something between false bravado and suicide for a
patient to give his first step within view of Angela's Twelve Steps poster.
Angela will leap square in the middle of your chest in a second if you try
and read the big first out loud. But the temptation to look can be over-
whelming. Minds have been bent trying to keep one eye fixed on Angela
while the other surreptitiously scans the poster. The resulting conflict
could make William F. Buckley, Jr. lisp.

Jake noted that Frank sat with his back to the poster. He cleared his
throat and began. "We admitted we were powerless over alcohol—that
our lives had become unmanageable."

There was silence. But they don't applaud in church, either.

"I took my first drink when I was fourteen. My father and mother
both were heavy drinkers, and there was always alcohol in the house. My
mother said all the alcohol was for entertaining guests, but we didn't
entertain much.

"At first I would sneak an ounce of whisky in a Coke just to see what
it was like. I would do this four to six times on weekends. In high school
I began to score pot and immediately went to three and four joints a
day, every day, in addition to weekend drinking. Every weekend during
high school I would drink between one and two six-packs of beer, in
addition to whatever I could steal from my father's liquor cabinet.

"Near the end of my junior year, my high school counselor confronted
me with my drinking, and I stopped. I continued smoking lots of dope…"

The story progressed, along with the use and the disease. Frank paused, turned a page, glanced at Angela, then looked back at his steno pad. "Because of something I did when I was twelve, I always kept tight control over my anger, but in the Army—"

"Just a moment, Frank." Angela leaned her chin on her right hand and looked at him. "What happened when you were twelve?"

"It was before I began drinking."

"What did you do?"

Frank closed his eyes, bit his lower lip, and sat silently. "I wasn't drinking then, Angela."

"Frank, do you know what we mean when we say 'alcoholic system.'"

"Yes. It's the effects—dynamics—between a number of related persons. Like a family."

"You said your parents—

"I didn't say they were alcoholics."

"Neither did I. Just think about it tonight. Agreed?"

Frank nodded. "Okay."

"Now, what happened when you were twelve?"

"I blinded a ten year-old boy."

"How?"

"I beat him with my fists."

"Why?"

Frank glared daggers at Angela, then closed his eyes. "He called me a nigger."

Angela nodded. "What happened when you were in the Army?"

"I got in a fight with my first sergeant and did three months stockade time. He made some crack about me. It wasn't racial. He didn't call me anything he didn't call everybody else in the company. I broke his jaw and put him in the hospital."

"Had you been drinking?"

He nodded. "Yes."

"Go on."

Frank looked at his notes. Jake saw that Frank's hands were trembling. He looked as though he were about to tip over into the abyss. "When I was discharged, I went to college to get my teaching certificate. In college I was drinking to the point of getting drunk and passing out every day. Two to three pints of whiskey every day…"

After college, the first of several teaching jobs. Frank flipped a page. "I was drinking and smoking dope every day and at work, averaging almost a fifth of scotch a day and at least ten joints. More, probably. I wasn't keeping count." He slowly shook his head. "I couldn't keep count." He paused as he mentally pulled up to the next category. "My preoccupation with chemicals began early. When I was fifteen I was constantly thinking about the weekends, looking forward to my first drink. Besides stealing from my father, I began hiding…"

Trying to quit in college. Failing. Trying to control the amount. Failing. As a teacher, trying to restrict use to weekends. Failing. Taking the geographical cure, moving from one school district to the next, moving from one state to the next. Trying to run away from the problems that were causing him to drink, not realizing that each time he would bring the problem—addiction—with him to the new location.

Effects on physical health. Frank was lucky. Only several bruises and broken bones. No liver damage. The degree of brain damage an unknown.

Sexuality and sex life. No longer a man. Instead, a terrified child, the act of love becoming a test, a judgment that he could only fail. The scenes in the bedroom became battles over the issue of who was to blame for their lack of affection, lack of love, the fights removing any excuse for either. He would stay up late at night, drinking, waiting for Mary to go to sleep so that he wouldn't have to face either fighting or loving. One day Mary was gone.

Feelings.

Jake watched as Frank's face underwent a radical change. His face became soft, vulnerable. "Whenever I was drunk, the only feeling I had was anger. When I wasn't drinking, it would be self-pity, shame, fear, more anger. I resented everything and everyone. I hated being resentful. I resented being resentful. I would drink and smoke dope to numb out the feelings. I preferred anger. Anger at least made me feel strong." He moistened his lips, his eyes looking blankly at the floor. "Then it was nothing but anger. Drinking or not. If I felt anything, it was anger. I would drink to hide from it." Another page.

Effects on social life and friends. Friends who didn't use or use to excess were no longer friends. But there were new friends. Dealers, bartenders, street warriors, junkies, the Leary generation. He cultivated white liberals who could ease their guilt to black America by giving drugs to Frank.

Spiritual life. God had singled out Frank Kimbal to withstand pain and degradation of a type and degree that went far beyond Job's little difficulties. God hated Frank, and Frank returned the sentiment.

Work and finances. Fired, asked to resign, quit. The kids knew he wasn't delivering his best, or even an adequate performance. He couldn't face them. The total of everything, chemicals, hospitalizations, lost worktime, loss of productivity, damages for accidents, court costs, treatment....

"Almost two-hundred thousand dollars."

Thirty values and how he had compromised them through chemistry. Honesty, responsibility, love, keeping promises, caring for children, citizenship. He lied, he stole, he cheated, he weaseled, he hated, he couldn't be relied upon to do anything but drink and smoke. In those times when he was employed, he no longer taught his classes—he terrorized them. The law was a laugh. He turned to the next page.

Insane behavior/destructive behavior against oneself or others. A driver cut in front of him in traffic. He became so enraged that he speeded up his car and rammed the car in front repeatedly until the driver lost control and ran off the road. A window in his living room was stuck. Frank freaked out and opened it with the television set. A waiter in a restaurant cocked an eyebrow at the wrong moment, Frank took offense and beat the man senseless….

Specific examples of things Frank did to hurt family members as a result of better living through chemistry. Embarrassments at parties, forcing his wife to lie, degrading her in her own eyes, hitting her, breaking her arm…

When he was finished, Frank closed his steno pad and leaned forward, his elbows on his knees. His eyes were closed and his head was slowly shaking.

Angela, her hands on the armrests of her chair, studied Frank. "What are you feeling right now?"

"Sad," he whispered. "Guilty, ashamed, betrayed. Hurt." Again he shook his head. "I've hurt a lot of people. I've been hurt, too. Hurt bad."

Angela motioned to D.T. to vacate the chair to Frank's left. D.T. stood and Angela took his chair, putting her arm around Frank's shoulders. D.T. slowly lowered himself into Angela's chair, looking somewhat uncomfortable.

Angela talked to Frank, her voice low, inaudible. Frank responded, his words thick. Then he cried. Angela patted his shoulder and rocked the huge man back and forth, holding open the gate for the tears, the pain. Like some parent had neglected to do twenty-five years before.

Jake remembered the hate in Frank's voice the morning before. The hate for Angela. But it wasn't hate for the woman, or her color. It was hate for the pain dammed up inside his heart. The pain flowed.

With Jake's new understanding came a new confusion. He was crying and couldn't imagine why. Angela looked around the group, beginning with Jake.

"Feedback?"

Jake hit the groupwad, blew his nose, leaned forward, looked at

Frank, and half-opened his mouth—

"Jacob Randecker, come to the nurse's station," blasted the intercom.

"What?" Jake looked at Angela. She nodded back and Jake stood and left the room.

At the nurse's station he and another patient were told to wait for an escort to the main hospital to get a chest x-ray and an EKG. Jake leaned against the counter, fuming.

—They could time these little outside events somewhat better.

Two things struggled into his awareness. First, what was going on back in group had become very important to him. Second, he was madder than hell.

38

Lunch at the Constipated Eagle.

From across the table, Roger watched Frank laugh and joke. The general consensus of the group's feedback had been that Frank had done a good job on his first step. He was in touch with his past and what it had been like. Angela had agreed. Frank was laughing. The reward for picking up the shit, sniffing it, and throwing it away for good. What had Martin, the return visitor, said in the lounge before lunch?

"You have to pick it up before you can let it go."

Roger had leaned forward, his gaze on Martin, his hands clasped together. "I have a hard time—an impossible time—letting go. Things keep coming back again and again, no matter how hard I try and keep them down."

"Roger, to me you sound as though you're stuffing, not letting go. If you stuff it, it keeps coming back because it never left in the first place. When you stuff it, you save it so you can feed on the misery forever."

Roger shook his head. "How can you tell the difference between stuffing and letting go?"

"For me I can tell by the amount of time it takes me. Stuffing is almost automatic. A bad feeling comes up and almost immediately I don't feel it. I put it down. Things I let go of take more time. I have to let myself feel whatever it is. I have to experience the anger, sadness, resentment, or pain, and realize that that's where I am right then."

Dave joined in. "Some of those bad things are more comfortable than an old shoe. Some resentments I have, they're awfully tough to put to rest."

Martin had laughed. "Everything I've ever let go of always had claw marks all over it."

Roger glanced at D.T. The surgeon was alternating between picking at his food and examining the chow line. There hadn't been any word yet on Mack's evaluation. Roger guessed that D.T. was in touch. He was listening to his family. It would be obvious to a steel post that D.T. was paying in catastrophic pain for each word of the information.

It's hard to believe, thought Roger, that in the long run stuffing hurts more than dealing with the pain. He looked at Candy. She was not looking for her husband and daughter. Her vision did not extend beyond the borders of her tray. The gay laughter of the day before had been replaced by brittle silence. Candy looked like she was about to snap.

The salt shaker was in front of Candy. Roger's ratloaf needed salt. "Candy?"

The woman started as though she had been jabbed in the back with a pitchfork. She swallowed and looked at Roger. Her face was frozen, but there was a double feature nightmare going on behind her eyes. "What?"

"Could I have the salt, please?" She turned her head, located the salt, and mechanically reached out, lifted it and transported it to Roger's hand. "Thank you."

Candy returned her concentration to her tray. Roger began salting his ratloaf. Candy was paying too, but for not getting in touch. With the same currency: pain.

—What did this morning's flogging bring back to me? What will I have to go through to get in touch? In touch with what? What dark horrors are lurking back there, pressing to escape into the sunlight?

—That nightmare of a morning at the seminary.

It had started with a toast at the faculty reception. The next thing he knew he was back in his room, sick. There was an empty bottle of Beefeater's on the nightstand, a pair of red panties hanging from the knob on the nightstand drawer. Roger had sat up, the pain in his head nothing next to the one in his soul.

"Dear God, what did I do?" Feelings of filth, unworthiness, horror pulled at him, threatening to drag him down into the slime.

He looked to his right. The bed was empty, but he saw tiny red spots on the sheet. A bullwhip was coiled around the bed's cornerpost. His heart—

Roger pulled his hand away from his chest and looked down. "Oh! Oh, no!" He was wearing a bright red brassiere. He ripped the thing from him and threw it across the room. Holding the covers to his face, he prayed. "God, oh my God—"

There had been snickers, then laughter. The door to his room burst open to expose four of his classmates, hardly able to contain themselves they were laughing so hard. Still holding the covers, Roger looked again at the room. It was his dormitory room. The bullwhip belonged to Allen. Who knows whose sister was going to come up short in the undergarment department. The spots on the sheet were red ink. The gin bottle was his.

"Mercy, Roger, you should see the look on your face!"

—A joke. It was a joke.

Roger had grinned and laughed. It would never do to break them in half and be accused of being a bad sport. Behind the grin and laughter was a strange feeling. It was satisfying, but too horrible to put into thoughts, much less words. Roger had been in combat in Korea, and had killed more than his quota.

—That thing that happened at the water hole—

But looking at his friends laughing, his own laughter mixing with theirs, for the second time in his life he wanted to kill. To murder. To litter the campus with corpses. To take every possible translation of the First Commandment and break it over his friends' bloody bodies….

The remainder of his drinking at the seminary had taken place behind locked doors.

He sighed and looked around at his group. That thing that had happened in Korea. No one could understand that. No one. Roger couldn't understand it himself, and he had been there.

—Better to just leave it be.

The most recent interview with Michelle bothered Roger. He didn't seem to have any answers for anything. Great stretches out of his childhood were totally blank. The blankness was interrupted by flashes of crying and screaming scenes, Korea….

He shook his head. There was nothing about the past worth remembering.

"What's with you and the girl, Ron?" Lydia's voice. Roger looked to his right. Ron was shrugging, his face slightly red.

"I like her."

Lydia, seated across the table from Ron, nodded and smiled. "I bet."

"What's that supposed to mean?"

"That means that I am willing to wager sound currency upon the proposition that you like the fair Paula. It also means that I think it just might be a little more than that."

"What if it is?"

"If you keep fooling around on the unit, you make it my business, as well as everyone else's in the group. You've been here long enough to know why."

Ron picked up his tray, stood, and moved to another table. As Roger turned back to his meal, he saw Mack Pennoyer approach the table. The boy nodded at D.T. and stopped next to him.

D.T. looked up. "How did the evaluation go?"

Mack bit the inside of his lower lip and nodded. "I'm coming in for treatment." He touched his father's shoulder briefly with his hand. "Just wanted to let you know."

A brief exchange of glances. He turned and went to the chow line. D.T. returned to his lunch, his tears confirming the smile on his face. Roger shook his head and pushed back his chair. As he carried his tray to the window, his own tears were just below the surface. Afternoon group would be a ball-buster.

"God," he muttered, "I can't take any more of this. I am weary of life in the middle of a soap opera."

But, as with most soap fans, Roger found himself being perversely drawn to the next episode. Will Mack the firstborn reconcile with John the contrite? Will Mitzi the martyr reach through her life of chaos and find love and happiness? Will Bobby the silent find his tongue and rip off D.T.'s head? Will the suffering Don and Ilene get fed up, smuggle a gun into group, and help Candy get in touch with a bit of reality? Stay tuned.

Roger disposed of his tray and dishes and headed for the elevators.

39

Back at the table, Candy had finished with her lunch. She sat back, lit a cigarette, and stared at the ceiling. She was remembering something. It had begun to gnaw on her while Frank was giving his first step. The memory. At lunch it had become slightly clearer. Katie Donovan, R.N. She had forgotten all about Katie. *They had been at Mario's having lunch.*

"You look terrible, Candy."

"I'm a little uptight. Sitting around the house polishing the washer is wearing thin."

"Why don't you come back to work? It'd be great having you back on the floor."

Candy nodded. "That might be just what I need." She thought a moment. "Yes. I'll talk to Don about it—" She laughed.

"What's funny?"

"I've been turning my crank all week. I'll have to check and see if Don and I are still speaking."

Katie reached to her purse, there was a click, then she extended her hand across the table. "Here."

Candy took the offering. When she looked into her hand there was a yellow tablet. "Valium?"

"Go ahead, I've got more. You need to calm down if you want to talk to Don about going back to work."

"I shouldn't."

"One won't hurt you. Just don't make a habit of it."

Candy rested her chin on the heel of her hand, her eyes closed, her cigarette burning unattended between her fingers. "Katie Donovan, you stupid asshole." She quickly looked around to see if anyone had heard her. No one was paying any attention.

Angela had suggested to Candy that she read a book. *Why Am I Afraid To Tell You Who I Am?* by Johnny Powell, Society of Goddamned Jesus. She had only read the first page. On that page was the answer to the book's question. "I am afraid to tell you who I am, because, if I tell you who I am, you may not like who I am, and it's all that I have."

Candy shook her head as she whispered, "It's all that I have, Angela. It's all that I have."

At the elevator, two elderly ladies in wheelchairs were awaiting transportation to the fifth floor. The fifth floor has nothing to do with the rehab unit. No one really knows what goes on up there, except that the patients all seem to be ancient, helpless, and in wheelchairs. They were always separated from the rehab patients. On the unit, the fifth floor was known as the Boneyard.

As Jake came up to the elevator, he nodded at the two ladies. One looked away while the other grinned timidly and wrapped her thin arms around her purse. Snake and his gang came up behind the two wheelchairs as the elevator doors opened. "Hey, Jake!"

Jake paused as Snake handed him his steno pad. "Hang onto this a moment while we give these two girls a hand."

Jake pushed the door-open button in the elevator while Snake and a genuine eye-patched pirate wheeled in the passengers to the Boneyard, their eyes wide. The wheelchairs were placed in back, and Jake released the door-open button as the last of Snake's seven biker buddies got inside. Jake turned and the wheelchaired pair was buried beneath biker beads, chains, denim, leather, and swastikas.

Snake called out from the back of the elevator. "Take a look at the new version, Jake. I hacked out all that shit about arson and killing those people, like you said. I want you to look at that part under insane behavior though where they say I tried to kill those three cops."

Another biker snickered. "Shit, Snake wouldn't kill no cops. That ain't nice. He jes' wanted to rearrange their parts."

Dirty laughs. Another voice: "I kilt a cop once."

Another voice: "Aw, that wasn't a real cop. You was only messin' on a county space cadet. Snake did some Pennsylvania state fuzz."

"Naw, it was California. You kin tell by the eyeshades."

Another voice as the doors opened for the second floor. "Shit, dickhead, you never killed no cop. I heard you was sleepin' with him."

"Mothafuckah, how'd you like me to strop my razor on your dick—"

The doors closed and Snake called out. "Would you look at it again, Jake?"

"Okay. I'll give it another squint."

"Snake, man, who in the fuck is this Jake?"

"Little bearded shit over by the door."

"You?"

Jake nodded. "Me."

"What are you, man?"

"I'm a writer."

"Shit, you say."

"It's the truth."

The guy scratched at his armpit, then his chin. "Shit, man, you fuckin' know, if I was a fuckin' writer, I'd fuckin' write a book about this fuckin' place."

The doors opened on third floor and Jake ran.

Later that afternoon there was a memo posted reminding the patients on the unit that patients belonging on the fifth floor, if they are waiting next to the first floor elevator, are to be left alone. A staff escort is needed to wheel them around, although the generosity of the rehab patients in offering their help is noted.

It seems that the two ladies, paralyzed by the sights and sounds of Snake and his buddies, refused to speak to anyone or to call out. No one is really certain how long they spent, wide-eyed and silent, riding up and down in the elevator.

40

At the nurse's station, third floor, Jake noted that counselor Harry Nast, known on the unit as Nast Ass, was leaning on the counter talking to the nurse named Tess. Tess pointed at Jake, and Harry faced him. "Are you Jake Randecker?"

Jake pulled to a halt. Warily he responded, "Yes."

Harry was very tall, with a coal-black Lincoln beard and eyes to match. "So you're Snake's literary advisor. I expected someone about two feet taller and about two hundred pounds heavier." He rubbed at his beard. "What week are you in?"

"First. Are you Snake's counselor?"

"Yes."

"I suppose it's a living."

"I'm glad Snake's found someone who'll be honest with him, Jake. But don't forget why you're here. Okay?"

"Sure."

Harry patted Jake on the shoulder and moved off toward the stairwell. Tess smiled at Jake and went back to work. Angela came out of the hideout, nodded and smiled at Jake, and headed north to her office.

"Why do I feel as though I have been the subject of a recent conversation?" Jake asked himself. "Paranoia?"

—Paranoia, my ass.

In the corridor between the third floor kitchen and east wing, Earl Nelson held the receiver to his ear and listened as his home phone rang. Two rings, three rings. Jake passed him on his way to the kitchen and slapped him on his shoulder. Earl nodded back as the next ring was interrupted. Alice answered. "Hello?"

"It's me, Alice."

A brief moment of shocked silence. "Hi, Earl. How have you been doing?"

"I'm doing great. I've never learned so much important stuff in such a short time in my life. And I feel terrific. How have you been, honey?"

"Why did you call, Earl?"

"Have you changed your mind about coming to family week? You and Joey? It's so important—"

There was a silence, a click, and then a buzz. He hung up the receiver and stared at its gleaming black surface. "What's the point? What's the point to any of it?"

He turned, went into the east wing hallway, turned at the nurse's station, and headed north. Once in his room, he closed his door and leaned against it.

He held back on the tears until he thought he would split down the middle from the Mary blue. He sniffed and opened his door. "Shit, I don't have to carry this by myself anymore."

He went in search of another recovering alcoholic with an ear and a few minutes to spare. He needed to hear someone say the words: pain comes, but misery is optional; nothing, including pain, is forever; alcohol does not kill pain, it only postpones it; if you find yourself in the bottom of a hole, stop digging; it's okay to hurt; it's okay to cry.

"It's not just sex, is it?"

Ron Steward, feeling nervous about being in Paula's room with the door closed, looked down at her and shook his head. "No, it's not. I don't buy this substitution thing, that we're just replacing our chemical with a person. I think I'm honest enough with myself to know at least that."

Paula closed her eyes, rested her head against his chest, and held him tightly. "I'd kill myself if we couldn't be together. I'm afraid."

"There's nothing to be afraid of. We run our lives, not the damned rehab."

"What about the halfway house? I have to go."

He shook his head. "No. You don't have to do anything you don't want to. It's an individual program, right? That's what they tell us. Well, we need each other. Anything that interferes with that is wrong." He held her by her shoulders, thinking of that terribly empty feeling called loneliness. "Can you imagine what it would be like out there alone?"

They held each other tightly. "Tonight, Ron. Right after first room check, okay?"

"Okay.

Lydia sat in the north wing lounge, smoking, and re-reading a letter from Walt. Angela had called him, he wrote, and he didn't know who in the hell that woman thought she was, but he would be damned if he'd drop everything he was doing to come to family week.

You got yourself into this, Lydia. Grow a little backbone and get yourself out. As for me being sick, don't you just wish that was the case—

She folded the letter and tucked it between the pages of her brown *A Day At a Time* book. She looked at the little book. It was time to get honest. With Walt she couldn't stay sober. It was time to leave.

She let herself remain open for the pain, for the despair, but there was nothing left to feel. She tried to feel pain. Deciding to leave someone after twelve years of marriage should cause something. She shook her head. There was nothing there.

But what now? She had spent her adult life as a "corporate ornament." A new life? Thirty-seven isn't the Boneyard. But doing what?

"I can't do anything." She opened the book and scanned the afternoon's reading.

For a good part of my life, I saw things mostly in negative terms. Everything was serious, heavy, or just plain awful. Perhaps now I can truly change my attitude, searching out the winners…

Today I will remember. I, too, am a winner.

Lydia sat up, reading and re-reading the line. *I, too, am a winner.*

"Yeah!" Saint Mary's was full of men and women starting over. Many of them—most of them—from scratch. "I can stand on my own feet. I can." She balled up Walt's letter and tossed it in the trash can. "Saint Mary blue, fuck you."

Jake settled in to listen to Mona, aftercare counselor, junky and alcoholic. The subject of the noon lecture was change.

"When you began controlling your feelings with chemicals, your emotional development stopped. If you started when you were fifteen, emotionally that's how old you are right now. Intellectually you might have gone on to get degrees, develop a career, or whatever. But emotionally you are back where you left off. You never learned to deal with emotions in an adult manner. This is what we mean when we say a person is fifty going on fifteen."

As Mona went on, Jake's reality seemed to bend. He heard her say that the way we see things causes our feelings and affects our behavior. If you want to change how you feel without chemicals, change how you see things. The most healthy road to follow is to see things exactly as they are—and to accept the things over which one has no control.

As Jake left the lecture hall, one stretch of the talk kept gnawing at him as he read the lecture outline in his hands. The feeling certainly was that he must be loved and approved by everyone. There were other, more acceptable, ways to phrase the sentiment, but in the end that's what it boiled down to. The same thing applied to the next item on the agenda: Life is fair. Or it should be. But it wasn't. Saint Mary's was full to the rafters with men, women, and children who had done their own research on that subject. But the feeling was still there.

Among the feelings that constituted the Randecker universe was the next proposition: he must be perfect and perfectly successful before he could think of himself as worthwhile. The awards, the success he had achieved, were nothing in his eyes.

He had been sitting at his desk, his Hugo Award, his Nebula Award, and his best new writer plaque arranged before him. He leaned forward and placed the University of Maine's distinguished achievement award next to the others. To the left of the awards was a stack of papers eighteen inches thick. Fan mail. To the right of the awards was a smaller stack. Favorable reviews of his works.

He sat back, examined the display, then tossed his checkbook in front of the pretty ornaments. The checkbook was very healthy. *He just couldn't understand why he was sitting there with a loaded rifle preparing to splatter his brains all over the wall.*

—It wasn't enough; it wasn't perfect.

Perfectionist. He had never thought of himself as a perfectionist. It's a stupid proposition. A guarantee of failure. Perfect does not exist. Thus the revised expression heard in the halls of Saint Mary's: "Practice makes adequate." But the feeling—the conviction that anything less than perfection is failure—was there.

The next proposition on the list. The belief that the past determined his present. Terrible things had happened to him. "I wouldn't be in this fix if—"

Jake smiled and shook his head. Back at military school, his old professor of military science had gotten exasperated with Cadet Randecker's excuses. *"If a toad had wings, Randecker, he wouldn't bump his ass every time he jumped!"*

Finally, the belief that there is one right and perfect solution to each of his problems. Jake had spent the better part of forty years trying to find those solutions. The feeling that such solutions existed was still there.

All of them, all of those feelings, in the lecture came under the general heading of "Common misconceptions, mistaken beliefs, unhealthy and unrealistic attitudes."

Outside of Angela's office, the concerned persons were already gathering. Mack looked thoughtful. Bobby looked frightened, as did his mother. Don was shaking his head at Ilene's discouraged pleading. At the sight of them, the tension stabbed into Jake's neck, instantly igniting a headache.

He smiled at them, turned into his room, and closed the door. After walking to his desk, he picked up his *A Day at a Time* book. He looked at the reading for the afternoon.

Perhaps now I can truly change my attitude, searching out the winners in The Program who have learned how to live comfortably in the real world—without numbing their brains with mood-altering chemicals.

Jake shook his head as he closed the book. Living comfortably in the real world. It sounded like such a colorless collection of words. There are worlds to build, giant problems to wrestle, wealth, fame, cities of knowledge to construct from the sands of....

Jake could list a thousand exciting goals he had striven for, had almost destroyed himself trying to accomplish. For most of them, even if he failed he could always point to good intention and the size of the enemy: War, crime, poverty...

—Living comfortably in the real world.

It wasn't a goal that would bring fame or alter the shape of the universe's future. It wasn't a brag item to have in one's goal collection. But Jake wanted it very, very much.

—To live comfortably in the real world.

It seemed so far away. Unattainable.

The cowbell rang through the intercom. "C'mon, Bossy," muttered Jake. "It's time to get our teats yanked."

41

Candy sat facing Don and Ilene in the fishbowl, her gaze again resting in that empty space between them. They were talking, but Candy was safely inside her amour. The horrible things they were saying couldn't touch her. Their words were only meaningless vibrations in the air.

—I can take it. I'll show all of them. I can take anything.

The muscles in her cheeks ached from smiling. But the smile stayed. It said better than any words: You can't touch me. Don was talking and Candy's gaze drifted to Ilene.

—The poor girl is suffering so. God only knows what Lillian and Angela had to do to get her to say all of those terrible things. Ilene would have never talked to her own mother that way on her own. She was always such a beautiful, loving, child....

Candy's eyes half-closed.

She rocked the baby in her arms and sang. A warm, gentle breeze pushed at the bedroom curtains. There was the scent of freshly cut grass in the air. The curtains were pale blue scattered with chains of bright white and yellow daisies. They matched the wallpaper. She had such fun decorating the room in preparation for their baby. The baby was perfect. Soft, pale skin, without a mark or blemish. That little curl of blond standing up above her head. *It was all so perfect—*

"Mother?"

Candy looked at the woman across from her. "Yes?"

"You're not listening. You're not listening to any of this."

Candy nodded slowly. She felt Angela's hand on her arm. "Are you hearing any of this, Candy?"

"Of course."

"How does it make you feel?"

"I feel sorry for them. I'm really sad that they would say these things about me."

"What things are those, Candy?"

Candy laughed, "Really, Angela. You know perfectly well. The things you and Lillian made up for them to say."

Angela withdrew her hand and rocked back and forth in her chair. "Candy, do you really want to end locked up in the back of a psycho ward?"

"No."

"That's where you are headed unless you start getting honest with yourself."

Candy frowned in confusion as Angela looked at Don and Ilene and then solicited feedback from the group. There were voices. Saying this, saying that. She looked back at Ilene, thinking that her daughter must be the most beautiful—

The night before Ilene was to marry Keith. There had been so many things to do, so many preparations. Keith's mother was no help at all. The woman didn't even have taste in her mouth.

Just a few Valium to help keep the lid on things. One, two drinks. Don getting angry. "My God, Don, I've been taking these pills for years. They are not a problem."

Argument. Don could be so unreasonable at times. After the argument, just one more Valium. Maybe another.

Sitting in her room, reading. Stopped and thought about losing her daughter. Keith, a nice enough boy, will take her to Atlanta. But there will be holidays. And Ilene promised she'd call.

Candy got up to look in on Ilene. There were a few finishing touches to put on Ilene's wedding dress. Candy picked up the lace, the card of pins, and her large shears—

No. Not the shears—

Candy realized that Brandy was talking to her. She smiled sweetly at Brandy and looked back toward Ilene. Her daughter was unbuttoning the sleeves on her blouse, folding the sleeves back, exposing her arms. "Look. Mother."

Candy frowned and looked. Her baby's beautiful, blemish-free skin had ugly marks on it. Some pale white, some a hideous purple. She looked up at Ilene. "How did that happen, dear?"

"Mother, *you* did this! That night. With your shears."

Candy closed her eyes and shook her head. "No, dear. How could you ever think—"

"Look!"

Candy opened her eyes. Ilene was standing, her blouse pulled out of her skirt and held up, exposing her horribly scarred torso—

Screaming. Claws, the girl attacking, the shears, down, again, down again, again, again—

Candy looked at her own hands. "No. No."

Angela had Ilene sit down. She turned and placed a hand on Candy's arm. "What's going on, Candy?"

Candy buried her face in her hands, and screamed. As she began calming down, the intercom interrupted. "Jacob Randecker, come to the nurse's station."

Jake shook his head. "I don't believe this," he muttered as he got to his feet. He worked his way through the chairs, and left the room.

Candy was numb. She saw Angela nod at Don and Ilene. They stood up and began moving their chairs to the circle. "Candy. Put your chair back."

"Yes." Candy put her chair back in its place and sat down. Vaguely it registered on her that the meatgrinder had begun on D.T. But she was confused about something.

—Why did Ilene have her blouse out of her skirt? In front of everyone. I must have been imagining things. That must be what it was. I was confused, imagining things.

She concentrated on D.T. and his family. Mitzi was letting him have it with a machine gun. Candy cried as Mitzi told about John smashing her in her mouth with his cast the night she was trying to keep the three men in her life from killing each other.

Still, every now and then, Candy saw those shears slicing down through the dark, then down, and down again.

It was Bobby's turn. He began crying and couldn't stop.

42

Physical examination, Doctor Hiller. After introducing himself, the doctor waited as Jake undressed. As soon as Jake had shucked his clothes, Tess stuck her head inside the examination room door. She grinned and waved at Jake. "Doctor, you have a telephone call."

The doctor left the room. Naked on the chair, Jake fumed about being stripped, exposed, then discarded for a lousy telephone call. Most of all he fumed about being pulled out of group. Important things were going on there, and here he was, naked and killing time counting his ingrown hairs.

He leaned forward, picked at one of his toenails, and stopped as he noticed a series of deep, yellowish scars covering both of his shins. He leaned further forward. "Where in the hell did they come from?"

The scars were very deep. It didn't look like the kind of injury that would pass without notice. He frowned, trying to remember. It was back there someplace.

The two acres of hilly lawn surrounding the house. Once a week during the grass season Jake would break out the ride-around mower, put a six-pack between his ankles, and attack the grass. He loved cutting the grass. It was a two-hour stretch of drinking that he could put in where no one would give him any shit.

Sometimes he would take a corner too fast and fall off. Then he had to race to catch the mower before it flew off the bank into the stream, or ran into a tree. He would be laughing. Faster and faster, up and down the steep slopes, weaving between the trees.

Last summer, flying along that one slope, the mower and he had rolled downhill, the mower finally righting itself and running over his legs. Jake caught up with it, climbed aboard, and finished cutting the grass.

That night. His trousers were shredded, and there was some blood, but nothing to go crying to the doctor about. Didn't hurt, and there were far too many things on his mind to bother. *But, brother, do I need a drink—*

"I'm back." The doctor came into the examination room and patted the table. "Sit here."

The doctor pounded, thumped, poked, and prodded. All Jake could think about, however, was how he had completely blotted out the memory of almost cutting off his own legs. He seemed to understand Candy just a little bit better.

"Up on the table and lie on your side.

Jake saw the doctor, wearing a disposable glove, greasing up his index finger. Jake grimaced as he got up on the table. "I really hate this part."

He got on his side and the doctor assured him, "There's nothing to worry about as long as you only see one of my hands. When you see both, you know you're in trouble." A cackle.

—Not a straight man in the joint.

After group let out, Jake stood at the entrance to the north wing lounge. Everyone seemed to have red eyes. Frank flopped into the easy chair and lit a cigarette. He blew out the smoke like he was trying to fog the room. Jake sat down in a straight-back next to him. "Heavy session?"

Frank nodded, his eyes closed.

Those of the group who didn't head for their rooms collapsed in the lounge. The family members went straight for the elevators at what appeared to be almost a dead run. Dave sat in the couch, still blowing his nose.

Jake tapped his fingers on his knee. No one was talking. It was like having the middle chapters yanked out of an important, exciting book.

—And for what? To get a greased finger stuck up your ass!

Jake stood, grabbed his cup, headed for the stairwell, and climbed to the fourth floor. As he entered the recreation room, he looked for a familiar face among the few that were there, didn't recognize anybody, and went to the kitchen for some coffee. Back in the recreation room, he settled into an easy chair with his coffee, and puffed at his pipe.

"Jake?"

He looked in the direction of the voice and saw an attractive young woman dressed in sweater and jeans. Her hair was bobbed into a glowing cap of auburn. She wore a fourth floor patient nametag. "Yes?"

She sat across from him, crossed her legs, and smiled. "You don't recognize me, do you?"

Jake blushed. "I'm sorry. I don't."

"Diane. Diane Cook?"

Jake frowned as he studied her. The magazine writer. She had been overhauled. Rebuilt. Pipes cleaned, dents hammered out, new paint and trim. "You look terrific. Absolutely beautiful."

She smiled widely. "Thanks. I feel good, too. One of the girls in my group is a hairdresser." She turned her head left and right. "What do you think?"

"It looks great. I'm not a short hair fan, either. But I think I just might change my affiliation."

"How have you been doing?"

"Me? Oh, okay, I guess. Right now I'm pissed off about getting yanked out of group for a physical. We're in the middle of family week. I wanted to be there."

"Awful, isn't it? It seems like you never catch up again. But it happens to everyone."

"It still pisses me off." Jake saw a half-familiar face moving through the lounge. A tall boy, neatly dressed, clean shaven, his hair trimmed short. I was Ken, the shaggy I'm fucked up on everything kid from evaluation group.

In ones and twos the lounge began filling up, every now and then another familiar face from evaluation group. Treatment hadn't grown any hair on the banker, but it had certainly put a smile on his face and a spring in his step. The pro athlete was laughing. Somewhere his shame had been left behind. The harried mother who had freaked and shredded her daughter's dress looked ten years younger—

"Jake?"

He looked at Diane. "Yeah?"

"What are you going bug-eyed about?"

"The people I was in evaluation with. I haven't seen them for a while. They've changed. They've changed a lot."

"So have you." Diane sat back in her chair and clasped her hands together. "Jake, what makes a story a story?"

Jake shifted into literary mentor mode. "A character, against great odds, strives toward a worthwhile goal and either achieves it or is defeated by the obstacles that have been placed in his path."

"What about character change?"

Jake nodded. "As a result of the events transpiring in the course of the plot, the character at the end of the story should be emotionally different from when he first walked on the stage. What's your point?"

"Don't you see it, Jake? You have one hell of a story here."

"That again?"

"Saint Mary's is in the business of changing characters. Against a background of horror and death, the goal is life. The disease makes each person's only obstacle himself. The only hope: a one-hundred-and-eighty degree change in character." She studied him for a moment. "What are you thinking on?"

Jake sipped at his coffee and looked around the room as he relit his pipe. "I was thinking that you're right." He took the pipe from his mouth. "But I don't know. All I can see right now are problems. I couldn't invent characters half as vivid as the ones right here. Using the ones here would breach anonymity, not to mention opening me up for a crowd of lawsuits. For example, what if I should happen to mention in this little tome the conversation we're having right now. How long would it take your little buddies back in New York to figure out what Diane did on her vacation last January?"

"Not long."

"How long would it take for you to grab one of the dogs of law and sic him on my ass?"

She nodded. "I see the problem."

"That's just one of them. I'd also have to be able to write the damned thing, and to be truthful, I haven't been able to write anything for a long, long time. Maybe it's the demon rum, but I suspect it's something more than that."

Diane cocked her head to one side, her face reddening a bit. "You know, Randecker, I did a little research on you."

Jake felt his defenses locking into place. "Oh yeah?"

"You're a pretty important writer. Awards all over the place, three books your first year. Next to you, I've just been fooling around." Diane suddenly looked very confused. "Why are you angry?"

"Angry?" Jake frowned and shook his head as he exhaled the breath he realized he was holding. "I don't know. I guess I'm not very good at taking compliments." He looked into her eyes. "I was watching your stock drop like a stone."

"Clarify."

"There were a lot of writers I once admired. Isaac Asimov, for example. At a party about two years ago, he said some very nice things about me. In front of a crowd, and in my presence. I haven't been able to take him seriously since."

"Ah, the Groucho Marx Syndrome."

"Come again."

"I wouldn't belong to a club that would accept me for a member. Quote, unquote."

Jake noticed Frank entering the recreation room and waved. "This is Frank, my roommate."

"God!" Diane replied. "God, is he *beautiful.*"

Frank stopped next to Diane's chair, grinning. "Were you talking about me, I hope, I hope? I'm Frank Kimbal."

"Diane Cook."

They shook hands and Frank looked at Jake. "Angela wants you down in her office.

"Why?"

"She doesn't confide in me."

"But why?"

"What'd I say?"

Jake stood and began trudging toward the door. His gut feeling was that of a ten year old kid being called to the principal's office. "I am thirty-nine." His revised gut feeling was that of a thirty-nine year old kid being called to the principal's office.

He looked back at where he had been sitting. Frank and Diane were already deep in conversation.

"Ann is coming for your family week."

Jake lowered himself into the chair to the right of Angela's desk. "Oh?"

Angela studied him. "How does that make you feel?"

"Feel?" Jake did a quick inventory, then laughed sharply. "I guess pretty confused. Frightened, grateful, disappointed, angry, a little nauseous." He laughed again. "I guess what I feel is panic."

"What are you laughing at?"

He thought for a second, then shook his head. "I suppose it's either that or scream, and screaming is so hard on the ears."

"It's a lot more honest."

"Laughing is all that got me through the past thirty-nine years. If I couldn't laugh at it I had to take it right between the eyes, and I got eyestrain."

"Jake, if you laugh when you should be crying, you don't deal with the pain; you hide it. When you hide it, it never goes away. It becomes agony in the bank, there to grow interest and be withdrawn anytime your disease wants to set you up to use. Feeling what needs to be felt at the time it needs to be felt is what we mean by being honest with yourself."

"Honesty is the best policy, right?"

She leaned back in her chair. "Jake, right now you look angry. Your hands are knotted up into fists, your face is red, you're sitting hunched over in your chair like you're getting ready to spring at an attacker. What's going on with you?"

Jake listened, and it felt as though a fist was lodged in his throat. "I don't know. I'm angry about…about getting yanked out of group for a lousy physical. You'd think they could time these things better than—"

"You want what you want when you want it."

"No, you don't understand, Angela—

"I understand very well."

"But—"

"I don't want to play games with you, Jake."

"But, dammit, I—"

"I said I don't want to play any games."

Jake sat back in his chair, a smile on his face. "Then I don't want to play either." The top of his head was close to exploding.

"Good. Was there anything else?"

Jake felt as though he was going to black out. "No. That's it. Thanks for the news."

"You're welcome."

She turned back to her papers and Jake walked into the hall. His eyes went in and out of focus with the blood pounding in his head.

—Honesty is the best policy?

A moment later, at the nurse's station, they were neating things up for the next shift, when the floor resounded with a horrible three-second long scream. Tess rushed from behind the counter and stopped at the center of the floor's X, checking each of the three patient wings and the hallway to the lecture room. There were several patients standing in each, frozen in surprise, looking back at her. The door to the men's showers opened and Jake Randecker stepped out into the hall, fully dressed.

"Gee, that felt good."

He turned north and headed toward his room.

43

Just before evening chow, Jake entered the third floor kitchen to fill his cup with what seemed like his millionth cup of Saint Mary's sludge. As usual, a couple of patients were camped out in the kitchen, working their jaws. Sitting next to the shelves of bread, cookies, and potato chips was a young man wearing jeans, tee shirt, and gloom. Leaning against the sink was an old fellow wearing jeans, a western shirt, and a face that was running for the Suffering Humanity Award.

The kid started. "This had to happen to me now. It's not like I got my fun in. I'm only eighteen and I had a whole life of drinkin' and druggin' ahead of me that's down the toilet. It's the shits."

Jake turned, placed his cup on the counter and opened the refrigerator to take out one of the small cartons of milk. He lightened his coffee as the old guy picked up the theme.

"Look at me. I'm sixty-two. My life's already over. What's the point of trying to do anything about it now?"

Jake picked up his cup, glanced at the pair, and shook his head. Welcome to the self-pity jamboree. "Well, I'm right in the middle, so I guess this program was designed for me."

A telephone rang. Jake pushed his way into the short corridor to east wing and stopped as one of the three patient phones rang again. He picked up the middle receiver and answered. "Third floor."

A woman's voice. "I'd like to speak to Amy Simon, please."

"Do you know her room number?"

"No, I don't."

"Hang on. I'll see if I can scare her up." Jake let the receiver dangle by its cord and went to the nurse's station. Marnie was standing behind the counter working her way through some patient files. Wayne, the male nurse with the black beard, was sitting behind the counter. "Could you tell me Amy Simon's room number?"

Wayne bent forward, scanned the intercom index, and pointed toward west wing. "First patient room on the left."

Jake nodded his thanks and walked to the room. The door was cocked open, the lights-were off. He knocked on the door. "Amy? Amy? Telephone."

Receiving no answer, he turned and moved off toward west wing's lounge. As he came to the entrance to the lounge, he saw four women watching the lounge's television. "Amy Simon?"

One of the four turned her head. "She's in her room."

He turned around and went back to the other end of the wing. As he came to the door he decided to give it one more try. He knocked and called out, "Amy?"

There was a radio on inside the room playing ancient acid rock. Jake pushed the door open more widely. "Amy?" In the dark there was an armchair facing away from the door. In the chair, wrapped into a tight ball, was Amy Simon. Jake stood next to her. She was crying. He felt his heart bend with her pain. "Amy, you have a telephone call."

She only cried. Jake squatted down next to her. "Do you want me to take a message?"

Amy just barely nodded and Jake went back to the telephone, took the message, and returned to Amy's room. Placing the message on her desk, he squatted down next to her and placed his hand on her shoulder. "Is there anything I can do?"

"Just leave me alone."

Jake withdrew his hand and stood, helpless, looking at the bundle of pain. "If...if you need someone, I'll be around. I'm Jake Randecker."

Amy didn't move or otherwise acknowledge the offer. Jake turned, quietly left the room, and stopped at the nurse's station. Marnie was still standing behind the counter working on the files. "Marnie, that girl in there is crying."

She didn't look up from her work. "Yes, she is."

Jake's head came back as he frowned. "I don't understand. Isn't there something you can do?"

Still not looking up. "Yes. I'm doing it. Was there anything else?"

Jake shook his head and numbly walked toward his room, blind, targetless anger bringing on an old familiar friend: rage.

"One minute." Jake turned back and Wayne was waving a white booklet at him. "Fill this out and return it within twenty-four hours."

Jake took the booklet and read its title. *Minnesota Multi-phasic Personality Inventory.* MMPI. The notorious Micky Mouse Penis Itcher had finally tracked him down. Jake nodded. Brother, are we going to have fun tonight.

Nate Koeber sat in the dining room saying hello to the salt shaker. "Hi, salt shaker." Hello to the table, to the walls, to the person sitting next to him. Alive. Wonderful alive. He nodded.

—Waking up a couple of times in a morgue, sheeted and toe-tagged can certainly make one appreciate living.

A bearded man sat down across the table from him. All he had was a cup of coffee and a case of the ass. Nate held out his hand. "Hi, I'm Nate Koeber."

"You want a fucking medal?"

The man sipped at his coffee as he kept glancing at his watch. He glanced at Nate, looked down, laughed, then looked back. "I'm sorry. I'm Jake Randecker. I'm just a little pissed."

"I sort of guessed."

"Nate, was it?"

"Yes."

"Nate, what is it with this damned place? It is filled to the light fixtures with hurting people, but all they can do here is kick them some more. I found a girl crying in her room." Jake laughed again, his eyes glistening. "I found her crying and I told a nurse about it. The nurse wouldn't do anything. Nothing!" He slammed his fist on the table. "Not a damned thing!"

Jake looked toward the door where the warden sat. The warden was the counselor or nurse delegated to keep an eye on the inmates while they ate and fink on those who didn't stay the required ten minutes. The warden, alerted by Jake's table-pounding, was looking in their direction. Jake stuck his thumbs in his ears, wiggled his fingers, and stuck his tongue out at the warden.

He looked at his watch and stood up. "That's close enough to ten minutes. If I stick around much longer, I'm going to go to work on the crockery.'

"Easy does it."

Jake bent over the table. "How would you like me reach down your throat, grab your asshole, and yank you inside out?"

Nate almost had a half-shrug out when Jake turned abruptly and stormed out of the dining room, leaving his cup behind. The warden was busily scribbling on her clipboard.

Nate raised his eyebrows and spoke to the salt shaker. "My good friend, I think that's what they mean when they talk about Saint Mary blue."

The salt shaker nodded sympathetically.

44

D.T. sat in his room, looking out of his window at the dark. Tomorrow would be his opportunity to respond to Mitzi and his two sons. But what was there to say? There wasn't anything, except I love you, I'm sorry, give me another chance.

Another chance. How many had there been? Thousands. But no one knew then what they were dealing with. No one knew how to fight it. But now that his family had finally been given the proper weapons, was there any will to fight remaining?

There was an angry voice in the hall. Sounded like Jake. D.T. stood up, walked to his door, and opened it.

"Fuck this place, fuck Bill W., and fuck the pink elephant he rode in on!" Jake was steaming toward the nurse's station and Brandy was standing in the hallway shaking her head.

"What's going on?"

"Jake's pissed off about something. The station told me to find him. They want him to take that twenty-minute test tonight after lecture. He almost took my head off." Brandy shook her head. "I'm afraid our boy

Randecker is on his way out of here."

"Buggout?"

"Either that or thrown out. He was threatening some acid-head down in the dining room at chow." She looked at D.T. "How are you holding up?"

"Okay, I guess." He pursed his lips and let his chin rest on his chest for a second. "Maybe not so okay. Could you stand a little talk?"

"Promise you won't jump on me for being in the counseling business?"

He stood to one side, held the door open, and grinned. "If I was going to jump on you, that wouldn't be the reason."

"Why, you dirty old man."

Brandy sat in the room's easy chair as D.T. closed the door and sat on his bed. They both lit up cigarettes. "Brandy, this whole family week thing—treatment…" He shook his head. "I'm all scrambled up. Before my life might have been a nightmare, but it was at least predictable."

She nodded. "It was certainly predictable. One of the most horrible forms of death ever invented. Are you trying to talk your way back into the fast lane?"

"No." He sighed, took a drag on his cigarette, and looked out of his window. "I looked at those people across from me in group this afternoon and they were a bunch of strangers. I don't know my wife. I don't know her at all. I don't know my sons. All the things I thought I knew are wrong. I don't know where I'll fit in now. My family." He looked at her. "I haven't been a father and husband for so long. Never. How can Mitzi…" His voice trailed off as he sat silently shaking his head. "In group this afternoon, Mitzi sounded like she hated me. She's never hated anything before in her life."

Brandy leaned forward. "D.T., your wife has hated, and hated plenty. You can count on it that the main object of her hate was you. You can't smack someone in the mouth with ten pounds of plaster without some ill feelings. She just never said it or let you see it. She's been storing it up for thirty years, and she let a lot of it out today. But what she's learning here is the difference between hating the behavior and hating the person. It will take her a while to learn the difference. Give her time."

"I don't know if I can stand it. Her hating me. Seeing her hate me."

"Give her time. How much time has she given you?"

"As you said, the better part of thirty years." He stood up, walked to his window and looked down at the snow. "Staying sober isn't going to be easy, is it?"

"Some people say once they got with the program, they never again had the desire to drink or use. Others seem to spend all their time white-knuckling it from one A.A. meeting to the next. I think the truth for most persons, at least at the beginning, is somewhere in between. It won't be easy. But it's what you have to do if you want anything else."

D.T. turned from the window and looked down at her. "Mack is going to be admitted into treatment Thursday. What can I do to make it easier for him?"

"You've already done it. There's nothing more. Just like you, he has to do it by himself, using the group and the program. Just be sure to show up for his family week." She smiled. "It's a hell of a disease, isn't it?"

D.T. nodded and turned back to the window and giggled, thinking of something Jake had said. "Somebody really ought to do something about it."

Cowbells. Brandy got up and stubbed out her cigarette in D.T.'s nightstand ashtray. "Shall we catch the evening show?"

"Like we had a choice." He put out his cigarette and followed Brandy into the hallway.

Candy sat on her bed in the darkness of her room, her arms wrapped around her knees. Fragments of memory flashed before her staring eyes. There were too many memories.

"I stabbed her. I stabbed my baby." So many other things. Burning

Don. Breaking his arm. Beating Ilene because…because she kept getting older, more beautiful, and Candy just kept getting older.

The door to her room opened. "Candy?" It was Marnie's voice. "Candy, it's time for the evening lecture."

Candy simply shook her head.

"You have to go to the lecture."

"Go away, Marnie. I know it's your job and everything, but just go away."

The door closed. "Did you ever think of turning on the lights when you're in the room and turning them off when you leave?" There were footsteps in the room, and a shadow sat on the bed next to Candy. "Talk to me. What is it?"

"I don't want to talk about it."

"You either talk about it, Candy, or hustle your little ass down to the lecture hall. Which is it going to be?"

"I'd like to talk about it, but I can't. Oh, Marnie!" She turned and buried her head in the nurse's lap. "I've done so many horrible things. I can't stand it! I just can't stand it."

Marnie reached out a hand and moved Candy's hair from her face. "What things?" Candy sobbed, her shoulders heaving. The nurse stroked Candy's cheek. "So you feel like nothing should be allowed to live that did the things you did."

"Why should it? They'll never forgive me. How can they?"

"Drugs, Candy. Drugs did it, not you." Marnie bit her lower lip, then closed her eyes as hot shame inflamed her face. "All of us do crazy things when we're high. That's why we can't drink or drug. You're not a bad person, Candy."

Candy sat up and looked at Marnie. "Marnie, I stabbed my own daughter. Not just once: I kept stabbing and stabbing—" She shook her head violently. "God, what kind of a thing am I?"

"You are a drug addict, Candy. A good person who does insane things when she's on drugs."

"I couldn't do those things unless they were in me, could I?"

"Acting against your values is one of the symptoms of this disease. I did."

Candy snorted a laugh through her tears. "Little miss goodie two-shoes. What kind of G-rated horrors did you commit?"

Marnie took a deep breath, let it slowly escape, and steeled herself for another peek into what she called her "fun chest." In A.A. and N.A. it is called her "story" or "adventure." That's how we help others, she reminded herself. It's how we help ourselves. We can't live in the past, but we can't afford to forget it. When you forget it, it tends to get placed in your "It wasn't all that bad" file.

"Where would you like me to start, Candy? When I whored around in junior high school to buy my shit? They used to call me the 'student body.' Isn't that amusing? Or if we're going to play my awful is more awful than your awful, perhaps I ought to get straight down to when my baby son had to have his foot amputated after I thrust it in some boiling water because his crying annoyed me. Or there was the time I killed my husband in a car accident—"

Candy picked up Marnie's hand and held it tightly. There was nothing said with words. But the touch spoke. It was something of gratitude, sympathy, understanding, love. Almost acceptance.

"How do you live with it, Marnie? How do you ever live with it?"

"Time. Time and the program. Unloading the shame and the pain in group. Accepting that I cannot change the past. Remembering that it's not anyone's fault; it's a disease. Living in the present. Taking responsibility for my recovery. Most importantly, learning how to forgive myself. But it takes time."

Candy sat silently, measuring the strength and power of those dark things hovering over her head. They were powerful, but they had been following her for too long. But to kill them, they had to be pulled to one's breast and smothered with light.

"Marnie, I began taking drugs when my daughter, Ilene, was seven.
It was Valium…" Candy talked for an entire hour, sitting on her bed,
holding Marnie's hand in the dark, doing again the first step that she
had lied her way through ten days before.

45

In the smoking lounge on the first floor, Jake, Earl, Lydia, Roger and three other patients were taking a test. Jake put down his pencil and fired up his pipe. The first ten-minute special was a vocabulary test. He had zipped through it in two minutes. The second half made no sense at all.

"Fuck it," he whispered.

He couldn't get the sight of that crying girl out of his mind. His heart had ached for how helpless he had felt. Now there was nothing left but anger. Anger at the clumsiness of the program. Anger at the heartlessness of Saint Mary's. Anger at the impotence of Jake Randecker. There were no locks on the door. His airline bag was on the top shelf of his clothes press. His ticket was in his wallet.

—Just have to call a taxi. That's all. Leave this goddamned nightmare behind.

"Time," called the nurse in charge.

Jake stood, picked up his paper and pencil, turned them in to the monitor, and sped for the stairwell.

Frank sipped at his coffee as he began working his way through the smoke-filled corridor to east wing. Chattering patients were lined up three deep to get at the phones.

"Hey!"

He saw Dave at one of the phones holding up the receiver. "Frank, you want to talk to Harold?"

Frank took the phone, placed his cup on the directory stand, and stuck a finger in his unoccupied ear. "Harold? It's Frank. How are you doing out there?"

"Hi, Frank. I'm doing okay. I miss you guys a lot, though. The real world sucks."

Frank frowned. "Hey, man, you got a problem you want to talk about?"

"I've already bent Dave's ear for the past half hour. It's just that I just don't seem to fit in anywhere. My boss and my family treat me like I'm made out of glass, and everybody around me is still playing all kinds of games."

"You've only been out one day, Harold. Give it some time. Go to a meeting."

"A.A.?"

"That's what I mean."

"Christ, Frank, after a month in the joint, I am about all meetinged out. Besides, those old alkys don't like druggies."

"Give me a break, Harold. You know better than that. There must be a Narcotics Anonymous meeting nearby."

"Maybe. But I don't have an N.A. directory."

Frank lowered the receiver, glanced at it, then placed it against his ear. "Harold, you have a telephone book. Call N.A. You are playing dangerous games, man."

"Hey, Frank." Harold's voice sounded a little hot. "It's an individual program. I'll do what I need to for me. Let me talk to Dave, okay?"

"Okay. Take care of yourself, man."

He handed the receiver to Dave. The union man took it and looked up at Frank. "What do you think?"

"I think…" Frank shook his head. "I think the only one who can work Harold's program is Harold." He picked up his coffee cup and pushed his way into east wing.

As he turned the corner into north wing, his head pounded. He felt like he wanted to cry. But there was nothing he could do. He remembered the very first sharing speech he had heard. His second day. The woman up front was saying how much she loved everybody there, and how much she wanted everyone to make it. "But the numbers don't lie. A third of us are already dead. No one knows who they are. It might be you, it might be me."

He laughed at himself. "Hell, I already have him dead and I'm throwing dirt on his face." He shook his head as he approached his room. Projecting. Trying to control the future.

—One bad day doesn't mean that Harold won't make it.

Frank reached out to open the door. He heard a voice, Jake's, coming from the other side. Rabid, incoherent anger. He pushed open the door and saw Jake's airline bag on his bed, clothing half-stuffed inside. Jake moved from his clothes press carrying an armload of shirts. He dumped the shirts on his bed.

Jake glanced at Frank, then turned back to the clothes press. Frank stood at the foot of Jake's bed. "Going someplace?"

"You're goddamned right."

"Where to?"

Jake tossed more clothing on the bed. "Anyplace away from here. I have had it."

"Sit down and let's talk."

Jake laughed. "I am all talked out. I am talked out, cried out, laughed out, pissed out, pissed on, pissed off, and on my way home!"

Jake crammed the remainder of his clothing into the bag, zipped it shut, and began putting on his coat.

Frank put his coffee cup down on Jake's desk. "I think we ought to talk."

Jake put on his stocking cap, picked up his bag, and headed for the door. Frank grabbed his shoulder, bringing him to a staggering halt. "I said we ought to talk!"

"Dammit!" Jake pulled away from Frank's grasp. "There's nothing to talk about. Me and this place have split the blanket!"

"Do you want me to sit on you, Jake?"

"You might be a big sonofabitch, Frank, but I fight dirty. Just stay the fuck outta my way."

Frank's head went back as he studied his roommate. "Five minutes. We talk for five minutes, then you can go do what you want."

"What if I refuse?"

Frank smiled. "Then you can go do what you want, but with a broken leg."

Jake fumed for a long moment, then dropped his bag on the floor. "Okay."

Frank watched as Jake turned abruptly and headed for the north wing lounge. As he picked up his cup and followed, Frank wondered whether he was helping or simply butting his head against that third that was already dead. He shrugged. Harold had sat him down to talk often enough, without knowing if it was going to do any good. Part of the tradition. Pass it on. Besides, there's something very threatening about seeing someone else fail. Very threatening. Frank took a deep breath and headed toward the lounge.

The halls were turned over to the emergency lights and the Nighthawks. The first of the night's three bedchecks was an hour old. Ron Steward crept down the north wing stairwell, stopped on the third floor landing, and looked through the firedoor's window. Frank and Jake were the only ones up. Ron opened the door and closed it as quietly as possible behind him. Frank looked at him. "What are you looking for, man? A discharge?"

Ron turned around and glowered at Frank. "You going to turn me in?" Frank sat back and studied Ron. "Is there something you want to talk about?"

"No. I'm hitting the sack." He waved goodnight and crept down the hall toward his room. There were the usual Nighthawks prowling the halls, but no one from the nurse's station was in a position to see him. He reached his room, opened the door, and closed it silently behind him. His heart was thumping against his ribs.

Paula had been in her bed, naked, holding up the covers. Ron had stared at her, his guts knotted by a rush of fear. Fear of what? He loved her. She loved him. There was no reason, but suddenly everything was terribly wrong—

Ron shook his head. "Dammit, what is happening to me?" He pushed away from the door, entered his bathroom, turned on the light, and pulled the accordion door shut behind him.

He looked at his image in the mirror. Cold fear was beaded on his forehead. He pulled a fresh towel from the rack and dropped it next to the sink. Turning on the water, he cupped his hands beneath the faucet and splashed his face. After drying off, he dropped the towel on the floor and leaned against the counter.

Her eyes, dark and hurt. "Ron, what is it? Ron?"

His throat had seemed paralyzed. He couldn't speak. He could hardly breathe. He began backing out of the room.

"Ron. Don't leave." She picked up her robe from the foot of the bed and held it to her breasts as she swung her legs to the floor.

"Ron?" She began crying.

Out into the hall, he ran for the north wing stairwell.

In the mirror a stranger looked back at him. All the confidence, all
the self-respect, all the peace that he had achieved over the previous
twenty-six days, gone. He looked at the counter. He squatted down,
then knelt on his right knee as he reached beneath the sink. He felt for
it, and after his fingers found it, he pulled it loose and looked at it: a tiny
clear plastic bag, a strip of adhesive tape placed across it.

The day he had been moved to third north he had taped it beneath
the counter. Just in case. A backup. He hadn't touched it since, had
almost forgotten it was there. Now he had it in his hand.

—Just to shut it all out. Just to drift away, calmness filling my heart.
"Shit"

He sat on the floor staring at the bag's contents. So alcohol's the big
problem, isn't it? Some alkys can handle pot, can't they? Pot only has a
psychological dependency, right? Ron shook his head, the tears streaming down his cheeks. "Damn. Damn, I hurt." His hands shook as he
tore open the bag.

He emptied the contents into the toilet, tossed the bag in, and
pulled the handle. The roar of the toilet's flushing filled the bathroom.
Again and again he pulled on the handle, the sound of the flushing covering his cries.

JANUARY 5TH

46

Morning group. D.T. did the reading: "Have I turned to a Higher Power for help? Do I believe that each man or woman I see in A.A. is a demonstration of the power of God to change a human being from a drunkard into a sober, useful citizen? Do I believe that this Higher Power can keep me from drinking?"

As D.T. read from the black book, Jake looked around. To his left, in Angela's chair, was a strange man. To his left sat D.T., then Lydia, Roger, Frank, Brandy, and Earl. Ron, Candy, and Dave were missing.

As the contracts began working their way around the circle, he thought about last night's talk with Frank. Again he felt like he was sitting in a rehab because he had been talked into it.

—I don't know how much longer I can keep the lid on this thing that is boiling over in me. I can't figure out if I want to die or kill—

"And your name?"

Jake frowned at the strange man. "Jake Randecker." He looked around and everyone was looking at him. "Oh. I'm Jake Randecker, drug addict and alcoholic." He blushed. "I really haven't thought about a contract."

The man nodded and smiled. "Perhaps you'd be willing to talk about your Higher Power this morning."

"Okay."

The man nodded again, placed the palms of his hands together, and faced the group. "I'm Barny Cole, alcoholic, your spiritual care counselor. Wednesday morning is spiritual care time, and we like to confine the subject to spiritual matters as much as possible. However, if someone has a problem on the gnaw, we can work on that first." Barny looked around the room. "Who's first?"

"I am." Earl was leaning forward, his elbows on his knees, his hands clasped together. "I can't get my wife and boy to come for family week. It looks like she's going to leave me." His head hung down for a moment, then he looked up. The groupwad began traveling in his direction. "I'm having a real hard time figuring out what the point of all this is."

Barny nodded. "Who are you here for, Earl?"

"I thought I was here for all of us—me and my family." He shook his head. "I don't know anymore. I feel like for the first time in my life I'm getting straightened out. I've got a handful of answers and now is when Alice picks to take off. It just isn't..." The farmer fell into silence.

Lydia broke the silence. "Were you about to say that it just isn't fair?"

"It isn't!" Earl sat up, his face flushed.

Roger looked across the circle at Earl. "So what's new?"

"What's that mean?"

"Where is it written that reality is fair?"

"Damn, Roger. She's been with me for sixteen years. Why'd she pick now—now when I'm doing something to end this damned nightmare— why'd she pick now to leave me?"

Brandy, seated to Earl's right, looked at the farmer and smiled. "Maybe this is the first time in those sixteen years Alice has had some breathing space."

"Brandy, did Al-Anon tell her to leave me?"

"No. Al-Anon doesn't tell anyone to do anything. If she leaves, it's her decision. But she's also a sick woman."

Barny leaned forward. "We're jumping the gun here. From what you said, Earl, she hasn't left yet. Has she?"

"No. But—"

"There's no buts. This is today. What do you have to do today?" Earl shook his head. "What about staying sober?"

Earl looked at Barny. "What about it?"

"If Alice leaves you, are you going to go back and drink?"

Silence. Earl rubbed his eyes. "Right now I don't know. I guess I better think about that."

"Here's something to think about, as well. If you go back to drinking because she leaves, you would have gone back to the jug had she stayed." Barny looked around the group. "Anyone else? Let's see, does anyone in this group have family week?"

"Me." D.T. raised his hand.

"John?"

D.T. nodded. "But I'm getting to feel sort of good about family week. Last night Brandy and I got together—"

"What?" Barny's face carried an expression of considerable alarm.

D.T. looked confused. "Brandy and I got together...Oh." He laughed and pointed across the circle. "Brandy."

Brandy waved at Barny, and Barny laughed as his face reddened. "I swear, one of these days I'm going to take a memory course." He nodded at D.T. "Continue."

"I was apprehensive about the lack of trust in me. I already was aware that my family had no reason to trust me, but still it seemed like an unpayable bill."

"Weighing you down?"

"Yes. But talking with Brandy helped put things into perspective.

This situation didn't develop overnight, and it won't be resolved in a week. Time."

Barny laughed. "Ah, yes, time. When I first came into the program I learned to hate that word." He glanced at Brandy, then addressed the group. "It's good that this group works together on its own time. There's nothing more important than being able to rely on the group."

Roger leaned forward. "Since this is supposed to be Higher Power time, I don't suppose that anyone would object if I touched on that subject."

Barny smiled. "You're Roger."

"Yes. This business about the group—relying on the group. God is my Higher Power. It's all the power I need."

"I see." Barny closed his eyes for a moment, sorted quickly through his mental files, then grinned. "You're Roger the minister."

Roger nodded, his eyes wary. "I'm not ashamed of my occupation."

"I'd be the last to condemn you for it, Roger. I'm in the business myself."

"Which denomination?"

"Old established firm. Roman Catholic."

Jake took another look at Barny. Crooked purple bow tie, brown and orange tweed trousers, green and black checked coat, pink shirt. A priest? Maybe for Ringling Brothers.

Roger sat up and crossed his legs. "Then you ought to understand what I'm talking about."

"Oh, I understand very well. Tell me, how does God talk to you?"

"How?"

"Does he send mail, shout in your ear, set fire to your huckleberry bush, first-run visions, what?"

Roger glared at the floor in the center of the circle, the steam almost shrieking from his ears. Then he closed his eyes, forced himself to look calm, and answered the question. "It's like when I have a problem—a question—that's troubling me. I pray to God and an answer comes to me. That's all."

"Roger, I'd like you to consider two things. First how can you tell the difference between God talking to you, and *you* talking to you? Second, is it possible that your god can express himself through your group?"

"I don't know about the first." Roger leaned back in his chair and glanced up at the ceiling. "As for the second, I suppose it's possible."

Barny nodded. "You better believe it's possible. The next time you think God is telling you to do something, check it out with the group. Okay?"

Roger nodded and Barny again surveyed the group, his gaze stopping on Jake. "Hi."

"Hi."

"Your name is Jake?"

"Yes. I was going to talk about my higher power, wasn't I?"

"Yes. What is your higher power?"

"Whatever works." It still didn't sound any better.

"Have you found anything yet that works?"

"Not a damned thing. But I'm still looking."

Barny rubbed his chin. "Do you think God might work?"

"I haven't seen his W-2 form."

"You might want to think about it."

"I will. I'll put my whole mind to it."

"Why do I feel like you're being just the least little bit sarcastic?"

Jake smiled, then laughed. "Probably because I was. Look, they say this isn't a religious program. I'm putting that to the test."

"There's a difference between God and religion."

"Not in my book."

"Jake, how well has your book worked in keeping you clean and sober?"

"My ass in this chair answers that, doesn't it?"

Barny rocked back and forth in Angela's chair. "You look angry to me."

"I am angry."

"What about?"

"I'm pissed at being made to feel like a leper around here because the big G sticks in my craw."

"Only you make you feel—"

"Right. Okay, I'm pissed at being treated like a leper. Is that better?"

Barny shook his head. "Jake, not for an instant will I grant you that you are being treated in that manner. But even if you were, so what? You don't have to own what others think about you. It can't be put any clearer than the Big Book puts it. Pick your own conception of a higher power. It doesn't have to be God, or a god or gods. But you need something that works where you don't. You know how well doing it by yourself worked."

Jake folded his arms and thought. All he had ever done during his entire life was own what others thought about him. How do you not own these things? There were other things he was pissed about, as well. His head was buzzing so loudly he was surprised when Frank interrupted his thoughts.

"Jake, would you mind me mentioning what we talked about last night?"

"Yes, I would." Jake looked around the group as he talked. "This is supposed to be an honest program. I'm trying to be honest. I could do like some and just mouth the words." He glanced at Lydia, who looked away. "But that would just be one more lie on top of my life of lies. When I am honest with myself, there simply is no cosmic creature out there running the show. You people can believe whatever you want. But I demand the same right."

Barny nodded at Jake, then let his glance slowly turn toward Lydia.

He kept looking at her. She aimed a hateful glance at Jake and returned Barny's look. She did not blink. "Okay. I've said that God is my higher power, and I don't believe in any god. It was an easy way out." She pointed at Jake. "I've seen the struggle Jake's been put through because he won't follow the party line, and—"

"Hold it—hold everything." Barny lowered his hands. "No one is trying to cram God down anyone's throat. There is no party line." He leaned forward. "But you're going to have to come up with a power greater than yourself. The group, the program, even," he grinned, "whatever works. If you could do it by yourself, you might not need a higher power. Jake's right about one thing: you sitting in that chair tells me that you can't do it by yourself. Lydia, since that's your third time in that chair, bullshitting yourself and the group about a fictitious god doesn't seem to satisfy the problem either. You're not here to get through a course or to convince the staff and your group that you are recovering; you're here to recover."

As Lydia responded, it suddenly occurred to Jake that Barny's bad memory bullshit notwithstanding, the priest knew every detail about every person sitting in the circle. It might have been fun to jump the cleric through a few theological hoops. One does not spend twenty years studying philosophy without acquiring a bunch of first-class goddie chain-yankers. Jake decided against it.

He folded his arms and sat back. Lydia was crying. D.T. was talking to her. Roger was angry, burning up energy in the direction of Barny, who wasn't noticing. Brandy was observing while Earl was feeling sorry for himself. Frank returned his look. What was in Frank's face? Concern?

Jake looked away, anger devouring his giblets. He looked at the black book in his hands, opened it to January 5th and reread the morning's thought.

Have I turned to a Higher Power for help? Do I believe that each man or woman I see in A.A. is a demonstration of the power of God to change a human being?

—No, I haven't. I just don't know where to turn. Whatever Works isn't working.

He had a strange feeling as a thought came into his head. He closed the book, withdrew his wallet, and took out the little white card printed with the Twelve Steps and Twelve Traditions. His eyes were drawn to Tradition Two. *For our group purpose there is but one ultimate authority— a loving God as He may express Himself in our group conscience."*

The group.

He replaced his card and returned his wallet to his pocket. Step Three was turning the old life and will over to "the care of God *as we understood Him."*

Barny had suggested to Roger that the minister might want to check out his messages from Above with the group. The group seemed to be Barny's rock-bottom expression of his god's wisdom and will. Not the church, not the Pope, not those little messages one gets on bended knee. Frank had said to take it to the group. The group.

—But what if you don't believe that there is some prime mover behind the group? Can't you just take the group conscience at the no-frills rate?

Jake shook his head. —Before I turn this ass over to the group, there's something I have to do first. I have to see it work before I'll believe in it.

47

At lunch Jake observed D.T. sitting with Mitzi, Mack, and Bobby. Their talking was animated, enthusiastic. Don and Ilene were eating alone. Candy carried her tray over to them, spoke for a minute, then Don stood and pulled out a chair for her. Candy sat down and talked while Don and Ilene listened. After a few moments, it was groupwad time all around.

Jake looked down and picked at the Constipated Eagle's special for the day: Terrieraki. It was either that or rat's ass: meatballs.

"What's red and green and runs around in circles at a hundred miles an hour?"

Jake looked to his left. Snake had his tray piled high with everything. "What?"

"Kermit the Frog in a blender."

Jake turned back to his Terrieraki. "How'd your first step go?"

"Okay. It went great. Thanks for the help. God, I feel better." Snake talked around a mouthful of something. "I don't know what it is, but I feel terrific. Like ten gallons of sewage was pumped out of my gut."

Jake grimaced, pushed away his tray, picked up his cup, and sipped at his coffee. "What's your Higher Power, Snake?"

"Why?"

"I'm shopping."

The biker shrugged, shoveled another fork full of fodder into his mouth, and frowned as he composed his thoughts. "I fooled around with that for a long time. Joked around. After getting jerked around pretty good, and getting damned scared, I settled on the group. You want to see my first HP?"

Snake reached into his hip pocket and pulled out a folded sheet of paper. He handed it to Jake. "I used to show that around when Nast Ass would get on my case about HP."

Jake unfolded the paper and began laughing. The drawing was really very good. It was Garfield the cat, a sinister expression on his face, in black leathers straddling a mean-looking Harley. He was carrying a jousting lance, and the flag that wafted from the lance's tip bore a Saint Mary's swastika—a reproduction of the blunt-ended cross that hung behind the nurse's station.

"You like it?" Jake couldn't get out any words he was laughing so hard. "It's yours." Jake dissolved on the table.

Noon lecture. Mark was on stage and he had some really lousy news for the inmates. "How you feel is up to you. No one makes you angry, no one makes you happy. All the things that you feel are your responsibility. Do you feel miserable enough to go out and have a drink that turns into a week-long binge? Don't blame it on your husband. Don't blame it on the wife, kids, your boss, or your dog. Just like no one can make you take a drink, no one can make you angry."

Earl shrugged and scratched his knee. He knew differently. He knew plenty of people who had made him angry. In fact, lecturer Mark was doing a pretty good job of it right now.

Mark leaned on the lectern. "Think of something that happened to you when you were very young. Something really lousy. Something that hurt you very much that someone else did. Pick something where the evil-doer is no longer around. Does everyone have such an incident in mind?"

Earl nodded. Sure. The old man drunk, wrapping his car around that rock, screwing us all out of a father.

"Okay, now think about the one that makes you the most angry. Is everybody angry?"

The audience snorted.

Mark held out his hands. "You just made yourself angry. When you are angry, you can make yourself not be angry. You are the doer. I didn't make you angry. The people you thought made you angry in the past aren't even here. You control your own thoughts. Does everybody buy that?"

Mark looked over the hall and Earl pondered the question.

—The old you can lead a horse to water, etc. No one can force me to think about anything. Okay. He looked back toward the lectern.

Mark folded his arms. "We agree, then, that each of us controls our own thoughts. Good. Now for the next step. Our feelings come from our thoughts. If your brain is not there to think, someone could hit your finger with a hammer, and there would be no pain. How many of you have severely injured yourselves and, as they say, felt no pain because your ability to think was crippled by a chemical?" He glanced at the few hands that were raised. "How many?"

More hands went up. "Everyone who has his hand up, put it down, and everyone who does not have a hand up, put one up." Around thirty hands were left standing. "Now I'll mention a few things, and when it applies to you, put down your hand."

Earl's hand, thanks to the job his sledgehammer had done on his shoulder, was already down. He sat back to watch the experiment.

"In the dentist's chair, you are having a particularly sensitive tooth worked on, but you feel no pain because the dentist is using nitrous oxide…"

All of the hands went down. "I see I won't have to go any further than that. Therefore, we are agreed, thoughts are necessary to have feelings. Feelings come from thoughts. Are there any problems so far?"

He looked around and nodded. "Very well. You control your thoughts. Your feelings come from your thoughts. Therefore, you—and only you—control your feelings."

Earl frowned. The frown grew deeper as Mark recited a list of common expressions. "Such as, you make me so angry! My boss makes me mad! The weather really makes me feel miserable. Snakes make me scared." Mark cleared his throat and continued. "Now what these things really mean are: I made myself angry because of what I thought about what you did. I made myself angry because of my reaction to what I think my boss thinks about me. I make myself scared when I'm around snakes—"

This is awful, thought Earl. All these years of mostly being miserable, and it wasn't my father's and mother's fault, it wasn't my sisters' fault, it wasn't my wife's fault. It was all me? It's not true that gray days make me unhappy? It's I make myself unhappy when there is an overcast? But why—

Mark was covering that point.

"Every self-destructive feeling you give yourself has what is called a payoff. There is a reward for going through the pain." Mark pointed at one of the frys. "What's the payoff?"

"I don't know."

"Do you ever get hurt, angry, depressed, miserable?"

"Sure.'

"And when I feel bad I…"

Silence. "When I feel bad…I drink. But—"

Mark shook his head. "That's it. No buts. If we reward anxiety with Ativan or Valium, we're going to be anxious a lot. If we reward our aches and sniffles with Nyquil, we're going to have a lot of colds. If we reward being unhappy with ethanol, we're going to be unhappy a lot. Our pay-off for being miserable is to go out and use. Therefore, we are miserable a lot. Just let that sink in."

Earl was rubbing his temples, his eyes closed. It's too simple, he thought frantically.

—It's not I drink because I have problems? It's I have problems in order to give myself excuses to drink? It's too easy an answer for an entire life down the toilet. It's too damned simple!

Afternoon group, Marnie and Lillian in attendance. First a reading from the brownie, then contracts. Then silence.

Angela glowered around at the group, missing only the family members. "Before we begin today, we have some housekeeping chores. I had a one-on-one with Ron this morning." She looked at Ron. "Do you mind if I summarize our talk?"

"No." His voice was very quiet.

"Very well. Group, I am angry. Disappointed." Her gaze went once around the circle. "Pissed off!" She clasped her hands over her belly and looked up at the ceiling. "How many of you knew about Ron and the girl from the fourth floor, Paula?" A few furtive looks, then everyone in the group raised a hand. "How many of you confronted Ron about this? One. Lydia. Not in group where it might have done some good." She faced Ron. "Did any of them know about the pot you had hidden in your room?"

"No. I don't think so."

Angela shook her head. "I am very concerned about you, group. Concerned. A working group doesn't act this way. When a working group finds a member killing himself, the member gets confronted." She pointed a finger at Frank. "Why didn't you confront Ron about Paula?" Frank swallowed, looked down, and shook his head. "I don't have a good excuse. It was—I guess it made me uncomfortable."

"Comfort." She looked at Roger. "What about you?"

"I didn't figure it was any of my business. We do have private lives."

"Privacy." She looked at Jake. "And you?"

Jake raised his eyebrows. "I'm new here. Ron's in his fourth week. What am I going to tell him?"

"Seniority."

She rocked back and forth in her chair. "You people seem to think that this is nothing more serious than a couple of kids grabbing some nookie in the back seat of the family Chevy." The rocking stopped, she leaned forward and swung her chair, slowly scanning the faces as she talked. "Ron isn't capable of handling a love relationship right now. He has all he can contend with learning how to handle himself. A love relationship to him right now is deadly poison." She looked up at the ceiling. "What did you almost do last night, Ron?"

"I had some pot stashed in my room. I was going to use—"

"Why?"

Ron's face turned bright red. "Paula and I, we were going to make love last night. I couldn't. I was afraid. It—"

"Do you know where Paula is right now?"

Ron sat up, his eyes wide. "No."

Again Angela surveyed the group. "Paula walked out of treatment last night. You people call it bugging out. Today Ron might be tossed out. If that happens, Lydia and Brandy can tell you that the chances these two have at staying clean are very poor." She swung her chair in Brandy's direction. "What's your excuse?"

"I don't have one."

Ron spoke. "When will I know if I'm going to be canned?"

"I have to discuss that with the staff. But your welfare is secondary right now. I will eventually want to know what this group plans to do to shape up its act." She faced Roger. "But first a word about privacy. Your business is the group's business, and the group's business is your business. We help each other. That's the only way that anyone has ever discovered to recover from chemical dependency. If you can do it by yourself, then be my guest. You don't need us and we don't need you. Leave the unit. Get out."

She looked around again. "If you can't do it by yourself, then you have to rely on the group. More importantly, the group has to rely on you. When you shirk your responsibilities, you threaten both yourself and the group."

Her gaze shot back at Roger. "If you saw a baby playing with a stick of dynamite, would you interfere, or would you avoid the issue by claiming that you were respecting the baby's right to privacy?"

"I'd interfere, of course. But—"

"But *nothing!* You are emotional babies. Addicts are emotional babies. You are not supposed to play with love during your first year of sobriety for the same reason you're supposed to keep out of drinking situations. They are dynamite. Just like the baby can't see anything dangerous in a pretty red stick of dynamite, the addict usually can't see the things that threaten him."

She held out her hands. "But the group *can.* In fact, the group is the only thing that can. If the group *won't* see, then the addict is blind." She stared Roger down, then took a deep breath, letting it out as she looked over the family members. "We can't take the time from group today to give this matter the thrashing it deserves. Count on tomorrow morning's group being very instructive."

She looked between Candy and D.T. "Okay, who's first?"

As Candy and her family pulled out their chairs, Jake mentally dabbed at his wounds. He felt sleepy, hurt, angry, ashamed. Rushed. From the frying pan into the fire with Angela swatting your ass with a spatula every lurch of the way.

Angela smiled at Don and Ilene. "Well, what's going on with you two this morning?"

Jake closed his eyes, thinking, if they're like any of the rest of us, Angela, they're still having muscle spasms from your opener.

"This is the day the patient is allowed to respond," Angela continued, "But, first, is there anything left that either of you want to say?"

Ilene glanced at Angela, then looked at Candy. "Mother, I'm confused. Today at lunch you were different than you were the first two days."

Angela patted Ilene's hand. "What happened? How was she different?"

"She was…I don't know how to explain it. She cried. I haven't seen her cry since I was a little girl. She said…" the groupwad zeroed in on Ilene as she whispered, "She said she loved me."

Angela looked across Ilene. "Don?"

He nodded. "All I can add is that she told me that she loved me, and that she was sorry."

"Candy?" Angela sat back in her chair. "I know you had a one-on-one with Dr. Caccia this morning. Would you share with us what went on?"

Candy reached out and took some tissues from the box on Ilene's lap. "We were talking about some of the things I've been allowing myself to remember. What to do about them." She glanced at Don and Ilene, shuddered, and closed her eyes. "I'm still having a hard time forgiving myself. I don't know if I can without…" She looked up and both her husband and daughter reached out, first holding her hands, then pulling her until the three of them were hugging.

As the three of them continued to hug and cry, Jake saw Angela's chair move back just far enough for the counselor to glance at Marnie. Marnie returned the look. Smugs all around.

There was some discussion about the past, the present, and the future, Candy's hopes for the future, and then D.T. and the Pennoyers were on.

As Jake listened to D.T. ask for forgiveness, and saw Mitzi and her two sons filling the request a thousand times over, he thought of Ann. It did seem like part of the obligation. Forgiveness. Before he could forgive himself, he had to hear it from Ann. But before it would mean anything, both of them had to admit to themselves and to each other what had happened. The complete, unabridged horror.

There was so much horror to wade through. Most of it hadn't even been remembered. Ann never said anything. A couple of times, as Jake was staggering his way from his office to the kitchen to get another drink, she had said, "Jake, don't you think you ought to do something about your drinking?"

"I'm doing it," he would answer, if he happened to be in a good mood. If not, he would begin peeling her self-respect like an onion until nothing remained except a huge, raw, throbbing nerve. He would jab at her vulnerability, curse her, scream at her, smash the things they both loved, just to—

The girl. The girl in west wing who was crying. Jake had seen her pain and his heart had gone out to her. Anything that would have helped her he would have gladly done. Anything. But, Ann. The pain he had inflicted on her. He loved Ann. He didn't know Amy Whatshername from a hole in the wall.

D.T. and his family were heading for the sidelines. Angela looked as happy as a clam at high tide. "Well, we have some time. Are there any old contracts pending?"

A few chuckles, then Roger began bellyaching about what Barny had said about his god in morning group, and the voices evened out into a buzz as Jake thought back to the conversation he and Frank had the night before.

"Don't bail out on the group, Jake. You'll only be hurting yourself."

"I can't hack it any more. This place is driving me crazy. What can the group do except hand out some more amateur psycho shit? I am up to here in having my brains, convictions, values and everything else scrambled. I'm tired, I hurt, I'm angry, and goddammit to hell, I am fucking fed up!"

"Take the thing that's eating you right now and lay it on the group. See what happens. Just stay one more day. Use the group. *That's what it's there for.*"

Use the group. That's what Barny was telling Roger to do this morning, and what the group was telling him to do again this afternoon. Even Snake had figured it out. Jake frowned.

—I have to see it work before I can believe in it, and before I can see it work, I have to try it.

There was a pause as Roger the minister's remains were swept under his chair. Angela looked at her watch. "There's still a couple of minutes."

Jake coughed. "Yeah. Well, I'd like to talk about something. Yesterday I answered one of the patient phones. When I went to get the girl the call was for, I found her crying in her room. I couldn't get anyone to do anything for her. I mean Marnie just—"

"Jake, are you upset because the staff at St. Mary's doesn't follow your orders?"

"No, I—

"You didn't get what you wanted when you wanted it?"

"I think we've had this conversation before."

In thirty seconds flat he was screaming at Angela, and at the end of two minutes he was sitting in the north wing lounge feeling as though he had been hammered into the ground. The memory was a blur of events and tangled feelings. Frank sat down in the couch across from Jake, his mouth curled up into a big smile.

"See, I told you it would work."

"Work?"

"You got her attention, didn't you?"

"I'm beginning to understand cannibalism, Frank. Eat me." Jake waved his hand toward Room 355. "What happened in there? There I was grooving on the good vibes, and the next thing I know Madam Guillotine is giving me a shave. I feel like I've been plucked, gutted, sectioned, and my parts put on sale for half price. What did she do to me?"

"That sweet old lady?"

Frank stood and wandered down the hallway, laughing. Jake shook his head and tried to relax, there remaining at least small hopes of limiting his flashbacks for the day to forty or fifty.

He took several deep breaths. Before she had dismissed him, Angela had asked: "Jake, do you have a problem with women?" He had opened his mouth to shout his denials, but Angela held up her hand. "Just think about it tonight."

—Talk about your off-the-wall questions.

Angela was standing in her doorway talking to Don and Ilene. Jake fixed the image in his mind and closed his eyes as he muttered, "There's only one woman I have troubles with. Bitch." Reluctantly he lowered his comment into his file of things he wished he had said at the time but thought of too late.

He glanced at the sparkles in the window frost made by the setting sun. Turning his head he looked at the wall calendar. "Oh no." He sank down into the chair. "This is only Wednesday."

48

Roger rolled over in bed and winced at the sounds of the plastic pillow covers. Reaching to the nightstand, he picked up his watch and forced his eyes to focus on the luminous dial. 1:07 a.m. He closed his eyes, letting his arm rest on the edge of the mattress.

"When am I ever going to sleep like a human?" He replaced his watch on the nightstand and rolled onto his back.

—Man, did Angela ever ream Jake a brand-new excretory opening in afternoon group?

Roger's feelings were mixed. Seeing Jake burn was wish fulfillment. But he understood how Jake felt. Jake had just tried to get help for that girl who had been hurting. Isn't that what he was supposed to do? And Angela wanted to know if Jake had a problem with women.

—It's not my problem, he thought, attempting to rid his mind of distractions.

"I want to sleep." He opened his eyes and looked at the patterns of light on the ceiling. Sleep would come with time. That return visitor, Martin, said it took him four months after treatment for the nightmares to stop and for him to get his first full night's sleep.

But Martin's nightmares were the ordinary using dreams. Wandering around old haunts, getting shitfaced. Roger's dreams were still about the waterhole. Korea.

He shook his head, rolled to his side, and spoke. His words weren't aimed at his old judgmental, punishing god. Barny had said that Roger would have to find something that would keep him sober. *"Design your own Higher Power. Give it the power to love you and help you."*

"Do you mean just out of my head?"

"Roger, God is big enough and powerful enough to fill any bill of particulars you can devise."

Roger put his words on display. Should a higher power with some compassion for Roger notice them, well and good. If not, nothing lost.

"I want this thing that some of the others have," he said to the darkness. "I want this ability not to take everything personally, not to have to put on an act, always hiding behind a collar. Peace of mind. Serenity. That more than anything. Peace of mind."

Everybody says the same thing: use the group. Frank was hanging from the edge of his chair in afternoon group. "For Christ's sake, Roger, get in touch with *something!*"

He wanted to. He wanted to so badly. To feel something besides guilt, anger, despair, fear. To feel something besides shame. He pushed himself up and leaned on his elbow as an outrageous thought crossed his mind.

—I don't hate Jake! I envy him! Jake can laugh.

Jake was hauling around as much angry garbage as anyone in the Animals. But he could laugh. Roger flopped down on his back. The feedback in group constantly told Jake that he was laughing when he should be doing something else, that his laughter was a defense designed to insulate him from his pain, that he needed to get in touch with that pain.

—But he can laugh.

"I want to laugh again. I need to laugh again." Roger felt his eyes moisten. "No, I really don't feel like wallowing in self-pity right now, thank you very much."

—Damn, but these nights alone get long. Sitting in a dark room alone with your thoughts. Prison solitary must be nine kinds of hell.

From the hallway came a thundering bellow: "Fuck the Minnesota Clean Indoor Air Act!!!"

A door slammed very loudly, its echo reverberating up and down the halls.

—That was Jake! "Getting in touch with his feelings."

Applause came from the other rooms. Roger began giggling, then laughed out loud, his hands joining the lusty applause. "Author! Author!" he demanded.

Tears streamed down his cheeks as his lungs fought for the air needed to feed his laughter. "Huzzah!" he shouted. "Bravo!" His arms fell to the mattress, exhausted. Light entered his room as the door opened. He squinted at the dark shape crouched behind the flashlight.

"Did you say that?"

"Say…say, what, man?"

The figure hesitated, then began withdrawing. "Forget it."

Roger wrapped his arms around his abdomen as he drew his knees up and gasped. "Oh, Jesus! Oh, sweet Jesus, it hurts."

49

Jake started awake, then settled his head back on his pillow. The dreams seemed to be getting stupider by the episode. Jake picked up his watch. 2:32 a.m.. Only an hour of sleep this time. "Unless I get my two hours in, I'm nothing the next day." Nighthawk humor.

This time the dream had been about Angela opening the top of his skull, sticking an eggbeater inside, and turning the crank. One needn't be Sigmund Freud to figure out that one. Jake noted with gratitude that for once his screamarama hadn't blasted his roommate out of the sack. Frank was asleep.

Jake sat up, crossed his legs and leaned his elbows on his knees.

Another night up. Another night sober and alone. Another night absorbing coffee, smoking, picking through the past, worrying about tomorrow, trying to survive the present. He toyed with the thought of giving his Minnesota Clean Indoor Air Act war whoop another try, but decided against it. Those who had managed to get to sleep would be after him with hot tar and feathers. Besides, he didn't feel like being funny.

Tired. In group Jake had said something that came out backwards. Gisel Apple, the freckle-queen interning in alcohol, asked for a clarification. Jake couldn't think of one and tried to explain that he hadn't been getting much sleep lately.

"That's just an excuse," Gisel had responded.

"What?"

"That's just an excuse for not getting in touch with your feelings."

"Just an excuse, eh?" A fantasy involving a wood-burning iron and a game of connect-the-dots with Gisel's freckles flashed by in the dark.

Jake counted on his fingers the hours of sleep he had managed to get during the past seven nights—

"That's right. This is my second week." Funny. Each day seemed a month long, but the week? Zip. "Suddenly I'm an old-timer."

No matter how he worked it out, he couldn't come up with more than ten hours of sleep. An average of less than an hour and a half per night.

What the hell. There was always his assignment for the night. "Do I have a problem with women?" He couldn't think of anything.

—It's my favorite form of protoplasm. "I mean I *dig* women, man, y'know?"

Before they had turned in for the night, Jake had talked it over with Frank, trying to see what Angela was getting at. He had said that he was shy with women. "But, then, I've always been shy with men, too. I can't think of any problems I have with women that don't apply equally to men, children, animals, and plants."

There were the questions about women on the Penis Itcher. The did-he-like-women questions. Was Mickey Mouse trying to find out if his penis itched for something more exotic than those of the female persuasion? He had answered them all in the affirmative. "Hell, man, I don't like them; I love them."

Frank had suggested that Angela's question might be about something other than sex. Jake couldn't imagine what.

Except for that one item on the Penis Itcher. He said it out loud: "My mother was a good woman. True or false." He sat staring at the statement for ten minutes before leaving the item blank and going on to the next.

Jake gathered his cup, smoking, and first step goodies. Slippers on the feet, robe on the back, got them rehab blues. He trudged down to the floor kitchen, filled his cup, and as he passed the nurse's station on the way to north wing he nodded at the nurse holding down the fort.

She smiled and nodded back. "It gets better."

"I read the advertisement," Jake replied.

Sipping his coffee, Jake reached the lounge, settled into the easy chair, put his feet up on the coffee table, and lit his pipe. He flipped through his steno pad, glancing with disgust at the several false starts he had made on his first step.

He couldn't even seem to track down his first drink or his first drug. When he was five, the guy who worked for his family thought it was cute to see a five-year-old staggering around drunk. Little Jacob liked the approval, and the beer, and the effect. Even before that there was the magic brown bottle: paregoric. The magic? The awful taste made the pain go away. It made his brain and the back of his head feel fuzzy. Licorice flavored tincture of opium. Alcohol and opium, what a drink. He still had a thing for licorice.

There was that time, not yet four years old, he woke up in a hospital from a drug overdose. He had been in a coma for two weeks. It had taken him days to relearn how to walk. The family story had been that he had gotten into Mama's sleeping pills. Even earlier, there was the story in the family about how baby Jake spent the first two years of his life puking. All the time Mama had carried him, she had been on morphine and cocaine. That was before they knew that shit in mama was shit in baby. So Jake had come into the world as a bouncing baby white knuckle.

Jake shook his head and closed the steno pad. He didn't even feel like working on his first step. He just didn't seem to fit the prepared pigeonholes. He looked at the windows in the lounge. They were thick with frost patterned into images that looked like tropical plants. Nate, the acid-head who had joined the wing that night, had really gotten into the windows. *Wowwwwww!* The idiot almost gave his nose frostbite.

Jake got to his feet, picked up his coffee and went to the balcony door. Half of the door's glass was clear, allowing a limited view of the city lights. It seemed so lonely, so far away, so dark, so cold. He thought of the girl, Amy, bundled in her chair, her pain drawing him like a magnet.

As he looked down at her, all he wanted in the world was to ease that girl's pain. Take it on. Do anything to rescue her. The love in his heart was an unbearable agony.

—Do I have trouble with women?

"Christ, Angela, it's the only value I have left that isn't screwed up." He shook his head and sipped at his coffee. Then a thought itched at the back of his head.

—What if Amy had been male instead of female?

He looked down in disgust at the boy wallowing in a sea of self-pity—

"Shit."

Jake backed up. He had dropped his cup, the hot coffee splashing on his legs. His head hurt as he put the cup on the coffee table and went to the tiny game closet to get some paper napkins. As he blotted up the spilled coffee, he looked again at Amy bundled in her chair, crying. There he saw pain, a call to rescue, an emotional blank check.

"But if I put a boy in that chair, crying…poor me, poor me."

Jake threw the wet napkins into the trash can, picked up his cup, and headed down the dark hallway for a refill. As he walked, his mind raced.

There were other women in his life. That editor who had screwed him sixteen different ways. Ann had been furious. *"Jake, you can't let her do this to you."*

"Ann, you don't understand. Felice has that entire editorial board to contend with, and as a woman heading a new department—"

"Why are you making excuses for her?"

"You're a woman. You should understand."

Jake inserted his cup in the coffee dispenser and pushed the button. He nodded. "If Felice had been a man, I would have killed the sonofabitch!"

There were others: Time after time, woman after woman, putting up with behavior he would never tolerate from a man. The more abhorrent the behavior in a woman, the more he would love....

"Love?" Jake sat down in the kitchen next to the tiny table. His stomach was writhing with self-disgust.

That "friend" he hadn't heard from for six years. Telephoned him from Florida. Her life was a shambles. Couldn't make the rent on her five-hundred dollar a month apartment, couldn't make the payment on her new Jaguar. The twenty-six thousand dollar a year job didn't pan out. The people there just didn't like her and she had quit. Just a couple of thousand would rescue her....

Without a second thought, Jake had promised to wire her the funds. Ann was outraged. It would take every cent of their savings.

"We can get by. Margie is in trouble."

"She could get rid of the car, couldn't she? She could move out of the Taj Mahal, couldn't she? She could stop walking out on high-paying jobs, couldn't she—"

"Christ, Ann, you're heartless. I don't like you this way at all."

Jake shook his head. The money hadn't been sent. Ann had put her foot down. But Jake had felt guilty ever since. He had resented Ann for it ever since. Hard hearted.

—But if my little Margie had been a man?

"I would have laughed at him."

Jake looked at his cup and was surprised to find it empty. He refilled it and pushed into the corridor. Once in the wing, he looked toward the nurse's station. The station lights surrounded by the darkness of the floor spotlighted the woman behind the counter. One of the graveyard nurses. He felt afraid of her.

She was older than most of the nurses and floor counselors. Her attention was concentrated on some papers. He turned the corner and made his way down north wing. He searched for why he had this bizarre view of women, this Jake Randecker the White Knight rescuing faire maidens in distress self-image. Where…

"How much sharper than a serpent's tooth is an ungrateful child—"

The voice, the words, were there. He stopped in the hallway and leaned against the rail. Thicknesses of obscurity seemed to part revealing endless spans of yesterday.

Her nightstand was a drugstore. She would sit holding court from her bed. Dirty feet from walking barefooted, ragged nightgown, straggles of hair, the smell of ancient cigarette butts. The perfection of his mother.

She was perfect. He loved her. A good boy loves his mother, and Jacob was a good boy. No…that's what he was striving toward. Never to be called sharper than a serpent's tooth.

She suffered so. All of her strange, rare, exotic illnesses. The quantity and degree of her vast collection of commonplace afflictions. Rashes, allergies, gall bladder, detached retina, heart, this, that….

Dad was nothing more than an irresponsible child. It was all Mama could do to hold things together, him living in Arizona, her living in Pennsylvania. But it was a home. A two thousand mile wide home.

"Jacob, why do your sisters hate me?"

"They don't," he lied. But it was a good lie for a just cause; it was a not-lie.

"Is it that they are simply thoughtless? Uncaring? I do it all for them, and you, and for that I am either forgotten or treated like some sort of monster. Am I a monster?"

"Oh, no, Mama. You're perfect."

She grew very red in the face and examined Jacob to see if he was making fun of her. "Come, now. Nobody's perfect."

Jacob noted that she was modest, thereby perfecting perfection. The proof. One who is perfect could never say so.

She would whine, and cajole, and order, and shout, and argue; an emotional Machiavelli piecing together and tearing apart what her children thought of themselves, each other, of the world, and especially of her. What was it that his older sister Marion called it?—Mind fucking.

She would manipulate one child against another, keeping everyone off balance, uncertain, insecure, in a constant state of terror. To survive as a child in that house, one had to instinctually read the mood of the moment and immediately conform. God help you if you laughed when everyone else was wallowing in depression. They became emotional chameleons.

When would she laugh? When would she condemn? When would she offer her love? When would she withdraw it? The rules, the circumstances, were always in a constant state of change. Jacob could never figure out the rules. Where should he be, who should he become, to be safe? Eventually he settled on becoming whatever anyone within his proximity wanted him to become.

Appearances. Convincing others that he conformed. I look, feel, believe, dress, vote, and want whatever you do. It was in the name of self-preservation that he had lost his self. It was in the name of love that he had entrenched himself in endless mazes of disguised hate.

Will Mama approve or disapprove? For the first twenty-four years of his life, this was the issue that shook the planet. This was the only issue that mattered.

That night on the outskirts of Augusta, Maine. The drive-in theater was advertising a picture. Its title: "I Dismembered Mama." Jake pulled over to the side of the road and stopped the car he was laughing so hard. *He was there forty minutes later, still laughing.*

That television show, *I Remember Mama*, was one of Mama's favorite programs. The mama in the series? A saint. An absolute saint. Jacob's mama didn't aspire to sainthood, though. She felt she had already achieved that. Just look at how she suffered. Always for them. She was waiting for her children to recognize her status and to treat her accordingly. She complained constantly because the worship of her children was never quite good enough.

"We tried. We tried so hard."

Jake shook his head, the tears running down his cheeks. Maybe there was some leftover groupwad in the lounge. He entered the lounge and sat in the easy chair. He pulled a sheet of groupwad from the box on the coffee table and blew his nose. He balled up the sheet, pulled another, and blew again. He leaned back, his eyes closed, his head slowly shaking.

"Oh this is a fun place!"

—What are you describing, Jake? The impatience, the grandiosity, the isolation—

"I lived for over twenty years in the same place and never met any of our neighbors."

He had asked Mama why once. *"They stole things from us, Jacob.* I'd be embarrassed if I walked into someone's front parlor and found my silver or my couch. Wouldn't you be embarrassed?"

"They all couldn't have stolen from us, could they?"

"It's a small community. I'm sorry, dear, but they all had to be in on it."

That afternoon Jacob said good-bye forever to beautiful little Lilly, his new friend. When Lilly wanted to know why, Jacob told her that her mother and father were thieves. *She had run home crying.*

Mama was always explaining, justifying herself, her behavior, her tears. Resentful, self-pitying, displaying her collection of miseries like the nail-holes in Christ's hands....

She was a shadow, backlit with the dim glow from the hall. As she tucked him in bed, he could tell she had been crying

"Mama, what's the matter?"

She finished tucking him in and paused. "Do you have any idea how sorry you will feel when I'm no longer here, when I'm dead?"

She turned, slowly entered the hall, and the room went black.

Jealous, envying, living in fantasy....

Watching the movie "Cheaper by the Dozen" on television. Mama began talking about when she was a little girl, abandoned by her parents. Her father was run off by Grandfather Merckle, a hard-driving, hard-drinking sonofabitch. Her mother became an uninvolved servant in her own home. Her mother's sister, Aunt Audrey, took command, alternately terrorizing and ignoring the little girl. Aunt Audrey used to have a drinking problem, you know.

Mama used to huddle in her covers at night and dream about the big happy family she was going to have. She would spin on about the big happy family, and how no one seemed to want it but her. Her kids just took all of this happiness she created for granted.

—Happiness?

The thought would race through Jake's mind before he could extinguish it with guilt and shame

—Lady, what in the ever-loving hell are you talking about? *Happiness? Are you insane?*

"What am I describing?" He shook his head. Grandfather Merckle's boozing begat Aunt Audrey the Awful, whose boozing begat Mama the Manipulator, who begat Jake the Jerk, who...

What had that one lecturer called the addictive family system of dependents and co-dependents? "A way of life that has been passed down from fist to mouth over generations." If one parent was addicted, the child's chances of becoming an addict are fifty-fifty. If both parents were addicted, the child's prospects of becoming an addict are certain enough to dispense with odds.

Mama always criticizing, constantly looking for flaws, nothing good was good enough. She was always arguing small ridiculous points as though her life depended on proving herself right and everyone else wrong, whatever the issue of the moment happened to be.

"The penny belt. A four-hour tirade for the sake of two lousy feet of Scotch Tape."

She could never be wrong. She could never admit to a mistake. She always had to be right. She not only had to be right, everyone had to admit that she was right. Not just the words. When you caved in and lied your ass off, throwing your values, integrity, and self-esteem down the toilet for the sake of a little peace and quiet, you had to be sincere.

"When you were right, you had to believe you were wrong. She could always tell when you were lying about your lie."

—Negative, insincere, envious, lying....

That woman on television being interviewed about teaching sex to your kids. The interviewer asked: "Is it ever too late to get into the game and teach your children these things?"

The woman shook her head. "It's never too late to be honest. You don't lie to your kids. I can't imagine lying to a child, can you?"

Jake never got to hear the remainder of the program. *He was laughing too hard.*

"What are you describing?" Jake asked himself.

The drugs on her nightstand. Thousands and thousands of dollars a year on prescriptions. She took the drugs because she was sick and depressed, and she was sick and depressed a lot.

Doctor Jim, every week, would come out, talk, shoot B-12 in her arm, and write her some more prescriptions.

"I'll be damned. Mama was working Doctor Jim for scripts. He certainly delivered, too."

The fight between Marion and Doctor Jim. "Doctor, don't treat me like a child. I know you can't keep shooting her up with dope and loading her with pills. Don't you see what it does to her?"

"Your mother is special, Marion. *She just doesn't react to drugs the way normal people do.*"

Jake shook his head. "He was certainly right about that." Poor Doctor Jim. He's dead.

"Why not say it?"

It was all there. All he had to do was say the words that explained it all. "A drug addict. Mama was a junky." She's dead, too. Heart failure. Sometimes known in the trade as an overdose. He lit his pipe. "And Dad? As long as we're facing up to all of this, what about Dad?" He died of liver failure, sometimes known in the trade as cirrhosis, or suicide by alcohol.

Mama was letting it all hang out that one time. "Yes, your father had a drinking problem. But he has it under control now. All he has now is his one Martini before dinner."

But there was never any problem finding nice sturdy liquor boxes to pack things in, was there? Jim Beam, Old Crow, and every brand of gin in the world. Long after Mama had told him about Dad's former drinking problem, Jacob had gone walking in the woods. He was thirteen and had been following a deer path that came close to the road to the upper house. Dad lived in one house, and Mama lived in the other. It had never seemed strange to have one's parents live in separate houses on the same property.

There was a bright glitter ahead. Jake walked up to it and saw that it was a waist-high mountain of empty liquor bottles. The bottle for Dad's one Martini was always at the lower house, and when it ran out, it went into the regular trash. Where had all these come from?

The burden of truth. Mama was wrong, Dad was drinking oceans of booze, and the owner of this truth knew that if it were acted upon, his world would end.

Jacob had cried, "No one's going to call my Dad an alcoholic!"

He picked up a heavy branch and began smashing the bottles. After they were all smashed, he covered the pieces with leaves and put the entire scene out of his mind. *The next time he allowed himself to remember the bottle mountain, it was twenty-six years later.*

Jake had read it a hundred times and had heard it in at least ten lectures. There ain't no such thing as a former drinking problem. Some alkys, though, get very, very good at hiding. Some alkys' families, though, put on some spectacular displays of denial. Hiding the booze, hiding the behavior, hiding....

"Wrong. Mama was wrong."

Father and mother, both dead from the disease. Jake's trouble with women? He had heard enough about co-dependency. He had been affected by the behavior around him and had bent reality to fit the laws of his universe. Mama was perfect, and he loved her. The only problem with this theory was that Mama was a drug addict and a chemical co-dependent. She was considerably less than perfect.

Jacob had hated her behavior. He had no way of making a distinction between the behavior and the person; therefore, he had hated her. But he twisted his mind until it saw and felt what it had to see and feel. She could do no wrong, and he loved her. The world twisted, cracked, and disintegrated to mold itself to these laws. The wrong, the problems, the addictions? They had never—could never—be seen. Anything wrong that could be seen?

"My fault. Always my fault."

—A good boy loves his mother. I was determined to be good. Nothing less than the perfection Mama whined and cried for. Perfect just never seemed to be good enough. So I quit trying, regarded myself as a worthless failure, and died inside from guilt. "The real bitch about this is that there's no one to blame. No one I can kill for what happened to all of us. That's the bitch!"

The bug. The disease. All the drunks and junkies at Saint Mary's were basically good people. Fine people. Even Snake had taken Bad Bob on and straightened out the man's shitty attitude. Because Snake cared.

Mama was a human being. A very sick human being, doing the best she could with what she had. In back of the disease was a good woman.

Jake took a deep breath. "So, where does all this leave us?" Jake stared at Angela's closed door. "Did I really have to know all of this shit?"

More groupwad. Then a sip of coffee. Then fire up the pipe. He sat back and looked up at the ceiling. "Where that leaves me is treating women I dislike as though I love them, and treating those that I like or love as though I hate them." And, he added wordlessly, getting some pretty bizarre results.

"Poor Ann. My poor Ann."

—Or in the words of a famous science fiction writer to his roommate: "I think that little old white bitch hit the nail right on the head."

—Talk about your off-the-wall questions.

He finished off his coffee, grabbed a handful of groupwad, pushed himself to his feet, and headed back to his room. As he opened the door a voice was speaking from the dark: "Jake? Jake? It's time to get up."

The call of the northwinged doorknocker.

"Okay."

He leaned against the doorjamb. "Well, well, well. I think I finally have something to try out in group."

He looked at Frank's sleeping hulk, then looked up at the ceiling. "Look, you sonofabitch, no more character insights until after ten in the morning. Okay?"

He pushed open his door, placed his coffee cup on his desk, and began removing his robe. As he threw the robe over the back of his chair, he looked up at the nailed Jesus hanging from the crucifix to the right of his desk. He laughed. "How does *that* make you feel, man?"

JANUARY 6TH

50

Jake was studying the floor on his way back from breakfast. As he passed the nurse's station, he glanced up and noticed Dr. Caccia leaning on the counter, studying a file. Tony Caccia noticed Jake and wreathed his face with smiles. "Jake, you're just the man I wanted to see."

Jake stopped next to the psychiatrist. He noted that Tony was still too happy. "Why?"

"Do you remember that twenty minute written test you took?"

"I remember."

Tony looked down at the file. His eyebrows were raised as he again looked at Jake. "The purpose of it was to test for brain damage. The results indicate extreme brain damage."

Jake leaned against the counter. "Tony, you have an absolute gift for timing." Jake thought back to the test, thought back to his state of mind. "I was pretty angry when I took it. Would that make a difference?"

"Maybe. Would you mind taking it again?"

"No." Jake went into the examination room next to the nurse's station. First side the vocabulary test. He maxed it. The second side had been the side that had made no sense the night he had been consumed with anger. He frowned as he pushed the paper away and dropped his pencil on the desk. This time all of the questions on the second side made perfect sense. He maxed it.

As he turned in the test, the conclusion was staring him right in the face. Angry, his words and mouth worked just fine, but the part of his brain that creates, that solves problems, shuts down.

He thought about it on his way to morning group. Before being led through Saint Mary's doors, every aspect of his life had been governed from a state of constant rage. And every single aspect of his life was screwed up. His life had been in the control of an articulate moron.

"Old saying: engage brain before operating mouth." He slowly shook his head as he walked the length of north wing. "But what do I do, then, with all of this anger that's eating me alive?"

The cowbells rang out the signal for morning group. There was the sound of cattle lowing—cattle that had smoked too much. Jake smiled as he saw the Animals mooing as they waddled into group.

The circle was small. D.T. and Candy were missing, having interviews with their respective aftercare counselors. Frank was being interviewed by Doctor Caccia. Dave was down at fourth step prep. Lydia was getting a physical.

Jake looked around, trying to remind himself that he was not the only bag of troubles in the room. Ron was glum. Brandy, doing the reading with a strong voice, looked determined to do something extreme. Earl had obviously been crying, and Roger looked like he was sitting on a ton of dynamite trying to decide whether to extinguish the fuse or run.

—I wonder what I look like.

Jake looked at Angela, wondering how anyone with both oars in the water could do this kind of work. Imagine coming to work every day and facing the convoluted bullshit of a room full of addicts. Jake pursed his lips and closed his eyes.

"I'm Brandy, drug addict, and my contract this morning is to talk about what I need from this group, what I need this group to be."

"Angela Gwynn, counselor for the group."

"Gisel Apple, alcoholic, intern."

A brief silence and Jake opened his eyes. "I'm Ron Steward, alcoholic." Ron shook his head, his glumness turning into anger. "I guess I'm just a plain addict. I don't have a contract."

Angela clasped her hands and rocked back and forth in her chair. "What do you need to work on, Ron?"

"I don't know that there's much point."

"You look disturbed about something."

He sat back in his chair and folded his arms. "I was supposed to get out today. Yesterday you told me to forget it."

Angela held up her hand. "Excuse me, Ron, but I don't like you putting words into my mouth. Now, what did I tell you?"

His face flushed as he again lowered his glance to the floor. "You said that you had talked to my parents, the staff, and the business office. The bottom line is my ass is in here for at least another week."

"Only if you want it."

"Sure. But if I cut out, it'll be against medical advice, and an AMA means that my dad's insurance won't pay for anything."

Angela tapped her fingertips against her chair's armrest. She thought for a long time, studying Ron's every movement. Suddenly she leaned forward. "Is that the only reason you can think of for staying here?"

"Yeah.

"Then you might as well take off and get out. Last night your father gave me permission to tell you this. His insurance doesn't cover any aspect of your treatment. Not one cent."

"He told me it did! That was the only reason I agreed to—he lied. He lied to me to get me in here."

"That's right. He lied to you to get you in here. How does that make you feel?"

Ron shook his head, shrugged, glared at the floor, and shook his head again. "I don't know. Grateful, I suppose, if—"

"Group." Angela sat back in her chair. After a brief moment of silence, she looked around the circle. "Where are you, group?"

Jake put his contract aside and looked at Ron. His face was red, the muscles in his jaw and upper arms were twitching, his right leg was rapidly jerking up and down, his eyes almost glittered. "Ron, to me you look angry—"

Ron sat forward, pointed a shaking finger, and glared at Jake. "What the fuck makes you think I'm angry?!"

Jake shrugged and held out his hands. "Oh, I don't know. Just a stab in the dark." The rest of the group laughed out loud.

There was a little more feedback, and the vote was unanimous. Angela asked Ron to talk on that peculiar form of gratitude he was feeling, and the contracts moved along.

"My name is Roger. I'm an alcoholic. My contract is to talk about something I did when—something I'm ashamed of."

It was Jake's turn. He felt lighthearted, frightened, almost as though he were taking that empty-handed leap into the void. "I'm Jake Randecker, addict, and my contract is to talk about what I was asked to think about in yesterday afternoon's group."

Earl was next. "My contract? I guess I want to talk—check out with the group—my reasons for leaving treatment." Jake looked to his left in surprise at Earl.

Angela nodded at Earl, clasped her hands over her belly, and cycled a deep breath. "Very well, who's first?"

Roger leaned forward, his hands hanging limply between his knees.

"I want to recover; I don't want to go back. But there's something that's been eating me alive for thirty years. It's really in my way."

Angela leaned forward. "Would you like to leave it here, Roger?"

He nodded. "Yes, but I don't know about saying it in front of—I mean, I don't know how anyone will react." He became quiet, his eyebrows raised. "I guess I'm looking for a guarantee."

"What kind of guarantee?"

"The wrong kind." He looked around the circle. "I feel afraid because what you think about me might change."

Jake studied Roger's face. The man was carrying a secret horror, a piece of the real man that Roger believed would cause the rest of humanity to shun him. Exactly the way Jake felt. He smiled and placed his right arm across Roger's shoulders. "Maybe it will change, Rog. But they tell me here that we're responsible for the effort, not the outcome. The outcome is up to whatever your higher power is."

Roger looked with confusion at Jake, then around at the group. He clasped his hands together and looked down at them. "It was in Korea, thirty years ago. I was a nineteen year old private in a newly integrated infantry company. My squadleader, Sergeant Stubbs, was from Tennessee. For awhile I was treated like a leper, but it all changed very quickly after that first Chinese wave assault. I was very good with that M-1, and I guess the squad figured they had more in common with me than they had with the Chinese. We became pretty close."

A single tear streaked down Roger's left cheek. "There was a waterhole. We had an unwritten agreement with the Chinese and we both used the waterhole. Once when three of us were filling canteens, we met two Chinese soldiers who were also loaded down with canteens. As we all filled up, we exchanged cigarettes, food, showed each other photos of family." Roger wiped the tear from his face with the back of his right hand.

"Stubbs, my squadleader, talked with me that night. He said the same thing probably goes on in every war. Back in the Second World War in Italy, Stubbs had met one German soldier so many times they had exchanged addresses. He said he still corresponded with the German, who operated a Wurzburg car wash. He showed me a picture of the German and his family. Stubbs didn't have a family of his own, except for the army.

"The next afternoon we found Stubbs and two other squadmembers dead at the waterhole. A fourth squad member, barely alive, told us a Chinese squad had been waiting for them. For the next two days, we covered the waterhole. Near the evening of the second day, nine enemy soldiers came to the waterhole. They did a quick search of the perimeter, then bent to filling their canteens and washing themselves and their uniforms. The firing lasted no more than three or four seconds. We killed all of them."

Roger leaned back in his chair, his eyes large and sad. He looked up at Angela. "Then we went down to where the bodies were and we cut off their heads." His voice became very quiet. "We took our bayonets out and sawed them off at the neck. We buried the bodies so they couldn't be found and arranged the nine heads around the waterhole. As a reminder." He glanced around the room. "That's all, except my drinking really took off starting with that night."

Brandy waited a moment, then began. "Roger, you look very sad. You must have loved your sergeant very much."

Roger closed his eyes, nodded, and cried. "I never let myself feel that. All I could feel was hate, anger. Revenge. But—"

He shook his head violently. Ron leaned to his left and placed his hand on Roger's arm. "What's going on right now?"

"I never talked about it. When I got home. I never talked about it. I wouldn't even allow myself to think about it. But the nightmares. The shame. I always felt guilty, dirty. I wanted to make up for it. To do good for the rest of my life to try and balance the evil of the past. But it just won't balance. I can't change the past. I don't want to live there anymore. I want to get better. I'm just tired of hurting."

Earl stood, picked up the groupwad from Angela's desk, and dropped the box on Roger's lap after pulling out a few sheets for himself. He sat back down, blew his nose, and talked.

"I know what you're talking about, Roger. About living in the past. That's where my address is. My father, he was an alcoholic. He died in a car accident. This is the day, January sixth. It's my birthday, you know." Earl breathed deeply.

"I loved him so much. He was wonderful. I blamed my Mom for it all. She's dead too. But in my head I'm always back there, trying to—" He shook his head. "Trying to fix it, trying to make it what it should have been, trying to change it, I guess. I can't." He shook his head. "I never talked about it, either. I figured if I didn't let myself think about it, I wouldn't hurt. But—" His eyes opened wide, his eyebrows up.

Angela smiled. "What's happening, Earl?"

"I feel like I just put down an anvil that I've been carrying around for years."

Angela turned from Earl to Roger. "How do you feel?"

Roger nodded. "Better. Much, much better. Almost human."

Earl leaned forward, his elbows on his knees. "In my contract I wanted to talk about my reasons for leaving treatment."

Angela raised her eyebrows. "Yes?"

"They stink."

"That's it?"

Earl nodded, leaned back, folded his arms, and crossed his legs. "That's it." He glanced at Ron. "How about you, spunky?"

"What about me?"

"Had any thoughts about bugging out?"

Ron nodded, then glanced at Angela and blushed. "I was angry. Angry at myself. I guess I never got past the bargaining stage with the program. I'll go along with this, but I won't do that. I just couldn't see—wouldn't see—" He shook his head. "It seemed so *right:* Me and Paula. I was so empty inside, lonely, and—now I don't know where she is, I don't know where I am."

Jake removed his arm from Roger's shoulders and shook his head. "Ron, where you are is in the middle of a decision. You have been handed another week to get your act together. Are you going to take it, or not?"

Ron nodded. "Yeah, I'll take it. I'll take it and any more I can get my hands on."

Angela looked from Ron to Brandy. "What's going on with you right now?"

Jake looked and Brandy's eyes were glistening. "Before I came in here this morning, I was getting ready to ask to be transferred to another group. I had gotten pretty tired of this bunch of—" She took a breath. "I felt like this group wasn't much of a group. I feel differently now...."

While she talked, Jake felt himself being moved to the edge of a very steep cliff.

—Pretty soon now it will be time to put up or shut up. Is this group going to be the elusive Higher Power? Are the things tearing up my guts of any interest to anyone? Most important: will talking to this sorry bunch of drunks and junkies do anything to ease the pain that is crushing my heart?

"Jake?"

"Yes?" He looked at Brandy.

"Jake, you look like you're about to explode."

He nodded, his gaze fixed on Angela's kneecap. "Yesterday Angela asked me if I had a problem with women...."

He talked about the night before. The things he remembered. The things he figured out. The things he had felt. The things he was feeling. All of it. In the tumble of words, the rotten scabs on long festering sores were painfully ripped open, the foul-smelling contents drained, the pain eased. He learned from Roger and Earl that the energy he was burning living in the past was all waste. That most of his life had been spent living, fighting, suffering in this fantasy of what was, trying to make it what might have been.

As they stood to close the session, holding hands, repeating the Serenity Prayer, Jake noticed that the weight he was carrying was considerably lighter. He entered the room with a warren of pains; he left with a Higher Power. Or, in his own words, silently spoken:

—It works. At last something works for Jake Randecker.

JANUARY 16TH

51

Sunday evening, ten days later. George McIntyre followed the nurse named Marnie down third floor's north wing. His arms were piled with his bag, clothing, and book issue. An occasional strange face passed going in the other direction. Always with a warm expression of welcome.

The mindless, dull-eyed grins of burned out retards, thought George. George's face remained impassive.

He looked again at the back of the nurse. While going through evaluation, he had heard too many stories about Angela Gwynn and her Animals. Now he had been condemned there. Members in other groups called the Animals bottom barrel bait, lost causes, hard nuts, the forbidden fruits. Rehab reprobates. That one junky in the fourth floor lounge had called them the Saint Mary Blues, which seemed to mean a spectacular form of failure.

The nurse turned toward the last room on the right, pushed open a door bearing one of the childishly drawn assistant wing leader posters, and George followed her in.

"Hi, Marnie."

"Hi. Jake, this is your new cagemate." She turned toward George. "Jake's in his third week. He also knows the Minnesota Clean Indoor Air Act's views on smoking in patient rooms."

"Can't blame me for Minneapolis's industrial air pollution."

The nurse put a hand on her hip. "Curious, though, how all the pollution seems to gather in here."

George stepped from behind Marnie as a bearded and bespectacled fellow got up off of the first bed, tossed a big blue book on the nightstand, and pointed toward the bed. "Dump your gear there. My name's Jake Randecker." The room was blue with smoke.

"George. George McIntyre." George noted that Jake's bed was closest to the shelves, closets, and drawers. He bent over, deposited his belongings on Jake's bed, and stood up. "Thanks. I'll get my things off right away."

Marnie knocked on the door. "Jake?"

"Yeah?"

"You'll introduce him to the rest of his group, won't you?"

"Sure."

"Don't forget to explain the smoking regs."

"I won't."

She waved and left the room. Jake quickly walked to his nightstand, opened the drawer, and extracted a smoking corncob pipe from it. He put the stem of the pipe between his teeth and grinned at George. "The Minnesota Clean Indoor Air Act, don'tcha know."

George grinned thinly. "My last roommate didn't smoke. He was a real prick about it. I don't suppose you'll mind, not if you smoke that thing."

A shadow seemed to cross Jake's face. "My last roommate smoked. A lot." Jake looked back at George, the sadness put on temporary hold. "He walked out of treatment four days ago. Come on and meet the rest of the zoo."

George followed, shaking his head.

—My god, what a moody klutz. Just what I need. Corncobs. The zoo.

He followed Jake around the corner into the lounge. There was Brandy, a semi-attractive blond wearing a lavender jogging suit. The name seemed even cuter when George learned that, besides being a patient, she was an alcoholism counselor. Brandy was the wing leader.

There was a happy-looking black guy around fifty years old named Roger. Roger was a Methodist minister, but was telling jokes usually restricted to high school locker rooms.

Jake pointed at Roger. "Before we send him back to his congregation, we're going to have to send him to a halfway house to clean up his language."

The other clergy was named Elliot Yates. Elliot was in his middle thirties, was down-the-nose quiet, and sat like he had a stick up his ass.

Nate Koeber, drug dealer; Linda Manchester, model; Lydia Marx, "looking for work." The farmer, Earl, was off the floor. George'd get to meet him later.

George nodded at everyone. They seemed harmless enough, if not particularly bright-looking. There didn't appear to be a creative thought in the crowd. Brandy seemed bossy and was probably the group's latent lesbian. The one called Lydia looked a little spaced out. Roger the minister was an overweight Uncle Tom, the group's latent Negro. Nate was a shallow street punk. The model, Linda, was delicious-looking, but from the way she talked she was about as sharp as a pound of wet leather, as Foghorn Leghorn used to say. The model was shaping her nails with an emery board.

The other clergy, Elliot, seemed forbidding, which was probably nothing more than a defense hiding a dull, dull personality. He didn't even need to meet the farmer.

—Yup, Elmer done bought me a new manure spreader. Takin'

Alvira to the dance in 'er. Yup, yup.

Jake took off to get some coffee, and George sat down in one of the straight-backed chairs. He looked at the back of his departing roommate. What about Jake? He looked like a junior high social studies teacher with delusions of intelligence.

The street punk, Nate, walked over to George. "What do you do, George?"

"Do?"

"For a living."

"I go to Boston University. I am working on my master's in journalism."

"Going to be a newspaperman, huh?"

"No." George smirked and shook his head. "I plan to be a novelist."

Nate pursed his lips and nodded. "You got a good roommate, then. Did you know that Jake writes?"

"Really? Writes what? Mobile home brochures, supermarket ads, that sort of thing?"

"He might have worked a few of those things in—in between his novels, that is." Nate smiled, then grinned. "Welcome to the Animals, fella. I just know you're going to have an absolutely marvy fun time."

George turned toward Linda the model and motioned with his head toward Nate as the punk shambled off. "Sensitive little shit, isn't he?"

Linda, never looking up from her nails, answered, "It's funny, George. Not funny, ha ha; funny strange. I see people wander in here, and from looking at them you'd never figure that they were in the Animals. Then the next thing you know the clown opens his mouth and I say, 'Oh, yeah. Now I know why. Welcome to the pen, turkey.'" She glanced up. "You're a nasty little asshole, George. Do something about it, will you?" She returned to filing her nails.

His face getting redder by the second, George stood up, walked from the lounge, and turned into his room. In a few minutes he had put his things away and was on his bed, his eyes closed, his lips silently framing the curses he had in his heart.

—I am in the wrong place. More than anything else in the world, I know that I don't belong here.

He heard Jake enter the room. "George, are you all right?"

"I am doing excellently, thank you." He heard Jake's mattress cover crackling.

—Dear God, he's sitting down.

"Do you want to talk about anything?"

"No." George rolled to his right and glared at Jake. "What is it with you people around here? Are you all frustrated psychologists? Do-gooders with no productive outlets?"

Jake's head went back, his mouth opened, and he laughed. When he calmed down he sipped at his coffee, then placed it on his nightstand. "I suppose it does look that way—like we were running around with couches on our backs yelling curb service—"

"That's *just* the way it looks."

Jake placed his hands on his knees and studied his new roommate. "We help ourselves by helping others, George. After you scrape off all of the trimmings, that's what it comes down to: helping ourselves by helping others."

"Jake, is it?" George sat up and faced his roommate. Jake nodded. "Well, Jake, perhaps some of us don't want your graciously offered assistance. Or need it. Perhaps some of us just want to be left the hell alone."

Jake got up, went to the door and closed it, then returned to his bed and fired up his pipe. "You sound as though you're having a rough time, George."

—Christ, talk about thick as a post!

George held out his hands and dropped them into his lap. "Dear God, what did I just *say?* If I want your shoulder to cry on—

"George." Jake puffed a bit, then removed the stem of his pipe from his mouth and pointed it. "If you don't need help, what are you doing here? You couldn't get a room at the Holiday Inn? You're in the Minneapolis area attending the National Assholes Convention, and you forgot to make a reservation at the bumwad factory?"

"Why I am here, Jake, is my business. I appreciate the offer. I really, *really* do. But, when I want your help, or anyone else's, I'll ask for it." George stretched out on his bed, his hands clasped behind his head.

Jake picked up his coffee, stood, went to the door, and opened it. He paused and looked back. "There are people in here that need your help, too, George."

Jake left the room, leaving the door open. George sat up, swung his legs to the floor, and sat with his hands clasped. He felt very guilty. Or angry. Or both. "Damn this place. Damn this place!"

He stood, walked to the window, and looked down at the snow beneath the lights. He had known it was going to be like this. He hadn't had any idea how bad it was going to be, but he had known it was going to be bad. He looked up at the dark sky, tiny sparkles of new snow reflecting the light from below. It was very, very cold. He felt the tears tempt his eyes, and he forced them back. He sat in the easy chair, closed his eyes, leaned his head against the back of the chair.

—I am so alone and this is such a nightmare.

52

Elliot Yates sat in the back row of the chapel, his eyes closed, his fingers tapping against the cover of his steno book. He had to keep his eyes closed. If he opened them, he would see the candle mounted on the wall to the right of the altar, and then he would remember that son of a bitch Randecker's smart-ass comments.

"God looks a little low tonight. Maybe He needs his wick trimmed. You can tell he's angry; look at him burn!

I have concluded that God uses. The grandiosity, impatience, attempts to control, playing God—"

Elliot opened his eyes and sighed. Eyes opened or closed, the words were still in his head.

—Irreverent bastard. Atheistic, godless bastard. The place is full of them.

Atheists, bikers, hippies, street punks, convicts, whores, drug dealers, homosexuals, junkies, and drunks. "I am not like them!" He was no falling-down, loud-mouthed, sour-smelling drunk. Except for that one time—

"Okay." He closed his eyes and nodded. He had admitted he was wrong doing services that time when he had a little too much to drink. But the payments and taxes on the house were past due. There had been another fight with Heather, his wife. The weather was a black day of freezing rain, and he just couldn't get Donny out of his mind. Donny needed another operation. Donny, that pain-filled lump of drooling vegetable matter that was his son. That drooling lump that he loved and ached for. That he felt so guilty—

"I was drunk. I was wrong to conduct services that way. I admit that."

He couldn't drive the memory of the intervention out of his mind. Heather had kept reading off his list of crimes. The other children, Joanie, Todd, and Lottie, their eyes wide and frightened, read off their own lists. Other times he had been drunk. The scenes he had made, the illnesses, the shame, the children and the wife that he had abused with his words. The children he had beaten. The strange man looked on. Dan something, the intervention counselor—

Elliot stood up. "I simply don't want to think about it." He looked guiltily around the chapel. Assured that he was alone, he resumed his seat.

Jake was an atheist. Elliot could understand the way he behaved. He just couldn't understand Roger Sanders. "The man is supposed to be a minister!"

Roger had been sitting in the lounge, and he had turned and frowned at Elliot. "Elliot, have you ever smelled mothballs?"

"Of course."

"How did you get their little legs apart?"

—The filthy jokes!

All of the Animals were acting like high school kids in a locker room. The lecturers had said that everyone in the place was emotionally arrested, but Roger was supposed to be a minister.

A dark thought flitted by, a thought that Elliot would not allow, a suspicion and a resentment that somehow Roger being black either explained or excused it all. But Elliot didn't have thoughts like that.

"I marched with Martin Luther King."

—*and Jake had laughed. "So did half the cops in Alabama."*

Elliot shook his head. He just couldn't get Thursday morning's group out of his head

—*Angela. What is she?*

"Elliot, you look like you're about to explode. What's going on with you?"

"My contract was to talk about this group."

"The group is present, Elliot, and can speak for itself. What about you?"

Elliot folded his arms, crossed his legs, and sat back. "I've been thinking about getting into another group."

Angela sprouted The Grin and began rocking back and forth in her chair. "Oh? Would you mind sharing your reasons?"

Elliot looked around the room. Jake the atheist; his houseboy, Roger; that slut, Linda—

"I simply think I'd be more comfortable in another group."

"Why don't you just go out and buy a bottle and be done with it?" The voice came from the return visitor, John, who had been inflicting his unwanted presence on the group for the past three days. He was tall, heavy, and sat in his chair with an expression of unending smugness.

"I didn't say I wanted to drink, John."

John grinned. "Now, Elliot, old boy, here's what I hear you saying. You are uncomfortable in this group. True?"

"Yes. That's what I said."

"Elliot, the process of change is painful—uncomfortable. If you are looking for a comfortable group, you aren't looking to get well. So, why not save everybody's time, go out and get your bottle, and be done with it."

"You don't understand what I—"

John bellowed forth a laugh. Angela was laughing as well, as though they shared a secret joke. John calmed down and shook his head. "Sorry about that, Elliot. There was a time when I was on a similar quest, as Angela remembers."

Elliot fumed, then held out his hand toward Angela. "Still, I'm uncomfortable."

Angela turned her head from Elliot and looked at John, just barely able to contain her laughter. John continued. "What makes you uncomfortable?"

"I just am."

"Bullshit."

Elliot, his face bright red, leaned forward and pointed a finger at John. "I don't like profanity!"

Then, in a horror-filled moment, John, his chin resting on his hand, his eyes half-closed, issued a stream of profanity that, that...

"...tits, cocksucker, motherfucker, shit, bullshit, bullshit, and more bullshit." John grinned. "It's called desensitization, Elliot. Now, if you're finished fucking around with words, what about this group makes you uncomfortable?"

"You, for one! Every other return visitor we've had asks permission from the group if they can sit it. You didn't! If you should happen to ask permission, I would refuse."

"Then I'd be a fool to ask, wouldn't I?" John sat back in his chair, his hands on his knees. "Elliot, I became a member of this group six months ago. I've paid my dues, earned my stripes, whatever you want to call it. You've been here almost a whole week and it looks to me like you haven't become a member yet—"

"But, still, other return vis—"

"I'm not responsible for others. I know I'm a member. There might be some basis, Elliot, for you asking *my* permission if *you* can sit in. I don't know about you."

While Elliot steamed, Angela picked up the pogrom. "I can assure you, Elliot, that this is not a comfortable group. If you do apply for another group, it will be against my advice."

Elliot did his best to look contrite. "I simply thought I might be able to relate better to a male counselor—"

Nate, the street punk, burst out in laughter. "Hell, Elliot, you just sunk your own ship. You couldn't get out of here now with a draft notice."

As the laughter subsided, Linda Manchester grinned. "Elliot, why does having a woman for a counselor bother you?"

"It doesn't."

"Bullshit," said Jake. "Look at yourself. Your face looks like a stoplight, your arms and legs are all wrapped around yourself, your eyes are narrowed—one might even say flashing. You are pissed, boy."

"Very well." Elliot looked around the group. "I don't like you people. Not at all. I can't relate to any of you. I thought I'd be able to relate to Roger, but no one laughs harder at Jake's anti-God jokes than Roger does. And you're supposed to be a minister—"

"Hold it." Angela scooted her chair across the floor. "Elliot, you're beginning to inventory the group. And you're being judgmental. Now knock off the games and tell us what you feel."

"Feel?" Feel. Elliot rubbed his eyes and shook his head. Feel. "Angry."

"What's under the anger?"

Elliot frowned at Angela. "Under it?"

"Often we use anger to mask our real feelings. What's under your anger?"

Elliot stared at the center of the circle. "I feel frustrated. Lost...frightened."

—I don't belong here! I don't belong with these people! I am not one of them!

Elliot opened his eyes and looked again at the candle—what Jake called Ignite-A-Spook. The feeling was there. All he had to do was say it. How do you feel, Elliot?

"I feel like killing Jake." There was more. "Linda." He felt threatened around her. As though he were in danger. The others—

"It's only for a month. I can put up with anything for a month."

He stood, made the decision that if it was at Saint Mary's it couldn't be a real chapel. Even Jake used it. He turned and walked out.

53

Linda Manchester put out her cigarette, closed her steno book, and looked around at the dark lounge. She was wearing the tan and black lace nightgown-robe combination that Nate, the Junkman, had nicknamed the Mankiller. Everyone had gone to bed except Jake. He was sitting at the card table playing solitaire, positioned so that he could look down the hallway.

"Jake, is it true that solitaire is masturbation for celibates?"

"No. Masturbation is solitaire for people who can't count higher than one."

"I take it your wife hasn't gotten in yet."

"Not yet." He shook his head, glanced down the hallway, then placed another card. "The plane's late." He looked toward the loveseat and shrugged at Linda.

"Are you worried?"

"I'm worried." He tossed the deck on the table, lit his pipe, and moved to the couch facing the loveseat. "There're snow and ice storms all of the way from here to Maine. I know I can't do anything about it, but I'm worried all the same." He wiped his forehead, laughed, and faced his wet palm toward Linda. "Will you look at that. I was all sparkly clean for when Ann showed up. By the time she gets here I'll look and smell like I've been sleeping in Godzilla's armpit."

"Does it hurt much—the flashback?"

He shook his head and reached for some groupwad. "I get stiff, aches in my neck and back. A low-grade headache. It's not intolerable, as they say." He mopped his brow and pointed at Linda's steno pad. "How's your first step coming along?"

"Not bad." She lit another cigarette. "Jesus, I never smoked so much in my life. Wouldn't it be hell to make it through here, get my medallion, and drop dead from lung cancer on my way out the door? Jake, are you giving first step tomorrow morning?"

"Yeah. Unless Angela decides my chain needs some more yanking instead."

"How come it took you so long? You're in your third week, aren't you?"

Jake leaned back in the couch and refired his pipe. "I had a lot of shit to clear off the decks before I could get started. I think I'm ready now, though."

"Nervous about it?,"

"Yes. That and family week starting tomorrow. Wondering where Ann is. God, it's going to be a sonofabitch in there tomorrow with me, Roger, Earl, and Lydia doing family." He shook his head and looked at Linda. "Do you have anyone showing for family week?"

"No. Not yet. The guy I live with is heavily into chemistry. I think this place gives him the willies. Angela said she'd talk to him, but I don't think it'll do any good." She looked at her steno pad. "I guess it isn't much of a relationship anyway. He was holding, so I moved in. I don't use anymore, so I guess I move out."

Jake stood, walked until he could look down the hall, then returned to the couch. He relit his pipe. "What did you think of my new roomie?"

"George?" She smiled and took a drag off of her cigarette. "I liked your old roomie better. George reminds me too much of myself when I first came in here. How is Frank? Have you heard from him?"

"I had a call this afternoon. He tried A.A. a couple of times, but said to hell with it."

"Is he back to drinking yet?"

"Not yet." Jake pointed at Linda. "What's the frown for?"

"I said something pretty shitty to George. I know it hurt, because someone said the same thing to me when I—"

She pointed her finger at Jake. "You! You said it."

"Said what?"

"You're a nasty little asshole, Linda. Do something about it, will you?"

Jake blushed, grinned, and shook his head. "I did apologize."

"You were right all the same. Still it was a shitty thing to say. Has George talked about it?"

"George says he doesn't need anyone right now." Jake slapped his palms against his knees in rapid succession. "But I certainly do. Christ, won't that plane ever get in?"

"How late is it?"

"The last I heard from the airport was three hours. That was an hour ago."

"What time is it?"

He looked at his watch. "Hell. It's past midnight. Sister, am I going to be in great form tomorrow. No sleep. A nervous wreck." He noticed her getting to her feet. "Turning in?"

"I'd like to stand watch with you, Jake, but I'm bushed. I think—or at least I hope—the Nighthawking is over."

She gathered her things and waved good night as she turned the corner. When she came to Jake and George's room, she looked in the open door. George was sitting next to the window in the easy chair, looking at the snowfall. She tapped on the door. "George?"

He turned rapidly. "Yes?"

"May I come in?"

George's discomfort meter began climbing. "If you want."

Linda entered the room and sat at the foot of George's bed. "I'm sorry for what I said to you earlier this evening."

He looked down and shook his head. "It was the truth."

"But it hurt all the same."

"It hurt." He sighed and looked out the window. "I've never been very comfortable around people. Especially..." He looked at her and turned red.

"Especially. what?"

He coughed and quickly averted his glance to the window. "People like you."

"Like me? What are people like me like?"

George sighed and turned back. "You know, beautiful, got-it-all-together, self-confident—"

Linda laughed until the tears came to her eyes.

"What's so humorous?"

"Oh, George, you are a treasure." She picked up some groupwad from the nightstand and dried her eyes. "When I showed up here, George, I was you in drag. Don't mistake the shell for the person. Whatever little self-confidence I've managed to put together has been put together since I came to Saint Mary's. If I had it all together, I wouldn't be here."

"Well , you are beautiful."

She smiled. "Thanks, but you'll learn more about that later. Before I forget, as long as you're Nighthawking anyway, Jake is having a pretty rough time. You might see if you can help out."

"He's having a rough time?"

"He gives his first step tomorrow and starts family week. Also, his wife's plane is around four hours late. Could you give it a try? I'm sure he'd appreciate it."

"Sure." George grimaced and shook his head. "I don't know why I always think that I'm the only one in the place with problems."

"It's called being self-centered."

"Ummm. Linda." He traced a circle on his knee with a fingertip. "That shell you mentioned. In evaluation they tried to get at me, and every time—"

"Every time they came close to getting behind that shell, you were terrified. Every time you felt horribly vulnerable. Every time you hurt. Yes?"

He nodded. "You've been there?"

She stood and put her hand on his cheek. "George, all of us have been there. That's why it's a disease."

A voice came from the door. "All patients are to be in their own rooms by midnight."

Linda stood and faced the door. It was Perry the male nurse doing room checks. She held her hand to her mouth in an exaggerated expression of having been caught at doing something illicit. She turned back to George, blew him a kiss, then opened all of the stops and sashayed to the door, her eyes half closed. Voom, voom, va, voom.

She stopped next to Perry. He swallowed and asked, "What were you doing in here?"

"Why, honey, hasn't this hotel ever heard of room service?"

She blew George another kiss, turned, tweaked Perry's scrawny beard, and bumped and ground her way down the hall. Before she reached her room, she heard George say to Perry, "What can I tell you? Some of us got it, and some of us ain't."

54

George saw Jake sitting at the card table, playing solitaire. He stopped next to the table and looked down at him. "I'm sorry I was turning my crank in there."

"Don't worry about it, George. It's all part of Saint Mary blue. As a man once said to me, the first few are Mary blue, but it evens out." George pulled out a chair and sat down. "I've heard that expression a number of times. What's it mean?"

"It depends on who you ask. For me it's an emotional state. A bottomless funk. Sometimes it's a hysterical laughing fit that turns on you in a second becoming the most severe pain you ever experienced." Jake glanced down the hall. "Just about the time you think you're caught in the middle of a sitcom because of the goofy things that go on around here, it turns on you. Saint Mary blue. A mix of belly laughs and death." He looked back at George and smiled. "For some others it's a color. Free waters, blue sky and stuff like that—"

"The ten will go on the jack over there."

Jake looked over the tops of his glasses at George. "You would like to get along with me, wouldn't you, George?"

"Yes."

"Then stay out of my wallet and my solitaire game." Jake smiled, tossed down his cards, and stretched his arms. "Are you Nighthawking or baby-sitting?"

"A little of both, I guess."

"Thanks. I appreciate it."

He looked down the dark hall to the lights of the nurse's station, then sighed. "Just about every time I think I've gotten it put together, something comes along, and I start unraveling again." He began gathering up the cards. "Tomorrow has me scared."

"Is family week really all that rough?"

Jake snickered. "George, did you come here through an intervention?"

"Yes. My wife and parents."

"How long did it last?"

"How long? I don't know." George rubbed his chin. "It seemed like it went on for an eternity. Half an hour, forty-five minutes, maybe. Why?"

"Try and imagine that same intervention with an expert jury of judges observing your reactions, occasionally dropping little comments about whether or not you are bleeding adequately and with sufficient sincerity. In addition to that, your family members have professional trainers who show them where, how hard, and how deep to stick it to you."

George moistened his lips. "It doesn't sound like a whole lot of fun."

"You haven't even heard the best parts, yet. For the first two days you have to keep your mouth shut. You have to sit there and absorb it. It goes on for an hour and a half a day, every day, for four days straight. Then, if you survive that, you get to do another hour and a half with the family group."

"Aside from that, Mrs. Lincoln—"

"—how'd you enjoy the play?"

George sat back in his chair and studied his roommate. "You weren't kidding, were you? About being scared?"

"Not even a little bit."

Jake tossed the deck on the table. "I don't think Ann can tell me anything that I haven't already told myself a thousand times. But I never heard it from her, understand? I think I still have this little fiction in the back of my head that says it really wasn't all that bad. That Ann never really got hurt." He leaned forward, placing his elbows on the table. "Beginning tomorrow that little fiction is going to be vaporized. Ann is going to tell me what I did, what I did to her, and how it hurt her. To be honest, I don't really believe I can live through it."

Jake thought for a moment and then laughed.

"What's funny?"

"George, we had a member in group, D.T., he was doing family week and said he didn't think he could live through it. He did, though."

"Where is he now?"

"D.T. go home." George winced and Jake took a deep breath, let it out, and nodded. "Yeah, by this time tomorrow I'll know I hurt her. About a thousand other fictions will be gone, as well. It took me almost two weeks here to figure it out, George, but I love my wife. I love her very much. I think the thing that scares me more than anything else is the possibility of losing her."

"Are you two separated?"

"Not yet." Jake held out a hand. "All of the fictions that get blown away don't belong to the patient, see? There is one fiction that they are very good at extracting from the spouse. Whatever else happens this week, Ann is going to leave here knowing that she can get along very well without me, if that's what she chooses to do. I've seen it happen with other families." Jake pushed around the cards on the table. "The roommate I had before you, Frank, he took off in the middle of his family week. He was a goddamned rock, George, and he couldn't take it."

"What's he doing now?"

"Playing Russian roulette with six loaded chambers. He's doing it his way. He already knows that his way is suicide. I really love that guy. The sonofabitch." Jake looked down the hall. George followed his glance and saw a man and a woman standing in front of the nurse's station. Jake stood up and placed a hand on George's shoulder. "That's her." He looked down and smiled. "Thanks for the use of the hall, George. You're going to do all right here."

Jake walked around the table and all but flew down the hall. George watched as Jake slid to a stop, gathered the woman in his arms and hugged her, then shook the man's hand. George thought, Jake was right about one thing: by helping others, you *do* help yourself. George was feeling strangely at peace. Maybe even a small particle of quiet strength, warmth. He shook his head. He didn't know what it was and didn't want to analyze it. He only wanted to feel it.

Halfway down the hall, a door opened and a man came out, paused to look at Jake and his wife, then turned and headed for the lounge. When he got to the entrance of the lounge, George recognized Elliot the Episcopal priest.

"Good evening."

George nodded back and Elliot sat down at the table and lit a cigarette. After he blew forth a cloud of smoke, he pointed his forefinger toward the nurse's station. "Look at Jake. Sucking up to his wife. Brother, is he scared about tomorrow. He'll probably bring her up breakfast in bed in the morning."

George stood up and looked down at the priest. "You're a nasty little asshole, Elliot. Do something about it, will you?"

He entered the hall, turned left into the room he shared with Jake, and closed his door.

"I've been afraid about coming here, Jake. They practically had to throw me on the plane. All these drunks and drug addicts here."

Jake put down her bag and unlocked the door to her second floor room. "They're a great bunch of people, Ann. Once you get to know them. During the week you'll get to know the Animals pretty well."

"Animals?"

He looked at her. "That's the tag we use: Angela's Animals." He felt his smile sag and disappear.

Ann's mouth was drawn back in a smirk. Her eyes were blank, humorless. Jake seemed to be standing in front of a fountain of sheer anger. Anger that became scorn. Scorn that became indifference. The thought passed. She entered the room and turned on the lights. "I want to get undressed and go straight to bed, Jake. I am very tired."

He stood in the open doorway, awkwardly trying to figure out what to do with his hands. There were so many things he wanted to say. But there had already been a lifetime of words. Words meant to manipulate, to express anger and pain, to drive her away, to insulate himself from her reality. There were no different words; they just meant something now. "I missed you, Ann."

She placed her small bag on the bathroom counter. "Could you put the suitcase on the other bed, Jake?"

He placed the bag on the bed and turned around. Maybe she didn't hear him. Maybe she did.

She emerged from the bathroom removing her coat. She tossed the coat next to the suitcase, opened the suitcase, and removed a nightgown. "What time is breakfast here?"

"Around seven-thirty."

She leaned over, gave him a peck on his cheek, then began unbuttoning her dress. "I really have to get some sleep. Good night."

"Good night."

Jake left the room, closing the door quietly behind him. He stood in the deserted hallway for a moment, then shook his head. "What in the hell did you expect, asshole?"

He thrust his hands into his pockets and headed toward the stairs.

JANUARY 17TH

55

He walked into the bathroom. The lights wouldn't turn on. Still there was a dim glow—just enough to see. A greenish glow, the shadows absolute black. The paint on the walls was cracked. Jake turned and looked into the mirror.

The face was his. It almost surprised him—

Suddenly the face was gone. All he could see was the cracked green paint. The open door where the greenish light came from. He walked toward it and was stopped. Reaching out, he felt the cold slickness of the glass.

Trapped. He was trapped in the mirror.

Ann came into the bathroom, tried the lights, and they went on. She looked at him, but her face registered no recognition. She began brushing her hair.

"Ann! Ann!" He slapped at the glass. "Ann!" He turned his head. The absolute black of nothingness was behind him. The only light was framed by the mirror's glass. He could see nothing back there but black.

"Ann! Please, Ann!"

No, wait.

There was something back there.

It had no shape but that of the unknown.
It breathed.
It made a scratching sound as it dragged its claws across a nonexistent
floor—
       "Ann! Ann—"

Jake opened his eyes and caught his breath.

The mirror dream again.

He had stopped trying to find a meaning in it. But Ann's face in the dream. There was something there.

He shook his head and wondered if Ann was getting any sleep. She had been tired when she got in. She looked frightened. That veneer of irritability that covered what? Anger? Hurt? Resentment?

Probably all three.

What would it all be like in afternoon group—her sitting before all of those strange people, trying to say things that she couldn't even say in her most private moments.

"Afternoon group is going to be a bastard."

Again he shook his head. Stop projecting. When it comes, it comes. Never trouble trouble 'till trouble troubles you. Fortune-cookie wisdom.

But that blackness behind the mirror. A creature of such malevolence that it couldn't even be imagined. Let's face it, a science fiction writer is up on his malevolent creatures. "One of these nights I'm going to hang in there long enough to find out what the dragon looks like." He didn't know what it was, but he called it the dragon.

"Jake?"

He rolled to his left. "Yeah?"

"I wanted to make sure you weren't just talking in your sleep."

"Been up?"

"Yeah. I've been thinking."

Jake picked up his pipe and lit it. "I'm awake. Did you want to talk?"

"If you don't mind."

Jake sat up. "After the dream I just had, I could use a break. Shoot."

He heard George move. "I've been thinking about what I've heard about family week. It scares me."

"It ought to."

George laughed. The laugh was nervous. "I was just about to ask you—hah!" There seemed to be tears in the laughter. "Have you stopped beating your wife?" A long silence. "Did you ever hit Ann?"

Jake pursed his lips. "There were some pushes and shoves. Sometimes she would get in the way when I was taking a swing at something else. I was more mouth than macho. But I suppose it all amounts to the same thing."

"Jake, I used to beat up on Barbara, my wife. Regularly. I don't like violence. I hate it. But…" George lit a cigarette. "Is that the kind of stuff that gets talked about in family week?"

"Yes."

"I don't think I can do it."

"Maybe you can." Jake looked at his watch. Just after three. He replaced it on the nightstand. "George, there's a couple of things to think about. First, family week isn't just for you. Barbara has a lot of sickness to get out. Old hates, old resentments, old hurts. What they say here is true: you can let go of all the shit, but first you have to pick it up and give it a good sniff." Jake relit his pipe. "That's the other thing. The first step is supposed to be your sniffing exercise. The ones that have gone through it say that a lot of the shame and guilt just drops away."

"Do you believe that?"

"I'll check in with you after morning group." Jake rubbed his eyes and stretched. "Are you going to try and get some more sleep?"

"No." George laughed. "God, I don't believe I'll ever get a full night's sleep again."

"They say give it time."

"And other great program clichés. Easy does it. One fucking day at a time. God, am I really condemned to live the rest of my life by a bunch of cracker-barrel homilies?"

"George, this is a rehab, not a literary seminar. We're here to get well. I picked on the same thing when I was looking for reasons why the program wouldn't work for me. I'd take a truth that works, call it a cliché, and then I wouldn't have to pay any attention to it. It's a head game. A good way to make yourself miserable. The only way a cliché gets to be a cliché is because it's true."

George stubbed out his cigarette and sat silently for a moment. "What do they mean around here when they say recovery can't begin until you run out of people to blame?"

"If you blame someone or something for why you drink, and if you can't change whatever it is, you have the perfect setup. You can't change the past and you can't change other people, therefore, you must continue drinking and drugging. Blaming is another head game. You'll hear Angela say it a hundred times: it's no one's fault; it's a disease. The most important one you have to stop blaming is yourself."

George snorted out a laugh. "Easier said than done."

"If it was easy, George, everybody would be doing it." Jake rubbed his eyes as he thought. Frank never did manage to stop blaming himself. He could say the words, but his gut feeling took over as he was facing Mary in the fishbowl—

Jake really felt ripped off. Frank hadn't stopped to say good-bye. He had simply walked out when no one was looking. He ran the memory out of his awareness and relit his pipe as George sat up and swung his feet down to his slippers. "Jake, what's this Angela like? Everybody around here talks like they're afraid of her."

Jake crossed his legs and leaned his elbows on the top knee. "What's Angela like?" He shook his head. "I'm afraid when I go in there, George. Every day, twice a day, I feel like I'm being put on trial for my life, and I just can't think of the proper defense. Angela is the Grand Inquisitor." Jake laughed.

"What's funny?"

"George, I just realized something."

"What?"

"I love that woman." Jake looked deeply inside himself. "She's good at what she does, George. Very, very good. Sometimes when I'm not hurting, I'll sit back and watch her work. I love watching her work. She plays that group like a symphony. She's the first person I can ever remember being proud of. Do you know what I mean?"

"Not really. I can't remember ever being proud of anyone."

"It's a great feeling. I suppose I'm a little overboard in this department. As far as I'm concerned, if Angela leaves the business, alcoholism treatment might as well close the door, turn the key in the lock and throw it away."

"That *is* overboard."

"Yeah. But the feeling's there all the same. I get angry as hell at her, or hurt, or ashamed, or a million other things. Like me acting the perfect asshole. Every time the look on her face is the same. She cares."

Jake turned his head toward his roommate. "George, for the first time in my life I am convinced that it matters to someone whether I live or die. If I live, it matters what quality that life will have."

"Jake, your wife must care. Your parents."

He nodded. "In my head I know they did. But in my gut, I still find it impossible to believe that it *really* mattered to them what happened to me. In my gut, though, I'm convinced that it matters to Angela."

"Jake, it's just a job. You make her sound like a bleeding saint."

He stretched out on his bed and looked at the reflections on the ceiling. Saint Angela. Well, if you're going to get into saints and such, you could do worse. How many times had he been asked in press interviews, "Mr. Randecker, who are your heroes?"

He would be nervous, because he knew that his answer would sound arrogant, and he didn't feel that way at all. "I don't have any heroes," he would answer. All it made him feel was very, very sad.

Now, he thought, I have a hero. Angels Gwynn. It felt very, very good.

—God, I love that woman.

"Y'know, George, it's very fortunate that Angela is twenty years older than I am."

"Why?"

"If she wasn't, I could be real mixed up right about now."

56

The morning group formed. Jake sensed a strange, tension in the air. The contracts went around, Angela welcomed George to the group, gave him his first step outline, addiction and recovery charts, and explained the ground rules for giving a first step. She nodded at Jake.

He took a quick look around the circle. Marnie, Tess, Coral from the fourth floor, Gisel, in addition to all of the Animals. God, thought Jake, they must have sold tickets. Hurry, hurry, hurry! Come and see Jojo the stupendous and amazing dogfaced boy! He dances, he prances, he will make you doubt your very own eyes—

Jake looked at his notes and thought, I didn't think it was going to be this hard. He glanced at George. George held his fist up over his head.

—Go for it. Thank you, George.

"I'm an addict, my name is Jake Randecker. This is my first step. 'We admitted we were powerless over alcohol—that our lives had become unmanageable.'" First hurdle passed. He looked down at his notes and took a deep breath.

"I was addicted to drugs when I was born. My mother was a drug addict and was on morphine and cocaine during the entire time she carried me. Ever since I can remember there was something to drink or medicine to take."

Beer, paregoric, champagne, nips of gin, Nembutal and Seconal, alcohol/codeine cough medicines, Jim Beam whiskey, codeine capsules, antihistamines, Darvon, yellow pills, white pills, blue pills, red pills, pink pills. Every pain had its potion, every problem its powder. He could not remember a period of more than a month during his entire life that he hadn't been using something.

"By the time I was thirty-three I was constantly taking Antihistamines and alcohol/codeine preps to relieve what seemed to be a never-ending cold. Antihistamines, two to three times recommended dosage; Nyquil, a twelve ounce bottle per night for up to two weeks at a time, five or six times per year; other alcohol/drug preps up to six times recommended dosages constantly. Codeine pain-killers, just as often as I could get them, four to six times the prescribed amount; nitrous oxide and sodium pentathol as parts of dental work. I liked the nitrous oxide a lot.

"After one three-hour session at the dentist's, I just didn't want to come down. I headed right across the street to the liquor store. I didn't come down until my heart attack. By then I was averaging a fifth of some kind of hard liquor per day. I was thirty-six and had my heart attack on my thirty-sixth birthday.

"In the hospital I was treated with morphine, Valium, and sleeping pills. Because I started going into blind rages which busted up a considerable amount of hospital furniture and a couple of nurses, I was treated with a mood-stabilizer, lithium. I was on Valium and lithium when I was discharged from the hospital. I freaked on the lithium. Entire piano pieces I had memorized were wiped out. I would sit all day, looking at the work I needed to do, not caring about it or anything else. I had such a bad reaction to the lithium that I stopped taking it.

"For approximately a month following my discharge, I was taking Valium. Instead of following the prescription, I would take them when I felt I needed them. When I was taken off of Valium, I began getting backaches. Then I was given a prescription for anxiety, called Ativan.

"The original prescription called for two one-milligram tablets per day. I used the entire two-week prescription in two days and got the doctor to increase the prescription, using two-milligram tablets, and more of them."

He was writing out the prescription. "I'm a little hesitant about this, Jake. It is a controlled narcotic."

"Hell, Doc, I'd sure hate to try and buy my way into today's drug culture with Ativan."

They both laughed—

"When I ran out of Ativan early one time I doubled up on the prescription by working it through another doctor and another drugstore. I had Ann, my wife, do the calling. I ran short again and took up drinking again to fill in the gap between prescriptions. When the prescription was refilled, I didn't stop the drinking.

"By now I was drinking nine to eighteen 16-ounce cans of beer per day in addition to approximately half a fifth of whisky or rum per day. Every day I was taking across-the-counter antihistamines at four to eight times package directions, and I was using a diarrhea medication containing paregoric almost every day, eight to ten times recommended dosage. When I told my doctor that I had stopped drinking, he gave me a prescription for Librium to ease the effects of withdrawal. I added the Librium to the Ativan."

As he turned the page, Jake shook his head. Saying it in front of the group was sure a lot different than putting it down on paper.

"In my early stage, I had no preoccupation with chemicals. They were just part of the environment. In my middle stage, however, I began looking forward to the end of the working day when my drinking would begin. It became very important to keep a supply on hand.

"By my late stage, waiting for that first drink of the day became a losing contest of wills. I kept moving the time for drinking forward.

Della looked at him, frowning. "It's nine in the morning. Isn't it just a little early to be working the beer?"

He looked up from the word processor. "I've been up all night. So this is still last night. This morning doesn't begin until I get some sleep."

"You're not kidding, are you?"

"Nope."

"Keeping a supply of Ativan on hand became an obsession. Being out of either alcohol or Ativan would throw me into a panic. I had to know it was there, just to keep from—"

He closed his eyes. The feeling was there, in his gut. The soft, dreamy monster would extend its claws and begin raking his heart.

"—Just to keep from screaming. In the middle stage, I tried to control my use of alcohol by quitting, switching back and forth between different kinds of liquor, beer, and wine. I never could stand the taste of gin so I switched to an old favorite of my father's. By the end of two days, gin tasted just fine. Switching became a regular routine by my late stage. A game. Controlling my use became as much of an obsession as using. I didn't make the traditional geographical moves; I couldn't work up the energy. But I used to think about them all the time."

The mountain fantasy. If he could just build a little cabin back there in the woods, away from everyone, especially away from Ann, he could stop. Things would get better. No interruptions, no pressures. "Physically, my use of chemicals contributed to my heart attack, being overweight, with constant back and neck pains from tension, migraine headaches, countless cuts and bruises, skin problems from stress and from poor hygiene, chest pains, anxiety attacks, rages—

Full of rage and terror, screaming at that doctor in the emergency room. "Where did you get your fucking degree, asshole? From a soap opera?

Did you intern at General Hospital? My chest hurts, and I don't want to answer your stupid fucking questions!" He pushed his way out of the door, his chest pains making him lighthearted.

"Jake!" Ann chased after him. "Jake, go back!"

"Fuck 'em!"

He got to the car, pulled open the door, and momentarily blacked out. *Awake, Ann's hand bleeding, the red before his eyes removing whatever pitiful restraints that remained. He got behind the wheel and drove home through the traffic jam at ninety miles per hour on the right shoulder of the road—*

"The effects of my use of chemicals on my sexuality and sex life. Love, what there was of it, was strictly physical. I couldn't even imagine a form of love beyond that, although most of the time that I was rejecting my wife, I loved and was loved by an army of fantasies. The prospect of making love to my wife sober terrified me. To justify this in my mind, what I felt was that she disgusted me, or hated me. The only time I would try to make love was when I was drunk. Most of the time I was drunk I simply couldn't perform at all. I would constantly flog myself because I was inadequate, afraid, a failure, not a man. Eventually I would hide in my office, drinking, waiting for her to fall asleep, avoiding the issue altogether.

"Emotionally, I automatically used alcohol and drugs to mask my feelings from myself and from others. I had frequent violent rages and was convinced I was going insane."

Ann was taking the broken pieces of the table out of the living room, the broken glass from the antique engravings crunching beneath her feet. Jake watched her, remembering the night before, the searing white-hot anger, destroying everything that came within reach, how reasonable and justified it all seemed at the time—

"Life was a never-ending wallow in black despair, depression, and self-pity. I could only express myself through anger, because it was the only emotion I could feel. Anyone who was close to me, I drove away. All they ever seemed to do was hurt me. Everyone seemed bent on hurting me. Day in and day out I lived in fear of others. I couldn't even go into my front yard for fear of what people driving by would be thinking of me, or what they might do to me. I had this constant feeling that doom was just around the corner. Something hideous was about to happen, I should be doing something to prevent it, but I never knew just what to do. I felt worthless. Nothing. A minus quantity. That no one did or could love me.

"But at the same time I felt like I wasn't getting my proper due. I just wasn't being loved and worshipped in the manner and to the degree that I thought I more than deserved."

—Jesus, this is really sick.

"On my social life...I had no social life. Because she was ashamed of me, my wife accepted no invitations and never invited anyone. We became hermits. I stopped seeing the people I knew, and meeting new people was too horrible even to contemplate. I dropped out of community activities and isolated myself from everyone. I withdrew completely.

Sitting alone in his office, staring out the window at the cars passing by, cursing them for not seeing his pain, trying to decide between another beer or the gun—

"I had no spiritual life. I was my own higher power. If I couldn't do it, then it just wouldn't get done. I could never do it, whatever it was. Since, as a higher power, I was failing, I thought of myself as a failure. Failing was the one thing I could not do and remain fit to live. I constantly played with the idea of suicide. Eventually I stopped playing. There were two unsuccessful attempts and failing at even that seemed to make me even more of a failure.

"Still, day after day I would sit alone in my office, constantly thinking of the pleasant neutrality of death. Death was such a positive move from where I was standing. It looked so attractive.

"As for work, everything I was doing to remodel our house and landscape our property eventually stopped. Simple everyday things that needed doing went undone. I lost interest in every hobby I ever had. My writing was cut to a third of its usual output. The writing started going very, very bad. I hated writing, so I quit.

"The effects on my finances. There are a lot of things in the writing business that depend on the breaks. But between the costs of chemicals, hospitalizations, treatment, damage, and loss of productivity, the cost is, conservatively, between a quarter and a half a million dollars.

"The effects on my character were considerable. Probably more than anything else, I value honesty. Honesty with myself, with my wife, with others. I lied to others, to my wife, to myself. It's important to me to pull my share of the load, to meet my responsibilities. I didn't—"

As he went through the thirty examples of values and how he had compromised them, his breathing became short, his manner agitated. On the outside he was crying. Inside he was no longer protesting or exclaiming in surprise. He was listening, dumbfounded.

"A gentle person, constantly resorting to violence. A good husband, constantly tearing down, manipulating my wife, diminishing her as a woman and as a human. Self-assertive, pushed around by anyone and anything. I valued sobriety. My father was a drunk, and I swore that was never going to happen to me."

He shook his head and turned to the next page. Examples of insane behavior, loss of memory, blackouts. "—in fact, when I showed up here, I was in a blackout. I kept going in and out. I didn't know what in the hell was going on.

"In my destructive behavior against myself and others—"

The fights, the abortive suicide attempts, threatening to commit suicide to force feelings from Ann, to manipulate her. Blaming her and her work for all of their problems, convincing Ann that she was insane, playing with loaded guns when drunk, driving drunk, injuring himself, because seeing him broken and bleeding hurt Ann—

"Poisoning myself with drugs and alcohol, knowing it was killing me, and not caring."

Jake turned the page for the big finish. Twenty-five examples of things he had done to hurt the ones close to him. He began, not quite understanding that the reason it was hard to read was because his eyes were filled with tears and his hands were shaking.

"At a party in our house when I was drunk, one of the children made a comment about the way I smelled, embarrassing Ann. At a science fiction convention, I was drunkenly holding court with other writers, embarrassing my wife so much that she left the room…abandoned her at one convention after another while I chased down the parties and the free booze. Hurting and rejecting her.

"In a drunken rage at home I trashed the furniture in the room she had worked long and hard to make attractive, hurting her. While I was breaking up the place, I called her vile names, meaning every word, hurting her very deeply.

"Another rage, hurting myself, wrecking another room that was partway remodeled, hurting her. When she tried to stop me, I pushed her away into some equipment, badly bruising her back and legs. But she kept fighting me, and in trying to stop me from throwing around a radial arm saw we have, I severely cut her hand."

So many conventions, so many parties, so many times Jake talking on long after he had nothing to say, so many times Ann creeping back to their room, praying no one would stop her.

Another rage, going to take the car, Ann standing on the drive in her nightgown in the snow, fighting him for the car keys. Dumping all of the financial responsibilities on her; embarrassing her when a class of computer students and their teacher came over to look at Jake's word processor. Beer cans all over the office, the stink in the air.

"Another rage...

"Cutting her off from her parents...

"Throwing a tantrum at a town planning board meeting, calling a dear friend terrible names...

"Hurting, angering, and embarrassing his secretary because she pissed him off for some unknown reason...

"Another rage, trashing his own office...

"Another rage, trashing his secretary's office...

"Another rage...

"Another rage.

"Another."

He closed his steno pad, a million images streaking through his mind. He heard a voice. Marnie. "Jake, you look very sad."

Gisel shook her head. "You're lucky to be alive."

Earl wiped a hand over his face. "Jesus, Jake, a lot of the things you did sounded psychotic."

Angela was looking at the floor immediately in front of Jake. She remained like that for a long while. She looked up at him. "I was just thinking of the cost of this damned disease." Her somber expression melted into a smile. "Do you know what they say in A.A., Jake?"

"What?"

"Alcoholics Anonymous has the highest initiation fee of any club in the world."

Jake nodded. The slogan makers had scored with that one. He looked at George. His roommate had his hand in front of his face, rubbing his eyes. Even Elliot was grabbing for the groupwad.

—I'll be damned. Not a dry eye in the house.

He looked at his watch. Fourteen minutes until the end of morning group. His number had taken over an hour. The feedback continued. The progression of the disease was there, the powerlessness, and the unmanageability. Jake was in touch with what it had been like.

A brief moment of silence.

Angela rocked back and forth in her chair. "Okay, gang. There's still some time left. Let's get working on some of those outstanding contracts."

57

Luncheon at the Constipated Eagle. Sowicide—pork chops—the entrée. No one seemed to be able to face the other selection: Caterpillar Stroganoff. Jake was only sipping coffee, watching the chow line. Ann, tall and blond with wide, frightened blue eyes, came to the tray stack. Her gaze swept the room, and when she saw him, she smiled nervously and waved. He waved back. Linda, sitting across the table from him, turned from looking at the chow line. "Jake, is that Ann? The blond?"

"Yeah."

Linda looked again, then returned to her lunch. "I don't know what you did to deserve her. She's beautiful."

Jake looked again. Ann had taken only a small salad and a cup of tea and was heading for a table away from the group. For the first two days, patients and family members are only allowed to meet in group. She was beautiful. He looked at Linda, who was also beautiful. But Linda was in the beautiful business. He had wondered if Ann would look good in group, if he would be ashamed of her. He closed and rubbed his eyes.

—For stupid thoughts, Randecker, that's a new low.

Fear of being ashamed. Why? Jake rubbed the back of his neck. He had scored an entire hour and five minutes of sleep the night before. He was still in shock from giving his first step, his neck was screaming and his headache was trying for new heights on the pain parade. He was sweating, his hands shaking, and he wanted to vomit. Muscle spasms in his chest were putting on a four star production of a mock heart attack, and for the first time in a year he was horny as hell.

He shook his head. "Oh, this afternoon is going to be an opportunity to grow."

Far to Jake's right, Lydia studied the chow line. Walt had said he was coming, but she couldn't imagine him rubbing elbows with a chow line full of junks and drunks, even though their numbers contained several captains of finance and industry, and all of them soberer than the crowd Walt usually ran with.

She sipped at her tea and shook her head. What would be the point of throwing her in the fishbowl with Wonderful Walter? His communication was all one-way. Walter talks and the world listens—or else. Her plate had a pork chop on it, and she picked up her knife and fork.

—Sowicide. I must stop listening to Jake before meals.

Sawing away on the chop, she glanced again at the chow line. Her silverware clattered to her plate. Walt was at the tray stack dressed in a knit shirt and slacks. He didn't look out of place at all. His eyes were red from crying.

—Crying?

Lydia sat back in her chair. Walt looked over the dining room, saw Lydia, and waved. His face even had a timid smile on it. Lydia dumbly waved back. She felt a hand on her arm. It was Brandy. "Lyd, what are you crying about?"

"Crying?" Lydia reached up and wiped the tears from her cheeks.

"I'll be damned. I *am* crying." She shook her head, picked up her napkin, and dried her eyes. "It's Walt. I was prepared for anger, indifference, even condescending amusement. I've been brushing all of that off for more years than I can count." She looked at Brandy. "I've never seen him sincere—no, that's not the word. Vulnerable. I'm not prepared for that. Not at all."

Walter smiled as he walked past the group's table. Again Lydia looked at Brandy. "Oh, shit! This changes all my plans!"

At a table away from the group, Earl Nelson pulled the letters out of his pocket and stared at the unopened envelopes. Alice and Joey wouldn't come. Angela had managed to guilt them into writing letters for family week. The letters had arrived five days before and were to be read in afternoon group. There was no requirement not to read them beforehand. Earl simply couldn't do it.

He told himself that he ought to read them before group began. Earl didn't like surprises. At least, not the kind that kept popping up in group. He whispered at the envelopes, "I love you two. I love you two more than anything else in the world. I don't know if I can live through what you have to say."

Still, there are enough things to contend with in group without surprises. He began opening the envelopes.

Back at the group table, Roger grinned broadly as Denise and Carmel came up to the tray stack. The grin vanished as he became aware that they had both been crying. Roger reached out his hand and placed it on his friend's arm. "Jake?"

"What?"

"They've been crying."

Jake opened his eyes and looked at the chow line. "Is that Denise? And Carmel behind her?"

"Yes."

Jake looked strangely at Roger, glanced again at the line, then back at Roger. "They're lovely."

"You don't have to sound so surprised. Of course they're lovely."

Jake shrugged and went back to his coffee. "I didn't mean anything by it. It's just that everybody around here is so damned down on themselves, it's a bit of a shock to find out that they belong to some beautiful people."

Roger waved and watched as his wife and daughter carried their trays past the group table. After they had taken their seats with Walter Marx and Ann Randecker, Roger poked Jake in the arm. "Your wife is beautiful."

"Yeah." Jake glanced back at the family members, then returned to his coffee. "She is. That surprised me most of all."

"Jake, how do you feel about this afternoon?"

He shook his head. "I've been through some hell in my life, like all of us. But this—" He looked at Roger. "I know it's just sitting in a chair and listening. But inside—" He turned back to his coffee.

"If you live through it, maybe you ought to get the Congressional Medal of Honor?"

"Close. I sure know what D.T. meant when he said he didn't think he could live through it. How are you doing?"

"I think I'm doing okay. I'm even looking forward to it."

Jake raised an eyebrow. "Don't ever lose your sense of humor, Roger. It's what endears you to us all."

Jake turned back to his coffee and Roger picked up his fork. He looked at his pork chop and frowned as his stomach began to quease.

—Am I kidding myself about what this afternoon will be like?

The answer was there in the Sowicide's congealed grease. He dropped his fork and picked up his coffee. He noticed as he drew the cup to his lips that his hand was shaking. Glancing to his right, he noticed Earl stand suddenly and leave the dining room. Earl's tray was still on the table.

58

Afternoon lecture, compliments of Nast Ass.

"When folks come to Saint Mary's, often they have a hard time putting this place into a comfortable pigeonhole. The word 'hospital' just doesn't seem to fit, somehow."

George snickered as Nast's comment brought back something. He had tried explaining on the telephone what Saint Mary's was like to his brother-in-law. *"It's sort of like a cross between Disneyland and Auschwitz."*

The voice on the other end had sounded puzzled. "George, that doesn't make any sense."

"Tell me about it."

Nast Ass grinned. "We once had a patient here that when she informed her husband that she wanted to come to Saint Mary's, he objected. He said that the only reason she wanted to come here was so she could lie around all day with little old nuns waiting on her hand and foot."

Laughter. The laughter the patients shared with every convict who was ever told that he lives in a country club and doesn't do anything but sit around all day and watch television.

"The only nuns I've ever seen on the unit were patients. We don't have starched Nightingales cooling your fevered brows. In fact, it often seems that the staff here is doing its best to see just how hot they can make it for you."

More laughter.

"When the family shows up, they don't bring you flowers, boxes of candy, and magazines, do they? They don't sit around your bed, pat your hand, and tell you that everything is going to be okay. At Saint Mary's the family gets treated, too. Easing your burden is not exactly what they're here for, as those of you who have seen a family week grilling know. You are here to recover from a disease; they are here to recover from the same disease.

"If you have to stick this place in a category, try this. Addiction has programmed you and your family into very self-destructive paths. Our job here is to interrupt that programming and provide you and your families with sane alternatives. If you are going to recover, you are going to have to give up your old ideas."

George shook his head, thinking, that's easy for him to say. He's not sitting where I am.

"Remember, your very best thinking got you here. Look upon treatment as a course you are taking in a subject that you have either never learned or have neglected for too long. Saint Mary's is a course in How To Be A Human."

There was applause and George joined the crowd moving out of the lecture room into the hallway. Hands thrust into his pockets, George looked at the floor as he walked toward north wing.

—What is going on here? This place isn't at all the way I expected it to be.

"George?"

He stopped and looked up. Tony Caccia was at the nurse's station plowing through some files. "Yes?"

"A penny for your thoughts."

"I can't make change." Tony laughed, and George shrugged and leaned against the counter. "Okay, I was trying to figure out what this place is about, what recovery is about. I thought stopping drinking was the treatment, but all of this other stuff, I don't know."

"Have you read the Big Book yet?"

George shook his head. "No."

"Read it. It's a real simple program discovered by two hopeless alcoholics who happened to stumble into each other and saw that by leaning on each other they were both still on their feet."

"Are you an alcoholic?" George asked the psychiatrist.

"Among other things."

George nodded toward north wing. "It's getting around that time."

"Okay." Tony Caccia turned back to his paperwork. "Try not to analyze it to death, George. Just let it work."

As he walked toward the north wing lounge, George pondered the amount of blind trust required to "Just let it work." He didn't know if he could do that.

Michael, the A.A. who had led the Sunday night wing meeting, was a computer programmer. He had said "No one has ever been too stupid to get this program, but plenty have been too smart." Michael had been speaking from experience, having spent eleven years drunk alternating between A.A., treatment centers, and the gutter before he managed to learn what Esau F. knew. Esau was one of the other A.A.s at the wing meeting. Esau was an American Indian, he was functionally illiterate, and what he said, "Keep the plug in the jug, go to meetings, ask for help," just about exhausted the man's English vocabulary. Esau F. had been sober for seventeen years.

George rounded the corner into the lounge. Jake, Roger, and Lydia sat together, smoking and drinking coffee as though the blindfolds were about to be placed over their eyes. For a brief moment there were nervous jokes, then the three became a watch-checking oasis of silence in the center of the lounge's chatter. George lit a cigarette and leaned against the wall, waiting for the cowbells.

—This is a scary place.

The door to the stairwell opened revealing a huge man dressed in a very natty gray suit and vest. He looked like a gorilla that sold insurance. He strode into the lounge and Jake stood up. "Snake?"

Lydia and Roger stood. "Snake?" they said together.

Snake hugged Jake, Roger, and Lydia all at the same time. "You didn't think I'd let you go in there without a rooting section, did you?" Jake looked very strange as he disentangled himself from the hug and they all sat down. "Snake, you coming back here to—I mean this—"

Snake bellowed out a laugh. "I'll be damned if I haven't thrown a wrench into Motor Mouth's gears."

Lydia placed her hand on Snake's arm. "I'm very touched."

Jake nodded. "Yeah, that's what I meant."

Roger grabbed for the groupwad and Snake glowered. "My god, what a bunch of crybabies. I'm back here after a week on the outside, and all you can do is bawl. Does anyone ask, 'How's it been, Snake,' or say 'Great threads, Snake.'"

Roger tossed his used groupwad in the wastebasket. "So, how's it been?"

"I don't want to talk about it." Snake laughed, but George noticed the big man had a glisten in his eye as he reached into his coat pocket. "Look, does everybody have a brownie?" George frowned until Snake held up his brown *A Day At A Time* book.

They all had theirs. George didn't have his and he went back to his room to get it. When he returned, Snake had his brownie open and was looking at Lydia. "You read August ninth." To Roger. "You take December fifteenth." To Jake. "You do February twenty-second." Snake looked around the lounge again. "Where's Earl? He's still in treatment, isn't he?"

Roger, leafing through his brownie, answered. "He's still here. I saw him leaving the dining room. He looked pretty upset."

"Unh." Snake stood up. "I'll be back." He walked past George into the hallway and continued toward the nurse's station.

George leaned against the wall and paged through his own brownie for the date Snake had given Lydia. The reading had to do with trying to overcome the fear of inadequacy by resenting someone else. He nodded, thinking that Snake had summarized Lydia on a page. She didn't hate Walt, which is what she kept telling everyone. She was afraid of having her own inadequacy exposed. Down at the bottom of the page was the remembrance: "As I build myself up, I tear down my resentments."

"Elliot Yates?" George looked to his left. One of the patients from Bill's group was standing next to him. He looked around the lounge. "Elliot Yates, telephone."

George gestured with his thumb. "Try his room." George sat down and turned to Roger's date, December 15th. It was a recipe for curing worrywortism. The reading was telling the minister that "the proven antidote to worry and fear is confidence—confidence not in ourselves, but in our Higher Power." George didn't see how it applied, but Roger had his eyes closed. He looked like he might be praying.

He looked at the reading for Jake, February 22nd:

I've since learned that many of my fears have to do with projection. It's normal, for example, to have a tiny 'back-burner' fear that the person I live with will leave me. But when the fear takes precedence over my present and very real relationship with the person I'm afraid of losing, then I'm in trouble. My responsibility to myself includes this: I must not fear things which do not exist.

George closed his book and thought. The fate of the world doesn't hinge on what happens in group today. Not even Jake's fate or Ann's. If he's going to get better, he has to hear what she has to say. If she's going to get better, she has to say what she has to say. That's all there is to it. The reading said it can be survived. If others can live through it so can George's roommate.

The cowbells rang and George stood up, thinking that this man Snake must be what they call a very spiritual person. A very caring person, as well. Maybe this is what Tony Caccia was talking about: drunks and junks leaning on each other, still standing on their own feet. "I don't know," he muttered. The old ideas seemed to be the only thing that had kept him alive for years.

—It's real easy for some writer to scribble down in one of these little books 'I must not fear things which do not exist.' It's a real easy thing to say out there. In here it's a different story.

Inside Angela's office, the chairs were being unstacked and the inmates and family members were beginning to sort themselves out into the chairs. Before entering, George saw Earl approaching at a fast walk, his face red. Down toward the nurse's station, the man called Snake was standing in the hallway. When Earl reached the doorway, George asked, "What was your reading?"

"What?" Earl looked down at George with angry surprise.

"Snake. What'd he tell you to read?"

"The bastard didn't tell me to read anything." Earl pushed his way past George into the office. George followed and sat down next to Earl. Earl leaned over and whispered into George's ear. "I'm sorry about snapping at you."

"It's okay."

Earl folded his arms and watched as the crowd finished getting seated. He turned to George. "I was bugging out. He told me if I didn't get my butt in here he'd hit the top of my head so hard I'd have to use my asshole for an ear trumpet—"

"Let's get going, group," said Angela. "We have a lot of ground to cover this afternoon." She looked at George. "Are you doing the reading?"

"Er, uh, yeah, okay." Trying very hard not to think of what Earl had said about an ear trumpet, George found the proper page and began reading:

"I have been told over and over again that I must constantly work to give up my old ideas. 'That's easy for you to say.' I've sometimes thought...."

George frowned at the words he had just read.

—This is a very scary place. Did someone arrange this, or am I just paranoid?

He felt a jab in his ribs. He looked to his left and saw Linda. "What?"

"The reading, George."

"Oh, I'm sorry." He looked up at Angela. "I'm sorry." He found his place and continued: "All my life, I have been programmed, computer-style; specific inputs brought forth predictable responses. My mind still tends to react as a computer reacts, but I am learning to destroy the old tapes...."

59

—Ann vulnerable. Not a numb lump of ice. She cries. She really has feelings. She walks, she talks...I can't believe it—no, I can believe it; I just can't stand it.

In the fishbowl, Jake sat, looking at Ann as she turned another page. The words that had already been said hammered against the inside of his skull.

"...*you were trying to get to the roof, threatening to jump. You were screaming horrible names at me...fucking bitch, icy fucking bitch. You were on the ladder and I was hanging onto your legs, begging, pleading....*"

Jake knew his shirt was soaked and that a twitch had developed in his left shoulderblade. He had tried to keep his facial features still so as to avoid any charges of attempting to control Ann by soliciting pity. His arms hung limply in his lap to avoid charges of appearing hostile or close-minded.

—Hell, I must look like I am totally fried.

He glanced at Angela, and Angela pointed at Ann. Jake turned his head forward, his eyes closed.

—Higher Power doesn't give me in a single day any more than I can carry. I do wish HP would recheck my load limit specs, though.

He opened his eyes. Ann was angry, which was wrong. Ann was angry at him, which was a double wrong. Jake had to keep his ass in the chair, his mouth shut, and his ears open, which is called Saint Mary blue, and—

"One night when you were drunk, we had a terrible fight. You ran out of the house and were going to drive the car. It was winter and very cold...."

Jake listened to the episode of the drunk dragging around the beautiful vulnerable half-naked asthmatic through the snow. Ann supplied some of the missing details: the six-inch long splinter that had gone into the skin of her thigh, him eating all of those pills and falling into bed, the next morning acting like nothing had happened.

He could almost feel the waves of revulsion coming from his groupmates. "You monster! Look at her, all blond pink and defenseless! How could you have done such a thing!"

—It's projection. I'm projecting what I'm telling myself onto others.

She was crying. And she was talking about crying. Simply because she hurt. She told him about the hundreds—thousands—of times she had crept off alone, like some wounded animal, to cry by herself. Never asking him for help or comfort, not believing he could deliver.

He remembered Amy Simon bundled in pain, crying. The feeling he had for Amy's pain he now had for Ann. For the first time in his life. His heart ached to relieve his wife's pain.

—At least I've got *that* straight.

To ease her pain, to help her get better, he had to sit there, listen, and take it. He had to get better himself. That meant sitting there, listening, taking it, and taking it in.

"One day we were driving in Augusta and you thought another driver had cut you out of traffic. You went...crazy."

Angela leaned toward Ann. "Tell him what he did. He might not know."

"You chased him up Western Avenue, running lights, honking, ramming his rear bumper. You chased him out of the city, trying to run him off the road. At one point we were just spinning around and around, then we were through a fence and stuck in a meadow full of cows."

"How did that make you feel?" asked Angela.

"No one should have to live in the middle of a horror show like that. I wanted him to—" Angela pointed at Jake. Ann said. "I wanted you dead. I just wanted you to drop dead."

Jake tried, but he couldn't remember anything at all about that incident. Another blackout. But he had done it. The truth had been there in her eyes, and in the tears running down her cheeks.

Ann reached for the groupwad and Jake thought of Frank's ex-wife, Mary. In the fishbowl, she had said much the same thing to Frank. Mary had been consumed with thoughts of murdering her husband, and with guilt for feeling that way. After group Frank hadn't cried, hadn't raged, hadn't talked with anyone. That night he simply packed his bag and left when no one was looking. Jake had been so angry at Frank. His anger was now all gone. Now he understood.

Angela rocked back in her chair and looked around the group. "Very well, is there any feedback?"

Jake tried not to feel like a sirloin that had been thrown into the middle of a pool of piranha.

60

After group Jake collapsed in the lounge and closed his eyes, trying to ease the tension in his neck. His guts were still writhing. Most of the things Ann had said were all mixed together in his mind—one enormous collage of pain, chaos, and horror. Only bits and pieces were clear.

Ann's wet eyes had looked at him steadily as she took a breath. "*And, Jake, I don't know if I love you anymore.*"

He had asked for it. Friday there had been the one-on-one with Angela. He had sat in his room's easy chair and Angela had sat on the foot of his bed. "*Your family week begins Monday, Jake. Where are you?*"

"Angela, I know how easy it is for me not to do what's good for me. The numbers for the people who don't bother with aftercare and A.A. are terrible. I know I need it. Right here, inside Saint Mary's, I can make all of the sincere promises in the world. But on the outside, I can talk myself into being able to get away with anything."

Angela folded her arms and looked deeply into his eyes. "Jake, what's really bothering you?"

He looked out of the room's window. "Ann. She's hardly ever said anything about my drinking. She didn't know about the drug problem anymore than I did. With all of the things I've done, she's never showed me that she hurt, or that she—Angela, against all reason, in the back of my head I am convinced that Ann will put up with anything from me. I need to be told that she won't put up with it anymore."

"I won't put up with this nightmare." Ann's wet eyes looked at him steadily as she took a breath. *"And, Jake, I don't know if I love you anymore."*

Jake opened his eyes and looked at Angela's door.

—Request made, considered, and granted. In bloody spades. "What if I have lost it all?"

During his second week, Brandy had asked him, "What if Ann leaves you, Jake? What will you do then? Go back to drinking?"

His gut feeling had been: "What's the point of being sober? If she leaves me, what's the point?"

"You can't do it for her, Jake. She isn't that strong; she isn't that powerful. You have to do it for you. For your reasons. Like the bumper sticker says, 'Ya Gotta Wanna.'"

"Brandy will be gone soon," he muttered to the empty lounge. The more he thought about it, the more he missed the ones who were gone. When he had shown up, they had been the old-timers. Harold, Dave, Ron, Candy, Frank—

"Jake, I don't know if I love you anymore."

Angela's doorknob turned, the lock clicking, and he pushed himself up from the easy chair and walked to the lounge's balcony door. He didn't want to see or talk to anyone who might come out of Angela's office. He looked through the glass at the city, not seeing it. He listened as Angela's door opened, footsteps and voices going down the hall toward the nursers station.

"What's the point?" he whispered "What's the damned point?"

In her room, Lydia was sitting on her bed trying to equate the

Walter Marx she had seen in the fishbowl with the Walter Marx she had been married to for the past twelve years. All of her plans for starting over—a new career, a new life—all scrambled.

"He *cried*."

—The superman, giant of industry, macho sonofabitch *cried*. "All on his own, he's going to bleeding Al-Anon."

She spoke to her room. "I don't know how to tell you this, Lydia, but that big asshole loves you."

—Loves me! He's trying to recover—change—himself. It ruins everything.

Roger pulled his cup out of the kitchen coffee dispenser with a shaking hand. He moved to the chair next to the table and sat down, sipping his coffee, holding the cup with both hands.

Denise had read off her list, talked about how she felt, crying the entire time. It hurt. It hurt worse than Roger ever could have imagined. But a greater pain had been waiting for him.

Angela had been patting Denise's shoulder as she looked at Carmel.

"Is there anything you want to tell your father?"

"No." Carmel's face showed no expression. Her eyes were half-closed, as though she were bored.

"This must have been a nightmare for you, Carmel."

"I suppose. That's in the past."

Roger studied his daughter. Had she forgiven him? Carmel looked back at him. No it wasn't forgiveness. She was like a person watching a hated enemy stand in the road as a speeding truck came down on him. She wouldn't call out. She'd just let physics and justice do their things.

Angela had tried again. "Carmel, your father needs to hear these things if he is going to get better. Do you want him to get better?"

Carmel just sat there, staring at him. Her eyes said: "Die. Die, you bastard. Die."

After group Roger had seen Denise and Jake's wife, Ann, hugging, comforting each other in the hallway. Carmel had disappeared down the north wing stairwell. He pushed himself up from the table and went into the corridor to east wing. God wasn't talking to him on this one.

Earl Nelson stood before his window. He looked again at the letters he had read out in group. From Alice:

I don't want you to come back. I hate you. I hate you for what you did to me. I hate you for what you did to us. I hate you most for what you did to my son. I have papers from a court. If you come near either of us, the sheriff...

Earl laughed bitterly. "I guess that's what those Al-Anon people mean by let go and let God."

From his son: ,

I don't think I have to explain my reasons. If I ever see you again, I will kill you.

Earl turned from the window, walked to his desk, and tucked the two letters inside his Big Book. He stared at the book for a moment, then headed for the door.

George McIntyre sat in the fourth floor recreation room talking to Linda and Nate. All three were shakily drinking coffee.

George sighed. "Christ, I didn't think I was going to survive afternoon group."

"Some heavy shit." Nate rubbed his eyes. "I thought I'd seen it all when Brandy went through family week. God only knows what I'm going to do. What'd you think, Linda?"

"That was before I joined the Animals."

"I mean about today."

Linda put down her cup and lit a cigarette. "First, I was thinking that no one could pay me enough to go through what any of them went through today. Second, I can't see how Angela can do this shit day after day. She is either the most put-together person I have ever met, or a real pervert."

Nate recited what had become the Party Line: "I don't drink or drug no more, man, but I'm really gettin' into pain, y'know?" He jabbed George's arm. "What's eating you?"

"Earl."

"I thought that shit was getting to you."

"Nate, I would have sworn that he was dying when he read those letters. God, I'd like to kill his wife and kid."

Nate laughed. "You're talking like an idiot."

"It's how I feel. We know Earl's a good man, and how hard he's trying. Why don't they give him a chance?"

Linda lifted her head as she noticed Brandy entering the lounge. Linda waved her hand and called out, "Over here!"

Brandy altered direction and stopped next to the three. "Get on down to the wing. We have a buggout."

George looked out of the lounge windows, noticing for the first time since awakening that there was an "outside" that had an existence independent of St. Mary's, and that a windstorm was blowing the loose snow into a horizontal blizzard.

"You coming?" Linda called from the door.

George turned and followed, teetering on the verge of prayer that it wasn't Jake who had bugged.

61

Angela Gwynn put on her thermal boots, scarf, coat, gloves, and fur cap. With the windchill, the temperature outside was reported to be seventy below. She picked up her purse and began entering the hallway.

Remembering the book she had promised Elliot, she returned to her desk and picked it up. Elliot's nine-year-old son Donny was retarded. Something the Episcopal priest had taken on as one of several punishments for his sins, as well as a sterling excuse to keep on the sauce. The narrow little tome answered the question "Why does God let these things happen?" with "Maybe there's not a Goddamned thing he can do about them." She went out into the hall, closed her door, and turned around. The lounge was empty. Even if no one else was there in the afternoon, she could always count on Jake being flaked out in the easy chair. This time the chair was empty. She looked down the hallway. Deserted. Heading for the nurse's station, she looked into the rooms along the way. All empty.

She stopped at the nurse's station. "Tess?"

Tess, seated behind the counter, looked up from her work. "Yes?"

"Could you see that Elliot Yates gets this?" Angela held out the book.

"Sure." Tess took the book and began writing a note.

"Where is everybody? North wing is deserted."

"I think somebody from your group said that they were all going outside for a walk."

"A walk?"

Tess nodded. "I think the whole group went. I know no one signed out."

Angela frowned. If they went as a group, they didn't have to sign out. "It's seventy below out there."

Tess shrugged, put the book aside, and turned back to some papers. Angela tapped her gloved fingers on the counter, then turned and headed for the elevator. She pushed for the first floor. The only place that the patients were permitted to walk was around the block surrounding the rehab center. Going beyond that limit was an ass-tossing offense.

The elevator doors opened and she turned left and marched into the lobby. Through the lobby's twin set of double glass doors, she could see ice dust blowing around a bundle of clothing that trudged by the front of the building. She went through the first set of doors, opened the second set a crack, and hesitated as the cold struck her nose, sticking her nasal membranes together.

She let the door close. Behind the first bundle of clothes came a second. With that fancy fur coat on top of everything else, the second bundle had to be Linda Manchester. When it came closer and she could see the person's eyes, she was certain. Wrapping everything about her more tightly and covering everything but her eyes with her scarf, Angela pushed open the door. "Linda?"

The furred bundle came to a halt. "Yes?"

"What are you doing out here?"

"Oh, Angela, it's you. I'm taking a walk. You know, exercise. The patient's handbook says we can take walks."

"It also says you can go sunbathing. Do you have any idea how cold it is?"

"There is a nip in the air, isn't there?" The bundle waved. "Well, I've got to keep moving. Nice talking to you."

Angela watched Linda's back until another bundle walked around her and said, "Have a nice day."

The voice belonged to the new group member, George McIntyre. She looked to her left. At the corner there was another bundle turning in her direction.

—What is going on?

She turned about, went back in the building, and headed for the garage.

62

In the dark of the cocktail lounge, Elliot Yates studied the glass on the table in front of him. The music was dreamy, the lighting soft, the drink was Johnny Walker Red. He was tucked away in a booth that removed him from public view. Every now and then the waiter would pass by, checking his glass, but that was all he had in the way of company.

—The waiter and five thousand ghosts. Perfect.

He whispered to himself, "I am a grown man. If I want a drink, no one can stop me. If I don't want to drink, no one can make me." He wiped the tears from his eyes.

—Who needs a damned place that makes you cry all the time? Who needs a house full of crude, rude drunks and junkies?

He leaned back against the soft upholstry, his fingers around the glass.

—All of them in the group, sitting in the lounge evenings, laughing and joking. Talking together. Friends.

"Why can't I be part of that? Why am I so afraid of people?" He noted that he wasn't afraid of them when he was in the pulpit. He only feared them when he was supposed to approach them as equals.

He noticed that the jerking of his hand had caused some of his drink to slop over the edge of the glass. He picked it up, placed the paper napkin beneath it, and rested the glass on the napkin. The whiteness of the napkin against the dark grain of the table seemed to throw a spotlight on the glass and its amber contents.

—It's only a drink. Hundreds of millions have just one. Just one, and then they go home to a normal family without totalling the car, or beating their children, blacking out for five days, or…

He folded his arms, his gaze still on the glass. "But I'm not normal." The lectures, the literature. Some of us got the bug. Addiction. One is too many and a thousand is never enough.

Slogan time.

"When you're sick and tired of being sick and tired." Elliot shook his head. "I don't want to be part of A.A."

—Part of a desperate society hanging onto life and reality by their fingernails. The white-knuckle serenity crowd, as Randecker put it. "I'd rather be dead."

The glass was right in front of him. What about that last time? He woke up in the morning convinced that he was dying. Later, at the hospital, they confirmed his diagnosis. He had been dying. Again he looked at the glass.

—Why the hell not?

He closed his eyes. They burned. From the smoke in the lounge?

No. Elliot was thinking about Jake. So much of Jake's first step—entire chapters—were from Elliot's book. He hated Jake so much, yet except for a minor theological point, they might have been twins.

—Hating someone who is so much like yourself means what?

He nodded. Another damned lecture. A form of projection where you see the things you feel in others, and hate what you see: yourself. He sighed and shook his head as a draft blew against his legs. He looked at his watch and saw that it was almost five o'clock. He had skipped before afternoon group. Wandered around. He didn't know how long he had been sitting in the lounge. The evening trade was beginning to come in.

—Pretty soon the bartender will begin charging me booth rent. I can't go back to Saint Mary's. They will have missed me by now. Besides, I can't face them. The group. Angela. Anyway, I must have been excommunicated by now.

Another draft on his legs. The place was filling up. He wrapped his fingers around the glass. Another failure.

—Before I didn't have the choice. Now I do. I can either leave this drink or drink it. But if I drink it, I will no longer have the choice.

"C'mon, asshole, make up your mind."

Elliot looked to his right. "Jake!"

Jake pointed at the glass. "Are you going to drink that, or what? Let me rephrase my question. Have you had any yet?"

Elliot shook his head and noticed Brandy reach out and shake Jake's arm, "I'm going to try and chase down Nate and Roger. Will you be all right?"

Jake nodded. "I'll be back soon, one way or the other." Jake pointed again at the glass. "Well?"

"Are you people insane? You could all get kicked out of treatment for this."

"No kidding."

"Why?"

"The Animals have a rule, Elliot. You forgot to say goodbye."

Elliot shook his head. "I don't understand. None of you people like me."

Jake sat down across from Elliot. "That's true. None of us knows you, and it's hard to like someone you don't know. But we don't have to like you; all we have to do is love you."

"You're not making sense."

"You're a professional Christian, Elliot. If you keep your head clear long enough, you'll figure it out." Jake nodded at the glass. "If you could have anything you want from that drink, what would it be?"

Elliot saw that as cold as it was outside, the perspiration was beading on Jake's forehead. Jake was taking a big risk. His question deserved an honest answer. Elliot looked down at the glass. "I want to drink...I want to drink like an alcoholic and avoid the consequences." He grinned at Jake. "Welcome to fantasyland."

"You said it."

"They'll kick me out for this." With his foot he pushed his bag out from under the table. "Even if I could get in undetected, how do I explain that?"

Jake got to his feet. "Mere detail, m'boy. Mere detail. What do you say?"

Elliot placed his fingers around the glass, waited a beat, then pushed it away. "Let's go home."

On the way back to the rehab center, Elliot learned more about Jake. Among other things, that he was not from Minneapolis and was very lost. After asking several persons for directions and taking a frantic bus-ride on the few busses that were still running in the blizzard, by five-thirty they unloaded in the snow next to a parking lot a block away from the center.

As they weaved through the parked cars, both of them moved strangely. Elliot because he was wearing all the clothing he had brought with him to the center. Jake because he was wearing Elliot's crushed bag beneath his coat.

They approached the center by detouring past St. Mary's College and joining the parade of Animals at the rehab center's side. Elliot followed the column while Jake went in the opposite direction. Every so often, one of the animated, frost-covered bundles would wave at him, and he waved back, his heart in his throat.

—They're doing this for me.

He cried. Once around the block, his toes so cold they felt like they were rattling around in his shoes, he could only imagine at how cold his group mates were. Jake approached from the opposite direction. "Okay. We're going in."

Jake turned around, and in minutes Elliot was inside the building, taking off his glasses. They were so fogged, he couldn't see through them. He followed Jake to the third floor, entered his own room, and shucked his extra layers of clothing.

As he stepped out into the hall, the cowbell was ringing for dinner. Lydia and Brandy were coming out of their rooms. Then Nate. George and Jake were walking past, and Elliot joined them. "Jake, all I want to do tonight is crawl into a hot bath and soak for hours. I'm freezing."

Jake nodded. "I bet." He looked at Elliot. "There's one thing you should do first."

"What?"

"After the evening lecture, go to every one of the Animals and apologize. The Animals have a rule. You can buggout and no one will try and stop you. But do it honestly. Say goodbye in group before you go."

Elliot nodded. "Okay."

"Another thing. Keep your mouth shut about this. You were right. We all could get tossed for this stunt."

"Elliot."

They froze as the voice came from the nurse's station. It was Tess. Elliot hesitated, then walked up to the counter. "Yes?"

Tess held out a book. "There's a note on it. Angela left this for you."

"Thank you." Elliot took the book, grinned and bowed. "Thank you. Thank you very—"

George elbowed Elliot. "Cool it."

They passed the nurse's station and went on down the stairwell to the Constipated Eagle. Tess finished watching the Animals pass by the station, reached down and dialed a number. Angela answered. "Hello?"

"This is Tess. When the Animals came back from their walk, they were all there. I just counted them. They were on time for dinner, too."

A silence. "Very well. It was just a thought. I'll see you tomorrow."

Tess said goodbye, hung up, then came from behind the counter and began checking the rooms. She knew the Animals were gone, but there was a fellow loose on the floor heavily into five-fingered discounts. When she was finished checking the rooms, she stood at the entrance to the lounge with a puzzled expression. Every bed in the wing had rumpled clothing piled on it.

She shrugged. "It's not my problem, how important is it?, one day at a time, first things first, let go and let God, easy does it, and something is definitely rotten in the state of Denmark."

63

North wing lounge, another day wrung to a close. George knew he was tired when he realized it was too much effort to smoke. "I am pooped." George looked to his right. Jake was flaked out in the easy chair. "Jake?"

"What?"

"Why don't you write a book about this place?"

"Stick it up your ass."

"No," George sat up. "I'm serious."

Jake opened his eyes. "Who'd be interested?"

"Nobody but alcoholics, drug addicts, and those affected by the bug, which automatically makes it a best seller."

Jake snorted out a laugh. "Hell, George. If I wrote up a manuscript that gave even a half-accurate impression of this zoo and the people in it, you know what the first editor who saw it would say? He'd say, 'What you've got here, Randecker, is a pretty good nurse romance story. Cut down the number of characters, clean up the language, take out all those jokes, put in more sex, and delete all those references to drugs, and I think you've got a sale.'"

George tapped his fingers on the amrest of the love seat and looked at his roommate. "You don't have a lot of confidence in your own writing, do you, Jake?"

Jake closed his eyes. "No. No, I guess I don't. It sells, fans say nice things, I get pretty awards, but no, I don't. It's all part of the inadequacy, low self-image schtick." He placed his hands together and looked up at the ceiling. "I know one thing, though. This place and being an addict have become such a part of my identity, if I did write it up and it was turned down, I think I'd feel like the whole experience was invalidated somehow." He lifted a hand and rubbed his eyes. "Anyway, I haven't written anything in a long time. I wonder if I'll ever get back to writing. A writer who doesn't write is…what?"

George leaned over and poked Jake's arm. "He's a retired man of letters."

A laugh, a shake of the head. "I don't know. For the movie, who would you get to play Snake?"

"Whatsisname—the guy who played the cop in Rambo."

"I know who you mean. Dennehy. Brian Dennehy. He'd be great. What about Brandy?"

George sat up. "How about Kathleen Turner?"

"Check. What about Ben Vereen for Roger?"

"If we could get him to put on about eighty pounds. We have to have Robert Blake as Nate the Junkman."

"Okay, Woody Allen as Elliot, and Maude's daughter—Adrienne Barbeau—for Lydia. Who would we get for Linda?"

"Cybill Shepherd. Tommy Lee Jones as Earl."

"Great." Jake nodded. "What about Angela? Who would play Angela?"

George shook his head. "That *is* a tough one." He thought. "I sort of have an image of Katherine Hepburn stuffed inside of Ingrid Bergman."

"With just a touch of Ma Kettle and the *Alien.*"

"No, I have the perfect one. Bea Arthur."

Jake nodded. "Bea Arthur. God'll get you for that, George."

"I'm serious. I can almost see it in my head."

Jake sighed, sat up, and lit his pipe. "And John Amos as Frank Kimbal."

"Your old roommate?"

"Yes."

"Why did he buggout?"

Jake shook his head. "My best guess is that too many things he would have liked to believe about his ex-wife turned out not to be true. Her name is Mary. For the couple of days she was here, I got to know her pretty well." He smiled. "Two days, George. That's one of the things that fascinates me about this place. My closest friends at home, folks I've known for many years, I don't know half as well as people here I've only known for a couple of days."

George nodded. "I know what you mean."

Jake leaned his head against the back of the easy chair, his eyes closed. "Mary is a very nice woman." He held his hands out and let them drop into his lap. "Frank is a helluva nice guy, and let's change the subject." He looked at George. "When are you going to stop screwing around in college and get to writing?"

George sat back, his face red. "I'm learning."

Jake smiled. "Well, George, you know what they say in the trade about college writing courses. Those who pass go on to become writing teachers; those who flunk out go on to become writers."

"Do you think I'm frightened of blank paper?"

"It's not up to me to do your inventory. Just remember that the bottom line in this business is getting something on paper. You can spend the rest of your life learning about it and not doing it. It's like this program. The only way to learn about it is to do it."

Footsteps in the hall. Tess looked into the lounge. "Jake?"

He sat up and turned around. "Yes?"

"Telephone. "

"Who is it?"

"I'm not an answering service. But it's a woman." The nurse put a sly look on her face. "She sounds very sexy." She raised an eyebrow. "I don't want to take your inventory, Jake, but it takes a real turd to fool around during his own family week."

Jake gathered his things and headed for the hallway, sticking his tongue out at Tess as he passed her. She followed him out, laughing.

George looked around the empty lounge, then picked up his steno book and first step outline. He shook his head and swore. He just couldn't seem to get any further on the effects of chemistry upon his emotional life. There had been plenty of effects, from spending half the time as a numb piece of meat to spending the other half in a walking rage. But there were all of those other things he didn't like: Self-pity, whining, manipulating, resentful, criticizing, negative, other-directed yet self-centered—

He had told Jake that he didn't like facing what he was.

"Neither does anyone in the joint. But see, George, it wasn't just you. It was you filled to the eyeballs with drugs. They call that stuff shit for a reason. When you're writing up your examples, try beginning them all with 'When I was drunk, I did so-and-so.' There's a big difference between George and George shitfaced."

George looked up to see Earl lowering himself into the easy chair. "How's it going, Earl?"

Earl frowned and took out a cigarette. As he was lighting it, the light came to George about one thing. Saint Mary's was the only place in the world he had ever been that when someone asked you "How are you?" he really wanted to know.

He remembered that one time seeing Brandy and Jake pass each other in the hallway.

"How's it going, Jake?"

"Fine."

"That bad, huh?"

"Well, I could say go wrap it around a trolly car and pound it up your ass. Would you prefer that?"

"It'd be more honest."

Earl was talking. "I guess I'm facing it. Alice and Joey are out of my life." He shook his head. "Shit, but it hurts. I'm not going to go back to the bottle over it. I think I'm finally here for me."

George listened, marveling in this wondrous new experience of knowing someone's real person. Not his shell clanking against someone else's shell. Knowing someone; and letting him know you.

George thought, if Randecker doesn't write the book about Saint Mary's, I just might.

JANUARY 18TH

64

Morning group. The groupwad was in circulation, trying to stem the group-wide case of sniffles. As Elliot began the reading, George finished blowing his nose and took a moment to study Angela. She looked different somehow.

She might have been trying to make a decision, or she might have been bored. Then again…she didn't exactly wear her emotions on her face. Perhaps a restrained Bea Arthur, if that wasn't a contradiction in terms. George looked at his roommate. Jake had been quiet ever since being called to the telephone late last night. George didn't think Jake had been to bed at all. When he had asked Jake about it, his roomate had simply ignored the question.

Elliot continued the reading. "Anyone who tries it, knows that the old alcoholic thinking is apt to come back on us when we least expect it. Building a new life is a slow process."

Elliot wound up the reading, blew his nose, and introduced himself. "I'm Elliot Yates, alcoholic, and my contract for this morning…is to talk about some guilt I have."

Angela nodded. "That sounds like a good one for you, Elliot." She turned her head, hammered Elliot to the wall with her expression, and looked to the next in line.

Roger jumped. "I'm, uh, Roger—Roger Sanders, and my contract for—"

"Roger, did you take the cure?"

His eyebrows went up as he looked at Angela. "Cure?" Angela looked at the ceiling and nodded. "Oh." Roger rubbed his chin. "I'm Roger Sanders, *alcoholic,* and my contract…"

George nodded as the contracts moved along, thinking, Angela is pissed.

"I'm Lydia Marx, alcoholic, and my contract is to talk about my family week."

Then it was George's turn. He finished blowing his nose again. "I'm George McIntyre, alcoholic—"

Angela leaned in George's direction. "And you have a *nice* day, George."

George felt confused, then cornered, then guilty as hell. "Er, my contract…uh, thanks, Angela. You, too—"

"Count on it."

George nodded again. Correction, thought he. Angela is *really* pissed.

The contracts finished going around the circle, and Angela sat rocking in her chair, her fingertips together playing spider-doing-pushups-on-a-mirror. "Before we start today, kiddies, I wonder if any of you know why I am angry." She looked around the circle, her eyebrows raised. "No? Well, you see, I am playing a game called 'guess why I'm angry.' You can't possibly know why I'm angry unless I level with you. That's why it's a game."

The spider collapsed on the mirror. "This group is playing a game with me. The game goes under several names ranging from 'nyah, nyah,

nyah, nyah, nyah' to 'I know something you don't know.' That is why I'm angry. Would anyone care to speak to this topic?"

Linda coughed and looked at Angela with red eyes. "I know what you mean. About games making you angry. But what if leveling—telling the truth—would bring dire consequences down upon our heads?"

Angela looked around the circle, ignoring Linda's question. "I don't want to play games, people."

Elliot coughed, turned red, and looked down at his *Twenty-Four Hours a Day* book. "My contract might clear up a few things. I walked out of treatment yesterday."

"That's why you missed afternoon group?"

"Yes."

"This is serious, Elliot. You know this means getting staffed, don't you?"

Staffed. Where everyone on your case gets together and gets *on* your case.

Elliot smiled. "I'm used to living with vast conspiracies against me out there." A few chuckles. He nodded. "Yes. I know."

Angela tapped her fingertips against the armrests of her chair. "What happened?"

"Happened?"

"Why are you here?"

"Oh. I, uh, changed my mind."

She looked around the circle. Everyone seemed to be looking somewhere else—anywhere but in her direction. The light dawned. "You know, group, if someone walks out of treatment, just about the most irresponsible thing I can think of to do is to chase him down."

"Hypothetically speaking," Roger added.

"Hmm." Angela looked at Linda. "Why would it be irresponsible, Linda?"

"We—I mean anyone who would do such a thing would be risking their own treatment, all that they'd worked for."

Angela looked at Nate. "Why are you here?"

"For myself."

"Can you control someone else?"

"Nope." He pursed his lips for a moment. "But I can let him know that I care."

She shook her head and looked at Jake. He looked preoccupied with something. "What about you?"

"Me?"

She looked up at the ceiling. "Group, I am very concerned about you. Why you are here is deadly serious business. I want to make clear right now that if I ever discover that anyone from my group has gone outside patient boundaries chasing after someone who has decided to leave treatment, I would most likely recommend discharge." She looked back at Jake.

Jake smiled sadly and looked at the floor. "I was just thinking that if I had managed to chase a buggout down, and he came back, and I had gotten away with it, I would be feeling pretty good about it. Hypothetically speaking, that is." He sat back in his chair, the smile gone. Tears brimmed in his eyes and he shook his head. "When I was steaming my way out of treatment, Frank chased me down. He threatened to break my leg if I didn't sit and listen to him. I did and I'm still alive." Jake looked out through the glass balcony door at the sky. Saint Mary blue. "Frank never gave anyone a chance to talk to him. He bugged in the middle of the night while I was out Nighthawking. The sonofabitch."

Angela scooted her chair across the floor and placed her hand on Jake's arm. "What's going on with you, Jake?"

He closed his eyes and shook his head. "Damn this disease. God damn it." He looked into her eyes. "It's a risk, all right. It's a risk chasing someone down. But I think it might not be so much how little we care about ourselves. I think it means how much we're willing to risk because that's how much we care about someone else." He rocked on his chair, the tears running down his cheeks. "I got a phone call last night. I haven't talked with anyone about it yet." His breath came out in a ragged sob. "Frank's dead. He drove his car off of some damned bridge yesterday. He was drunk. Mary called me."

Angela motioned to Brandy to vacate the chair to Jake's right. Angela sat in Brandy's chair and put her arm around Jake while Brandy stood, looking down at them, her hand on Jake's shoulder. For a long time there was nothing but the sound of Jake crying. Angela spoke quietly, "No alcoholic ever dies in vain, Jake. Somewhere, perhaps right in this room, others will take that death to heart and try that much harder because of it to build a new life."

George watched them. Saint Mary blue. A barrel of laughs with a kick in the groin for a punchline. He could feel it. Brandy was crying, too. Roger. Earl. He saw a tear work its way down Angela's cheek. George had never met Frank. But the man's death was getting through to him.

—There but for the grace of God go I.

George looked within himself and found the part that had been missing in his awareness of the bug.

—I don't want to go back to what I was. I don't want to die. And I'm scared.

The talk in the lounge before afternoon group was somber. Those who had met Frank recalled what he was like, remembered his stories, his mothball and Superman jokes, the new life he had wanted so badly. Early on Jake dropped out of the postmortem. He sat in the easy chair, looking at the people in his group.

Angela's Animals.

Brandy, Lydia, Roger, Earl, Nate, Linda, Elliot, and George. The ones who went before: Harold, Dave, Ron, Candy, D.T., and Frank.

He opened his steno pad and began writing.

I care about them, these refugees from the fast lane. I have never cared about anything or anyone as much. It goes beyond just the Animals. Snake, Robby, Diane, Bob, D.T.'s son Mack—all of them. Even Amy and Ron's friend, Paula. Where is she now? Alive? Dead? It matters to me.

The staff that crews this ship of drools: Marnie, Coral, Barny, Tess, Bill, Mark, Angela. That mag writer, Diane, showed me that this is a place of change, and reminded me that change is the entire stuff of a good story, and I have heard from everyone here: "If I was a writer, I'd write a book about this place."

I want to write that book. There's a story here that is busting my gut I want to tell it so badly. So many things.

To the straights, hey, we aren't bad people; in fact we are some of the best people I know. Underneath all of the bullshit, everyone in this place is a fine person. Even me.

—That is a radical concept: Jacob Randecker is okay. Even me.

To my brother and sister drunks and junks, there is some hope. It isn't easy and there's no guarantee, but the first gamble we all took was stepping outside of the womb. The bug only guarantees one thing: let him run around free, and you will die. Saint Mary's only guarantees one thing: to give you a start at arresting the bug and building a new life.

But how could I write such a book? How could I picture this place even half-accurately with made up characters? Violating anonymity I couldn't do. Each and every one of these persons fills a very special place in my heart.

If it wasn't for anonymity,, I could sit down and pound out a book about Saint Mary's in a week—

Jake looked up and saw the concerned persons gathering outside Angela's door. Ann had been crying, and Roger's wife, Denise, was talking to her. Lydia's husband, Walt, was listening intently to both of them. Carmel was on the other side of the door, leaning against the wall, first glowering at Roger, then looking away. Her tears were left defiantly on her cheeks.

Jake turned back to his pad.

Ann is changing, too. I know nothing about her. But I see the family members hanging together, leaning on each other, being concerned about each other, just like the Animals do. They've said it a thousand times: the family has the bug, too. We are all in this together. We are all fine people— worth loving, worth caring about.

How could I ever make such a book believable? Angela, what goes on in group, Snake, and all the others. Nate waking up toe-tagged in a morgue— twice. All of the stories. The civilians just wouldn't understand.

Right now there are cowbells ringing. Who would believe cowbells? No one seems to know how they came here. Soon the Animals will herd into Angela's room, and I will find myself sitting in a chair facing Ann. She may have reached a decision to go for a divorce, and may very well tell me that. I will sit there with my mouth shut and take it—

"Jake?"

He looked up from his pad. Angela was standing in the doorway, holding the door open with her back. "Are you part of this group?"

Jake pushed himself to his feet and smiled. "Yes, I am."

He entered the room and the door closed. Angela and Jake took their seats, and the circle was complete.

In the center of the fishbowl's circle, Jake looked at Ann. She seemed less frightened, less defensive, less restrained than on Monday. She was comfortable with her group, now. Now she had friends—broth- ers and sisters—who understood, who were going through the same thing. She had more trust in the group, in the process. She was beginning to understand the purposes of laying out before the patient exactly what life with him had been like. He needed the information; she needed to dump the pain.

To Jake it was a blur. It wasn't a case of letting go; it was sensory overload. Angela leaned back as a searing pain stabbed into Jake's neck.

"When you introduced yourself in group yesterday as a *drug addict* and alcoholic, I was shocked—horrified. You had *me* arrange the second prescription through another drug store and had *me* pick up your pills! That's a Federal crime…."

And more. "It got so that I knew what every day was going to be like. You'd storm around the house in the morning, begin drinking around noon, and then we would fight all night."

Angela looked from Jake to Ann. "How did that make you feel?"

Ann's eyes filled with tears. "Jake…I wished you had died when you had your heart attack—"

—Oh, damn. Just when I think it can't get any worse, it gets worse. But she'd have to be an idiot to feel differently.

"We'd go for so long without making love. I thought you were having an affair, but I couldn't see how, because you never left the house, but we never—"

Angela nodded at Ann. "He was having an affair, Ann. His chemicals were God, life, and lover to him." She looked at Jake. "True?"

Jake nodded, wondering silently if there was any life possible after this ordeal.

—You're a nasty little asshole, Jake. Do something about it, will you?

He looked down and noticed that the scar was still there. On her hand.

—Was that when I pushed her into the saw or slammed the door on her hand that time in the parking lot? Isn't that one esteem-building question to ask oneself?

Jake stared at Ann with pain-glazed eyes. He could see her lips moving, could feel his body wincing at the words, but couldn't understand what was being said. He rubbed his eyes.

—Can anything be worth this?

A pause.

Feedback from the group. Jake's head was numb, the room spinning, sharp pains in his chest. The body was telling the head, "Hey, boy, I can get you out of this." But the head replied to the body, "If I die, I die, so shut up."

Silence.

Angela spoke to Jake. "I saw you in the lounge after the family session yesterday. What were you thinking about?"

Jake frowned, trying to remember.

—Oh.

He looked at Angela. "Ann means so much to me. I was thinking what if I have lost it all. Lost her—"

"Jake!"

Hands reached out and grabbed his arms. Ann, still seated, pulled him toward her. He stood, crouched over her, and held her tightly. Her body shook with sobs.

Jake was confused. Embarrassed. Frightened. Sorry. So terribly sorry.

Reality became wet tears, desperate kisses, and whispered words of love too long unused.

Healing began.

ONE YEAR LATER, JANUARY 9TH

65

Jake sat in the otherwise unoccupied north wing lounge making notes, slightly distressed at how inaccurately he remembered the place. Angela's room number was 355, not 356. His room number had been 356. The tiles on the floor were gray, not light green. He looked up at the acoustic tile on the ceiling. The wormy pattern he had remembered very accurately.

"Jake?"

He saw Ann standing in front of the stairwell door. "I'm heading down to my group now. Do you want to meet at our room before lunch?"

"Okay." He waved, she waved back, and disappeared down the stairwell. Ann looked happy—was happy.

On the way to the Portland Jetport, he had heard her singing for the first time in twelve years. There had been some fights, some chilly moments, some painful growing and sorting out of roles to do. There was a lot left to do.

—Look where we are now. Singing again.

Jake sat back in the love seat and fired up his pipe. The lounge, Saint Mary's, being there with Ann, none of it seemed strange at all. It was like coming home. He shook his head and returned to his notes.

A familiar voice. "Ward Owens?"

Jake looked toward the lounge entrance. It was Marnie. "Hello, hello."

"I was looking for—" She frowned. "Jake?"

He stood up, walked over to her, and stuck a thumb behind his return visitor's nametag. "One year return visit."

They hugged, and Jake wondered again why it had taken him so long to discover this glorious alternative to shaking hands. He held her at arm's length. "I bet you thought I was back on a retread."

"It's happened before. It's too bad you weren't a week earlier. You just missed Roger and Nate."

"How are they doing?"

"Good." She smiled. "You're looking pretty good, too. Did Ann come with you?"

"Yes."

"Good. I'm glad to hear that." She glanced around the lounge. "I'm trying to track down one of the Animals. Ward Owens?"

Jake shook his head. "I haven't met anyone in the group yet."

Marnie patted Jake on the shoulder, turned and headed toward the nurse's station. She snagged one patient who was leaving his room, and Jake went back to the love seat and resumed his note taking. After a few moments a woman entered the lounge, sat in the couch facing the love seat, and nervously lit a cigarette.

Jake nodded. "Hi. My name's Jake."

She issued a brief smile. "I'm Pat. Are you new on this wing?"

"I'm back for my one year return visit. I went through last January."

She shook her head. "I don't know if I'll ever make it." She put her feet up on the coffee table. "Hell, I'm in my second week and I haven't even started on my first step yet."

"I was in my third week before I gave mine."

Her eyebrows went up. "Really?"

He nodded. "For the first three weeks I thought I was taking stupid pills. I couldn't seem to understand anything. It gets better."

Pat was silent for a long time, then she looked at Jake. "Tell me the truth. Is it hard?"

"Is what hard?"

"On the outside. Staying sober."

He reached into his pocket and let his fingers touch his one-year A.A. chip. Next to it was his one-year N.A. keytag. They had been presented to him by his home groups in Maine for one year of being sober and clean. Their history covered an endless succession of meetings, a lot of close calls, some terrible moments, some hard decisions. It meant discipline, forming new habits, new friends, a new relationship with Ann, and lots and lots of growing pains. The two tokens represented a million victories apiece.

"Sometimes it was hard, but only when I was making it hard on myself. It's been the best year of my life. I could drop dead right now, and it would have been worth it."

The lounge began filling up. Cigarettes, coffee, talk. A woman in her teens sat next to Pat. A young man with long blond hair sat at the card table across from an older fellow wearing banker's casual. Jake closed his eyes and listened.

"I'm not letting anybody shove God down my throat."

"—Angela on my ass—"

"I really don't think I have a problem with pot."

"—I think everybody made a mistake about sending me here. I don't belong—"

"I just don't seem to be able to get into that first step."

"—don't see how I'll ever live through family week."

Home again, home again, thought Jake. He felt someone sit down next to him. He looked and saw that it was the woman called Pat. She smiled timidly.

"Are you going to be here for the week?" Jake nodded. "We didn't make our last return visitor feel very welcome. He only sat in on one group. Where are you from?"

"Maine."

Pat looked away, then lit another cigarette. "That's a long way. Are the return visits worth it?"

"They're worth it. I've been stuck a few times, and the return visit blasts me loose. It also gives me a chance to see how far I've come."

"Have you been doing A.A. as part of your aftercare? I don't know if I'd fit in with those people."

"Yes, I'm in A.A. and N.A. both. Those people are a great bunch, and they're keeping me alive. I just started going to Al-Anon, and my wife and I go to a growth group."

"That's a lot of meetings."

He nodded. "I might just trade them all in and start up Anonymous Consolidated: 'We do it all.'"

Pat laughed as Angela's door opened for morning group. Jake stood. "It's that time again."

She reached up and grasped his hand. Something desperate was in her eyes. "Is it really worth it?"

He held her hand in both of his. "Believe it. Until you know it, believe it."

Then there were cowbells.

Morning Group.

Ward Owens massaged the back of his neck in an, attempt at relieving his tension. He could feel his heart beating rapidly.

—It's time to put up or shut up.

Ward looked at the faces in the circle as the contracts crept slowly around the room. There was a new face. Ward moved his fear sideways, changing it to anger.

Angela introduced herself as counselor for the group and looked at the new face. He smiled and looked around the circle. "My name is Jake Randecker, I'm an addict. I became a member of this group last January, and I'm back for my one-year return visit. My contract is to tell you a little about myself, and about what the past year has been like."

Ward leaned forward and glared at Jake. "Aren't you going to ask the group if you can sit in?"

"No."

Ward's face flushed as his eyes grew hooded. The rest of the group looked very uncomfortable, but Ward wasn't paying attention. He looked around at his fellow group members and back at Jake, pointing his finger. "I'm afraid I'll have to insist."

Jake glanced at Angela who was busy studying the air vent in the ceiling. The visitor smiled and looked back at Ward. "Everybody has to have a hobby."

"I insist that you ask the group's permission."

Jake scratched his beard, then leaned forward, his elbows on his knees. "I have no intention of asking."

Ward turned his head toward Angela. "I want him out of the group!"

Angela lowered her gaze until she was looking at Ward. "You are talking to the wrong person." She swung her chair around until she was facing Jake. She smiled. "Welcome back."

"Thank you. It's good to be back."

Ward sat back in his chair and folded his arms. "I don't believe this!" He looked at the other members of the group. "Well?"

Scotty looked from Ward to Jake. "I'd like to know why you won't ask permission."

"I became a member of this group last January. Group members don't have to ask permission." He looked at Ward.

"I find this most uncomfortable."

Jake nodded and laughed. "I just bet that you do."

Ward noticed that Pat was grinning in his direction with evil delight.

Angela clasped her hands over her belly and swung her chair around. "Who wants to begin?

Ward glared at Jake, then settled his glare on Angela. "I'll start," said Ward. "Last Friday in morning group you asked me to think about whether or not I belonged here. Am I unique, you wanted to know."

Angela pursed her lips, her gaze fixed on Ward's eyes. "Have you reached any conclusions?"

"I think so. I don't think I do belong here. This program might work very well for religionists, but that I'm not. All of this capital 'H' capital 'P' Higher Power shit—"

The return visitor burst out in laughter. When he calmed down he held out a hand toward Ward. "I apologize. Go on."

"What's so funny?"

"You just remind me of someone. A very unhappy fellow I knew a year ago."

Angela raised her eyebrows and looked at Jake. "Now, who might that be?"

"Me.

Ward shook his head and sat forward in his chair. "Look, I'm not you; I'm not anything *like* you or anyone else around here. And I'm happy that way."

"Happy?" Jake shrugged. "Maybe you should tell your face. You look sort of resentful to me."

"Look, you sonofabitch, I don't have any resentments!"

The laughter from the group filled the room. When they calmed down, Angela turned toward Jake. "Did Ann make the return with you?"

"Yes. She's with her family group right now."

"Will you be here all week?"

"Yes."

"Sometime this week, then, the three of us will get together and talk. How have you two been doing?"

Jake grinned. "Terrific."

Ward snorted out an enraged laugh. "I do not believe this! I wasn't finished!"

Angela slowly turned her chair until she was looking at Ward. "You said you don't belong here. What more is there to say?"

"I wanted to explain—"

Angela scooted her chair across the floor and stopped in front of Ward. She then issued The Curse. "Ward, maybe you ought to go outside and suffer some more."

Ward felt lightheaded. He closed his eyes, opened them, and folded his arms. "Maybe I should. When they put this program together, they certainly didn't have me in mind."

Angela looked around the circle. "Where are you, group?"

Silence.

Angela moved her chair back in front of her desk and kept looking around the circle as she talked to Jake. "This group is different than the one you went through treatment with, Jake. Tell them a little about your group."

The return visitor talked about the Animals. The tough love, the caring, the sharing. He paused, then looked around the circle. "In fighting this disease, I can't think of a more valuable tool than group. I'm concerned for you if you're not allowing yourself to have this tool. We had a good working group. We worked hard for ourselves and with and for each other. Now, a year later, a third of them are in the toilet."

Angela held out her hand. "Tell them what you mean by in the toilet."

"Back to using. Or dead." He glanced at Angela, then leaned forward and looked at the floor. "Even though we're spread all over the country, we've kept in pretty close touch."

Angela studied Jake. "I knew about Linda and Ron. Who else?"

"D.T.—John. He's back on the sauce. His son, Mack, is still clean, though. Dave wrote me some time ago that Harold went back, lost his job, and disappeared. And Brandy."

The return visitor looked at the floor, almost on the verge of tears. Jake looked around at the faces in the group. "Brandy was an alcoholism counselor. She was one sharp lady. She knew what was at stake, and she didn't want to go back. She died from a drug overdose two months ago. Sometimes it's a lot of laughs around here, but you are all fighting for your lives—or should be."

He smiled at Angela. "Everyone else seems to be doing pretty well. You know Nate is in vocational school, and George finally sold his first short story. Candy and her family are doing great. Earl's a college freshman now. Do you believe that? Roger, Elliot and the others are okay."

He paused and Angela placed her hand on his arm. "Thinking about Frank?"

"Yeah." Jake sat back and looked at Ward. "Ward, I want to tell you about a book that I'm writing. It takes a group of patients through treatment here at Saint Mary's—"

Angela sat up. "You're going to do the book?"

"I already have forty thousand words done on it."

Angela nodded and glanced at Ward. "I'm sorry for interrupting. Go ahead."

Jake clasped his hands together. "When I went through treatment, almost every time I told someone I was a writer, the next thing I would hear would be 'If I was a writer, I think I'd write a book about this place.' At first, I wasn't interested. I wasn't going to be here that long. Then I was too sick. Then I was too busy getting well." Jake leaned back in his chair.

"When I finally did want to write that book, I had a problem I couldn't see any way around. All of the ones I went through treatment with seemed so vivid, so special, so unique. How could I make up characters like that? See, I couldn't use the characters of the men and women I knew because of anonymity."

Ward folded his arms. "What does that have to do with me?"

"Ward, when I came back for my three-month return visit, I was in for the shock of my life. I didn't have to worry about anonymity at all. When I attended patient group on that visit, I found the same cast of characters sitting in this circle as the one I went through treatment with. The same thing on my six-month visit. The same cast of characters. Ditto on this visit. In fact, we are all so unique, we ought to be issued uniforms."

"Now, wait—"

"No, Ward. You wait. That's why it's a disease. I'm an atheist, and I played the same game you're playing right now: why the program won't work for me. People who believe in a god play it a different way. But we all play it."

Ward shook his head. "Well, I don't think I'll see myself in any of your characters. If I do, I'll sue your ass off."

Jake smiled. "You're already there, Ward. Before I ever met you, I put you in. You're me." He looked around the circle. "Every one of you is in the book. There are minor detail differences, but you're all there. To repeat, that's why it's a disease. That's why it can be treated." He looked back at Ward. "That's why the program can work for you, if you'll let it."

Ward leaned forward, his eyes narrowed. "I still don't want you in this group."

Jake sat back and grinned. "You might as well get used to it, laughing boy. This is *my* group."

Ward folded his arms and sulked. Angela rocked back and forth in her chair, her fingertips together playing spider-doing-pushups-on-a mirror. The spider collapsed. "We have important work to do in here today, group. Get on with it."

The banker-looking fellow coughed and held up his steno pad. "My first step?"

Angela issued The Grin. "Alex, do you really think you're ready to give your first step?"

The one called Alex did a quick inventory of his soul. He shut his eyes, swallowed, and took that empty-handed leap into the void. "Yes. I think so."

Angela's chair rocked back and forth as she studied the air vent in the ceiling.

"We'll see, Alex. We'll see."

The End